Nadine Gonzalez is a lawyer and a romance novelist. *Kirkus Reviews* has described her work as 'sleek and entertaining…[with] vibrant settings, appealing characters, and a sexy and nuanced love story.' Nadine lives in Miami with her husband and their son. For more information visit her website, nadine-gonzalez.com

Shannon McKenna is the *New York Times* and *USA TODAY* bestselling author of over twenty-five romance novels. She ranges from romantic suspense to contemporary romance to paranormal, but in all of them, she specialises in tough, sexy alpha male heroes, heroines with the brains and guts to match them, blazing sensuality, and of course, the redemptive power of true love. There's nothing she loves more than abandoning herself to the magic of a pulse-pounding story. Being able to write her own romantic stories is a dream come true.

She loves to hear from her readers. Contact her at her website, shannonmckenna.com, for a full list of her novels. Find her on Facebook at Facebook.com/authorshannonmckenna to keep up with her news. Or join her newsletter at shannonmckenna.com/connect.php and look for the juicy free book you'll get as a welcome gift! She hopes to see you there!

Also by Nadine Gonzalez

Miami Famous
Scandal in the VIP Suite
Exclusively Yours
Unconditionally Mine

Also by Shannon McKenna

His Perfect Fake Engagement

Discover more at millsandboon.co.uk

WHAT HAPPENS IN MIAMI…

NADINE GONZALEZ

CORNER OFFICE SECRETS

SHANNON MCKENNA

MILLS & BOON

First Published in Great Britain 2021
by Mills & Boon, an imprint of HarperCollins*Publishers* Ltd
1 London Bridge Street, London, SE1 9GF

www.harpercollins.co.uk

HarperCollins*Publishers*
1st Floor, Watermarque Building,
Ringsend Road, Dublin 4, Ireland

What Happens in Miami... © 2021 Nadine Seide
Corner Office Secrets © 2021 Shannon McKenna

ISBN: 978-0-263-28294-8

0521

MIX
Paper from
responsible sources
FSC™ C007454

This book is produced from independently certified FSC™
paper to ensure responsible forest management.

For more information visit: www.harpercollins.co.uk/green

Printed and bound in Spain
by CPI, Barcelona

WHAT HAPPENS
IN MIAMI…

NADINE GONZALEZ

To my editor, Errin Toma, thanks for coaxing the best possible story out of me. There would be no Miami Famous series without your vision. I am looking forward to our future projects.

Special thanks to my agent, Jessica Alvarez. I am thrilled to join your team.

To my sister, Martine, thanks for your friendship and your love. To my lively family, particularly those on the group chat, thanks for sharing the highs and the lows.

As always, this novel is dedicated to Ariel and Nathaniel. Without your love, none of this matters.

BASELICIOUS

The prodigal son returns! Alessandro Cardenas ("Sandro" for his stans) was spotted at MIA late last night. The Academy Award winner and avid art collector is back in the Magic City for Art Basel Miami Beach. The weekend-long affair is a mix of glamour, culture and drunken good times that can only happen in Miami. Get ready! A-list celebrities will descend on our city to feast like royalty and party like beasts. Unlike the others, however, Cardenas may actually give a damn about art. The actor will donate a painting from his private collection to raise funds for Caribbean islands devastated by last summer's hurricanes. The international art fair starts tomorrow evening with a star-studded, invitation-only event. The rest of us will have to pay full price. Hopefully, we won't have to wait too long for another Cardenas sighting. We expect to run into the hottie at his favorite after-hours club, TENTEN, sometime between 4–6 a.m. #SandroFever

—@Sunshine&Wine_IG

One

Angel wasn't in the habit of taking impromptu midweek boat rides, not anymore anyway, unless there was the promise of a major payoff, like a free night's stay on Grand Bahamas Island. And yet here she was on a Wednesday evening, on the deck of a speedboat, slicing through the bay, hair, scarf and the skirt of her dress flapping in the wind as sunset poured out its colors.

She was on her way to Fisher Island, a private residential enclave for the ridiculously rich. The barrier island off the coast of Miami Beach was accessible only by boat or aircraft. Anything the select few residents could ever want or need was ferried or flown in. For the residents, this was part of the appeal. For the random mainlander dispatched at the end of a long workday to deliver goods and services, it was an inconvenience, a pain, an encroachment on personal time, a—

Ouch!

The boat skipped on the choppy waves, tossing Angel on her side. The helmsman shouted for her to take a seat. She sat on the banquette and gripped the rail. You're lucky to be here, she reminded herself. This "plum" assignment had fallen on her lap due to a series of unfortunate events. Earlier today, Justine Carr, the art gallery's sales director, was dashing across Lincoln Road for a quick cup of coffee when a Mini Cooper hit her. Her injuries were not life threatening: a broken ankle and a bruised ego. The ensuing turmoil, however, was like nothing Angel had ever seen. It was Art Basel week, all-hands-on-deck week, no-time-to-mess-around-and-get-run-over-by-a-car week. After some quick reassignments, Angel, the newest member of Gallery Six, was tasked with picking up some of the slack.

The boat slowed and pulled up to a marina crowded with various yachts and the like. A man rushed forward to assist her. Angel handed him her metal briefcase instead. Then she slipped off her Louboutin mules and leaped off the boat unassisted. She was, after all, a lifelong Floridian.

A golf cart ride later, Angel arrived at Villa Paraiso, a bay-front compound that could have been copy/pasted from the hills of Capri. They drove through the gates and along a palm tree–lined path. After a brief interaction with the property's chief of security, she was allowed entrance into the main building. An elevator took her up to the penthouse on the tenth floor.

A housekeeper greeted her at the door, asked for her name and led her into a large living room. "Please wait here," she said.

Catching her breath, Angel took in the panoramic views of the bay she had just crossed and the skyline of the city she had left behind, all of it spread out under an orange-vanilla swirl sky.

Paradise, she mused. Only a quick jaunt across the bay. Who knew?

She placed the case with the painting on a console table and checked her appearance in the mirror hanging above it. She was a disheveled mess. The midi-length linen dress was wrinkled. Her hair… *Oh, God, my hair!* As she raked her fingers through her tangled chestnut-colored waves, she was forced to admit the boat ride had done some good. She was radiant! Her tawny brown skin glowed and her light eyes shone clear and bright. Fresh air was a hell of a boon.

She ought to get out more often.

There was plenty she ought to be doing more often: dating, sexting, socializing, jogging, maybe even scuba diving. All this focus on her career wasn't healthy. After, she promised herself. After…

Music, laughter and the smell of something delicious drifted in from somewhere. Was the client hosting a party? If he were, she wished he'd hurry up. The sooner they wrapped up this deal, the sooner she could get back to her life. So what if it involved eating crackers out of the box while waiting for the next installment of *My Ex Is Getting Along Just Fine Without Me* to upload on YouTube? That was her business.

She had expected a quick, discrete exchange in a home office setting. To her understanding, this was the standard practice with most collectors. Then again, this client was anything but standard.

To Angel's supreme irritation, her heartbeat ticked up with anticipation. Meeting with a buyer, no matter how rich, handsome and famous, should not provoke a flurry of butterflies. What next? Was she going to ask the man for an autograph? She was not going to make it in this business with that mindset. This was her new career path. Dealing with the rich and famous was part of her job now. She could not afford to fail.

Last Tax Day, after her ex had moved out, Angel had come to the conclusion that her lifestyle could not be sustained on a starving artist's income. She had to face facts: her dream was dead and the time to mourn had passed. But if she could not sell her own art, what was stopping her from selling the work of other artists? Within weeks she'd landed a job at a prestigious Miami Beach gallery and earned enough to save up for Phase 2 of her plan. She wouldn't earn a commission on tonight's transaction, but she'd earn bonus points with her boss if she concluded the sale.

Angel checked her phone for the time. Only five minutes had passed. She had to chill out—famous people kept regular people waiting all the time.

Her trained eye zeroed in on the artwork. The space was, at its core, a gallery showcasing the homeowner's eclectic pieces, all periods and trends colliding. She went over to a pair of framed paintings on a far wall. One was of a red apple hanging from a tree branch. The other was of a woman sleeping in a garden. She was naked if you looked past the strategically placed fig leaf. Angel was trying to decipher the artist's signature when she heard the blunt sound of bare feet on tile. She glanced over her shoulder.

There he was, standing motionless by the sliding glass doors that opened onto a terrace. Whatever remained of the day's sunlight spilled onto his broad, bare shoulders. He was practically naked—if you looked past the damp swim trunks, which wasn't hard to do.

Tight and trim, he had the body of a lifelong swimmer. And it seemed to Angel that he had just emerged from the sea. His chest and limbs, sculpted and defined, glistened with water. His wavy black hair, cut close to the scalp, glistened. His bronze skin, touched by sunlight, glistened. With all that glistening sparkle, it was disquieting to meet his blank expression. His handsome face was impassive. From brow line to jawline, broad nose to full mouth, he gave nothing away. Was he perplexed to find her here? He'd been expecting Justine. Had anyone warned him?

But a sheepish grin quelled her fears.

"Sorry, I was expecting…" He paused to slip on a rumpled white shirt. "They said your name was Ángel and I figured…"

He figured she was a man. Common mistake. She'd gone to school with at least three guys named Ángel. To set the record straight, she stepped forward and introduced herself properly, business card and all. "Angeline Louis, sales associate with Gallery Six," she said. "Angel, for short."

He took the card and ran his thumb over the gallery's embossed logo. Under his breath, he repeated her name. "Angel." Why that moved her, she couldn't say. Then he introduced himself. "Alessandro Cardenas."

She would have liked to say: I know who you are. But

that wasn't technically true. She knew his name, age and ethnicity: Alessandro D. Cardenas, thirty-two, Cuban American. She'd seen most of his movies, including *Shadows Need Light*, the indie film for which he'd won an Independent Spirit Award, a Golden Globe, and an Oscar for best supporting actor. She was familiar with the brands he promoted, his political leanings, and she could name a few of his famous exes. He was a sex symbol, a social media star and a darling of the critics, in that order. And, it seemed, he was a serious art collector. That was a lot to know about someone you'd never met. More than she knew about her next-door neighbor.

"A pleasure to meet you, Mr. Cardenas."

"Don't," he said. "Sandro…for short. Never Alé. When I was a kid, I had a cat by that name. She strayed, but she'll always be the one."

That didn't sound right. "A kid named Alessandro had a cat named Alé?"

"Short for Alley Cat. But I was ten, and a little narcissist."

"What's changed since you were ten?" Angel asked. She doubted that he'd grown out of his narcissistic tendencies.

He dropped her card on a low marble coffee table. "For one thing, I'm not little anymore."

Amen to that!

Despite her best efforts, her gaze swept down the length of his sculpted body. It was a shame that he'd covered up on her account. His shirt was as rumpled as her dress. However, the white cotton beautifully highlighted the sun-kissed patina of his skin.

Okay! Stop!

Not five minutes ago, she'd been nervous to meet him. Now they were chatting freely as if hanging out at a poolside bar. There must be a happy medium where she was more polished and professional, and he less naked and wet.

Angel took a moment to stitch her frayed wits together.

But he wasted no time snipping the thread. He looked her dead in the eye. "*Temptation*."

"I'm sorry. What?" Had she wandered onto the set of a nineties Calvin Klein ad?

"The diptych." He pointed to the paintings that she'd been studying. "The first is Eve in her garden, the second is the apple hanging out of reach."

"Temptation," she repeated.

You didn't need a degree in biblical studies to catch the symbolism, but a few functioning brain cells would help. She should wrap this up before she made a fool of herself. She went to the console table and retrieved the metal case. "As you requested, I have here—"

"Have you eaten?"

"Excuse me?"

"We just came back from the pool and were about to have dinner. Would you like to join us?"

Just the mention of dinner provoked a rumble in her tummy. Whatever was on the grill smelled divine. Even so, she had a job to do. That meant no ogling the client, no chitchatting with him and definitely no joining his friends for dinner. Those were the rules. Right?

"Sorry. I have a boat to catch."

"We can take you back at any time—unless you need to get home. In that case, I won't keep you."

Tomorrow was Art Basel's grand opening. The day promised to be long and grueling. She had to help with the final touches on the gallery's viewing room in advance of the star-studded VIP event. Angel had intended to spend the rest of her night accessorizing the outfit she'd selected. Then she was going to repeat the process with a backup outfit.

"I shouldn't," she said.

"Oh, you should," he said. "The chef from *Diablo* is at the grill recreating his bar menu classics. You won't want to miss out."

The metal handle of the case with the painting almost

slipped from her hand. Had she heard him correctly? Myles V. Paquin, known as MVP, was a Miami culinary sensation and a master of fusion cuisine. His restaurant in the Design District, *Diablo*, was a hot spot. It wasn't Michelin star-rated or anything, but it was *the* place for brunch and dinner. She had wanted to celebrate her thirtieth birthday at the restaurant this year but no luck. Not one seat was available.

"You came all this way," he said. "At least let me feed you."

Angel swallowed the last bits of her resolve. Not only was she staying for dinner, if he kept this up, she might eat out of his hands.

Two

Angel was in paradise.

Chef MVP fussed over kebabs on a massive grill. Grammy winner DJ Jordan regaled the table with tales of drunken nights in Ibiza. Fashion models Jenny Xi and Rose Rachid, an exceptionally attractive couple, shared recipes and real estate investment tips. Alessandro (she refused to call him Sandro) played the role of the solicitous host. He was the life pulse of the party, readily sampling Myles's spicy grilled corn, laughing at Jordan's corny jokes, and asking Rose follow-up questions. At some point he passed Jenny the name and number of his real estate agent. As he juggled those tasks, he kept Angel's wineglass full and encouraged her to sample every dish. All of this took place on a terrace that stretched out beneath the stars.

During dessert, he pulled up a chair next to hers. His bathing suit was dry and the buttons of his shirt had been left undone. Relaxed and happy, he looked centerfold ready.

"Do you like working for Gallery Six?" he asked.

He was probably just making conversation, but he'd hit a sore spot. Gallery Six was one of South Florida's premier galleries, one of only two that had been invited to show at Art Basel. Truthfully, it was a bit pretentious for Angel's tastes, but she wouldn't complain. Not everyone got to follow their life's true calling or succeed at the career of their choice. "It's an exciting place to work," she said. That wasn't too far from the truth.

"Have you worked there long?"

"Under a year." Angel took a sip of wine. Their conversation was getting lopsided. She ought to reciprocate, show some interest in his work. "I liked you in *Shadows Need Light*."

Myles passed along two dessert dishes with slices of coconut flan. Alessandro handed her one. "Do you like me in person, though?"

He was more beautiful on the big screen, but much more interesting to look at in real life. Either way, she liked him just fine. Still, it was more fun to tease him. "You know what they say about meeting your heroes."

He narrowed his eyes at her. "Should I be flattered you ever considered me a hero, or disappointed I fell short of your expectations?"

Angel wasn't disappointed. She was well fed and having an amazing time. "You met my expectations," she said. "And thanks for dinner. It was awesome."

"It's not over. Try the flan."

It turned out to be the best advice. The flan was light, creamy and delicious. "I know you're a big movie star and everything, but how did you get Myles Paquin to cook your dinner? I can never get a reservation at his restaurant."

"Myles? He's my cousin!"

"Oh?"

She stared at the chef but could not pick up a trace of familial resemblance. Myles was the color of brown sugar with long, thick, wavy hair that deserved its own social media channel. Still, she wasn't so closed-minded to rule out their family ties. "Are you a clan of prodigies, by any chance?"

He licked the back of his fork. "More like a clan of delinquents. We grew up on the same block. His mother is my 'aunt,' just not really."

"And you're still close after all these years?"

"I can't shake him loose."

Angel was envious. She did not have a bench of childhood friends to call up at a pinch. It was her fault, for spending most of her free time in her artist's studio. And by studio, she meant her bedroom.

After the plates were cleared away, DJ Jordan was the first to leave. Despite his occupation, or maybe because of it, he was an early sleeper. "Peace, bro!" he shouted on his way out.

"Peace!" Alessandro called back.

Shortly thereafter, Rose picked up her miniscule purse and announced that she and Jenny were heading out. She was a stunning black woman, long and lanky. She wore her hair braided in neat rows gathered at the nape of her neck. Her accent was decidedly French.

"Cool meeting you," she said to Angel. "Love your name, by the way. Is it short for Angela, Angelica, Angelina…?"

"Angeline." The name had been in her family for generations.

"That's French!" she exclaimed. *"Tu parles Français?"*

Angel had to focus to generate a somewhat decent answer. *"Un peu… Je suis Haitienne…mais Americaine."*

"Je suis Marocaine," Rose said with a laugh. "Don't worry. I won't torture you with any more French." She planted a kiss on Alessandro's forehead. "We're still on for tomorrow."

Alessandro joined his hands behind his head. "We'll see."

"Oh, don't start!" Jenny scolded. She draped an arm around her girlfriend's waist. "Gigi will be here tomorrow and she'll set you straight."

Rose beckoned to Myles, who was absently scrolling through his phone. "Hey you! We might as well take the same ferry off Fantasy Island."

"I don't ferry," Myles said. "I have my boat."

Rose and Jenny rejoiced.

"Aren't you suddenly more attractive!" Rose cried.

"It's not a yacht," Myles warned.

"Never mind yachts," Jenny said. "Let's go!"

The three headed inside the penthouse, calling out, "Ciao!"

"Kisses!"

"Later!"

Alessandro waved goodbye to his friends. "Get outta here! Be safe!"

Angel watched them go. They could not have been more obvious. Alessandro's friends were clearing out to give him space to...what?

"They know their way out," he said. "You don't have to look so concerned."

She was concerned, only not for them.

He studied her in his quiet way. "Let's play a game. Up for it?"

The only game she ought to play was one that resulted in her transferring ownership of an oil painting and him transferring funds into the gallery's account. Win-win. Angel wasn't so green as to ignore the timeworn principle: no deal was done until money had exchanged hands.

Maybe it was the food, the wine, the flan and the whole dolce vita vibe, but yeah...she was up for it.

"You tell me one secret or embarrassing thing about yourself, and I'll do the same. It doesn't have to cut deep. You don't have to unearth a childhood trauma. Just something. Okay?"

She reached for her wineglass. This game did not sound fun. "You go first."

"Okay," he said. "When I was fifteen I stole a car, stripped its tires and sold them in under an hour. I used the money to buy a PlayStation."

The look on her face must have given him ample ammunition to come after her. "God, I can't believe you bought that!"

"It's not true?"

"No way!"

In her defense, he'd established the rules. "This is a bluffing game?"

"I never stole a car," he said. "I've never stolen anything. I went to a high school for performing arts and did community theatre!"

"What's the point of this game?"

"I know what I look like and what people think when they see me."

His view must be distorted because from where she sat, he was *Temptation*. "Community theatre?" she said, trying to make light of the whole thing. "You're losing street cred in my eyes."

"I'll take that chance." He paused "You're safe with me, if that's what you're wondering."

How could Angel make him understand? A man's penthouse apartment did not rank high on the designated safe spaces for women. Either way, her unease wasn't rooted in fear. She needed clear boundaries, signs, guideposts, a rulebook and adult supervision to be alone with him.

"That's not what I'm wondering," she said.

"What then?"

"To be or not to be?"

He laughed. "What?"

"You're not the only one who's dabbled in theatre."

"So we have that in common," he said. His voice was rich and sweet and he served it up like coconut flan.

Angel studied him openly. This man had poured her wine, fed her heirloom tomatoes and left the table to retrieve clean utensils when she'd dropped her fork. She'd been convinced that he was showing off for his friends. Now, though, his audience had cleared out. They were alone and he was not letting up. Alessandro Cardenas was still flirting with her, and she did not know how to deal.

"Alright," she said. "I'll confess to something bad."

His gaze flickered. "You? Angel? *No me digas*."

"When I was fourteen, I stole blue nail polish at a dollar store."

"Wait a minute," he said. "I confessed to grand auto theft. That's a felony in some states. And you give me dollar store nail polish?"

"You confessed to nothing!" she fired back. "And FYI: I wasn't shocked at your made-up juvenile delinquency."

He tilted his head and peered at her through his long, thick lashes. "No?"

"I promise," she said. "I wasn't prepared, that's all. You said no childhood trauma."

He leaned back in his chair. His shirt gaped open. That smooth expanse of skin was just an arm's length away.

"I said it to reassure you. You looked so scared."

"If I look *scared*, it's because I'm way off course here!" she snapped. "I'm on the clock. And yet, here I am, out here, playing games with you!"

She could get fired for this. When celebrities stopped by the gallery, the sales staff was never allowed to get too close. They were supposed to maintain an attitude of professional indifference at all times.

"And yet, here you are playing games with me," Alessandro repeated, as if the actor in him could not resist the chance to pump her words for full dramatic effect.

His eyes lingered on her face. For the first time that night, Angel heard the soft murmur of the surf. It had always been there beneath their chatter and laughter. The question she'd been truly turning in her mind bobbed to the surface. She dared to say it.

"Why does it feel like you don't want me to go?"

His gaze flickered, a ripple in the sea. "Because I don't."

Angel exhaled, feeling better with it all out in the open. But he looked pensive. He stood up and extended a hand. "Come on. I'll buy your painting and take you home."

Her heart sank. He'd come to a conclusion about her. What was it? That she was too small town to play at his level, too uptight, too *scared*. But wasn't she all those things?

She ignored his outstretched hand and stood on her own. The time for fun and games was over.

"You're under no obligation to buy it," she said. "You haven't even seen it."

"I'm familiar with it."

The case with the painting was where Angel had left it. If anyone had walked off with it, her boss would have sold her on the black market to recoup the cost. He sat on the arm of one of the two suede cloudlike couches. Under his watchful gaze, she punched in the pin, released the lock, and reached in for the eight-by-ten-inch framed oil painting. "As requested: *El Jardín Secreto* by Juan David Valero."

The small painting wasn't as pretentious as *Temptation*. Did it merit a *Miami Vice* sunset speedboat trip across the bay for an in-person delivery? Maybe not. Juan David Valero was a respected but obscure artist from Cuba who had passed away decades ago. Very few high-profile collectors were clamoring for his work.

Earlier, Angel's boss had sent her a prepared statement via text message. She pulled out her phone and read it aloud.

"The midcentury Cuban artist is best known for his renderings of daily life in 1950s Havana."

She glanced at Alessandro to gauge his reaction. The set of his jaw led her to abandon the prepared statement. She pocketed her phone. "It's no *diptych*," she said. "But I love that the artist's only ambition was to share a tender memory."

His expression softened. Encouraged, Angel continued. "The artist renders landscapes in muted shades of green and yellow and blue. That's unusual in Caribbean art, which is usually bursting with color. Valero was a Cuban exile. I believe he used color to communicate his nostalgia."

"He was depressed," Alessandro said flatly.

Angel studied the little painting with new eyes. The garden was bursting with red bougainvillea, but always tucked away in the shade. All the beauty in the world was veiled in darkness. "It's possible. I'll admit I'm not too familiar with this artist's body of work."

"It's fine."

It was not fine. She would have done her homework if she'd had the time. "I'm standing in for Justine Carr. It was all very last minute and—"

"Angel, trust me. It's fine," he said.

"Alright." She handed him the canvas and, to her disappointment, he placed it on a side table without so much as a glance.

"Why do you even want it?" It was such a modest painting, so unlike the artwork on display in the house.

His gaze slid down her body, liquid and hot. "We want what we want."

"I want a straight answer."

"You got one."

Angel took a breath. Her job wasn't to talk the client out of the sale. "We're asking forty-five grand."

"And that's what you'll get."

In her opinion, he was overpaying by ten grand. But he hadn't asked her opinion. Plus, in the spirit of Art Basel, overpaying for stuff was part of the fun. He reached for his phone and completed the transfer of funds. She received email confirmation. Her boss sent her a text message with a thumbs-up emoji. She handed over the envelope with the bill of sale and certificate of authentication. It joined the painting on the table.

Angel could now confirm that reports of Alessandro Cardenas's appreciation for art were greatly exaggerated. He was likely collecting random pieces for the same reasons rich people did anything: the tax break. *El Jardín Secreto* would probably end up buried in Freeport art storage in Delaware.

"We're done," she said.

"Seems so," he said. "But what's the matter? You don't look happy."

She snapped the case shut. "I'm thrilled."

"You don't look it."

"It's just…art is personal to me," she said. "I understand that for some it's strictly an investment."

He steepled his fingers. "Go on."

"I'd prefer to sell you a piece that would…" She grappled for the right word. "I don't know…"

"Spark joy?"

His snarky tone pissed her off. "Yes! Pinwheels of joy! Why not?"

He grinned. "It's sparking something!"

That devious grin! It poked out when you least expected it, like the sun in a rainstorm. She had to drop this. What did it matter if he loved the painting or not? Whether he sold it on eBay or hung it in his bathroom, it was none of her business.

Her phone buzzed in her dress pocket. Angel reached for it, needing an excuse to look away. There was a chance it was a text from her boss with a follow-up question. It wasn't.

NEW POST ALERT! @CHRIS_UNDERWATER posted a new video to his channel: DEEP DIVE, A FRESHWATER EXPLORATION

Angel stared at the screen. Eyes stinging, she swiped away the alert. She was suddenly furious with herself. Her ex was off living his best aquatic life. Here she was with a man who was making it very plain that he wanted to dive into her body. All she could do was think up excuses to say no. Is this who she wanted to be? The woman who rushed home to popcorn, boxed wine and YouTube? The woman who, decades from now, would sit on a rocker and tell her knitting circle about the night she'd met a handsome movie star and was too much of a mouse to make a move? She was worried about losing her job, too, only that didn't seem as important anymore.

Alessandro fished a set of keys from a copper bowl on the coffee table. "I'll take you home."

"No."

He went still. "No?"

"I'm in no hurry."

A series of unusual events had landed her here tonight. She'd stay and explore every avenue. Tomorrow she'd walk away, *run* away. But tonight, she'd play the role, be whomever she needed to be to take this chance.

Three

If Sandro believed in divine intervention and the like, he would have thought his grandfather had sent him an angel to guide him. Not the kind who comes in peace, but the other kind.

Earlier, his driver had called to inform him that the gallery rep was on the way up. Then his housekeeper texted: Ángel is here. Sandro and his friends had returned from a swim. He'd thought nothing of grabbing his rumpled shirt off the back of his chair and racing in from the terrace. He came skidding to a stop when he saw her. In her white dress and standing just where the sunlight slid across the terrazzo floor, there was something unearthly about her. Her honey-brown skin was aglow and her windswept hair, dark and wavy, had spun sunshine into a halo around her head. She looked up from the paintings that she'd been studying and fixed her steady, light-filled eyes on him.

Angel…short for Angeline.

He had no choice but to revisit his stance on divine intervention.

She had wanted to get straight down to business and wasted no time presenting the case with the painting he'd requested. He hadn't wanted her to open that case. Like a ticking time bomb, it had the potential of blowing up everything. Instead, he'd asked her to stay for dinner.

Sandro lived a YOLO lifestyle in Los Angeles; it was the Hollywood way. Now or never. Maybe he'd forgotten how to be around normal people. People who didn't jump into bed with the first attractive person they met. Unfortunately, they didn't have the time to get to know each other better. He was in town for only a few nights. On Monday he was flying back to California to start rehearsals for his next film. Sandro had come home to relax and hang with friends, not to find a lover. Since he'd laid eyes on Angel, he'd wanted to know if that option was on the table.

Now she wanted to stay. At last, the opening he'd been waiting for and, for some reason, he was hesitant. It came back to his first impression: she was a normal person, here to do a job. Shouldn't he leave her alone?

Take the gifts of this hour. That was his motto. *Just take it!* All night, he'd been so impatient to touch her, to feel all that glowing brown skin. If she could light him up with just a look from across a room, he wondered what other tricks she could do. He wanted his other senses satisfied. Touch, taste, smell—yes, he wanted her scent on his hands. But he couldn't overlook the glaring signs hinting that something was wrong.

He pointed to her phone. "What was that?"

She feigned innocence. "What was what?"

"That message upset you. It's obvious."

She shoved the phone into a pocket of her dress, as if to bury the evidence. "It was my alarm, reminding me of something I no longer have to do."

This angel was a little liar. "I should have asked if someone was waiting for you at home."

"No one is waiting for me anywhere."

"In that case..." He dropped his keys into the bowl. Then he led her back outside, not to the terrace where they'd had dinner but to the rooftop deck with its bar, lap pool, hot tub, outdoor shower and endless views. He pulled a fresh bottle from the stocked wine cooler beneath the bar, and poured two generous glasses of God-knows-what. They went to stand by the balustrade, facing the night.

"You have the best views," she said.

It was a quiet night. Sandro turned his back to the view and admired her instead. Tousled hair, eyes like topaz, lips wet with wine, he liked this view better.

"I had my eye on this place for a while," he said. "Bought it days after I signed a major endorsement deal. The sad truth is that I don't get to spend more than two weeks at a time here. I'm either in LA or on set. Most of the time my niece crashes here."

"I want to pity you," she said with a smile. "But it's so damn hard."

"Not looking for pity," he said. "I'm trying to tell you something."

She took a sip of wine. "What's that?"

He was momentarily distracted by the way the delicate gold chain she wore pooled at her collar. He yearned to lean in and kiss that spot. And for the first time all night he suspected that she might want him to. Before he did anything, Sandro had to make a few things clear.

"This trip will be shorter than most and I'll be gone in a few days."

She glanced up at him sharply. "Why would I need to know this?"

"Because I want you to have all the facts." Sandro wanted her to come out of her shell and play, but only if it felt right. "There's an upside: nothing you do or say tonight will matter. You can throw caution to the wind."

"First of all, everything matters. Second, what do you think I'm doing here?"

She pressed a palm to her chest as if to attest that her presence on his rooftop deck was proof positive she'd stepped so far out on a ledge she could not take one more step.

Sandro wasn't buying it. He pointed to the phone she'd hidden away. "I think you're hiding the truth in your pocket."

She let her head roll back out of sheer weariness. And this time, he could not restrain himself. "May I touch you?"

She gave him a hard look. He expected her to throw the contents of her wineglass in his face and he braced himself. To his relief, she nodded.

He leaned in and kissed where the thin gold chain grazed her collar. She didn't pull away. Instead, she brought the flat of her palm to his cheek, keeping him close.

"You can talk to me, Angel," he whispered against her warm skin. "I won't tell anyone."

"You'll judge," she whispered back.

She was trembling.

Sandro buried his nose in the hollow of her neck. "You don't know me. I don't judge."

"And I'll never know you," she said. "Isn't that the point? In a few days, you'll be gone."

"In a few days, you'll have forgotten me."

"Do people forget the great Alessandro Cardenas?"

He pulled away from her and leaned against the balustrade. "When he's not putting on a performance, they do."

"Ah!" she exclaimed, as if she'd spotted the North Star or something.

"What is it?"

"It just hit me! I can be whomever I want and you can be yourself. Win-win."

Clever. He hadn't thought about it that way. "I like the sound of that."

She let out a shaky breath and when she spoke her voice was as fragile as a blade of grass. "My ex-boyfriend followed his bliss halfway around the world. Now he posts about his adventures on YouTube."

"You loved him?"

With so much to unpack, why had that been his first question?

"I used to."

"What's his bliss?"

"Marine biology, specifically coral ecology."

Sandro couldn't even diss the guy. The coral reefs were in peril and the jerk was doing something about it.

"I followed him from Central Florida to Miami so he

could wrap up research for his PhD. Then he packed up for Australia for a postdoc residency."

"And left you behind."

"Something like that."

Sandro did not want to know the answer to his next question, yet he had to ask. "Was that message from him just now?"

She moved away from him, walking backward. "If I were just dodging his messages, there'd be nothing to be embarrassed about."

He went after her. "Embarrassed? Now I need to know."

"Alright!" She took another sip of wine. "So I mentioned he started a YouTube channel. I get alerts each time he posts a new video."

Sandro barked out a laugh. "You little stalker!"

Her jaw dropped. "That's *not* what I'm doing!"

"That's exactly what you're doing."

"No!"

"Yes, my angel," he said. "You're cyberstalking your ex."

She groaned and pressed the wineglass to her forehead.

He took the glass from her and used the rim to raise her chin. "Admitting you have a problem is the first step to recovery."

"Oh, shut up!" She swatted him away. "It's just… He's exploring caves and sampling lagers… I don't know. His life seemed so interesting. Maybe I was keeping tabs."

"Hey! We've all been there."

"Really? Who have you stalked recently?"

Sandro shook his head. "In the interest of privacy, we won't name names."

She stared wide-eyed at him. "Interesting."

"Not really." In recent years, he'd learned to cut his losses. Which was what Angel had to learn.

She absently slid off her shoes and immediately lost a few inches. He wanted to fall at her feet.

"Since you're an expert, what's the next step?" she said.

"Aside from the usual blocking, unfollowing and deleting the app."

"All good precautions," he said. "What are your thoughts on rebound sex?"

She coughed. The nervous little sound echoed in the night. "I'm neither for nor against it."

"That's the cure," he teased. "Give it some thought."

Sandro walked over to the bar and set their glasses in the sink. She was hung up on her ex. Did he want to get mixed up in that? On the other hand, what did it matter to him? *If he followed his own logic, in a few days none of this would matter.*

Everything matters.

Angel stood with her hands in her pockets. "Are you offering your...services?"

He went to her and leaned close. This time he kissed the corner of her mouth. "When you put it like that, it sounds as dirty as it should be."

She went perfectly still. He breathed in her sweet floral perfume and he had his answer. He wanted to get mixed up in whatever this was.

"I wouldn't say no," she said.

That was a start. "I need you to say yes."

She took one step closer and whispered her answer. "Yes."

When Alessandro Cardenas offered sex, even obliquely, you said yes and dealt with the fallout later. That was only common sense. Right?

In a restroom off the pool deck, Angel was having a moment. She splashed water on her neck to cool down. She could lose her job over this. If word got out that she slept with clients, what other reputable gallery would have her? Her professional reputation would be destroyed before she had a chance to build it up. Angel dabbed her face and neck with a towel as these thoughts assailed her. Then her fingers lingered at the spot that he had kissed and, just like that, she was on fire again. There was no way she was backing out.

It wasn't like she hadn't considered rebound sex before he'd offered it. It was item No. 5 of her five-point plan to get over Chris. *#5 Get back on the saddle.* Only she hadn't even made it to *#2 Reconnect with old friends.* So this felt like jumping the gun. Then again, item No. 1 was to follow her bliss, and this oddly fit the bill.

God, but when he kissed her…the way he said her name…there was no way she could have said no.

For now, they were going for a swim.

Angel tied her hair in a topknot and stripped off her clothes. After a quick consultation in the mirror, she let out a resigned sigh. A runner since high school, her body was strong with a fair amount of curves. Right now, though, she might've regretted gorging on Chef Myles's food if it hadn't been so damn delicious! In a rattan basket, Angel found a collection of swimsuits, all new with tags. Alessandro had explained that his niece was a travel blogger/social media influencer and received tons of free clothes, some she made available for last-minute guests. She picked a one-size-fits-most black bikini with string ties, slipped it on and headed out the door before she lost her nerve.

He was nowhere to be found. The rooftop deck was deserted. She walked over to the pool's edge and for a minute she imagined him hanging out with his friends, lazily worshiping the sun while the others laughed and splashed around. The sound of pouring water caught her attention. She followed it to a manmade waterfall tucked away in an alcove. And there he was, naked, leaning forward with a hand pressed to the stone-paved wall as water rushed down the mountainous terrain of his back. She didn't have to imagine anything anymore.

She did not dare move.

He spotted her anyway and stepped out of the water stream. "Found everything you needed?"

She nodded.

He reached out and rested a hand on her hip. It was warm and wet and she didn't realize until too late that he was tugging at the string holding the bikini bottom together.

"And you thought you'd need this?" One sharp tug and the bit of triangular fabric fell away. He then worked on the strings tied below her shoulder blades and lifted the bikini top over her head. "You won't need this, either."

Her heart thundered in her chest as he guided her into the shower. He held her by the waist under the heavy stream. Water poured down her back and between her breasts. He drew her to him, kissed her then gently eased her back into the stream, letting the rush of water do its job. The pressure beat down on her. He drew her to him once again and smoothed back her hair. Angel had to blink to see clearly. His face was inches from hers. Drops of water clung to his lashes and shone like glass beads. She had no idea what other people thought when they saw him, but she thought he was devastatingly beautiful.

Inhibitions thoroughly washed away, Angel mingled her fingers with his and guided his hand between her thighs. Water poured down their bodies, but she wanted him to discover the wetness there. His touch made her delirious. She shut her eyes and tipped backward.

He drew her back and held her tight. "Stay close."

Angel whimpered. He pressed a kiss to her ear and, voice gruff, murmured, "What do you need?"

More of this! All of this! Warm water, cool breeze, moonlight, his touch, all of it! Those words were crammed in her throat. She couldn't speak.

He gathered her hair and tugged on it. "Talk to me."

"I need you."

Oh, girl... What had just come out of her mouth?

There was no time for regrets. He crushed them all with his kiss.

Four

With a hop, skip and a jump, Angel had landed in bed with a notorious Hollywood heartthrob. The chorus of internal voices that had egged her on last night wasted no time shaming her in the morning. She'd obviously lost her mind. Had she risked her job for a one-night stand? She'd let a sweet-talking celebrity turn her head. The man had flown down from California to party all weekend and she'd offered herself up as a favor!

These thoughts invaded her mind before she even opened her eyes. It was 6:00 a.m. She knew it without having to consult her phone or watch. Angel woke up every morning at six, often to start her day with a quick run or to prep a canvas for later that night. It had been months since she'd done either of those things, yet the habit remained. Alessandro was sleeping beside her, his breath crashing in even waves. Angel listened, her own breath rising and falling, keeping time with his.

She was wading in dangerous waters. The sounds of his breath, his warmth, his leg thrown over hers, the citrusy scent of his sheets—together they had the force of an emotional riptide strong enough to pull her under. She wanted to cuddle close to him and fall back asleep. Maybe later he'd wake her with demanding kisses.

She wanted to do it all again.

For that precise reason, she had to get the hell out.

Running had always been part of her hastily hashed plan. Putting the plan in motion was tricky. She hadn't thought it would be this elaborate, a hug and a quick kiss goodbye at 2:00 a.m. at most. But after they'd made love on his bedroom floor, he'd scooped her up and carried her to bed. She'd plunged into a deep sleep.

Thanks to top-notch blackout drapes, the room was plunged in darkness. Without risking a glance at her bed partner, Angel slipped out from under the sheets. Where had she left her dress? And her shoes? All she had within reach was the large white towel he'd wrapped around her body before they took off running from the rooftop deck to his bedroom for quick access to his stash of condoms. The towel lay crumpled now on the wood floor as a cruel reminder of just how *fun* last night had been, how much more fun they could have this morning if she could bring herself to stay.

Stick to the plan.

Angel grabbed the towel, wrapped it around her body and tiptoed out of the room. She hesitated a while, her hand on the knob, her forehead pressed to the closed door. Privately she thanked him, wished him luck and said goodbye.

It was better this way, and by "better" she meant "easier" on her.

Angel turned away from the door and toward more practical matters. Finding her clothes would require no less than a scavenger hunt. She'd changed out of her dress in the rooftop restroom, but had stepped out of her heels well before that. Where had she left them? She gingerly made her way down the hall to the main living area. Which way to the roof? She couldn't remember. And how would she even get off this damn island? It wasn't as if she could order an Uber.

Help arrived in the form of the housekeeper. At this early hour, she was humming to herself while watering a bird of paradise in a massive white planter. She turned from her task. The look she gave Angel loosely translated into, *"¡Ay pobrecita!"*

"Good morning," Angel said, her dignity in shreds.

"Come," she replied. "I have everything you need."

Her name was Maritza. She'd gone on the scavenger hunt.

and collected Angel's things, including the metal case that she'd forgotten all about. It cost north of two hundred dollars and the gallery would have taken it out of her salary.

Burning with equal parts gratitude and humiliation, Angel changed in a powder room off the foyer. When she emerged, she asked Maritza how she might catch the ferry.

"I can arrange for a driver to meet you in the lobby. Is that okay?"

Angel was dangerously close to tears. "That's great. Thank you so much. For everything."

Maritza escorted her to the elevator and left Angel with a pat to her shoulder.

A golf cart ride to the marina, a race along the dock to catch the ferry already pulling away, a quick leap on board, and Angel had made it out of paradise. She took a seat on a wood banquette and kept her gaze fixed on the Miami skyline. Her fellow passengers were properly dressed and likely returning home from night shifts as nannies and security guards. Out of respect, Angel resisted breaking into hysterical laughter.

It had been a night of firsts. First one-night stand…with a celebrity. First time she'd ever ducked out on a man without so much as a kiss goodbye. First orgasm in an outdoor shower, which was a weirdly specific category but nonetheless true. First full night's sleep since Chris's departure. First time she'd opened up about Chris to anyone.

Angel hadn't confided in anyone about the breakup, mostly because she'd lost touch with most of the friends she'd left behind in Orlando. As for family, that was dicey. Her older sister, Bernadette, was judgmental as hell. Newly married, she had cautioned Angel not to trail after Chris to Miami. *He won't marry you*, she'd proclaimed, as if marriage were the ultimate goal in life. When news of their breakup got out, Bernadette had wasted no time sending an "I told you so" text.

She hadn't gone into details with Alessandro, but it had

felt good to release the pressure valve. Chris Moyer, a native of landlocked Nebraska with a lifelong fascination with the sea. This had led him to Florida to study marine biology. A native Floridian, Angel had always taken the beaches for granted. She and Chris had met in graduate school. He was pursuing a doctorate; she was wrapping up an MFA. Theirs was an opposites attract sort of thing, but they truly could not have been more different. A pragmatic guy with single-minded focus, Chris had never aligned with Angel's fluid views on life and career. He had short-and long-term goals that extended into the next decade or two. Angel could not see too far into the future and took each day as it came. In the end, though, this attitude hadn't served her and she was actively working to change.

On her thirtieth birthday two things happened. Angel could not get a reservation at *Diablo* and a gallery turned her down for a group exhibition. Chris had patiently waited until the next day to announce that he had accepted a post-doctorate position in Australia and didn't think it was a good idea for her to come along. "This was fun," he'd said, dismissing three years of a committed relationship with three one-syllable words.

This. Was. Fun.

Fun was dinner under the stars, playing bluffing games, talking to the point of revealing too much, holding back only to spill everything out with no regrets. Fun was a first kiss under a manmade waterfall followed by a mad race to the bedroom on bare, slippery feet.

Angel lowered her head in her hands. Bernadette was right. The last thing she needed was fun. Her fun career in the arts was a flop. The fun ride of her last relationship had ended in a ditch. For the sake of her sanity, all the fun she'd had last night had to be shelved away.

In a few days, you'll forget me.

Oh, how she wished that were true.

Five

Angel was gone. Sandro woke up sure of it.

He shot up, sent the sheets flying and scrambled out of bed. In a move that ended up saving him time, he yanked back the thick curtains to let in some light. From his bedroom, he could see as far as the marina. He caught sight of her tiny frame racing barefoot along the dock, shoes cradled in her arms, hair in the wind.

This little angel is bad.

He watched the ferry fade into the distance and sighed. It was for the best. Sandro had an eye for beauty, and sometimes it led him astray. Right now he couldn't afford the distraction. He was on a mission in Miami, an unpleasant one that required a level head. Yet, as distractingly beautiful as Angel was, she had not wasted his time. She had delivered the painting and the certificate of authenticity that wasn't worth the card stock it was printed on.

It surprised him that for all her keen-eyed observations, she was clueless regarding the nature of her errand. She had not connected the dots between him and the artist Juan David Valero. Sandro liked her all the more for it.

Alessandro David Cardenas was the grandson of Juan David Valero. His favorite grandson, by all accounts. At his death, Sandro had inherited the bulk of his paintings. A fire had destroyed half and Alessandro made it his mission to preserve the rest. He had repurchased anything he could find on the market, which wasn't much. His grandfather had not been, by any stretch, a commercial success. And yet new pieces kept cropping up. It wasn't until a friend had very proudly unveiled a Valero original purchased while on a fishing trip in Miami that Sandro began to suspect these new pieces were fakes. The painting of the Havana Harbor at dusk had all the trappings of his late grandfather's work—the broad brushstrokes and the muted color palette that Angel had so beautifully described—but there was something "off" about it. That was all he could say. Sandro's friend, a Cuban attorney from New Jersey, had all the best intentions. He had not wanted to embarrass the guy, so he kept his suspicions to himself. He did get the name of the Lincoln Road art gallery that had sold him the painting and made some inquiries.

What role, if any, did Angeline Louis play in this? None, he'd decided, and shut the door to any doubts.

Sandro went to the old wood desk that used to belong to his grandfather, flipped open a notebook and drew her face from memory with an ink pen. He did not want to forget her. He sketched her angular face, almond-shaped eyes, flared nose, and heart-shaped mouth. What that mouth had done to him...

He dropped the pen, the memories flooding back. The attraction between them had been there, whole and intact, the instant they'd met. He thought her beautiful from the start, but once she had started describing his grandfather's work, from the muted color palette to the emotional undertones, he found her riveting.

The scripted speech had irritated him. He'd held the hands that had mixed those paints and didn't need a lecture. Still, he'd appreciated the way she went on to present his *abuelo* as a person, not merely a signature on a canvas. She'd looked for nuance and meaning in the composition, color palette and even the brush strokes. Then he'd reminded himself that what she was so poetically describing was in all likelihood a cheap fake. His reaction had upset her. He liked that she cared so much.

He just liked her.

For all her good intentions, Angel was wrong about his grandfather whom she'd painted as a romantic figure, struck with nostalgia—the classic affliction of the Cuban exile. Juan David, JD to the family, had fled Castro's Cuba in 1970, leaving behind his country, his family, and a fiancée whom he loved. That was certainly enough to cripple any man. It took years for Sandro to acknowledge the deeper truth: his grandfather was flat out depressed. He would have benefited from therapy and medication if his machismo hadn't prevented him from seeking help.

It certainly didn't help that the old man felt like a failure. Having dedicated his life to his art, JD never made a penny from it. And that was why Sandro was determined to prevent anyone from exploiting his work after his death. He would protect his legacy no matter what.

Sandro slipped on shorts, grabbed his phone and went to the kitchen for coffee. Maritza was there and had already poured him a cup. She was spooky like that.

She put the cup on the island counter before him. "Your friend is gone."

"Ah!" he said. So that's how she'd managed it, with Maritza's help.

"She is a very nice girl, very pretty, very polite."

There was a not-so-subtle reproach in her voice. "And I'm not nice?"

"You are a Hollywood playboy."

Did she think he'd kicked the very pretty, very polite girl out of bed? "She left me! I was sleeping and she took off. *You* helped her."

Maritza joined her hands as if in prayer. "I am not telling you how to live your life. I only said that she is a nice girl."

"Who's a nice girl? You can't mean me." His niece, Sabina, entered the kitchen. She was wearing the same outfit that she'd worn when she'd left the day before. "What did I miss? Did Tío have a girl over?"

"Good morning," Sandro said. "And never mind that."

Maritza poured Sabina a cup of coffee and discretely

backed out of the kitchen. He had the suspicion that his housekeeper didn't think his niece was "nice."

Sabina stirred sugar in her coffee and confronted him. "What's that in the living room?"

"What's what?" Sandro asked.

She brushed a lock of black hair away from her face. "The painting by JD. Where did you get it?"

Sabina was his half brother Eddy's daughter, but she looked more and more like her mother who had tragically passed away when she was twelve. Eddy had since remarried and moved to Tampa. Sabina did not get along with her stepmom and stayed on Fisher Island whenever she was in Miami. Her official occupation was travel blogger.

Sandro put down his mug. "Why do you need to know?"

Sabina continued her interrogation. "Why did you buy it? What's your plan? To put it away with the others?"

The "others" were in storage, except for the few in his LA home. "Does that bother you?"

"Art is supposed to be on display for people to love and admire," she said. "JD wouldn't want you to hoard his work like that."

He wasn't hoarding anything. And what would she know about it? His grandfather died two years after she was born. "If you have so many strong opinions, why don't you paint yourself? You used to back when you were in high school."

"I used to pole dance back in high school, too," she said. "For the exercise."

Sandro sipped his coffee. This conversation had taken an odd turn.

"Daddy thinks it's selfish of you to hide JD's work, and I agree."

So it was *Daddy* now? She hadn't called her father that in a while. Interesting that his niece's change of heart coincided with the one time that she and Eddy were taking sides against him.

"So I'm selfish," Sandro said. "I can live with that."

She slammed down her tiny spoon. "You're a big deal now! Why not use your platform to promote his work? Let people discover it. You'd be surprised how much they'd pay—"

"No."

"Okay," she said. "If you're not interested, let me try. I'll never be as big as you but—"

"No."

As the eldest grandchild, Eddy had happily inherited their grandfather's fishing boat. Sandro had inherited the valueless art. There had been no formal reading of a will, but as boys they'd agreed to this. The boat had been sold for scraps years ago. The art, however, would outlast them all.

"Why?" Sabina snapped. "You do it for your friends? Why not your family?"

"What are you talking about?"

"Myles's restaurant! Jordan's DJ gigs! You promoted them and they blew up!"

If he were petty, he'd add her travel blogging career to that list. "I don't promote them. I attend their events on my own time. I can't help it if my friends are talented."

"So what do you call going live on Instagram at *Diablo*'s grand opening or at Club TENTEN when Jordan has a set?"

"I call it living my life." What would be the point of promoting his grandfather's paintings? He had no intention of selling them. His hope was to pass them on to his kids…and his niece. Anyway, it was much too early for this conversation. "Sabina, I can't deal with you right now."

"You won't have to. I'm only here to pack a bag."

He had been looking forward to spending time with her today. "Don't go. You just got here."

"Don't take it personally. It's work. Soho House is hosting influencers this weekend for Art Week. And spare me the sad puppy eyes. Sounds like you won't be lonely." She grabbed a banana from the fruit bowl Maritza kept full and swirled out of the kitchen. "Catch you later, Tío!"

Sandro felt the stab of heartburn. This day wasn't supposed to have started with him arguing with his niece over his grandfather's paintings, and no amount of coffee was going to fix that. It should have begun in bed with Angel. But he'd been cheated of that experience and it was making him cranky. There was no other way to put it, really. He'd been cheated.

The door to Sabina's bedroom slammed shut. What was he going to do about the growing gulf between him and his family? He hated to draw this parallel, but since bringing home the Oscar two years back, his relationships with his few remaining family members had deteriorated. His brother rarely called and now he was filling Sabina's head with ideas. It saddened him. With his father long dead and two-thirds of his relatives back in Cuba, many he would likely never meet, Sandro didn't take family for granted.

His phone buzzed with a text message. He welcomed the distraction. At least he could always count on his friends. Georgina Garcia, better known as Gigi, was the daughter of a former Dominican baseball star. Sandro was lucky to count the trust fund baby–turned–film studio head as one of his best friends. He had worked on one of her first projects and his performance had earned her studio its first Independent Spirit Award. It had also gotten him a meeting with the director of *Shadows Need Light*, the biopic of Cuban cinematographer and activist Néstor Almendros. He'd cinched the role of Julio, one of Néstor's lovers and a fellow gay rights activist.

Gigi was in Miami for the same reason everyone was in Miami. The text message read:

Tonight's itinerary: Cocktails at Pérez Museum, Basel event for one hour tops, dinner at the Mandarin and after-party at the Aston Martin Residences. Are you in? Or are you in???

Sandro was about to reply when his agent, Leslie Chapman, called with the classic combo of good news and bad news. A standoff between the director of his next film and the production company had resulted in more setbacks. Rehearsals were delayed until after the holidays.

"What's the problem?" he asked. This was meant to be his first big budget fantasy movie in which he played a space pilot.

"Money is the problem."

"What's the good news?"

"You've got some time off," she said. "Yay!"

"Come on, Leslie! What am I going to do with time off?"

Sandro knew that most people didn't react this way to the prospect of free time. However, he wasn't wired like most people. He worked. That's what he did. Day in, day out, around the clock, he worked. On short breaks like this one, which were few and far between, he connected with friends and partied hard. That was how he liked it. Everything in balance.

"For God's sake, man! You're home on a private island in Miami. I'd trade places with you in a heartbeat. Plus it's December and before you know it, the—"

"The holidays? If you tell me to spend time with my family, so help me—"

"Boy, please!" Leslie cried. "I was going to say the Golden Globe nominations are around the corner. I've got a good feeling. Take some time to relax. It's going to be wild after that."

It was Leslie's job to dream big. Sandro had no reasonable expectation of a Golden Globe nomination for his supporting role in a series that had aired on a new streaming platform. He'd been snubbed for the Emmy, after all. That didn't bother him too much. His pride in his work wasn't contingent on winning a gold statue. Leslie was right on one point: he *was* home. A little solitude wouldn't kill him.

There was the pool, and if not the pool, the beach. *And Angel... Don't forget Angel...*

"I'll send you scripts to read and look out for a television appearance on a holiday special. Or maybe a late-night talk show. How about Fallon? Would that cheer you up?"

"Don't bother," he said. "I'm going to take your advice."

Leslie hollered over the line. "Am I dreaming or what?"

"It wouldn't kill me to slow down."

"Damn straight! And I like to keep my clients busy. You know my motto."

Sandro chanted, "You make money, I make money."

"And we all go home happy, baby!" Leslie chimed. "Except today I recommend that you *stop* working. Just. Stop. There's such a thing as burnout."

As a black woman in Hollywood, Leslie understood the business better than most. She knew how hard it was to break past stereotypes and score the types of roles that got an actor noticed. Sandro was a trained actor, but he would have been stuck playing the bad boy boyfriend or "some kind of Latino" for life if he hadn't signed with Leslie. Now that his career was on track, he was in a strike-the-iron-while-it's-hot frame of mind. When you came from a long line of starving artists, to be at long last bankable meant everything.

He said goodbye to Leslie. Maritza returned, cleared away his coffee cup and put a glass of water in his hand. He was no match for the women in his life today.

Sandro left the kitchen for the rooftop deck. Leslie's words echoed in his mind as he climbed the stairs. *You're home.* In recent years, he'd felt most at home on a movie set. That left him feeling adrift when he wasn't at work. Nothing balanced about that.

He grabbed a net and scooped out a few leaves floating on the pool's surface. He hadn't come up here for pool maintenance. He needed a visual aid to relive last night.

May I touch you?
Please.
He stretched out on a lounge chair and finally replied to Gigi's message. He was all in. Except for the drinks at the museum part. They could count him out of that. He had something else in mind.

Meet up with you at Basel.

Six

For four days in December, Miami Beach was the epicenter of the art world. Art Basel drew a wealthy, well-heeled crowd with money to waste on or to invest in, depending on whom you asked, modern art. A convention center the size of a warehouse was divvied up into viewing rooms, similar to booths at any bazaar worth wandering in. Each exhibitor's room rivaled the other, some were stark and spare, others were kaleidoscopes of colors and light. But each showcased carefully curated collections from around the world. A Picasso, a Warhol, a Lichtenstein print, a bedazzled Buddha, a miniature porcelain toilet, or a bust of Columbus made entirely of chewing gum—it all counted as art. And Angel was here for it.

Too bad she was too distracted to appreciate it fully. With every blink of the eye, she was back in paradise, kissing Alessandro Cardenas under a waterfall. The memory was tangible; she could feel the water rush and swirl between her breasts and his hard body pressed against hers.

Angel massaged her temples in a fruitless effort to erase the memory. *Oh, God! Please. Let me forget.*

Her mental state wasn't lost on her boss. "Angel! You're as shaky as a Chihuahua! Please calm down."

Perfect! The night had not yet begun and Angel had managed to piss off Paloma. As the newest member of the Gallery Six team, she wasn't part of the elite sales force led by the flame-haired Paloma Gentry. Angel was meant to stay behind and man the Lincoln Road shop like a sad and sorry Cinderella while Paloma, Justine and the rest had twirled in the Basel spotlight. Justine's accident had thrown a wrench in that plan. Paloma (real name Paula) was so brittle, you'd think Angel had ordered the hit on her top salesperson. It was unfair. What had she done except be helpful? She'd successfully closed Justine's last deal, getting top dollar for the Juan David Valero painting. And here she was tonight, looking damn good in Miami's answer to Millennial Pink and glowing like never before. She'd gone the extra mile and added some temporary golden highlights to her wavy brown hair. Bottom line: she was ready.

Was she just going to gloss over the part where she had sex with the client straight after closing the sale? Yes, as sure as the sun set in the west.

Paloma clapped to get her attention. Wearing all black and a ton of gold jewelry, red hair pulled into a severe bun, she had gallerista style down pat. "We are competing with galleries from Europe and all over the world. We have to measure up. Celebrities can smell nervousness. It's a turn-off."

"We wouldn't want to do that."

"No, we wouldn't," Paloma said. "Listen. I know you're a bit rough around the edges. That's understandable. A degree in fine arts doesn't prepare you for the art world. But you're going to give me an ulcer if you don't calm down."

Angel took offense at that. Her edges were smooth as silk, thank you very much! Besides, this wasn't her first Basel. It was her second. Her first visit to the art show dated back to when she qualified for a student discount, but still.

"Go and grab a drink at the lounge before the night gets going and the A-listers show up."

According to Paloma, there was Europe and the rest of the world, A-listers and ordinary people who weren't worth her time. But for all of her poise and polish, Paloma came undone when any B-lister wandered into their gallery.

She had almost made it to the exhibitors' lounge when it

struck her: one of those highly anticipated A-listers could very well be Alessandro. She'd sort of ruled that out, since he'd had his art home delivered and all. But he was in town for Art Basel and this was the premier event. Why wouldn't he swing by with his colorful friends?

Angel dashed over to the bar for that drink she now sorely needed. The bartender gave her a choice of red, white or rosé. She picked the latter—strong enough to mend her nerves, but too light to mess with her head. Despite everything, Angel had to perform tonight. She had a job to do, a boss to impress and a commission to earn. The extra earnings would go a long way to help her relocate back home to Orlando.

Whenever Angel got to this point of her loosely strung plan, she felt a strange pang in her chest. Why was she having second thoughts about moving? Miami was an expensive city and with such stiff competition, she'd likely never get ahead here. She wouldn't miss the gallery. She would, however, miss Miami and its thriving art scene. Only this city wasn't her home and had never been her dream until Chris sold her on it. For that reason, and that reason only, she wanted a fresh start. She needed one.

A man approached the bar and, of the choices of red, white and rosé, opted for Patrón. There was nothing earth-shattering about that except for the man's deep, rich voice. Angel shivered. It couldn't be. She risked a sideways glance and found herself staring into a pair of dark eyes set in a face so ruggedly handsome it made her want to laugh and cry at the same time.

"Hello, Angel."

She died.

The last time she'd seen him looking this good, he was lording over her from a billboard, sporting a Rolex and a smile, while she stewed in traffic on I-95. Last night, at home in damp swim shorts and a crumpled shirt, he was amiable and approachable. She'd come close to forgetting his celebrity status so many times. Tonight, in what looked like a Tom Ford charcoal gray suit, clean-shaven, clear-eyed, he was killing her. Since she was hyperventilating, she had no choice but to accept that she was fangirling…hard. So much so that when the bartender placed her glass before her, she promptly knocked it over.

"Dammit!"

Alessandro closed the gap between them. "Are you okay?"

Her primary concern was for her dress. It was a Cushnie classic, rented from a designer clothing website. As she frantically brushed away the few drops that had splashed onto the silk-draped bodice, she spit out a jumble of words. "Yes. Sure. I'm fine. Yup."

Oh, joy! One look into his eyes and she'd suffered a mini-stroke. She might as well admit it: Paloma was right. She was a nervous wreck, shakier than a Chihuahua, not quite ready for primetime, golden highlights and all.

He handed her a cocktail napkin. "Here you go."

She wanted to thank him; instead, she reprimanded him. "What are you doing here?"

A slow smile crept to his lips. "Drowning my sorrows in tequila."

She doubted that very much. "The VIP lounge is down that way."

"Can't I hang out here?" he asked, lips twitching with that smile. "I promise I won't cause trouble."

Angel stared at him. She'd kissed those lips. She'd done more than that, but that was as far back as her mind would safely take her. "Obviously, I can't chase you away."

"True," he said. "But you could always run. Again."

"I didn't run…" Angel's voice sounded foreign to her own ears, so she thought it best to shut up.

The bartender who'd been minding his own business until now rushed forward. "Mr. Cardenas! You are welcome here, sir!"

Alessandro brought a finger to his lips. "Keep it quiet. I'm flying under the radar."

Now that was a waste of time. A star-studded international art fair was not the place to go incognito. Besides, any radar sweeping the area tonight would gravitate to him. Who was he wearing? What was he buying? Who was he taking home? Et cetera.

"I didn't mean to make you feel unwelcome," Angel said, mainly to appease the bartender. "Just wanted to point out that there's a full bar in the VIP."

He didn't have to settle for red, white or rosé when the exclusive collectors' lounge was top shelf only.

The bartender wouldn't hear it. "Never mind that. We can get you anything you want. Patrón Platinum, of course. We have an excellent limited edition—"

"Silver is fine," Alessandro said. "On ice." Then he turned to Angel. "What were you drinking?"

"The young lady was enjoying a rosé," the bartender replied on her behalf.

"Not sure she got a chance to enjoy it."

The mess on the counter was wiped away and a fresh glass, poured from a far superior bottle, was set before her. The drinks were free. Alessandro slipped a fifty-dollar bill across the counter and the grateful bartender took the tip— and the hint—and backed away.

"Missed you this morning," he said. "Missed me?"

Angel let out a shaky breath. Why did she like him so much? "Listen, I didn't run out on you. I was late for work and…you were sleeping and… I didn't want to wake you and…that's all."

"That doesn't answer my question."

Two women sporting matching silver bobs and chatting excitedly approached the bar.

"I do want to highlight the pieces from our new artist," one said. "That should be our focus. What do you think?"

The other woman stared blankly. "I, uh… Sandro?"

Ah! Poor thing! She'd gone brain dead. Angel knew the signs.

He said hello and the women swooned. Angel took Alessandro by the elbow and steered him to a cocktail table.

"How did you find me?" she asked. She thought she might bump into him before the end of the night, but this felt targeted.

"I'm here to meet friends," he said. "I took a wrong turn somewhere and ended up at the wrong bar—and there you were."

He hadn't been looking for her, after all. Her "check ego" dashboard light flashed red. "I'm glad we ran into each other. I meant to apologize for the way I left."

It was a big fat lie, necessary only to salvage her pride. If he could act cool and collected, so could she.

He picked up his glass and gave the ice a rattle. "Whatever you say."

Angel watched him over the rim of her glass. He hadn't bought a word she'd said. "Okay. I left the way I did because I didn't want to drag things out," she said. "I know the rules."

"What rules?" he asked. "There are none."

It was highly possible that in Alessandro Cardenas's happy-go-lucky world there were no preset rules. He did as he pleased.

"The rules of the one-night stand," she explained.

He sipped his tequila slowly. "I'm trying to remember the last time I had one of those. It's been a while. Generally, my lovers want to keep me around."

Angel went very still, his words painting visions in her mind. His lovers were braver souls than she'd ever be. Although she hated the cowardly way she'd ducked out this morning, she did not regret much else. This was not a game she could play, not anymore. She was happiest and most secure when in a stable relationship, which meant she tended to keep random boyfriends long past their expiration dates.

It also meant that she tended to choose partners with an eye for long-term compatibility. That simply wasn't the case here. Even so, she couldn't let him score this point.

"My lovers have never complained," she said.

This was true. If there were a Good Housekeeping Seal of Approval on keeping a lover happy, even if just temporarily, she would have earned it. And so would he. He'd left her blissed out. Which raised the question: Had she seriously cheated herself out of early morning sex for the sake of keeping her emotions neat and tidy?

He leaned close and whispered, "I believe it, Angel."

With him so close, she yearned to touch his face, to feel the smooth skin that was rugged the night before. She wanted him to kiss her neck again, to turn back time and relive it all, to have him take her home.

"Alessandro, I have to go…" she said plaintively. "I've got to get back to work before I get in trouble."

"What kind of trouble?"

"The kind you get into when your boss gives you a five-minute break and you hang out at the bar with your ex-lover for about a half hour!"

"I'm your ex?" he said, indignant. "After just one night?"

Angel dropped her hands onto the tabletop in despair and almost knocked her glass over again. Good thing it was empty. "It is what it is. Now I have to go."

Alessandro drained his glass then stood up straight and tugged at the cuffs of his shirt. "Okay. Let's go."

"Where are you going?" she asked.

"I got you in trouble. I'm getting you out of it."

She started to back away. "How?"

"I have my ways."

"Are you nuts? My boss can't know!" she protested, on the edge of panic.

The wicked grin came out to play. "Know about what, Angel?"

She glared at him. Was it too late to ask him to stop calling her by her nickname? Angeline was her grandmother's name and her world wouldn't stop spinning if he called her that.

"I can be discrete," he said. "Can you?"

Angel pinched the bridge of her nose. Which god had she angered to deserve this?

"Do you want my help or not?" he said.

She looked him in the eye, prepared to turn him down. He shoved his hands in his pockets and waited for an answer. The gesture caused his unbuttoned shirt collar to split and reveal the dip in his brown throat. She faltered. Why lie? She wanted it oh so very much.

Seven

Paloma was darting around their booth like a goldfish in a bag of water. When Angel approached, she snapped. "Where were you?" Then she got a glimpse of her companion and went pale everywhere except her cheeks that remained orgasm pink, courtesy of NARS Cosmetics.

"Look who I ran into," Angel said innocently.

"Sorry if I've kept Angeline away too long," Alessandro said. "I've been to this circus so many times, you'd think I'd know my way around. She was a big help."

Paloma rushed forward. "The convention center is a madhouse maze. Good thing Angel is resourceful."

Angel sighed with relief. No one short of an A-lister could have saved her from Paloma's wrath.

"I'm Paloma Gentry. How may *I* help you?"

Alessandro's response was polite but firm. "I'm with Angeline. Thank you."

Paloma looked as if she had to gulp for air. "I'll leave you to it."

Paloma went to her minidesk, set up like a throne in a corner of their viewing room. If a side-eye could kill, Angel would have had a gash across her throat.

She turned to Alessandro. "Thanks for using your influence to aid and assist the underprivileged."

"You're welcome, Angeline," he said. "I do what I can."

She had to stop flip-flopping on this, but she wished he'd quit calling her Angeline. He was doing it deliberately, to put distance between them, and all of a sudden she didn't like it.

"Alright," he said. "I think you're in the clear. Show me what you've got."

A personal challenge lurked in his words, and she took

it up. Angel looked around and picked a piece at random. Their collection was a little mix of everything, curated to draw in the social media crowd. Their featured pieces made for good Instagram content, but there were some hidden gems as well.

Angel led him straight to the crowd pleasers: neon text art with catchy phrases. "Here we have *YOLO*, by a young local artist." She pointed to the bold yellow letters with the poise of Vanna White.

Alessandro was nodding, as if YOLO were gospel. "I've got that tattooed somewhere."

She stifled a laugh. "No, you don't."

He slid her a glance. "How would you know?"

Heat rushed to her cheeks. Now she was turning orgasm pink. "I can't get into it right now."

"Want to get into it later?"

His gaze stayed on her, holding her in place—otherwise, she would have gone to pieces. "I'm working."

He pointed to the large yellow letters. "You only live once, Angel. What time do you get off work?"

"This thing ends at midnight," she said, before she could think better of it. She did not want to encourage him. "Let's continue."

Angel hurried along with the tour. She showed him an acrylic on canvas painting of a lemon and a lime, titled *Lemon Lime,* a collage of a bull dog, titled *Bruce*, and a flashing neon sign with the words: *Sorry. It's Me, Not You.*

He paused at that one. "The last time I used that excuse it didn't go so well."

"Bad breakup?" she asked.

"Is there any other kind?"

For once, Angel didn't spiral backward into a whirlpool of her tragic memories. Instead, she flipped through a mental catalogue of the gorgeous actresses and models that Alessandro had been photographed with over the years. Something inside her shrank. Under ordinary circumstances her self-esteem was rock solid, but nothing was ordinary about this.

"May I ask you a question?" she said.

"You can ask me anything."

Paloma chose that moment to return with champagne. "Mr. Cardenas, for you!"

Only a flicker of his lashes betrayed any trace of impatience, and Angel was sure Paloma had missed it. He accepted the flute of Veuve Clicquot, thanked her and dispatched her with a nod. He did not drink from the glass, but he used it to point at her. "You were saying."

Angel took a breath. She was just going to come out with it, before Paloma swung back around with an offering of pigs in a blanket or whatever. Who knew when they would speak again? "Please, don't get me wrong."

"I'll try not to."

"What do you want with me? There are so many more... fascinating women here."

Alessandro studied her a while before turning his attention to a glass sculpture of a dolphin. "You know what I was doing six years ago?"

"I don't."

"Serving drinks to fascinating women."

"You were a bartender?" Could he mix a decent margarita? Not too sour. Not too sweet?

"I was a bartender and a waiter and everything you can think of," he said. "These fascinating women were not interested in struggling waiters/actors."

"You're not struggling anymore." Angel felt the need to point this out in case he hadn't gotten the memo. Maybe his accountant had failed to inform him, but his net worth was up there.

He ran a thumb along the smooth curved lines of the sculpture. She wished he wouldn't touch the art, particularly because it reminded her of the way he had touched her.

"Here's something that might interest you." She led him

to the opposing wall, where a series of black-and-white photographs, titled *Devastation*, were on display. The series featured photos of Haiti after the 2010 earthquake, Bahamas after Hurricane Dorian, and Puerto Rico after the island was hit last summer by both varieties of natural disasters. "These photographs cut to the heart of the climate crisis by laying bare the consequences."

Alessandro studied each print. "I'm interested."

"Oh? You have the option of acquiring the complete series or just one or two pieces. It's up to you."

"The series is not complete," he said.

"What do you mean?"

"Where is Cuba after Hurricane Irma?"

He was Cuban. The missing photograph must be jarring to him. "Arranging last-minute travel to Cuba is difficult, particularly after a disaster."

"Difficult, not impossible."

Wonderful! She'd managed to insult her ex-lover with her activist art.

"I'll take it," he said, surprising her. "The whole thing."

"Don't you want to know how much it costs?"

"I'm sure you'll tell me."

"Each original photograph is nine thousand dollars."

"Sold."

The words she uttered next made no sense. "You don't have to do that."

"Why not?" he said.

She looked around to make sure Paloma wasn't within earshot. "If you're doing this to help me, you've done enough. Just look at this crowd."

Their little viewing room was drawing people in and the object of their curiosity wasn't the art. Angel had noticed a few well-heeled attendees angling camera phones, sneaking photographs. So much for the 1 percent living above the fray!

"What makes you think I don't want it?"

His tone made her question what exactly he was talking about.

"I only meant, you don't have to pretend."

"Pretend to want the things I want."

They were in their own private bubble now. The growing crowd fading to nothing.

"You should be sure..." She hesitated. "Before mistakes are made. It's a substantial investment."

"It's good work and I have plans for it."

"In that case, I'll ring you up."

"Angel," he said, stopping her before she could turn away. "You fascinate me. And I don't think this is a mistake."

Stunned, Angel picked a distant point to stare at. Unfortunately, the point was part of a gigantic mobile and now her whole world was spinning.

"I get that you don't want things to get messy, and I can't promise you that they won't. Given the chance, wouldn't you want to make a mess with me?"

Paloma, proving that she could be counted on to kill anyone's joy, returned, this time with an offer. "By any chance, Mr. Cardenas, are you interested in acquiring any more of your grandfather's artwork? We were delighted that Angel was able to finalize the sale in Justine's absence. But Justine is just a phone call away."

Excuse me? What? His grandfather?

Paloma likely did not miss Angel's confounded expression, nor did she miss the opportunity to school Angel in front of a client. "Juan David Valero is Mr. Cardenas's grandfather."

"I see." Why was she only learning this now? Why hadn't Justine given her the heads-up? Or Paloma included that nugget in the prepared statement she had texted her? And for the love of God, why hadn't Alessandro *told* her?

"If you are interested, just let me know. We don't come across a Valero too often—that's safe to say. Still, Justine could make some inquiries. Are you interested?"

"I am." Alessandro handed her a card. The way she beamed at it, you would have thought he had handed her the winning Powerball numbers. "If you find anything, get back to me."

"Sandro! Finally! There you are!"

Angel turned in time to catch the green-eyed brunette elbowing her way through the crowd. Wearing Chanel from head to toe, she looked…rich. Her face was expertly painted with shadows and highlights accentuating her delicate features.

"Gigi," Alessandro said with zero enthusiasm. "You've found me."

Gigi pulled out her phone and placed a call, canceling a search party. "I got him. Meet you at the entrance in five."

"You make it sound like I'm a fugitive," Alessandro said.

"We had to split up to look for you," she said reproachfully. "You weren't answering your phone."

"Sorry. It's off."

"You're not buying more art, are you?"

"I am."

"You are?" This was news to Paloma.

"Yes," Angel said, her voice shaky. "Mr. Cardenas is interested in *Devastation*."

"What's that?" Gigi asked.

"A photography series," Paloma informed her.

"Oh, good. So long as it's not that stupid banana taped to the wall." She tapped Alessandro's arm in a chummy way. "Have you seen it?"

"Nope," Alessandro said. "You've seen one, you've seen them all."

Everyone laughed except for Angel. She did not find him funny, not when he'd withheld information that was pertinent to her job. It explained so much. His blatant disinterest. His insistence that he was "familiar" with the painting. He could have expounded on that.

He was looking at her, his expression contrite. "Angeline, should we finalize the sale?"

"No need!" Paloma chimed. "We have your information and we can handle things on our end. I will send you an electronic invoice. Once settled, we'll have the photographs shipped to your home address."

"That was painless!" Gigi exclaimed. "Now let's get out of here before you buy anything else. We're late for dinner."

Alessandro rested his eyes on Angel, his gaze soft.

She pasted a smile on her face. "Thanks for your business, Mr. Cardenas! Always a *pleasure*."

She couldn't help but torture him a little. Unfortunately, she'd drawn the attention of his friend. She focused on Angel as if seeing her for the first time. Then her lips curled up in the faintest smile. "Hi," she said. "I'm Georgina."

Fascinating women... "I'm Angeline."

"Nice to meet you," she said. "I'm Sandro's friend. We're just friends. We go way back."

Alessandro looked up and away. "I think she got your point."

"Just making sure," she said. "Now I hate to do this, but we really have to go. We've got reservations. Friends are waiting."

Alessandro sought her eyes as if to communicate a quiet apology. Angel stiffened and looked down at her hands. Then Gigi tugged at his arm and led him away, all the while cooing, *"I approve! She's beautiful!"*

Paloma rushed off to finalize the sale. If she'd picked up on anything, she didn't seem to care. Only Angel stood bolted in place. She watched Alessandro go and didn't turn away until he vanished into the crowd, until he was lost to her.

Eight

The six of them were seated in a private dining room at a round table beneath a massive chandelier. The lights were dim enough to hide Sandro's discomfort. His friends were roasting him tonight.

"I caught the vibe between them within a nanosecond," Gigi said. "And he was so shy around her. It was *adorable*!"

Sandro had never been shy a day of his life. But by the time Gigi had come around, he'd been actively avoiding Angel's gaze. The revelation about his grandfather had not gone over well.

"We met her last night," Jenny Xi said. "It was riveting to watch."

"They were on fire," Jordan said.

"I liked her," Rose said. "Why didn't she join us?"

"She's working tonight," Sandro said.

"Ah! La pauvre!" Rose lamented.

"Pobrecita!" Rolando Ramirez echoed in Spanish. He was the front man of a local band that had just picked up its first Latin Grammy. Sandro, Jordan and Rolando had attended the same high school for the performing arts and, by all accounts, were doing pretty well.

"Don't feel sorry for her," Gigi said. "Apparently, she's very good at her job. She sold Romeo here a series of photographs at ten grand a pop."

"Nine grand," Sandro corrected. "And it's for the cause. I'll be auctioning them off tomorrow."

"That's so good of you!" Gigi cried. "Tell me again. Why aren't we a couple?"

"Back off," Jenny Xi said sternly. "I'm Team Angeline."

"So am I," Rose said. *"Absolument."*

"Me, too!" Rolando said. "And I've never met the woman. But I'm married and I want you guys to catch up."

"Sorry to disappoint you all, but she wants nothing to do with me."

"A woman turned you down?" Jenny looked doubtful. "Hard to believe."

"I promise you it's happened before," Sandro said, putting a playful spin on a painful subject. "Gigi, will you have me?"

"No, thanks. I'm Team Angeline, too." She raised her wineglass. "And I'm all for raising money at auction. For the cause!"

"For the cause!" they cheered.

Gigi's father was a famous baseball star, but he'd made his fortune off the diamond by investing in Florida real estate. Her mother had organized tomorrow's fundraising auction. It was a ploy to draw attention to her newly renovated Miami Beach hotel. Sandro didn't mind playing along for a good cause. His contribution was a mere drop of rain in the ocean. The press made a fuss about it when, really, he was doing the bare minimum. This was the only part of fame that truly bothered him. Acclaim, adulation, loss of privacy—all things he'd prepared himself for. This was the life he'd wanted and he had zero qualms about it. But when they put him on a pedestal like some kind of benevolent god, he made sure to set the record straight. A flawed man, he'd let people down, broken hearts, and was known to hold a grudge. He wanted the public to celebrate his work, not to conflate him with the heroes he portrayed.

He'd complained once to Gigi and she put it all in perspective. "In five to seven years' time, when you're teetering on forty, no one will give a damn what you do. So hang in there, buddy. This too shall pass."

She was right. Only well-respected veteran actors got the opportunity to age in the business, snapping up the few good roles available. Sandro wanted a long career and to work in the industry for as many years as he'd waited tables and mixed drinks until 2:00 a.m. These were the years and he had to make them count. That left little time for relationships. He wasn't even thinking about marriage. Oddly, that thought brought him back to Angeline.

She had a sensitive heart, which she could not hide—not from him, anyway. Her emotions pooled in her eyes. For that reason, guilt and regret churned in his gut all evening. Sandro hadn't missed her hurt expression when the gallery manager brought up his grandfather. At the time he could not pause to explain, not with the manager dangling red meat before him. She could find him more paintings. Wasn't that interesting? And then Gigi had arrived.

"It's bad luck not to toast," Rose scolded him.

Sandro looked around the table. His friends were holding up their cocktail glasses, all waiting on him. So he raised his glass to the cause. When Gigi went on to discuss their plans for the rest of the night, Sandro tuned her out.

He had to get to Angel. He owed her an apology.

His angel was blond tonight, a detail that he had somehow missed earlier. Standing in the light of the streetlamps, newly added golden strands shimmered down the length of her wavy hair. The December night air had a bite to it. She tightened the belt of her white trench coat. All around her, people were chatting and laughing. She looked serious, brows drawn as she studied her phone. Was she still receiving alerts on her ex? It was her prerogative. Rebound sex wasn't magic. So why the pang of jealousy? When she looked up from her phone, she looked lost and, frankly, sad. Whoever had caused her to feel that way could die a slow and painful death.

If only he didn't have a sneaking suspicion that he was the one to blame.

He got out of his borrowed car and leaned against the door. He was double-parked and blocking the flow of traffic. The only reason the crossing guard wasn't having a fit was because the Bentley was a beauty. The guard might not know who Sandro was, but he knew that he was *someone*. Sandro had always hated guys who pulled stunts like this, and yet here he was.

The event had wrapped up a while ago, but chaos outside the convention center had not died down. Angeline stood apart from the crowd, staring straight ahead. She had a way of folding within herself. Earlier, when he'd spotted her at the bar, she'd had that same unsearchable look on her face.

Then suddenly her gaze sharpened with recognition.

"Alessandro!"

She shouted his name, drawing the attention of a few people. He didn't care. He was transfixed with the woman making her way toward him, her eyes brilliant with anger and her hair, caught in the night breeze, flapping around her face.

"What are you doing out here blocking traffic?"

She was so practical. It was adorable. "I was hoping for a chance to speak with you."

Going by her body language alone, he expected her to say, "Get lost. I never want to see you again." Instead she said, "My Uber canceled, I need a ride home."

Sandro held open the car door. "Get in before they tow me away." She glared at him again before climbing into the back seat. He got behind the wheel just in time to hear her sigh with relief. In the rearview mirror, he watched as she got settled.

"Did you have a good night?" he asked.

She fastened her seatbelt with a snap. "I had a long night."

"Where do you live?"

"Key Biscayne."

"That far?"

"Is that a problem?"

"It's a long commute for you. That's all I meant to say." He put the car in gear. "Do you have a car?"

"I do," she said. "It's been leaking oil and I don't have time to get it repaired this week."

He could offer to have it repaired or he could offer to drive her around this week. He was tossing around these options in his head when she leaned forward and proceeded to give him instructions. "Make a right at the light and head to West 41st Street."

"If I needed directions, Siri, I would have asked."

She let out an exasperated gasp, implying that he was behaving like a typical man.

"Before I worked my way up to bartending, I delivered takeout," he explained. "I know this area like the back of my hand."

"Okay, fine," she said. "But every other week a road closes and the map changes."

Good point.

"You don't have to keep doing this," she added.

"What?"

"Spinning the tale of your humble roots," she replied. "It's as if you want to prove that you're an ordinary guy, all the while driving a car that costs more than a house. It's jarring."

Another good point. Although, he hadn't been aware that that was what he was doing. He wanted her to like him, to trust him. Was that wrong?

"This car belongs to Georgina's mother," he said.

"Relatable," she said. "Last week I borrowed my neighbor's scooter so I could run an errand."

Traffic was crawling at a snail's pace, which explained why her ride might've canceled. As they sat in the dark, motionless car, silence took over. He chanced a glance at the rearview mirror and their eyes met.

"Hi, Angel."

She did not blink. "You lied to me."

"I withheld information," he said. "That's not the same."

"You let me make a fool of myself, rattling on about your

grandfather's nostalgia." She turned to the window with a huff. "You must have thought I was an idiot."

Humiliation rang through her voice. A half-assed apology wasn't going to cut it.

"I'm sorry," he said.

She did not respond. Sandro stared at her until the blare of car horns jolted him into action. The light had long turned green and the drivers behind him were impatient. He focused on his driving, checking on her from time to time. Her body language was not encouraging. She sat with her arms folded across her chest, the collar of her light trench coat—her only nod to winter—drawn close to her throat. He waited until they were cruising on the highway before he spoke again.

"Why do you think you never heard that Juan David Valero was my grandfather?"

"Because I'm a novice who didn't prepare?"

"Because I've kept it hidden for the most part."

She leaned forward and gripped his headrest. "Then how did Paloma know? I'm sure Justine knew!"

He had no clue. And yet Paloma's sudden expertise on all things JD was suspicious. "My grandfather, the great painter, died penniless. But he left me his greatest treasure."

"His art?" She was still gripping his headrest, but her voice was less harsh.

"That's right."

She fell back against the seat. "Oh… I thought…"

"You thought what?"

"Nothing."

She was not getting away with that. He'd shared something personal. She could reciprocate a little. "Tell me."

"I thought you didn't care about art."

"What made you think that?" he said.

"Last night you barely looked at the painting."

"Now you know why," Sandro said. "I was familiar with

it, just like I said. And you could've given me the benefit of the doubt. I traveled across the country for an art show."

"That means nothing."

Yet another fair point. The city was crawling with celebrities, none of which were even remotely interested in art. Most would spend their days on the beach and nights at the clubs. But most people knew where he stood.

"Angel, I come from a long line of artists, going back generations. They were not famous and they didn't win awards. They were dedicated and serious." Before she could say anything, he added, "That's not another anecdote to make me relatable. It's the truth of who I am."

She did not say much the rest of the way. Gradually, the tension drained from the car. He felt comfortable with her. It had been this way since, well, yesterday.

"Head onto Rickenbacker, then a left on Galen Drive."

Sandro followed her directions without objection, sailing over the bridge that arched over the dark bay. Was he disappointed that the long drive had turned out to be not all that long? Yeah, particularly because he was certain Angel would not invite him up.

She lived in a rental community named Coral Rock. She used a clicker to raise the gate arm and pointed to the nearest available parking spot in the large flat lot. As expected, she thanked him for the ride and reached for the car door handle.

"Angel…"

She silenced him. "It's pointless, Alessandro. You and I…we orbit around different suns."

"Why is that a problem?" he asked, arguing even though he knew that letting her go was the best thing to do.

She reached forward again. This time, she lightly raked her fingertips through his hair. Sandro shivered at her touch. He took hold of her hand and brought the palm to his lips. Her rose-scented perfume filled his nostrils.

"I'm glad you came by," she said. "Not because I needed

a ride, although that helped. But I needed to make sense of what happened tonight. Thank you."

She gently freed her hands from his and slipped out of the car.

The five-story building was pistachio green. The apartment doors opened onto a breezeway corridor. Sandro watched as she climbed the stairs leading to the top floors and waited until a light came on in a third-floor apartment. *It's over.* Then he pulled out of the parking lot and drove into the night.

Nine

"Angel! What's the matter? Why are you hyperventilating?"

Angel was jogging along the bridge when her phone buzzed in her hand. It was Justine Carr. No matter the circumstances, she managed to spike every encounter with a bit of drama. Angel adjusted her earbuds. "I'm fine, Justine. Out for an early run, that's all."

After a fitful night, Angel had given up on sleep. She swapped her pajama shorts for running shorts and took off into the dawn. One of the perks of living in Key Biscayne was the scenic path over the bridge to the sandy beach that doubled as the neighborhood's dog park. A run had a way of clearing her head, something she desperately needed. He was haunting her. Last night she'd done the sensible thing and ended their affair—and even that was too strong of a word. It was a hookup gone awry, and not for the reasons she'd allowed him to believe.

He had been less than forthcoming about his grandfather, but she sort of understood why and had accepted his apology. What she could not get over, however, was her own treacherous heart. Standing on the curb last night, despairing that her ride had canceled due to overwhelming traffic, she'd looked up, seen him and instantly felt safe. He was here, and he'd take care of her.

What fresh batch of nonsense was that?

He was not the hero in her melodrama. She had no business feeling warm and gooey inside, no business hearing a choir of angels when he said something as simple as "Hi."

She had to get herself together and fast before she hopped onto the first ferry back to Fisher Island.

"Wish I could go for walks," Justine said wistfully.

Angel had forgotten that she was on a call. "How are you feeling?"

"Like an idiot, but I'll survive."

"Anything I can do for you?"

"You can attend tonight's event at The High Tide."

"Why do I have to go?" she whined. Great, she was a whiner now.

"Because I can't!"

"Why can't Paloma go? She's the manager."

"Paloma is pulling long shifts at the convention center. Then she's meeting with a private client. Besides, we need someone who'll stand out. Paloma is pretty much useless after ten p.m., or haven't you noticed?"

"I haven't, to be honest."

Justine let out a heavy sigh. Originally from Monroe County, she had the pronounced drawl of a kid who grew up in the Lower Keys. "This is Basel, the big time, and we all have to do our part. Paloma is running the show. I'm processing the orders from home. It's your job to go to the parties and represent us. We can't be absent from the scene. We expect you to take photos for our social media accounts. If you're smart, you'll make some contacts."

"Fine. I'll go."

"Quit moaning!" Justine said. "If I were your age and had your legs, I'd have the city at my feet. Don't forget to stop by the gallery to pick up the invitation, along with your commission."

"Commission for what?"

"The Cardenas deal," Justine replied. "You know what? I don't think fresh air is doing you much good."

It scandalized Angel that she should earn a commission for *all the things* that she had done. She might have to pass on that.

"Justine, did you know…"

"Know what?"

"Nothing. Never mind."

Angel ended the call. She walked along the bridge, stopping at the halfway point to watch the boats crisscrossing the bay. Even though she'd wanted answers, discussing Alessandro's private business seemed wrong. It didn't matter what Paloma and Justine knew or when they knew it. He was not comfortable with anyone knowing about his grandfather. If Angel owed him anything, it was discretion.

Sandro arrived at the Lincoln Road gallery shortly past seven. At this early hour, the open-air mall was deserted, except for a few joggers. The designer shops and restaurants were all closed, and so was Gallery Six. Paloma Gentry greeted him at the door.

"Thank you for accommodating me," Sandro said. He could not swing by during regular hours without drawing too much attention. Lincoln Road was nothing but a backdrop for people watching. He had to get out before the sidewalk traffic picked up and he was spotted, photographed, hounded. And lately, if he patronized a business, even if just to pick up a pack of gum or beer, it was perceived as an endorsement. Since he would rather not endorse Gallery Six, discretion was in order. He could have sent a proxy, but he felt as if he owed it to his grandfather to handle this himself.

"It's no trouble," she said. "I live above the gallery."

She locked the glass door behind him.

Gallery Six was smaller than he had imagined. They'd made the most of the viewing space— paintings cluttered the walls and the floor was dotted with sculptures and art objects displayed on pedestals. At the register was the usual assortment of postcards and Miami Beach souvenirs. He found himself wondering where Angeline Louis fit into all this.

Paloma invited him to her office and offered him coffee or tea. He wasn't going to make a social call out of this. "No, thank you."

"Very well." She opened what looked like a filing cabinet and pulled out a small painting, no bigger than an iPad. His grandfather liked to paint on a large scale. This seemingly endless parade of miniatures was grating on him.

"This is *La Playa*."

Alessandro took the canvas from Paloma. It was, as its name suggested, a rendering of a beach in thick swirls of oil paint. The sky was a hazy blue gray, and in the foreground the waves thinned and spread onto pale blond sand. Seagulls, a lone palm tree and a little boy taking a nap, completed the composition. It was a signature Juan David Valero piece.

Although his grandfather never regretted fleeing Communist Cuba, he spent his entire adult life longing for the idyllic settings of his childhood. But something was off about this painting. The small size was only part of it. It didn't move him like his grandfather's other paintings never failed to do. It didn't bring back his grandfather's voice, his paint-stained hands or the smell of turpentine that clung to his clothes. That wouldn't make sense to anyone else. It was part of the bond that they'd shared and, he knew now, his father and half brother had envied.

"You say my grandfather painted this, but I've never seen it, or even sketches of it."

"That's not unusual. It dates back to before you were born."

"Where did you get it from?" he asked.

"A private collector who prefers to remain anonymous."

Paloma backed away from him and went to stand behind her desk. Her auburn hair was the color of autumn and she wore it in a tight bun at the base of her neck. Her eyes were a watery blue.

"That's convenient."

"Selling off art is like pawning the family jewels. It's unseemly and you wouldn't want your friends to know. Our clients can count on our discretion." She flashed a toothy, shark-like grin. "Trust me. It's best for everyone involved. I can answer any questions you may have. You have concerns about the provenance of this piece?"

"I do."

"Alright." Paloma let out the weary sigh of the expert having to explain basics to the novice. "We work with industry experts. Every piece comes with a certificate of authenticity."

The certificate was BS, and she knew it. A painting wasn't a designer purse.

"Is the seller in financial trouble?" Sandro asked. He was just fishing around here. Paloma was a stone-cold professional. There was no getting water from rock.

"Why does it matter? Are you worried the seller didn't value your grandfather's work?"

No one would value his grandfather's work as much as he did. His interest had to do with his aversion to being duped. But he'd gone far enough with this. He wished he could walk out and leave the painting on her desk, but he couldn't do it. Fake or not, *La Playa* belonged to him.

"How much?"

She looked him dead in the eye. "Thirty-five thousand."

Sandro didn't flinch. "Ring me up."

The High Tide was high glamour. Angel opted for a slinky LBD, a little *blue* dress. The dress was basically a variation of the pink one she'd worn the night before; only this one was a thrift shop find. She finished off the look with a swipe of red lipstick and heels. Faking confidence was an art form.

In the elevator taking her to the hotel's rooftop deck, Angel mapped out a strategy. She decided to ignore Justine's advice. What was the point of networking? She didn't know anyone, and no one gave a damn about her. She'd snap photos for the gallery's social media accounts, maybe even a livestream, and then she'd call it a night.

When the elevator doors slid open, she stepped into a wondrous world. Angel followed the other guests through a forest of papier-mâché palm trees, past a waterfall cascading into a white marble basin and around the pool-turned–dance floor until she found the bar. After quickly perusing the cocktail menu, she ordered a lychee martini. While she waited, she cast a look around at the moveable feast of ridiculously attractive people, not the least of which was the bartender. She recognized actors, models and opera singers. She spotted Julian and Nina Knight of Knight Films, a Miami power couple, holding court by the fountain. When her phone buzzed in her purse, Angel was grateful to have a genuine reason to stare at her phone—anything to keep from gawking.

Justine had sent her a text message:

BIG NEWS! AC is auctioning off Devastation tonight. Make sure you take photos so we can remind everyone where he got it!!!

AC? It took a minute for her brain to make the connection, but once it did, Angel shoved her phone in her purse as if it were radioactive. The part of her that had chosen to wear the dress, the sexy heels and the Fenty by Rihanna red lipstick had known there was a chance he'd be here tonight. It was one thing to suspect. It was another thing to receive written confirmation.

The bartender placed a decadent cocktail before her. "Here you go, gorgeous."

Bless his heart. She tipped him well.

Angel scanned the crowd. If she had eyes on him, she could stay out of his way. She'd hide behind a papier-mâché palm tree if need be. Then she'd take the photos and tiptoe out before he ever knew she was here. That was the plan.

"ANGELINE! Guys, look who's here!"

Angel closed her eyes and kissed her plan goodbye. Suddenly, she was pulled into a group hug with Jenny Xi, Rose Rachid and Georgina Garcia, air kisses all around.

"What are you doing here alone, *ma chérie*?" Rose asked. "Where is Alessandro?"

"I'm working tonight," Angel said, setting the record straight while trying to sound as cool as these women looked.

"You're always working!" Georgina said disapprovingly.

The woman was wearing this season's Dior pantsuit. Maybe, for her, work was voluntary rather than a mandatory activity.

"Put your Blackberry away," Jenny said. "Your squad is here!"

"What are you drinking?" Rose asked. "It looks delicious."

"A lychee martini."

"And that's what I'm having," Jenny said. She took Rose's hand. "We'll be at the bar."

Angel was left alone with Georgina in Dior, who was now demanding Angel call her "Gigi."

"Okay, Gigi," Angel said tentatively. "Where's Jordan tonight?"

"He's playing a set at The Zoo," she said. "We'll meet up with him later. But forget Jordan. I want to talk about Alessandro."

And I don't. Wasn't the whole point of small talk to avoid hot-button topics?

"He's here, you know. I'll give him a call, if you like."

"Don't bother!" Angel practically shouted the words. "I'm here for work. Remember?"

Gigi tossed a lock of caramel brown hair over her shoulder. Angel had never seen anyone so impeccably groomed, not up close anyway. Whoever did her highlights was a skilled artist.

"About Alessandro," she said. "He and I have some history."

Angel's throat tightened in the way it had when she'd watched Gigi and Alessandro walk away together last night. Soon, she'd be gasping for air.

"I was into him, and he didn't feel the same," Gigi said. "That's our history. The end."

That could mean any number of things. When had she figured out he wasn't into her? Had they been dating awhile?

"He starred in one of the first movies I produced."

"*Downward Spiral.*"

"You've seen it?"

"It's one of my favorite films."

Gigi seemed genuinely pleased. "Thank you! It's a classic immigrant story. That's why I found it so compelling."

"Alessandro is great in it."

"He's great in everything," Gigi said matter-of-factly. "He's very serious about his career. Our working relationship was important to him. So I asked myself, was it worth it to muddy those waters? The answer was no, and I don't regret it. We're the best of friends *and* we have a great working relationship. I'm very lucky."

Lucky didn't scratch the surface. She was fortunate, privileged and clearly had the sort of upbringing that gave her the confidence to just speak her mind without fear of blowback.

"There's something else," she said.

Angel didn't want to know anything else, but that wasn't going to stop Gigi.

"He never looked at me the way he looked at you," she said.

"You're wrong," Angel said with a nervous hiccup of a laugh. "He didn't look at me in any particular way. A lot was going on last night and—"

"I'm not wrong," Gigi said flatly.

Angel took a long sip of her martini to hide her burning cheeks. Rose and Jenny returned with an extra cocktail for Gigi.

"The bartender is so hot, I almost climbed over the bar," Jenny said.

"She's not joking," Rose said. "I had to hold her back and remind her of our burning love."

Gigi tossed her head back and laughed. "Should we find out when he gets off work?"

A hush ran through the party crowd as musicians walked on the stage at the far end of the deck. After a quick sound test, the guitarist approached a microphone.

"That's Rolando!" Jenny whispered to Angel. The name didn't ring any bells...until it did. Rolando y Mafioso had had *the* hit song of the summer.

In a smooth baritone, Rolando said, "Ladies and gentlemen, beautiful people, give it up for my brother in the struggle, Alessandro Cardenas."

Alessandro joined the band on stage to thunderous applause. He held up a glass half-filled with amber liquor and ice, and saluted the audience.

The drummer got things going. "One! Two! One! Two! Three! Four!"

The band launched into a Buena Vista Social Club staple. Alessandro swayed with the tempo for a while. He approached the microphone, opened his mouth, and started to sing. His voice was raw honey.

Angel felt sure she was going to die.

"Oh, yeah," Gigi said. "Give him a fifth of rum and that happens."

Fingers curled around the stem of her glass, Angel tuned out everyone who was not Alessandro. Wearing black, like the rest of the band, his shirt was fitted and neatly tucked into his trousers, and yet he'd somehow neglected to fasten most of the buttons. He looked delicious. A golden spotlight added shimmer to his bronze skin. Eyes closed, brows drawn, he sang and seduced his audience. The tempo picked up suddenly and one of the backup singers took off on a reggaeton tangent to the delight of the crowd. Then a trum-

peter stepped forward for a solo that wrecked Angel's heart.
All the while Sandro stood to the side, grooving in a world
of his own. She focused on the way he moved, and remembered how they'd moved together. She'd done everything to
squeeze that memory into a small space and lock it away.
Now she wondered why she had ever wanted to.

Gigi approached again. "I never looked at him the way
you do, so maybe that was my mistake."

Angel swiveled around to confront her, only to find Gigi,
Jenny and Rose smiling at her without malice. They were
harmless. She was ready to drop the act. Besides, Alessandro had returned to the microphone and let out a low,
plaintive sound. His voice was smooth, but it also had grit.
It wrapped around her, tugging her to him. Angel handed
Gigi her cocktail glass. She moved toward the stage, angling
her way through the crowd and leaving her newly acquired
squad behind. She was vaguely aware of shouts and high
fives. She heard Gigi pronounce triumphantly: "My job is
done!" But nothing could tamper with the immediacy of
Alessandro's voice.

Angel crossed the covered pool and with each step she
had the sensation of walking on water. The instant he spotted her, his onyx eyes turned glossy. With the very next step
she was walking on air.

The way he looked at her!

When she reached the stage, Alessandro neared the edge
and hunched low. The sleeves of his shirt were rolled up to
the elbows. All she'd have to do was reach out to feel his
warm skin. How she'd held back from doing so was anyone's guess. He sang the last lyrics of the song just for her.
The full meaning of the Spanish words escaped her, but she
understood the longing they conveyed.

Life may have given Gigi the option to muddy the pro-
verbial waters—Angel had no choice. She was neck deep
in mud, and drowning fast.

Ten

Tonight, his angel was a devil in a blue dress.

Once the music died, Sandro tossed his microphone to Rolando and leaped off the stage. This impromptu jam session had taken him back to their high school days and he'd enjoyed it. The payoff, however, was greater than he could have ever hoped. If he believed in miracles, this would count as one. He was sure he'd blown it with Angel. He'd been pouring out his heartache on stage when she cut through the crowd. It was like a scene from a goddamn movie.

How would the night end?

The applause was thick and a small mob pushed toward the stage and gathered around him. Angel was cast aside in the melee. Sandro reached out and took hold of her hand before she slipped away. The band launched into one of their latest hits and his newly acquired fans dispersed. Sandro gently pulled her to him and pressed a kiss to her temple. "Want to dance?"

She nodded and they took off with a whirl, as much as space permitted on the crowded dance floor. His moves were less than smooth. He was nervous and his joints were stiff. Plus the effort he put into holding her at an appropriate distance was going to kill him. But that lasted only until another couple bumped into them, pushing Angel into his arms. He tightened his grip on her waist to steady her and, once he had her in his arms, he could not let go. She pressed her forehead to his chin and her breath fanned his throat. He rocked her slowly until finally, *finally*, she looked up at him. The heat in those light brown eyes told him that he was not alone in this private torture.

There's my angel.

He placed a hand on the small of her back and guided her off the dance floor. They made their way to the bar. The bartender motioned to him. "One more round, Mr. Cardenas? You too, miss?"

Once Sandro gave him the okay, they got settled at a quiet corner of the bar.

"How did you learn to sing like that?" she asked.

"My grandfather listened to old school boleros on the radio while he painted and smoked and smoked and painted. It's basically all he did."

"You have a beautiful voice. Have you considered—"

"No, I'll keep my day job. Thanks. But I'm available for private functions."

She laughed, doing away with all the acrimony of the previous twenty-four hours. Or so he ardently hoped. "Can we start over, Angel?"

Their drinks were served promptly. She reached for hers with a shaky hand. She had not been this nervous back when it was just the two of them at his place.

"Am I asking too much?" he said.

She took a sip from of her cocktail and lowered the glass. "No, you're not. I'd like that, too."

To seal the deal, he leaned close and kissed her.

When the music died down, the band announced a break for the art auction. She pulled her phone out of her purse. "I have to take photos. That's part of my official duties for tonight."

A roster of wealthy people had donated artwork from their private collections. The donors were invited on stage to drum up interest in their offerings. Sandro did not budge. You could not pay him to leave Angel's side. Good thing he didn't have to.

She kept her camera trained to the stage and nudged his flank with an elbow. "Shouldn't you head up there?"

"I sang for them. That should be enough."

"But I want a photo of you."

He reached for her phone, reversed the camera to selfie mode, moved close enough to drop his chin on her shoulder, and snapped a photo of the two of them. "There you go."

She stared at the phone screen a long time. There was no denying they made a handsome couple, Sandro thought. The proof was in her hand.

"I meant for the gallery," she said, her voice thin. "They would love a photo of you with the art."

"They're not going to get it."

"The first piece is a series of photographs titled, *Devastation*," the auctioneer announced. "Here to present it is the artist."

The photographer was a young woman from the Bahamas. She wore a simple white dress and her hair fell in long box braids down her back. After thanking Sandro for the opportunity to address the influential crowd, she spoke of the importance of recording the devastation caused by climate change. "We cannot afford to bury our heads in the sand. Future generations will judge us for our inaction."

Bidding began at fifty thousand dollars. A fierce war between three buyers hiked up the price. The collection of photographs sold for one hundred and ten thousand dollars. Angel recorded it all on video, then switched off her phone and rushed to hug him. The hug was cruelly brief.

"Did you arrange for her to be here tonight?" she said.

"I might've put in a call."

"That's so good of you!" she cried. "This sort of exposure can really help an artist in the long run."

Sandro's mood fell. Everyone was in agreement. He could use his celebrity to lift a struggling artist—or reshape the legacy of a dead one.

She rested a hand on his arm. "Are you okay? Did I say something?"

"*No, querida*. It's fine."

And just as quickly, she withdrew her hand.

* * *

Angel flinched as if she'd been burned. He'd called her *querida*. She knew it meant nothing, maybe just another word that he tossed around. But her reaction was over-the-top. She had slept with this man, and yet the unexpected use of an endearment had shot straight to her head.

After the auction, Gigi, Rose and Jenny swarmed them. "Hey, you two! There you are!"

Alessandro let his friends plant kisses on his cheeks and even sample his drink.

"It's a wrap," Gigi said. "We're heading out to meet Jordan at The Zoo. Are you two coming?"

"I can't," Angel said. "I have to work in the morning."

Gigi turned to Alessandro who gave her a pointed look. She smiled. "I didn't think so. Don't forget tomorrow's party at Garage."

"The club?" Alessandro asked.

"No," Jenny replied. "An actual parking garage. What will these crazy kids come up with next?"

"It's not an ordinary garage," Rose said. "It was designed by Swiss architects."

"Sounds like fun," Alessandro said dryly.

"I'm attending that one," Angel said. "You know, for the gallery."

Alessandro flashed that grin. "In that case it really does sound like fun and I'll be there."

The squad made a grand exit with loud goodbyes and air kisses.

Alessandro turned to her. "Do you need a ride home?"

"I can manage," Angel said. What she meant was: *Take me home. Now!*

"No way I'm putting you in an Uber, if you could even find one."

"Well, there's no rush. I don't have to leave right now." She was acting like an octogenarian, and that wasn't even fair to the eighty-plus crowd. Some might be out partying right now.

The band resumed. Alessandro suggested they find a quiet corner. They wandered off to a remote seating area tucked beyond the cluster of papier-mâché trees.

"I have to ask," he said. "Was I any help?"

"What do you mean?"

"With your rebound efforts. Did I help any?"

Angel nearly spit out her second lychee martini.

"The way you left, I wasn't sure how effective I'd been."

"You know why I left. Let's not go there again."

"You didn't even say thank you," he said, indignant.

"As in…thank you for your service?"

"You wouldn't have to stand on ceremony or anything."

"I wouldn't dream of it."

"I've been dreaming of you."

Angel went soft everywhere. Did he know the effect he had on her? His next careless words proved that he didn't.

"If rebound sex doesn't work out, there's always revenge."

"You've been giving this some thought."

"Have you considered posting that photo of us?"

That quick selfie had astonished her. She and Alessandro looked good together. And not only that, they looked comfortable with each other. A stranger could tell that they were intimate. The fact he'd suggested that she use it as fodder to get back at her stupid ex saddened her. It revealed something about him. He'd grown accustomed to people using his celebrity to further their own causes in both positive and negative ways.

"Thanks for the offer," she said. "You should know that I'd never use you like that."

"What if I want you to?"

Angel set her drink down on a low table and reached for him by the loop of his belt. "Stop."

She did not want to hear any more talk of rebound tactics or revenge plots.

He took her face in his hands; his eyes were as black as the ocean. "Fine. I'll stop, but the offer stands."

"What do you get out of this?" she asked. "Just curious."

"I get you."

"You already have me."

Alessandro crushed her mouth with a kiss. They toppled onto a nearby chaise in a tangle of limbs. He nudged aside the silky ruched bodice of her dress and the lace of her bra. His teeth closed tightly on a nipple. Angel wanted to cry out with pleasure, and then she remembered where they were.

"We can't do this here!"

Alessandro slowly drew away from her. "But we're doing this?"

Now she cupped his face. "If the offer still stands."

He got up and pulled her to her feet. "Let's get out of here."

It was YOLO all the way home, in a convertible with the top down.

Sandro was driving his own car tonight, a compact Alfa Romeo that suited him far better than the borrowed Bentley. The leather seat cradled Angel and the breeze teased her hair. Sandro took on the curves of the highway, one hand on the wheel and the other on the clutch...or on her knees, or burrowed between them, or traveling up the length of her thigh. Angel couldn't wait to get home but she never wanted this ride to end.

By the time they'd made it to her place, Angel was drunk with desire. She had thought the last time was *the* last time. It had been a surreal experience. He was practically a stranger and his touch felt new. How would it be different this time? The man kissing her neck while she fumbled with her keys at her apartment door did not feel like a stranger.

"Need help?"

He meant with her keys, not her mental state.

"Thanks. I can manage."

She could *not* manage. He waited patiently for one second for her to get it together. Then he took the key from her, inserted it into the tricky old lock, and deftly turned it until it clicked. Damn it! Why was that hot?

She ushered him into her living room. "Next you're going to tell me that you worked as a locksmith before hitting it big."

"A janitor."

"The tenants must have loved you."

She switched on a lamp and lit the candle on the dining table for ambiance. Basically, she did not know what to do. Alessandro roamed around, exploring her space in very much the same fashion that she had explored his. If he were looking for signs of her personality, the only ones he'd find were her potted plants and her framed paintings. Although she liked the furniture, every piece a flea market or Craigslist find, it all belonged to Chris. He had no need for it in Australia.

Angel stepped out of her heels and tossed them onto the rug beneath the midcentury coffee table. When he approached one of her paintings, a simple but colorful landscape hanging over her desk, she went for a quick and easy diversion. Her blue dress joined her sandals on the floor. Alessandro must have heard the whisper of silk because he immediately turned to face her.

"Um… Do you want a house tour, a glass of wine or… what?"

There was something uniquely empowering about being on her home turf.

Alessandro turned his back on the painting. "Option 3, if that's alright."

"Option 3 it is, but you're overdressed."

"I'll take care of it."

While he stripped off his clothes, Angel thought it might

be best to shut her blinds. She walked over to the window. He grabbed her by the waist, backed her onto the window-sill and stripped her of her lingerie. Alessandro Cardenas was deliciously naked between her thighs. The man was cut from bronze, all hard planes and sharp angles, and every square inch of him taught and tight. To keep him there, she wrapped her legs around his thighs.

He cupped her face and ran the rough pad of his thumb over her lips. "My angel is bad tonight."

Now, she could admonish him for the simplistic characterization of her sexuality—or she could just be bad.

Angel tightened her legs around him. Fingers woven in her hair, he tugged her head back and kissed her. His hands left her hair and roamed over her body. These were not the hands of a stranger. He knew where and how to touch her, cupping her breasts and teasing her nipples until her back arched and her head slammed against the windowpane.

He slid two fingers inside her. "Did you think about me last night?"

"What?"

"Last night. Did you think about me?"

He was stroking her and her mind was singularly focused on his hands, not his words. "Last night was...last night."

"Now tell me. Why did you run away?"

The truth spiraled out of her. "I was scared."

He rubbed his nose to hers. "Scared of me?"

"Scared of *this*!"

He could do with that information what he liked. She was scared of the pull he had on her. It was pure burning emotion, defying logic or reason, and it made her do the unthinkable.

But Alessandro didn't seem bothered by this revelation. Or maybe he already knew. He seemed to have her figured out. He kissed her again and again while his fingers explored deeper. Angel arched forward knocking a decorative crystal off the edge of the sill. It dropped on his foot. That didn't bother him, either. He laughed it off and pulled her to her feet. "Why can't I ever get you in bed?"

That first night at the penthouse, they'd gotten only as far as the rug on the bedroom floor and crawled into bed afterward where they promptly fell asleep. At least here, at her place, there wasn't too far to travel to find the nearest bed.

Angel led him to her bedroom. Along the way, he stopped to pluck a foil packet from the pocket of his trousers, which he left strung over an armchair. Good thing he'd planned ahead because she didn't have condoms in the apartment. She hadn't needed any for a long, long time.

Her bedroom was dark except for the pale glow of the table lamp in the front room. She poured herself onto her bed, while Alessandro remained standing at the foot. He tore open the foil packet and spoke deliberately. "Yesterday morning, I woke up wanting you. Last night I stayed up fighting the urge to show up at your door. And tonight when I saw you, I knew there was no other possible outcome than this." He looked her square in the eyes. "So, yeah. It's scary, Angeline."

"Don't call me that."

Angel closed her eyes as soon as the words leaped out. What had possessed her?

Alessandro went silent a moment. "Don't use your name?"

"Never mind." She sat up straight and took the condom packet from his hand and finished the job—the less talking the better. "I'm so ready for you."

He eased her onto her back and crawled over her. Angel was murmuring nonsensically. "Yes. Yes. Don't. Yes." He entered her inch by inch, deliberately, cruelly slow.

"What do you want me to call you?"

Her words turned into whimpers.

"If not Angeline, then what?"

Angel gripped his arms. "Forget it."

His tactics were more advanced than hers. With a slight

shift in position, he sank in deeper inside her, leaving no room for self-possession. "You like it when I call you Angel? Is that it?"

"Call me yours."

He went still. Angel squeezed her eyes shut again. She was not going to make it through the night.

"My angel…" He brushed his parted lips to hers. "And what does my angel want?"

Angel was near delirious with pleasure. "She wants you."

They'd made love before, but it was in her simple room, her plain bed, that they truly became lovers.

Eleven

"This is the part of the rom-com when you make me pancakes."

"Even if we had the time, I couldn't bring that fantasy to life. I'm no cook. Why do you think I value Myles so much?"

"Protein smoothie it is," she said with a shrug and gave her state of the art blender a whirl.

With the first rays of dawn streaming through Angel's kitchen window, their day began with coffee, quiet conversation and now protein shakes. She was dressed for work, looking elegant in an emerald green dress. Her hair was brushed into a high ponytail and gold hoops hung at her ears. The color in her cheeks and that coy smile were all his doing, or so he liked to think.

Sandro had yet to put on his pants. After their shower, he was feeling lazy. All he wanted was to fold back into bed with her, but she was focused on heading out the door. Paloma was expecting her at the convention center in an hour. Sandro had offered to drive her to work. She'd accepted with one caveat: he had to drop her off one half block away from the convention center. "I can't be seen with you."

When Sandro thought of the lengths people went to in order to be seen with him, this just cracked him up. "You want to hide this?"

Wearing only his boxer briefs, he turned to give her a look at the goods. Her gaze swept over him appreciatively. Those luminous brown eyes got him every time.

"You're my client," she said.

"I'm more than that."

"No one needs to know that." She poured him a glass of the shake she'd taken such pride in whipping up. "More importantly, Paloma doesn't need to know that. Now drink up and get dressed."

"My poor Angel, how can you stand Paloma?"

"I can't!" she confessed with a horrified laugh. "Which is why I need a new job."

He was relieved to hear it. Gallery Six was shady. He couldn't come out and tell her. For one thing, he had no proof. And what if she let it slip? He did not want to tip off *la Paloma.* "We'll get on that as soon as this fair is done."

"*We* won't be doing anything. You'll be gone and I'll be packing up for Orlando."

He couldn't believe how deeply those words cut him. She was dismissing him and had very concrete plans on how to move on. "This is the first I'm hearing about Orlando."

"That's where I'm from."

"Don't you like it here?"

"I do."

"This apartment is great." He meant it, even though he was desperately grasping at reasons for her to abort her plans. "I've lived in Miami my whole life, for the most part, and I've never met anyone who actually lived in this area."

"Chris picked this apartment."

Chris...

She took a long sip from her glass as if stalling for time. "It's close to the university's school of marine science," she said, finally.

Ah. Now for whatever reason he didn't think the apartment was so great. It was old and dated. He reached for her hand. "Just so you know, I'm not leaving right away. I'm sticking around awhile."

"Why?"

"Film production delays. Plus, my agent seems to think I need a break."

"Do you need a break?"

They stood at opposite sides of the kitchen island, hands linked. "It wouldn't hurt."

She drained her glass, avoiding his eyes. "I don't leave for Orlando right away. The lease doesn't lapse until March of next year."

He could work with that.

If Sandro were brave enough to be honest, and bold enough to hope, he'd admit that his meeting Angel felt fortuitous. It felt like the beginning of something good—if they didn't mess it up.

Angel took their glasses to the sink. "You know that thing I said last night? I don't know why I had you call me that…it was crazy sex talk."

A lot of crazy sex talk had gone down last night. He wasn't ready to take any of it back.

He grabbed one end of the dishrag she was holding and used it to draw her to him. "You mean when I called you mine?"

She nodded slowly before putting it in words. "Yes."

Sandro watched her struggle, but he would not relent. "Do you want me to stop?"

"No."

"Come here, my angel."

She melted into his arms. He held and rocked her, stroking her back, until someone simultaneously knocked at her door and rang her doorbell. Then a strident female voice called out, "Angeline!" and a few words in French that he did not understand.

"Angeline! *C'est ta marraine!*"

Damn it all to hell! It was Angel's godmother. Not the "fairy" kind who made your dreams real with a wave of a wand, but the Haitian kind who snooped, meddled and reported back to your mother.

Angel gripped Alessandro's shoulders, her fingers digging into his flesh.

"Listen to me. I want you to go into the bedroom and not make a sound until I come get you. Do you understand?"

The actor gave her a look of hurt betrayal. "You're determined to keep me in the closet."

"We're not yet at the point where you meet my crazy family."

"When do you think we'll get to that point?"

"Never!" Angel said. "Now go and hide. I'll pump up your deflated ego after."

His eyebrows shot up. "By any means necessary?"

She was shaking with bottled-up laughter. He was impossible. "Just go!"

Alessandro blew her a kiss before disappearing into the bedroom. Angel was still grinning when she opened the door to her mother's cousin Hélène Roger, or *Tati* Hélène, as she liked to be called. A petite woman with smooth dark brown skin, she wore pastel pink scrubs and a matching cardigan with a brown leather Coach bag tucked under her arm.

"Tati Hélène! What brings you here so early?"

Her godmother presented her with a pair of stacked Tupperware. "You missed Charles's retirement dinner. I brought you some food."

How thoughtful. But Angel suspected her mother had dispatched her ally to check in on her child who'd been "abandoned" in Miami by the boyfriend that she had never liked in the first place. Stunts like this made her plan to move back home less and less enticing.

"So heavy. What's in this?"

"Just a little something. *Lambi en sauce, salade Russe, macaroni au gratin…*"

"Wow! Thanks!" Conch in Creole sauce, rice and beans, beet and potato salad, and her godmother's famous mac and cheese: a feast in takeout containers. "Sorry to have kept you waiting. I was getting ready for work."

"Is that what you're wearing to work? *Ah, non!*"

Angel glanced down at her dress, purchased on a whim

off Instagram. She was headed to the cocktail party in the Swiss-designed parking garage straight after work. The dress struck the right balance with its capped sleeves, bias-cut skirt, and high slit over her right thigh.

"Don't worry," Angel said. "This is very appropriate for an art show."

Before her godmother could tell her to find a "good" job in hospital administration, Angel took the food into the kitchen and arranged the containers in her mostly empty refrigerator. She had no doubt her godmother would be back within a week to collect the prized containers.

"I'll get these back to you," Angel called out from the kitchen. "I promise!"

She returned to the front room to find her aunt examining a pair of tailored black trousers. Angel stopped midstride and came close to toppling forward. She raced through hundreds of possible explanations, settling for the most probable one. "Those belong to Chris."

Tati Hélène shot her a look that said she wasn't born yesterday. "This is quality. Chris never wore anything this nice." She held up the pants as evidence and Angel prayed another condom wouldn't come tumbling out. "That boy only wore khaki pants, even to your cousin's baby shower, and he was *not* this tall."

"That's why he left them behind," Angel said, no longer able to hide her irritation. She was a grown-ass woman in her own rental apartment. Why should she have to explain herself? This would be the part of the sitcom where the main character would tell her busybody godmother to mind her own business. Angel, however, was not born into a sitcom prototype family. Her parents, aunts, uncles, and honorary aunts and uncles were from Haiti. She and her cousins were first generation American who gave their parents ulcers with their "American" lifestyles. Dating, pursuing careers outside of the medical profession, marrying foreigners, and best of all, "living in sin," were all signs that they'd lost their way.

"Tati Hélène," Angel said as respectfully as possible. "I hate to rush you, but I am going to be late for work. You don't want me to *lose* my job."

Those proved to be the magic words. Losing a job, or *pèdi travay*, was a calamity no Haitian immigrant would wish upon anyone.

"Okay, okay, I'm leaving." Tati Hélène shuffled to the door. "*Bonne journée, ma cocotte.* And wear a sweater, at least. It's December."

"I will. Don't worry," Angel said. "*Merci* for the dinner. I'll eat it tonight."

With that, Angel ushered her godmother out the door and went to join Alessandro in the bedroom. He was standing by her dresser studying a painting on the wall. It was one of her few from childhood, a bougainvillea vine creeping over a cement wall. Angel handed him his pants. She wondered how much he'd heard or understood of her conversation with her godmother, but the devilish grin he flashed her confirmed that he'd heard and understood *everything*.

He fell onto the bed and joined his hands behind his head. "There better be enough food for two."

Angel rolled onto the bed and cuddled next to him. "That was just a preview of my family. Trust me, you wouldn't want to meet them."

He tucked her to him. When he answered his tone was surprisingly solemn. "I would, actually. Family is important."

She raised herself onto her elbow and studied the near-naked man in her bed, seeing him with newfound appreciation. Chris had never wanted to spend time with her rambunctious family. Toward the end of their relationship, she'd had to resort to bribery. "Come with me to my cousin's baby shower and I'll go with you to see the hundredth *Star Wars* movie."

He smoothed her hair. "Come on, let's go. I don't want you to lose your job."

Angel checked her watch. "I'm going to be late, and Paloma will kill me."

"No way. I'll get you there on time."

And he did.

Twelve

"We cannot certify the authenticity of *El Jardín Secreto*." The expert had called while Sandro was running lines over Zoom with his acting coach.

He stepped out onto the terrace for privacy, even though he was home alone. The authenticator explained in detail how they'd come to their conclusion.

"It all comes down to red paint?"

"That particular pigment was not commercially available until 1985. There's no way your grandfather could have found it for such liberal use ten years earlier."

The blooming bougainvillea flowers had betrayed the secrets of the garden. Funny.

"We wish we had better news for you, Mr. Cardenas."

"It's the news I expected."

Over the last few days, Sandro had managed to put the painting out of his mind. He hadn't wanted the results back this soon, either. It forced him to link Angel to the gallery that sold him a forged copy of his own grandfather's painting, a thing he did not want to do.

"Most professionals would try to avoid this common mistake. This leads me to think we're not dealing with a professional. How would you like to proceed?"

"I'm not sure."

"You may file a police report. We find that most of our clients don't."

Most wouldn't for the reasons Paloma had so eloquently explained. They wouldn't want their neighbors to know they'd been conned.

"More often than not these cases are not prosecuted, even

with the best of evidence," the authenticator continued. "Either way, our discretion is guaranteed."

Sandro ended the call and pocketed his phone. The cloudy morning sky mirrored his mood. Who would go through the trouble of reproducing the old man's paintings? Who had suddenly expressed interest in their market value? And called him out for not doing more to increase it? All signs pointed to his brother. Sandro wasn't delusional. Ed didn't have the skill to reproduce an original stick figure, let alone an oil painting. But he could have hired someone to reproduce the paintings and pass them off to galleries. You didn't have to be a genius to work out that plan.

He was going to have to pay his big brother a visit.

Two hours later, Sandro landed in Tampa. Good thing his brother's tire shop wasn't too far from the airport. A driver was waiting to take him there and back. The car hadn't slowed to a stop when he pushed open the door. When he burst into the small shop, welcomed by the smell of grease and rubber, his brother proved that Sandro wasn't the only one with theatrical inclinations.

"Well if it isn't the King of Hollywood!" Eddy bellowed from behind the cash register. "To what do we owe this honor?"

The few customers threw glances their way, but none likely recognized him. He was just another Latino guy in the ball cap, sunglasses and bland T-shirt. "We need to talk."

"Nah," Eddy replied. "I need to take care of my customers."

"Eddy," Sandro said through clenched teeth. "I came a long way."

"Is that right?" Eddy said. "Well, take a damn number."

Balding, paunchy, with a lined face, Eddy looked older than the seven years he had on Sandro. But he'd had a difficult life. Their father's death had hit him harder. Sandro was only four at the time and had been living with JD since he was two. In the family, they said their dad had died of stubbornness, having refused to go to the ER when a minor cut turned into a raging infection. Sandro was deemed too young to attend the funeral. All he knew was that his father, like his mother, had stopped coming around. It was complicated, as was his relationship with this half brother whom he had once worshipped.

Sandro went over to the waiting area and flipped open a frayed copy of *Car and Driver*. He was going to sit here until—

The staged sit-in didn't last long. Eddy waved him over. His office was down the hall. It was large enough for a desk and not much else. Still, Eddy had managed to squeeze in a recliner for himself.

"Welcome to my humble abode. Have a seat."

Sandro lowered himself onto one of the two guest seats that lined the wall. There was little legroom, but he made it work.

"Coffee? Tea? Or what do you guys drink in California? Green lettuce juice? Is that it?"

"I'm good, thanks."

"Yeah. I can tell you're good."

"Why the attitude?" Sandro asked, point blank.

"It's not about nothing," Eddy said. "You show up here unannounced. You don't ask about Linda."

"Oh? How is she, by the way?"

"She's a certified substitute teacher."

"Give her my best."

"I will."

"Can we knock this off now?"

Their relationship had not been considered loving. As the illegitimate child of their dad and his mistress, Sandro was by default the black sheep. The power dynamic had shifted over recent years, with Sandro gaining confidence and asserting himself.

"Sabina tells me you two have talked about JD's paintings, wanting to see them in the world."

"Don't know why you're hiding them. Are you embarrassed?"

"Don't go there," Sandro said quietly.

Eddy looked down at the points of his shoes. "Just asking."

"What do you care? You've never cared."

"That's what I don't like. Righteous attitude. You're not the only one who loved JD."

"I don't question that. Just your interest in the paintings."

"I've got no interest in the damn paintings. You've seen to that."

"Seeing how you've wiped out more than half of them, I don't know how you can complain."

"There you go, blaming me for that fire again!"

"Whose cigarette was it?"

"It was an accident."

"You tossed a cigarette into a shed full of turpentine and other explosives."

"It was an accident," Eddy repeated.

Straight after their grandfather's wake, his friends had gathered in the yard outside JD's painting shed. One tossed cigarette had set the shed ablaze. "Accident or not, the result is the same."

"Why are you here?" Eddy asked. "You didn't come all this way to fight about the fire or JD's paintings."

"Actually, yeah, I did."

Sandro opened the duffel bag he'd brought with him and pulled out *El Jardín Secreto*. He dropped the painting on Eddy's cluttered desk.

"What's this?"

"A fake."

"No me jodas," Eddy murmured. "How do you know?"

"An expert analyzed it."

"How does the expert know?"

"That's what he does."

"Or he's taking your money and feeding you bull."

"It's a fake."

"Okay...so what?" Eddy said. "What do you expect me to do about it?" Sandro stared at him. "You think I have something to do with it? You think I have an art studio at the back of the shop?"

"I'm not saying that. Just wondering if you know anything about it."

"I don't."

"Are you sure?"

"Get outta here with this mess! You show up—unannounced—and freaking ruin my day."

"Sorry," Sandro said, unfazed. "That wasn't my intention."

"The result is the same."

Sandro did not budge. He sat stewing in frustration. This was plainly going nowhere, but was he really going to leave without answers?

Eddy shooed him off like a stray dog. "Go on! I got a shop to run!"

The shop was nearly empty. There was no way Sandro could remind him of that without coming off as an ass. He stood to go.

"And take that with you," Eddy said, sliding the painting across the desk with the tip of a logo pen. "Don't plant it on me."

Just when Sandro reached for it, Eddy stopped him. "Wait." He studied the painting for a long moment, his eyes wistful.

"What is it?" Sandro asked.

Eddy shook his head. "Like I said—you weren't the only one who loved JD's work."

Sandro snatched the painting off the desk and shoved it back into his bag. "It's a fake. Remember that?"

"Says you and your expert," Eddy said. "But you gotta admit. If it's a fake, it's a damn good one."

"I'll pass that message along when we catch the forger."

"You won't."

"Why do you say that?"

"A hunch."

Sandro leaned against the doorway. "A hunch?"

"Who really cares, anyway?"

"Someone is making money off JD. That doesn't piss you off?"

"Imitation is the sincerest form of whatever."

"Bullshit!"

"Here's some advice."

"I'm listening."

"Go back to California or Cannes or wherever you spend your time. We've got enough problems. Leave us nobodies alone."

The question was cued up, ready to roll off his tongue. *Do you hate me that much?* Only he knew Eddy didn't hate him. He envied him, and that was just as bad. This shop had been his older brother's dream and he'd built it from ground up with little help from anyone. Sandro couldn't imagine him living any other life yet the resentment was there, palpable, weaving itself within their conversations. Eddy had been fine with him being a struggling actor, waiting tables and cleaning rest rooms. Sandro was often the butt of jokes at holiday reunions. So much so that he had stopped attending. Once his career picked up, though, Eddy's attitude changed. The entrepreneur now referred to himself as a "nobody." Ridiculous.

Sandro turned to leave. "Good seeing you again."

"You look good, bro!" Eddy called out. "Keep up with that keto diet!"

Thirteen

"That seems to me like an unfair cultural appropriation..."

A string bean of a man in a tweed jacket frowned at a painting of an American pop star reimagined as Ganesha. Angel bit back a smile and wandered to the next exhibit. On her half-hour break she liked to wander through the halls, soaking up as much art as possible. The next room featured a life-size glass house. The manager was on his mobile phone, hustling. "We're everywhere. So wherever you want to be, we can get you there."

Angel felt a tug at her heart. Was that how it felt to be celebrated, promoted and valued? That sort of overture could potentially take an artist from anonymity to hot commodity. That was the dream that she had walked away from. She had locked away those ambitions to embrace her new career path. So much so, she hadn't even wanted Alessandro to look at her paintings. She hoped to keep her failures hidden, if only for the short while they had together. Things didn't have to get that deep.

Her phone buzzed in her hand. Alessandro had sent her a photo, and all the overconceptualized artwork in the convention center faded to black. It was a screenshot of an Instagram post from two summers back. He was standing on a dock at Fisher Island wearing a black T-shirt and cargo shorts.

She'd saved his phone number under the name BEST MALE LEAD. The text message that followed read: I look good in shorts, too.

Angel was fully aware that she was texting and flirting

like her teenaged self. That awareness didn't prevent her from throwing herself into it.

ANGEL'S PHONE: I like you best without pants.

BEST MALE LEAD: My wicked Angel... I'll be late for the parking garage party.

ANGEL'S PHONE: Long day in paradise?

BEST MALE LEAD: Difficult day. Won't bore you with details.

Angel stared at her phone. She wished he would bore her with details. She wanted to know the not-so-glamorous side of him. What wore him down? What weighed on his mind?

BEST MALE LEAD: Please don't run off with another guy.

ANGEL'S PHONE: This is a work event. I'm not going to cruise celebrities.

BEST MALE LEAD: Celebrities don't worry me. It's those starving artists...

ANGEL'S PHONE: Ah! The ones with goatees...

BEST MALE LEAD: I used to be a starving artist.

ANGEL'S PHONE: No goatee?

BEST MALE LEAD: Didn't need one. It would be a crime to hide this face. May I take you home later tonight?

ANGEL'S PHONE: I'll think about it.

BEST MALE LEAD: Think about me without pants.

Angel laughed. The real crime would be to not take this man home tonight.

1010 Alton Road resembled a cement origami structure. It cost the owner fifty million dollars to build and the average motorist thirty dollars to park. The ground floor was dedicated to retail space. But the party was held on the top floor. It was redesigned as a sculpture garden against the backdrop of unobstructed views of Miami Beach. In short, it was fabulous.

A popular DJ was spinning, so there would be no surprise live performances tonight. She was grateful; her heart couldn't take it. But she was excited beyond reason to see Alessandro again. No matter that they'd been apart for only a few hours. She was even excited to see his crew of friends. Angel stood at the entrance and scanned the crowd composed of collectors, curators and the artists that they all coveted. A few people outside the industry caught her eye: a street-style photographer and his fashion blogger girlfriend, a famed performance artist and activist, and an art critic for the *Times*.

And there he was.

Another thing her heart couldn't take? Seeing her "date" and his ex huddled up in a corner. Although the woman had her back to him, Angel recognized her right away from her famous cropped blue hair. Actress/musician Chloe London was one of Alessandro's most famous exes.

In a stunning plot twist, after all the drama about Chris, he was the one to introduce an evil ex. Although there was no evidence that Chloe London was evil, apart from the fact that she'd starred as an evil witch in a Disney movie. But by all accounts, except maybe that of Alessandro's publicist, the breakup had been brutal.

Angel did not know what to do with herself. Thankfully,

a waiter swung by and offered her a glass of champagne, which gave her something to do with her hands. She was being ridiculous, overly dramatic and a touch possessive. In his world, where there were no rules, he could do what he wanted. There would always be something or someone more exciting to catch his attention.

Angel could map her thoughts from the dangerous turn they had taken to the ditch where they were headed. Pump the brakes! She was here for work—even if her work consisted of snapping a few photos for the gallery's Instagram account.

And then Alessandro looked up. While nodding in agreement at whatever Chloe was saying, he scanned the entrance as if searching for someone. When his gaze settled on her, he brightened and the search appeared to be over.

Sandro hadn't thought he'd make it back from Tampa on time, but good thing he had. He would not have wanted to miss Angel's grand entrance. She stopped his heart in her "nothing" dress paired with tall suede boots. He stirred with impatience, eager to get away from Chloe and to get his hands on Angel. He listened as Chloe updated him on the recent shenanigans of her toy poodle. Then he begged off as tactfully as possible. He'd lost sight of Angel for a moment and when he finally spotted her, her quiet anxiety roared loud in his ears.

What was she thinking?

"Hey, you," he greeted.

He refrained from touching her. She'd made it clear that they weren't "out." And he was okay with it. Really, he was. Once the press got wind of their affair, things would get complicated very quickly. Flying under the radar was likely the smartest thing to do. He only wished that she weren't so adamant about it.

She gave him an empty smile. "Hey! You made it."

"I couldn't wait to see you." Sandro hadn't even gone

back to the island to change. He'd thrown a blazer over his T-shirt and jeans and hoped his smile made up for it. "If your godmother saw you without a sweater, I'm not sure she'd approve."

That got her laughing. And he was relieved, mainly because he had a clue as to what might have triggered her initial reaction.

"You're not going to let this die down, will you?"

"I love your godmother."

"You love that she loved your pants."

"That, too." He motioned for her to follow him. "Come with me. I found a private spot for us to talk behind that giant penis."

Angel whimpered with suppressed laughter, her eyes bright with tears. "You're the big penis! It's a statue of a double helix!"

"It's whatever you say it is. You're the expert."

He drew her close and hugged her, rubbing the small of her back. "Have you eaten, babe?"

"I'm sure there's a bacon-wrapped date with my name on it somewhere."

There was more than that. He'd checked out the spread. "I'll make sure you're fed," he promised. "Everything okay, otherwise."

"Everything is fine." She eased away from him. "And you?"

"Yeah," he said with a shrug.

She nodded. "Cool."

He couldn't stand it, all the things they weren't saying were piling up. Sandro cut through it and addressed the "ex" in the room. "That was Chloe London I was speaking with just now. We used to..." He couldn't finish the sentence. What had he and Chloe been up to those few months they were together? Killing time?

"We don't have to go there," she said. "It's fine."

It wasn't fine. "You're big on rules. How about this for one? We tell each other the things that matter." When she moved to protest, he stopped her. "Don't tell me this doesn't matter."

She grabbed his hand. "I'm trying to tell you it's not necessary. The press coverage was thorough."

"The press?" According to the "press," Chloe had cheated and dumped him for her ex. It was no wonder Angel didn't want to talk about it.

"You shouldn't believe everything you read online."

"It wasn't online, it was in *Vanities*."

Sandro stepped back. Her hand slipped from his. He was so offended that he switched to Spanish. *"No me digas que crees—"*

She reclaimed his hand. "I told you the sordid details about my breakup. It's only fair that you get to share yours."

"There was no breakup," he said. "We were never together, not in a real way. I had time on my hands and she was on a break from Tyler. When they got back together, I was filming in Toronto."

Angel's expressive face went blank and he understood his mistake. "It's nothing like us."

"Isn't it?" she said. "Some brokenhearted woman needs a distraction and you offer yourself up as a chew toy." She poked him in the ribs to drive the point home. "You're not a chew toy for the brokenhearted."

"Is that what you are?" Sandro asked. "Brokenhearted?"

With Chloe the answer to this question didn't bother him. She was a good person with a kind heart, but her thing with Tyler was their business. He hadn't cared enough to get entangled in it. But with Angel, it weighed on him a little too heavily. He hated that she was still stuck on her ex. She only had to mention him and jealousy shred his insides. Plus he could not remember the last time he'd had to compete for a woman's attention and he was clumsy at it. His flippant offers for rebound sex were nothing but a facade, a lid covering a pool of want. He wanted her. Why couldn't he just say, "I like you"?

Sandro leaned against the penis statue, wondering when and where exactly he'd lost his balls. He missed it when Angel's cool nonchalance turned to hot anger.

"I was never brokenhearted, you big dummy!"

He snapped to attention. "Okay…"

"Chris and I were on our last legs by the time he left. We weren't talking. We weren't having fun. We weren't much involved in each other's lives. If I'd had my act together, I would've left him long ago."

He stopped her. "Angel, the look on your face when you got that alert."

There was nothing an ex could post that could upset him if his feelings weren't involved. He certainly wouldn't sign up for alerts.

"I was upset, yes!" she admitted openly. "It was an intrusion. I was just getting to know you and it pulled me into the past. What bothered me, really, was the way he'd ended things. As if he were destined for greatness and I was dead weight dragging him down. It was humiliating. And I felt like…"

She struggled with the last word. Sandro said it, so she wouldn't have to. "A failure."

She nodded. "I'm thirty. That's an age when you ought to have your shit together."

"I wouldn't know about that."

She groaned. "At thirty you worked three jobs."

"And had four roommates."

She made a face. "That sounds terrible."

He kissed her; it was long overdue. "It was terrible."

"Maybe in the spirit of competition, I got obsessed with

keeping score. I used Chris as a visual aid. His videos showed me how far off track I was."

"Or you think you were," he corrected.

She made a gesture as if to say, tomato/tomahto, it was all the same.

"Hate to say this, but Chris reminds me of this tool." He knocked on the double helix penis and she burst out laughing. His fear that they'd taken things too far tonight gently subsided. He drew her tight and kissed her as if they were alone, back at his house or her apartment, and not at a raging party with a frenetic DJ upping the ante with every track. He wanted to get out of here, but she still had work to do. He couldn't keep her tucked away for much longer.

Just as he was about to propose they rejoin the party, she held him tighter. "I've never told any of this to anyone."

"Oh, my angel…" He felt honored, flat-out honored, that she had trusted him enough to confide in him. "I'll keep your secrets."

She whispered back. "And I'll keep yours, just so you know. You can tell me anything."

Had they just exchanged vows? Exciting…

"Listen to me." He eased her away and gripped her shoulders. "I've lived in California long enough to know that we have to end this session with an affirmation."

She laughed, all the while wiping at her eyes with the back of her hands. "Alessandro, you're the only one who can make me laugh and cry at the same time."

Good, he thought. It was a sign that he was getting to the heart of her. "Repeat after me. I'm not a failure."

She took a deep breath. "I'm not a failure."

"Good girl."

"Not so fast! Now it's your turn," she said. "Repeat after me. You're no one's chew toy."

Over the years, Sandro had coupled up and split up more

times than he could count. His work always came first. He could always count on his friends to fill the time between jobs. His life had been a wild spin and he'd enjoyed it. Angel made him want to step off the carousel.

"I'm no one's chew toy, except yours."

She rolled her eyes at him, but he could tell that she loved it. "That's progress, I guess."

"Some might call it a major breakthrough."

"They'd be wrong," she said. "Now come on. You promised to feed me. Let's go."

She'd grabbed his hand and didn't let go, not even after they'd emerged from their hiding place. They made a meal of the array of appetizers and, an hour later, were still holding hands when Gigi, Rose and Jenny made their grand entrance. Sandro held her purse while she went around snapping the photos for her gallery's social media accounts. Finally, when she was done, she curled an arm around his neck and whispered, "Take me home."

In the elevator, at his request, she raised the hem of her dress to show him how far high those sleek boots reached. He pinched her thigh. She laughed all the way down to the ground floor valet station. But Alessandro kept sinking deeper into an emotion that he was afraid to identify.

ART BASEL BABE WATCH

So far, the men have brought the heat during Basel. Top on our list is Alessandro Cardenas. Although he has not yet been spotted at the after-hour clubs with his usual crew, here he is on opening night looking like a boss in a Tom Ford suit. Next, the actor sports a more casual look, in a black shirt and trousers, while serenading some lucky girl at The High Tide. Is there nothing this man can't do? Obviously not! We hear that there are some production delays with his next feature. Here's hoping that he spends his free time on the beach, so we can catch a glimpse of the body under the clothes. #SandroFever

—@Sunshine&Wine_IG

COMMENTS:
@thebitterandthesweet: Who is the basic chick he's serenading?

Fourteen

Art Basel, closing night...

Someone ripped the banana straight off the wall, peeled it and gobbled it down to the great consternation of the crowd. There went the most photographed banana in the world. It was instantly proclaimed performance art.

Paloma sold *YOLO* to a young gay couple from Lisbon.

Justine was feeling well enough to attend the night's big party, albeit with a foot in an orthopedic boot. Which meant Angel had the night off. As soon as she learned the news, she called Alessandro.

He answered on the second ring. "Tell me you were there when that guy ate the banana."

"Ugh! I didn't make it in time." She'd heard the commotion, but Gallery Six's viewing room was halfway across the convention center. "I got a picture of the duct tape on the wall. It's posted on Instagram."

"Good job," he said. "So, what's on the agenda tonight?"

"Nothing! I have the night off."

"Angel…" he said in his teasing way. "Don't play with my emotions."

"I wouldn't!"

She had made it to the break area: an indoor park complete with artificial trees and a spread of fake grass. She took a seat on a bench.

"I'm taking you out," he said. "What would you like to do? Just tell me and I'll make it happen."

Angel turned the question in her mind. "There's one thing."

"What?"

"We'd have to move beyond Basel," she said, dropping her voice to a whisper. "Only the top one percent of artists gets the chance to show here. For the rest, it's every man for himself."

"Or woman," he said.

"No," she said. "It's even worse for women. Say nothing of the nonbinary! Nobody cares!"

"I care," he said. "And I can't go to another Basel party, I swear to God. I'm done. Let's branch out. Want to go to Wynwood?"

She was always taken aback at how well he knew the city. She had half expected him to suggest Ocean Drive. "And Little Haiti. There's an art scene there, too."

"Just you, me and my driver," he said. "Is that alright?"

"I don't know," she said. "Are you sure you want to be out with someone as basic as me?"

She heard him snap to attention, or had he dropped the phone? "Why would you say that?"

"It was a joke," she said. "Someone left a comment on an Instagram post and—"

"*No me digas*, Angel!" he said. "What are you doing reading comments?"

Increasingly, he broke out in Spanish. Angel wondered if this meant that he was more comfortable around her. She hoped that was the case, even though now he was clearly exasperated.

"It was right there. There was no missing it."

"I pay someone to monitor social media," he said. "It doesn't look like I'm missing out on much. Who would call you basic? You're so beautiful, half the time I can't even look at you."

Angel hadn't been fishing for a compliment, but Lord, she'd caught Moby Dick. "It didn't bother me, really. My self-esteem is rock solid."

"Alright," he said, although he didn't sound convinced. "So…you, me and my driver. Sounds good?"

She rose from the bench. Her break was nearly over and Paloma would kill her if she returned late again. "Sounds great."

"Angel, have you met Gus?"

"We've met," Angel said. "You were waiting at the dock when I arrived that first night."

Gus was bearded, bald and built like a linebacker. Angel understood that "driver" was code for "bodyguard." For Alessandro to venture into the city on a warm December night, he needed security. Was this something that she would have to get comfortable with? *No, Angel! Stop! Dead end ahead!* Alessandro would be leaving soon enough. She'd register with a dating app and find a nice boyfriend who did not need an armed guard on a date. The end.

Was Gus armed?

Alessandro took her by the waist and guided her into the car. "First stop Wynwood?"

She agreed. "I don't know where you'll park this beauty."

"It's arranged," Gus said. "We have a spot in a garage."

By "garage" Gus had meant an actual mechanic shop owned by a buddy of his and located one block away from the popular Wynwood Walls. The Alfa Romeo pulled up to a metal drop gate smeared with graffiti. It rose to allow them passage and fell like an iron curtain behind them. The garage owners rushed forward to greet Alessandro and escorted their trio through the front of the shop and out onto the sidewalk. Although it was dark, Alessandro slipped on sunglasses. They were like any other couple, strolling hand in hand, with a bodyguard in tow.

Every square inch of Wynwood was coated in spray paint. Every back alley brick wall was a street artist's canvas. The murals varied in style, but the point was to provoke. Whether it was a pair of widespread angel wings or a play on a political slogan, all that mattered was that it stood out.

With so much art on the streets, they avoided the galleries, preferring to stroll the sidewalks.

Angel squeezed her date's hand. She was of average height when surrounded by average people, but at his side, she felt small and dainty. Then Alessandro popped the traditional third date question: "Your place or mine?"

"Well...mine, obviously. Yours is an ocean away."

"It's across the bay, not the straits," he said. "I can get you back in time for work in the morning if you're concerned."

That was always a concern. But she had an idea. "I open the gallery in the morning, but I have the next two days off."

He pulled her into a side street—with Gus standing guard. "Two whole days? No obligations?"

"None."

"Then what's to stop you from coming with me to paradise?"

His gaze lingered on her mouth, anticipating her answer. Angel couldn't help licking her lips. "Nothing."

He kissed her full on the mouth. "Pack a bag. But don't pack too much—you won't need it."

They'd made it to the main attraction. "The Walls" was an outdoor grand scale art space for graffiti and street art. Securing a wall was a competitive process and some of the world's most celebrated artists had been featured. Alessandro mentioned that he'd attended the grand opening. "No one thought it would take off like this."

They stood before a mural of a bird perched on barbwire. The bird had blood-red feathers and his eyes were dots of coal. The opposing wall was painted pink with the words *I'm beautiful, damn it!* Mothers and daughters, sisters and girl squads waited in line for a chance to pose for photos, using the mural as a backdrop.

"This is how people consume art now," Angel said. "It's more immediate and interactive. Much better than a stuffy gallery."

Alessandro looked at her, his expression soft. "Do you like your job at Gallery Six?"

Angel laughed nervously. "You asked me that already."

She'd done a competent job for the gallery these last few days. Was he picking up some other vibe?

"Your answer was bull, and you know it. I want the truth."

She scrounged around for some scraps of truth. "Let's just say, it wasn't my first career choice. I'm still new at it. The gallery itself is a bit much and a little too concerned with its celebrity clientele—no offense."

He took none. In fact, he seemed relieved.

"Look," she said. "I just need something to work. Okay?"

"Okay."

They migrated to the next mural, a dazzling geometric abstract which, upon close inspection, was composed exclusively of stick figures in various sexual positions. Angel could not focus on it. She was stuck on something he'd said. How had he known her first answer was BS? At the time, they hadn't known each other that long.

"How do you know me so well?"

He shoved his hands in the back pockets of his jeans, feigning boyish innocence. "Reading your body language is not the same as knowing you."

"You always get to the heart of me."

He cocked his head, coal black eyes steady on her. "That's the objective."

He was so damn sexy! Angel forgot where she was and, more importantly, whom she was with. She took his face between her hands and drew him into a kiss.

Their audience swooned.

They were not an average couple on an average date. They were tropical fish in an aquarium, floating around to the amazement and astonishment of a crowd. Someone shouted: "That's Sandro!" A woman screeched: "I knew it!... Who's the girl?"

Alessandro groaned. "Blown cover. Let's go."

That proved to be difficult. The crowd pressed around them. Gus tactfully drilled a tunnel for them to move forward. Armed security guards rushed forward to assist. Sandro appeased his fans with handshakes, smiles, and kisses blown into the air. Angel was in shock. Up until now, their public outings had been limited to controlled environments where celebrities like him were free to roam outside of their gilded cages.

The garage was not far. They were able to duck in and disappear.

"This doesn't always happen," Alessandro said apologetically. "Most times I blend into a crowd."

Angel was doubtful. Could this be his one blind spot? Once upon a time, he might have blended into a crowd like this, but not anymore. She wondered who among his friends would volunteer to tell him the truth.

"Where to now?" he asked.

"You're up for more?"

"Baby, the night is young!"

The endearment tossed out casually set off a glitter bomb in her chest. *What has this man done to me?* Angel had to do better. She couldn't let him get to her like this. What was she going to do when their love affair ended with a great big Hollywood kiss?

They all climbed into the car.

"Where to?" Gus asked.

"*Papaya* on Northwest Second Avenue," Angel replied. The gallery showcased Haitian art and she would be remiss not to stop by during Art Basel week.

"I know it," Gus said. "Let's go."

"We call Gus 'GPS' behind his back," Alessandro said.

"And to my face," Gus chimed good-humoredly.

It was the last Angel heard his voice during the ride. The city was marred with traffic and the short drive took longer than it normally would. Nestled close to Alessandro in the back of the car, fingers intertwined and speaking softly, Angel didn't mind.

"Before we were so rudely interrupted, you were going to tell me all your secrets," he said, speaking in that quiet way of his that made her tremble.

"Funny. That's not how I remember it."

"Here's your chance," he said. "Tell me something real. Not the stuff I can guess at, but what you keep hidden from everyone."

There were no skeletons drying out in Angel's closet, only her twin pet demons: inadequacy and failure.

Gus turned onto 2nd Avenue. Located at the corner, Papaya was as colorful as its name. The exterior walls were painted a rich apricot hue. Hand-painted palm trees soared up its facade from the ground to the roof. The one-story building blended nicely with its surroundings. The mini-mart next door was peacock blue with the words *BON APPÉTIT BONNE SANTÉ* stenciled in gold, a neighboring property's privacy wall featured religious iconography in primary colors, and the restaurant across the street was a vibrant red.

It occurred to Angel that there was something she could share with Alessandro. *Papaya*, her favorite art gallery, was the appropriate place to do it. But now that they'd finally arrived, Angel had second thoughts.

Fifteen

The goal was to get to the heart of her. Yet whenever he tried, asking direct yet simple questions, she looked as if she might crawl out of her skin. Whatever she was hiding behind her painted facade was tormenting her, and he hated it. To force it would be a mistake. So he let questions go unanswered and tried to read the coded messages in those steady brown eyes that still got to him, even now.

So far, he'd gathered that deep inside she felt like a failure. Tonight, he learned that she desperately needed *something* to work. Having been there himself, he knew it was a dark place to be.

They'd arrived at the gallery. "Let's go."

She grabbed his arm just as he prepared to bolt out of the car. "Wait! I should walk you through this."

The neighborhood was hosting an art walk. She stared out the window at the lively party scene. Sandro was slightly offended. Did she think the Little Haiti crowd would scare him? Or did she worry he'd reject the art she took so much pride in? Either way, he had to stomp those fears.

"I grew up in the Little River area just miles from here," he said. "You're not going to explain anything to me."

"Wow." She released him. "Is there no situation you can't spin with a folksy tale of your humble roots?"

"Apparently not."

Angel was actually wringing her hands. "I might have hyped it up a bit," she said. "This is not a fancy gallery by any stretch. But I want to support them."

"Okay, let's support them."

"Whoa!" She gripped his arm again, tighter this time. "By *support* I mean showing appreciation for their work.

Please don't think I brought you here to buy out their inventory."

"Angel! You're taking the fun out of this."

"I'm just saying! You tend to show off a little."

He tended to show off a lot. That was the performer in him. But he didn't have to buy out a business's inventory to show his support. "If I like something, I'll buy it. Plus, there are other things I can do."

"Like what?"

"You'll see." He opened the car door, stepped out and assisted Angel. She was dressed simply in a silky blue top, which she wore with fitted jeans and barely there sandals. Her brown waves gathered at the top of her head with a clip. Although she was not one to layer on clothes, he had already formulated a plan how to best undress her when he finally got her alone. The jeans would have to go first. The top would fall away once he tugged at the ties at the nape of her neck. Then he'd snatch away that hair clip. He imagined her waves would cascade around her shoulders. Only then would he work on the lacy strapless bra that he'd gotten glimpses of earlier.

But first they had to get through this gallery tour. It meant something to her, and he was going to show up for it.

The glossy Alfa Romeo standing idle at the curb had drawn some attention. When Alessandro and Angel emerged from it, excitement crackled through the gathering crowd. He was not as famous as Angel seemed to think. He was nowhere near a household name. Most people struggled to remember his name or recall which movie they'd seen him in. He hoped his next movie, a big budget adaptation from a popular fantasy trilogy, would change that. He could have ducked into the gallery before anyone had figured out who he was, but he gave it a minute. Soon enough, a young woman cried, "I love you, Sandro!"

Without missing a beat, he called out, "Love you, too!"

And that triggered an uproar and a blaze of flashing camera phone lights. Before they got swamped, he grabbed Angel's hand and headed inside. A security guard ushered them into the reception area and locked the door behind them. He turned to Angel and met her knowing gaze.

"I know what you did there."

"I don't know what you mean."

"Tomorrow's headline will be Hollywood Discovers Artsy Gallery in Little Haiti."

He bent forward and kissed the tip of her nose. "Or something like that."

She mouthed the words *thank you*. Sandro wanted to kiss those lush lips. He could hardly wait to get her back on Fisher Island. All that time alone together, he might die of happiness.

When they entered the first viewing room, the gallery owner nearly fell off the stack of wood crates where he sat, drinking beer from a bottle and chatting with friends. He knew Angel and extended a warm welcome. He gave them the tour and explained the objective of the space was to promote up-and-coming artists, boost the culture and build community. The paintings were not unlike those his grandfather might have painted, scenes of Caribbean life, beaches, gardens, outdoor markets, women in recline, women at work, women dressed in white, dancing to bongo drums. Sandro took a moment to speak with the night's featured artist who was eager to share that he had been to Cuba last year as part of a cultural exchange program. Sandro posed for photos with the artist, the owner, the security guard and nearly everyone else who'd found themselves locked in the small gallery space with them. All the while Angel was beaming at him. He'd do it all again if it made her look at him like that.

When the frenzy died down, she asked the owner if they could have some time alone in one of the smaller viewing rooms. The space was immediately cleared out. As soon as a pocket door slid shut to offer them ultimate privacy, she backed him against a wall and kissed him fiercely. His hands found their way under the hem of her silky top, in search of skin. Was a gallery tour all it took to get her hot?

"You are so easy," he said when she broke away.

"And you were so good out there!"

"I wasn't putting on an act," he admitted. "This art is more accessible than half the things at Basel. It's the sort my grandfather would make."

"It's the sort my parents would hang on their walls." She pointed to a still life of tropical fruit. Bananas, oranges, pineapples, watermelon and mangoes were lumped into a large basket. The colors were subtle, all shades of yellow and green. "As a kid, I used Crayola paints to copy still life portraits like this one. I made copies of the art in my family home. That's how I taught myself to paint. I worked hard to re-create them, almost obsessively. They were more beautiful and interesting than anything in my coloring books."

Copy... Re-create...

A question fell from him. "You paint?"

"I have a masters in fine arts to prove it," she said with a sad little smile. "Not that I'm doing much with it."

"Those paintings in your apartment…?"

She turned away from him, nodding.

"Why didn't you ever say anything?"

"What's to say? The thing I dedicated my life to is nothing more than a hobby now."

"Why did you quit?"

She did not answer. Could this be the secret that she had been hiding so deeply? A hidden shame? He took her gently by the shoulders and made her face him. Tears glazed her eyes.

He pulled her close. "Don't cry, my angel. It's okay."

She spoke into his shirt. "This is stupid! I'm over it. Really, I am."

Sandro couldn't let her lie to herself. "No, you're not, babe."

She gripped at his sleeves. "Why can't you lie to me?"

Sandro held her tight, laughter rumbling through their bodies. He kissed her hair. Later, he'd ask for more details. He might suggest that she had given up too soon. He'd encourage her to try again. For now, though, he'd rock her and make her laugh. He'd quiet the voice repeating her words.

I worked hard to re-create them, almost obsessively...

The emotional heavy lifting had taken its toll. They dropped Gus off at his downtown condo and drove to her apartment in silence. Back at her place, Angel poured him a glass of ice water and straightened things out in the kitchen. Then she headed to her room, promising to slip into something more comfortable if he were good.

"I'll be good!" he assured her.

Sandro circled the living/dining/home office area while he waited. She kept the light to one source, a table lamp near the entryway. Like last time, he was drawn to a framed painting on the wall over her desk. It was a seaside landscape brought to life in swirls of blue. A few palm trees. A little boy crouched on the sand.

She stuck her head out the door. "We can order pizza if you're hungry."

Her voice died when she saw what he was up to. This time she didn't panic or try to steer his attention away from the painting. She stepped out of the bedroom, her feet and her legs bare. All he could think was that she'd denied him the pleasure of peeling off her jeans.

She stood behind him, wrapped her arms around his waist and pressed her cheek to the space between his shoulders. "I was ten when I painted that."

"Only ten?"

"Yup. My dad is from a coastal town named Saint-Marc. This is a copy of a postcard that I found tucked in one of his books."

"Have you ever been to Haiti?"

"Never," she said. "My grandfather on my mom's side is a political exile. Back in the sixties he was a little too vocal about the dictator. One night, he was arrested, but put on a plane to the Bahamas. He got off easy because his family was well connected."

Sandro guessed the ending. "He swore never to go back and forbade his children from ever returning."

"So you know how it goes."

"Oh, I know. Sounds very familiar."

Sandro perched himself at the edge of the desk. He gathered the hem of her silky top into a fist and drew her to him. "We're both connected to an island home through pretty pictures."

"It's sad when you put it that way."

"It's sad any way you put it."

She leaned into his chest and kissed his neck. The slightest touch sent rings of heat through him. "Is it tough to turn the charm on and off like that. Wherever we went people wanted a piece of you."

"It's what I signed up for. Was it tough on you?" He was already thinking long-term. Would this be a problem in the future?

"No. I always have the best time with you."

He tugged at the ties of her top and the flimsy thing fell to her waist. Her breath came quick and shallow, raising her chest, offering up her lace-clad breasts and then quickly withdrawing the offer, over and over again. Beside him on the desk was the glass of ice water. He reached for it and swiped it against a budding nipple. Angel shuddered and arched back. He caught her by the waist and drew her back to him.

"I've changed my mind." He treated the other nipple to the same torture. "I'm going to be bad."

She disentangled herself from him and stumbled back,

brown skin prickled with goose bumps, wavy hair loose, liquid brown eyes blazing.

She slipped her thumbs underneath the waist of her panties and with a dip of the hips, lowered them to her ankles. She kicked them aside and fixed her gaze on him. Those haunting eyes urged him to be whoever he needed to be, good or bad, so long as he kept his word.

Angel led him to the couch. In the back of his mind, doubts were piling up. The trip to the gallery had opened up her world. This last conversation had revealed facts that he should not ignore, and yet he planned to. When he held her trembling body and sank inside her, he was thoroughly convinced that it was worth it.

I made copies.
I worked hard to re-create them.
Almost obsessively.
This is a copy.
Oh, my angel...

Sixteen

Myles sat in the quiet kitchen with his coffee mug and his recipe cards, jotting down edits to the day's menu. Sandro sat across from him at the stainless steel counter, coffee cup in hand, brooding. At this hour of the day *Diablo* was empty and calm. It was Myles's favorite part of the day. The guy fed off peace and quiet. Too bad for him it was Sandro's favorite time to visit. He'd stopped by after dropping Angel off at the gallery. As per usual, Myles brewed him a cup of coffee, spread butter on fresh baked bread, and left Sandro to eat in silence. Today was different only because the silence had gone prickly.

"If you don't tell me what's bothering you, I'm going to kick you out."

Sandro did not respond. He focused on ripping a chunk of bread to pieces, then the pieces to pieces.

"Is it that girl?" Myles asked.

Sandro wiped his hands of the crumbs with more force than the task required. "Yes."

"I like her," Myles said. "You two got a nice vibe, but you just met her. Shouldn't you chill a bit?"

"It's not a cake, man. You don't just pull it out of the oven and set it aside to chill."

Myles ran a hand through his hair and tightened the elastic that held his mane together. "You know what? You're right. I don't know crap about relationships. I'm staying out of it."

"No, you're in," Sandro said. "I've got to talk to someone."

"Then talk."

Myles tapped the butter knife on the counter to edge him

on. Sandro took a breath and dove in. He told his old friend about JD's paintings, the sudden appearance of fakes on the market and Angel's infinitely small role. "I don't think she has anything to do with it."

"You don't know," Myles said. "You don't know either way. Not enough time has passed. This girl is a stranger."

"She's not."

"She is," Myles insisted. "Having said that, what does your gut tell you?"

"That she has nothing to do with this."

"Then why haven't you told her any of this? You're here, telling me this shit, and you should be telling her."

Sandro was still salty for having been thrown out of his brother's tire shop. "You're my best friend," he said. "Who else am I going to talk to?"

Myles held up his hands in the universal sign of *hold your fire!* "I was just trying to make a point, not cast doubt on the state of our union. It's strong, man."

Sandro curved forward and pressed his forehead to the cool stainless steel countertop. "You think I should tell her."

Myles gathered his recipe cards in a stack and whacked him over the head with it. "There's nothing else you can do."

Sandro swatted his hand away. "Got any of those chocolate pastries I like?"

His friend got up from the stool. "It's called *pain chocolat*. Expand your vocabulary."

Myles had spent two years in Paris studying culinary arts and returned a snob. "Whatever. Just warm it up."

"I want you to consider something," Myles said when he returned with the warm pastry. "Miami is a cesspool of corruption. They've got this angle on you. Some unknown Cuban artist linked to a big Hollywood star. That's gold. They start a whisper campaign. Suddenly everybody wants a Valero original. They get some guy holed up in a warehouse cranking these things out. What do you think you can do about it?"

"So what are you saying? I should do nothing? Just give up?"

"Never give up, man. But you may be playing whack-a-mole. Don't you got a couple more Oscars to win?"

"I could just go public with it," Sandro said. "Let people know that they're buying fakes."

"That's a PSA some people might appreciate," Myles said. "You could pull JD's pieces out of storage and show them what the originals look like."

Every sign was pointing in this direction. "Like a gallery show."

Myles yawned. "Those things are so fucking boring. You're an artist. Can't you think of something more creative?"

Sandro nodded. Note to self: *Think of something more creative.*

"Now... about Angel."

Sandro piped up. "Yes?"

"Can't really help you there, but do you really think she's the one holed up in a warehouse pumping out these paintings? Yes or no?"

"No," Sandro said without hesitation.

"There's your answer."

Sandro folded his arms. That was his answer. Deep inside he knew that he could trust her. They'd exchanged vows, promising to keep each other's secrets and tell each other the things that mattered. He had to hold on to that.

"You've got to tell her, man," Myles said. "Otherwise, it's not fair to her."

Sandro stuffed his mouth with chocolate pastry and chewed. His quiet and wise friend was right, as always. *"Gracias, hermano."*

"Anytime."

"So, how's your mom?"

Myles shrugged. "She's got those back aches, you know."

Sandro nodded. He knew that Myles was a good son, a

good friend, a good uncle to his nephew, a good cook and a good-looking guy. "Tell me something. Why are you still single?"

"Shut the hell up."

Sandro finished his pastry in two bites and wiped his mouth. Now that he'd sorted things out, he was famished. "What do I got to do to get a *croqueta* around here?"

Angel was dying at work. Alessandro had dropped her off at the gallery and would return later to take her with him to Fisher Island. In the meantime, she had nothing to do but sell postcards, T-shirts and trinkets to tourists. It was a slow day at the gallery. The desire to buy art dissipated just as soon as the Basel big tents came down. And she was fine with it. She could not focus on anything except tonight, tomorrow and the day after that. She and Alessandro would be alone for two delicious days. It might change her.

Angel was falling for him, dropping through the clouds and too blissed out to worry about the landing. She could not help but compare this affair with long-term relationships that had not felt this good, this comfortable. It had nothing to do with his celebrity status or star power. She was drawn by his vivacious spirit and generous heart. She loved the way he flirted, all his pet names for her and the jokes they shared. She loved the way he made love to her, the way he freed her so that she could make love to him without inhibitions. All this was going to end soon. She wasn't prepared. There was no way to prepare for a fatal crash.

During her lunch break, Angel looked both ways before crossing Lincoln Road to grab her usual chicken Caesar wrap and iced coffee. She found a bench in the shade. People-watching was her favorite pastime and the open-air mall was ideal for this. She watched the crowds of stylish shoppers and visitors from all over the world. When she was done eating, she took out her phone and sketched the lively scene on a drawing app.

Her phone buzzed in her hand with a FaceTime request. It was her mother. *Her mother!* Angel repressed the urge to chuck her phone into the trash. She tapped the button and her mother's broad, brown face filled the screen. Likely calling from work. Her hair was brushed neatly in a bun. She wore her usual diamond stud earrings and wine-colored lipstick to elevate her physician's white coat. Her mother had kind eyes and a broad mouth that was always quick to smile. Angel favored her father, though. He had the glamour of a sixties era crooner with wavy, slicked back hair and a trim moustache.

"Bonjour, ma fille!"

"Bonjour, Mom."

"Ah! You remember your mother. Praise God!"

"Don't start. You knew I'd be busy this week."

"Busy with what you call work, yes, I knew that. But you managed to find the time to run all over town with a movie star. Imagine my surprise!"

Oh…shit!

"It's not what it looks like, Mom. Entertaining celebrities is part of my job."

"Then get a new job."

Not this again.

"Mother, I'm a thirty-year-old woman," Angel said. "My job is my business."

It irked Angel that as she made this impassioned declaration, she sounded as peevish as a thirteen-year-old. Her behavior wasn't much better. She was lying and hiding just like when she was a teen. Angel lived her life under the dome of her parents' disapproval. Immigrants with a strict code of conduct, they'd expected their daughters to focus on their education. No parties. No proms. No dating. No boyfriends or boys as friends. In order to get around their parents' rules, and to enjoy their high school years, she and Bernadette had resorted to flat-out devious behavior, sneaking around and covering their tracks.

Alessandro had asked why she'd given up on her dreams so quickly. She'd given herself a full decade, her twenties, to achieve success. When he shared the stories of his waiter/actor days, Angel felt a pang of envy. He'd had the freedom to fail over and over again until he got it right. He didn't have exacting parents to account to. No one faulted him for the sacrifices that he was willing to make in pursuit of his dreams. Things were different for Angel.

Often her mother had bemoaned Angel's so-called lack of ambition. Once, at Thanksgiving, she'd decried the poor return on her parental investment. "All that we've done for you girls, private schools, tutors, extracurricular activities, and not one of you followed in our footsteps. Bernadette, you could have been a pediatrician." Bernadette was a nurse practitioner, which was okay, just not good enough. Say nothing about Angel's so-called "career in the arts."

Angel's definition of success was grafted onto her parents' standards. Following one's bliss was not part of the equation. At thirty she needed something to show for herself: a stable source of income, a home, a husband, a few kids on the way. As of today, she had none of those things and, frankly, didn't care. After work, she was sailing off with her movie star lover to a secluded island for a nonstop sexfest. That was the plan, and she could hardly wait. Her mother would just have to deal.

"You know what, Mom?" she said. "I'm not paid to entertain celebrities. I don't know why I said that. Alessandro is my boyfriend."

As soon as those words flew out she had wanted to recall them. He wasn't her boyfriend—no matter how good it sounded.

Thankfully, her mother didn't seem to buy it. "Uh-huh."

"Okay. So maybe he's not—"

"Angeline, *those* people don't have girlfriends or wives. *Those* people only want one thing—a good time. *They* don't care who they hurt or use."

Those words ran through her like a freight train. Alessandro certainly loved a good time. He didn't use women, though. He cleverly offered them the opportunity to use him. This way, he could walk away feeling as if he'd done a public service. *You didn't even say thank you.* Angel had known the rules from the jump. She'd signed on the dotted line.

"Mom, you don't have to worry about me."

Her mother took a sip from a Styrofoam cup. "Okay."

Angel was all too familiar with that clipped tone. "My lunch break is over. I have to go."

"Okay."

"Love you."

Her mother let out weary sigh. "Love is what's killing you, Angeline."

Seventeen

Dawn left behind nothing but pristine light. Angel shielded her eyes with a hand, but otherwise she was perfectly comfortable aboard the same boat that had transported her to paradise that first time around.

Their trip had been delayed another night. The night manager had failed to relieve Angel and she had had no choice but to pull a double shift at the gallery. She'd been too tired, too frustrated with her job, too emotionally drained from her argument with her mother and too eager to collapse into bed with Alessandro to consider packing a bag. Alessandro had picked up dinner at *Diablo* and they'd spent another night at her place, finally setting off at dawn. They were rewarded with a fresh sky and crystalline bay all to themselves.

This time the golf cart was waiting at the dock and Alessandro took the wheel. At Villa Paraiso, they bypassed security and rode straight up to the penthouse without having to check in with anyone. In the elevator, he dropped her bag and kissed her until they'd arrived at the penthouse.

"This is your home for the next forty-eight hours," he said.

"I think I'll like it here."

He gave her a tour, starting from a stark white kitchen that he planned to renovate someday, a viewing room with projector and screen, the main sitting area where they'd first met, a home office and a guest bedroom down the hall from the master suite. "This is where my niece stays when she visits."

"Will she be coming by?" Angel asked, nervous at the prospect of meeting this niece who meant so much to him.

"I'm not expecting her. She's made herself scarce these last days."

He shut the door to the guest bedroom and leaned on it. She'd caught his grim expression. "Family drama?" she asked.

"Family BS, more like it," he mumbled. "But don't worry. I won't burden you."

Angel understood all too well. She was still trying to tunnel her way out of the pile of BS her mother had dumped on her yesterday afternoon. *Love is what's killing you.*

"Family is a blessing and a curse," she said.

They looked at each other and let the silence tell the story and fill in the gaps. There was no need to get into that now.

"I envy your friendships, though," she said. "Your friends are cool."

"My friends are pretty damn great," he said. "And they like you."

She waved the comment away. "They hardly know me."

"Trust me on this—they like you," he said. "We all like you. Hell, even Maritza."

His housekeeper? She couldn't possibly!

"You're mistaken," Angel said. "I was a hot mess the last time I ran into Maritza."

"She didn't mention it," he said. "She said you were nice and polite."

Angel looked down to the oak wood floor, hoping to conceal a silly little grin. "Well, that's nice."

"Hey," he said, "I have a proposition for you."

"No!" Animated by an irrational impulse, Angel rushed to silence him with a hand pressed to his lips. "No propositions! No revenge plots! No offers for rebound sex! You like me and that's enough. I like being liked."

He pried her hand away. "That's not what I was getting at. I only meant to tell you that I've given Maritza a few days off because I wanted to be alone with you. Absolute isolation. But not having Maritza means *not* having Maritza. I don't know how to turn on our stove. So there's the issue of meals. We have options. There are several restaurants on the island. We can check those out or order in."

"Oh," she said, embarrassed at her gross overreaction to what amounted to a what-would-you-like-for-dinner-type question. "Let's order in. Definitely. Absolute isolation. I like the sound of that."

"And Angel?"

"Yes?"

"*I* like you, very, very much."

Angel went to him and took his hand. She liked being liked in general, but this was special.

"I should have said that the first night instead of inventing bullshit reasons for you to stay. All that talk about rebound sex was just…"

"What?" she asked in a whisper.

"A way to…"

"Get me naked?"

He laughed and pressed his forehead to hers. "Get you to stay."

That first night, she would have played any game he'd wanted just for the chance to be with him, get to know him, touch him, taste him. "I like you, too," she said. "Much more than I thought possible."

He burrowed his face in her neck. "What does that mean?"

Angel slid her hands under his shirt. "What does it matter now?"

"It matters if this is going to last beyond these few days."

Needing to focus, Angel stopped her wanton exploration of his skin. "You mean *us*?"

"Who else?"

Angel let out a breath. Now was the time to say the things that mattered. "At first it was just a game, a little fun. Not anymore."

He kissed her slowly and for such a long time, she melted into him. "My angel…" he whispered against her lips. "This was never a game."

"There still have to be rules."

He pulled away from her. "You and your rules!"

"They work!"

He grabbed her wrist and kissed her open palm. "Can't we just enjoy this?"

"That sounds like YOLO!"

"Not YOLO, I promise." He laughed. "I know how much you hate it."

"I should have bought that piece just to remind you."

He leaned in and kissed her. "You don't have to do that. I remember everything about you. What you love. What you like. What you hate."

Well…she hated uncertainty. At the risk of sounding needy and clingy, Angel asked the question burning inside her. "What happens when you leave in a few days?"

"Weeks," he corrected. "I can stay through the holidays."

"Oh?" In the greater scheme of things it didn't move the dial much, but it bought them time. A new fragile leaf of hope sprouted inside her.

"Eventually, I'll be leaving for New Zealand. When the shoot wraps, there's no reason why I couldn't return here instead of LA."

"Or I could visit you in California," she proposed, so eager to meet him halfway it killed her. The need to keep him in her life bordered desperation, and wasn't that what her mother had tried to warn her against?

"If you do," he said, "I'll make each day beautiful for you. I promise."

A shiver ran through her. In no time, he had her out of her clothes. He made love to her, her back against the wall, her legs coiled around his waist. And before she knew it, Angel was saying yes to something that she did not fully grasp.

Sandro watched her sleep. A part of him worried that if he did not keep watch, she would run away again. Yesterday had been a sun-filled dream. They'd spent the entire day poolside. After a swim they shared a lounge chair. Stretched out on their backs, fingers linked, he told her about his father who'd been married when he'd met his mother and how his grandfather had stepped in to raise him when both his parents had shrugged off the responsibility. It turned out to be the best thing that could have happened to him. He grew up in a house with no rules and plenty of freedom to experiment and try on new hats. It allowed him to thrive as an artist. His grandfather, as moody and temperamental as he'd been, was Sandro's whole world as a child. His parents had all but abandoned him. Which brought him to a truth he hadn't yet fully acknowledged.

"People ask me to promote my grandfather's work and I can't do that without exposing my parents for who they were," he said. "As it is, nobody cares about my childhood. There's no way to introduce JD without the whole mess with my parents spilling out."

Beyond the biography his publicist had crafted, which stated that he was "born and raised in Miami," there wasn't much information about him out there. Nobody cared about his early life. They only wanted to know whom he was sleeping with at any given time.

She rested a hand on his chest, strengthening their connection through touch. "Where's your mother today?"

"In Pembroke Pines, married, with two grown kids," he said. "I'm the mistake she's left in her past. Although she did write when I landed my first major role."

By contrast, Angel's upbringing was exceptionally strict and proper. It seemed to Sandro that her mother was a little too involved in her affairs. Both her parents were physicians and they had done their best to stifle her creativity. They considered her MFA degree a waste of time and money. They disapproved of her "bohemian" lifestyle. He guessed that she'd given up on her art in large part because of familial pressure. When he tried to get her to admit it, she sat up on her knees and begged him to change the subject.

He obliged by bringing up Gallery Six. Understandably, she didn't want to talk about work. He dropped that topic, too. He couldn't avoid it for too long. He had to tell her that the painting she'd sold him was a fake; he owed her that much. He remembered how she'd reacted when he'd withheld his grandfather's identity. How much worse was this?

The news would affect her in more ways than one. She'd have to come to terms with the fact that her employer was dealing fakes, either knowingly or unknowingly. Angel would have some choices to make. Would she ignore the facts and keep her job? Would she confront Paloma and potentially lose her job? He wasn't comfortable with either option. For sure, he'd like her less if she didn't take this seriously. And yet, he didn't want her to lose her job because of him.

There was a lot to consider. He couldn't just spring the news on her. After the week she'd had, it would be cruel to dump it on her now. She needed this reprieve. He needed this time with her, untainted and untouched by the outside world.

Last night, they'd ordered gourmet pizza, ate dinner at the kitchen island, silenced their phones and went to bed fairly early. She stirred beside him now.

He rolled over to her, drew her into a spoon. His palm found the curve of her breast. Their breathing synched. A moment later, she lifted her head off the pillow and her whole body went stiff.

"What's the matter?" he asked.

"Nothing," she said. "I'm fine."

Fine was code for *I'm freaking out.* He knew that much.

"Want to run away again?"

"Don't be ridiculous!" She set her head back down but did not relax.

"Something is bothering you." He kissed her neck and her shoulder muscles knotted up. "You're tense."

She turned around in his arms and faced him, the tips of their noses touching. "This feels good."

"And that's bad?"

"It feels too good."

"No such thing as *too good*, Angel," he murmured sleepily.

She broke away from him and sat up, drawing the sheets over her chest, which was completely unnecessary. It was still dark; he could make out only the lines of her body.

"This feels too good for what it is," she said. "Does that make sense?"

So early in the morning, nothing made sense. "What time is it?"

"Six. I always wake up at six."

"Always?" he asked, groggy.

"Always."

"Well, not today. Come to me." He reached for her and pulled her deeper into their cocoon, drawing the heavy blanket around them. It didn't solve the real problem. She was still tense. He kissed her forehead and smoothed back her hair. "You're afraid of getting hurt again. Is that it?"

"Of course I am!" she exclaimed. "What about you? I could hurt you. Or don't you think that's possible?"

It was not only possible; it was highly probable. What was she going to do when he left? Sit around and wait? "Angel, you could tear me to shreds, and I'd take it," he said. "Notice I'm not the one who wants to bolt."

She closed her eyes. The flutter of her lashes tickled his chin. "Sorry. I like to panic first thing in the morning."

Maybe it was time that he made his wants clear. "I want to take the risk," he said. "I want to be the man in your life, and in your bed. I want to wake up beside you whenever I can. And I want to be good to you."

"Good?" she said. "In what way?"

"In any way you'll let me, my angel."

He couldn't bulldoze his way into her life, particularly

because he was not in a position to promise the usual things: Friday nights at the movies, Saturday night dinner dates and Sunday picnics at the park—or whatever it was people in love were doing these days.

Love. Was that what this was?

She crawled on top of him, sat up and pinned him down between her thighs, pushing away sheets, dismantling the cocoon. In the glow of the thin rays of light sneaking into the room, she was magnificent. Waves of hair framed her face. The smooth lines of her body silhouetted against the light.

"Do you panic every morning?"

"Like clockwork."

"Damn."

"It'll pass," she said. "Physical activity helps."

Well…he was her chew toy.

"Have at it," he said.

Their gazes held and she bent forward to kiss him. Before their lips touched, she whispered that she wanted to be good to him, too.

GOLDEN GLOBES NOMINATIONS

Best Performance by an Actor in a Supporting Role in a Series, Limited Series or Motion Picture Made for Television

Brad Baxter, *The Hit Job*
Alessandro Cardenas, *Black Market*
Zach Harris, *The Agency*
Nicholas Jones, *Good Vibes Only*
Robert West, *Moving Target*

Eighteen

No matter what, Angel could not snuff out a looming sense of doom. It was ridiculous. Everything was perfect. Swimming all day, talking all afternoon, a glass of wine at sunset, sketching by the pool while her lover studied lines, gourmet pizza for dinner delivered to their door—Angel had never had a more perfect day. Waking up beside Alessandro was a gift tailor-made for her. And yet she could not relax. The tension just wouldn't ease up. *I want to enjoy this. Why can't I?*

She blamed her mother. She'd poisoned her mind.

Or was it Chris?

And if no one was to blame, then what was wrong with *her*? Couldn't she be happy for a while?

They'd made love in the early morning and fallen back asleep. The house was peaceful, but her thoughts raged. Then it happened: the equivalent of a five-star alarm.

Alessandro's mobile phone started buzzing and chiming like a vengeful bumblebee, so much so it spun off the nightstand landing onto the wood floor with a thud. Somewhere in the distance a landline telephone started ringing nonstop. Angel shot upright, heart pounding. "What is it? What's going on?"

Alessandro, unruffled as always, rolled over and scooped his phone off the floor. He tapped the screen and scrolled through his messages and alerts. A lazy grin spread across his face. "Holy shit! I got a Golden Globe nom."

Was that all? Angel fell back against the pillows, relief rushing through her. She'd nearly had a stroke, there! She shoved her dark thoughts to the back of her mind and offered him a bright smile. "Congratulations! That's exciting!"

"Thanks." He chucked the phone and pounced on her. He was most handsome in the morning, scruffy and disheveled. She did not take this for granted. "Be my date, babe."

"For what?"

"The Globes."

Wow! It wasn't the prospect of walking the red carpet that excited her. Actually, she might turn that down. The award shows typically aired in February. Alessandro was making plans for several months out. That realization set off pinwheels of joy.

"I have a ball gown in the back of my closet," she said. "It'll do."

"No…" His hands explored her naked body under the sheets. "I like you in those light silky dresses."

"You do?"

"Oh, yes…" He kissed her neck and the rough skin of his cheek scraped the tender skin just below her ear. "The ones with the thin straps… It drives me crazy."

"Will you wear a blue suit?" she asked. "Like the blue Tom Ford you wore to the Emmys?"

He kissed the tip of her nose. "That was Armani, but sure, whatever you like."

"May I choose the tie?"

"May I tie you to the bed post with it afterward?"

"Or maybe I'll tie you."

"I knew it." He dipped his head and kissed the hollow of her neck. "You're no angel, and I love it."

Angel broke out in laughter. The dark clouds that crowded her mind quickly dissipated.

"Come on!" he said, pulling away. "Let's celebrate."

"With champagne?"

"Overrated," he replied. "With coffee."

She slipped on a T-shirt. He pulled on a pair of board shorts. They puttered barefoot down the hall to the bright, immaculate kitchen. Angel wandered over to the picture

window. She stretched and did a few rounds of sun saluta-
tions while Alessandro proceeded to brew coffee. Essen-
tially he shoved a pod into a fancy machine. Nevertheless,
she still felt like the most cared for and pampered woman
in the world.

"What got you nominated?" she asked, gliding from
downward dog to upward dog. The aroma of coffee filled
the kitchen.

"*Black Market*, the FastFlix miniseries."

"Oh, no! I haven't seen it!"

He pulled a milk frother from a drawer. "What?"

"Sorry! I don't have that streaming app!"

She wasn't the least sorry. Angel had no intention of sign-
ing up for another streaming service. Enough was enough!

He held up the frother. "My ego is as fragile as you'd expect, and I hate to say it—I'm hurt."

"Awww!" She rushed over to hug him. "I love your work.
You know that."

He leaned into her. "Go on. Stroke my ego."

"Sure," Angel said, pushing him away. "But first, coffee."

He retrieved a glass bottle of milk from the refrigerator. "Myles taught me how to make a decent cappuccino."

"Then that's what I'll have."

"One cappuccino coming up."

She watched as he methodically poured frothy milk into
two coffee mugs and handed her one. Then he stepped out
of the kitchen to return his agent's calls. Angel searched
around for a television remote and switched on the flat
screen mounted on the wall in the breakfast nook. She took
her coffee to the marble-top table and flipped through the
channels. The local TV networks might replay the award
nominations, if only to celebrate their local boy. Channel
3, Channel 6, Channel 7, Channel 10…and wait… A headline grabbed her attention.

*Days after Art Basel, allegations of fraud rattle the art
market.*

The news anchor, a young man who'd risen in visibility thanks to his coverage of the last hurricane, promised more details after the commercial break. Angel sipped her coffee, which was delicious, and waited. Which gallery had messed up this time? Art dealers never learned. Greed was at the rotting core of the art market; that was the unvarnished truth. It filtered every transaction with suspicion. Just last year, one of the oldest, most prestigious galleries in North America had to shut down when it was caught peddling a fake Rothko. Angel had absolutely no sympathy for...

"FBI raids Miami Beach art gallery, a Lincoln Road staple for over two decades...

"Gallery Six, named after the six daughters of Florida billionaire Lawrence Saxton, was raided early today. The feds seized computers and records. At the heart of the scandal is Paloma Gentry aka Paula Claire Gentry, arrested at dawn under allegations of money laundering. Ms. Gentry joined the gallery in 2012."

Nineteen

"What did I tell you?" Leslie said. "That award is as good as yours!"

"Calm down. It's an honor to be nominated."

"That's BS and you know it!" Leslie scoffed. "Plus the field is weak. I like your chances."

"Whether you win or not, we should capitalize on the pre-award show craze." This was Cameron, Sandro's publicist. Leslie had conferenced her into the call. The women worked as a tag team. "I'd like you to post a candid photo or a short video, maybe a TikTok, of your reaction to the news. You know the drill."

"I know the drill."

"I'll line up interviews and keep you posted," she said. "You may want to consider coming home now."

Sandro's mood fell flat. "Is that necessary?"

"Uh, yeah!" Cameron said. "We'll want you to do the late-night talk show circuit and maybe even *The Talk* or *The View*. It might be a good idea to start with the New York circuit since you're on the East Coast."

"Don't sign me up for anything yet. Give me a couple of days."

"First you didn't want time off and now you're begging for more time?" Leslie intervened. "You're no better than my kids."

The sound of breaking glass reached him from the kitchen. Had Angel hurt herself? "Ladies, I gotta go."

"What did I say?" Leslie said. "Just like my kids."

Sandro rushed into the kitchen. Angel was at the round table near the window. Her cup was shattered on the floor, a puddle spread across the tile. Angel hadn't budged. She sat very still, staring at the television screen. Nothing special was on, just an auto insurance commercial. Sandro had to wonder if she was losing her mind.

"Angel!" He sidestepped the mess. "Babe, are you okay?"

She turned to him, blinking, snapping out of whatever trance she'd been in. She stood and opened wide eyes to the mess at her feet. "Oh, God! Look at this! Sorry!"

Sandro pressed a hand to her forehead. "Look at *me*. What's going on?"

"I have to go."

"What?"

"I have to go. I'm so sorry, but I have to go."

She wiggled free from him and headed out of the kitchen. He chased after her, genuinely panicked. "Angel, talk to me. Where are you going?"

She burst into the bedroom and whirled around, searching for articles of clothing. "I have to get back to Miami. You have to help me get off this island."

"Why?" he demanded.

"It's crazy!" She got down on her hands and knees to reach for a pair of sandals under the bed. He recalled that she'd kicked them off on the morning of her arrival and that's where they'd landed. "The FBI raided the gallery!"

Sandro snapped out of his own trance. "What are you talking about?"

She stood and faced him. "Paloma was arrested this morning!"

"Shit!"

"I have to go back."

"To do what? Bail her out?"

"No! Be serious."

She darted into the bathroom and started shoving mini bottles into her zipped pouch. She paused only to gather and secure her hair into a ponytail. The blond, face-framing wisps had long faded. She looked exactly as she had the day they'd first met. Glowing brown skin. Messy hair. Guarded expression. Like that first day, she wore white. Except this time she had on one of his many cotton T-shirts.

He crowded the door. "I am serious. What do you expect to do for them?"

She grabbed her toothbrush. She was intent on leaving and Sandro felt the first stirs of panic.

"It's the gallery," she said. "It's my job. I have to find out what's going on. Do I even have a job anymore? Don't you think I should find out?"

"No. I think you should stay away from those criminals."

She zipped the pouch shut, pushed past him and shoved it into her travel bag open at the foot of the bed. "Sandro, this is bad. This is really bad. Last year one of the biggest galleries in New York shut when it was caught selling fakes."

"All the more reason for you to stay away."

"Here's the thing," she said, folding a bathing suit into the bag. "I've worked with these people. Paloma is a lot of things, but she's not a criminal. This has to be a mistake."

Sandro couldn't take it anymore. "There's no mistake."

She went still for the first time since he'd found her at the kitchen table. Brows drawn, she turned to him. "How are you so sure?"

Oh, Angel.

Sandro felt sick. He'd been waiting for the perfect time to come clean. The time was now and it was far from perfect. One thing was certain: Angel would not forgive him.

Moments later, Angel hollered at the top of her lungs. "You let me sell you a *fake* painting!"

The look in those clear brown eyes told him just how betrayed she felt.

"I didn't know it was fake. I had my suspicions, but I didn't know for sure."

"The only reason you bought it is because you suspected it was fake!"

"Suspected, yes," he said. "I had no proof."

"But then you had proof and you *still* didn't tell me." She covered her eyes with her hands. "I can't believe it. All this was going on and you didn't tell me."

"I wanted to catch the people involved without involving you. You worked for them. I couldn't be sure—"

"Of my involvement?"

"No!" he protested. "Let's just say, the less you knew the better."

"We were sleeping together!"

"We *are* sleeping together. Don't go putting us in the past tense."

"Here I thought we were growing close."

"We *are* close."

Sandro hated himself for how meek and desperate he sounded. He could have told her, but their relationship had been only days old. It would have shattered this fragile thing between them.

He went over to where she stood at the foot of the bed. "I only ever wanted to shield you from all this."

"Shield me? Don't you think it would have been smarter to warn me about the possible risks of working in a den of thieves? You knew I was trying to get my career on track. I could have gotten out before the scandal broke."

She had a point there. "I didn't think—"

"No, you didn't!"

"Angel, I'm sorry. This whole thing is one big cluster…"

Angel wasn't listening to him. She bit into her lower lip in that way she did whenever deep in thought. "That first night? Were you trying to keep me around to pump information out of me?"

Emotion rumbled through him and left him trembling. "Don't do that," he said through clenched teeth. "Don't make that first time into something ugly. If I'd wanted information, I would've asked straight up."

That night, he hadn't wanted to talk about the painting at all.

"Tell me the truth," she said. "Part of you suspected that I played a role in this."

"No. Never."

"Not even when I showed up at your house with a forged painting?"

Sandro dug his hands in his pockets, unbothered. "Not even."

She took a step closer, wielding a forefinger like a sword. "Lie to me now and I'll never trust you again."

In an odd way, the threatening statement gave him hope. He wouldn't lose her over this. It wouldn't break them.

"The thought crossed my mind once."

She lowered her hands to her hips, looking formidable. "When was that?"

"When we went to Papaya, and you told me how you taught yourself to paint."

She crinkled her nose. "I don't follow."

"You copied the paintings in your parents' collection. You reproduced them."

"Oh, God." She folded over and fell onto the bed, looking gutted. "That night we'd shared so much. I opened up to you."

"It was a passing thought. It never sank in."

"I told you about my family, my grandfather, my dad's hometown…" She mumbled the words, speaking mostly to herself.

Fear kicked him in the gut. This could very well break them. "I was confused. That's all."

"We made love."

He joined her on the bed, sitting beside her. It was time to come clean and still he kept one more thing from her. He had fallen in love with her that night.

"Stay," he said. "We can talk this through."

"We had rules, Alessandro," she said. "We promised to tell each other the things that mattered. Didn't you think this mattered?"

This time her words were sharp and clear. It was his turn to ramble. "I did. I didn't know. I…"

Her phone blinked on the bedside table, catching her attention. Ignoring him, she got up to retrieve it and stared at the screen before raising it to her ear. "Hello."

Sandro heard the muffled sounds of a man's voice. Angel said, "I'll be there." She lowered the phone and turned to him. "I can't stay. The FBI wants to question me."

Twenty

Clearing her name with the FBI did not matter as much as clearing her name with Alessandro. Angel sat stone-faced through the interview and tossed out perfunctory answers to their questions. She had consented mainly to avoid hiring an attorney and because she had nothing to hide—two of the worst reasons to risk self-incrimination, that was for sure. When she stepped out of the nondescript building in Downtown Miami, there he was, still waiting, two hours later.

He wore his cap, sunglasses and the plain clothes that allowed him to blend in. When he hugged her she did not pull away. Angel needed to be held. She was emotionally drained.

"If they try to pin this on you, I'll hire a team of lawyers. You are not taking the fall for those people."

She pulled away and looked up at his face, his strong features lined with concern. "How do you know that I'm not one of those people?"

"Angel…"

She was serious. How could he ever really trust her? It was upon her to clear her name. She could tell he was anxious to sweep the dirty business under a rug and move past it. But that was impossible.

Angel waited until they were in the car before she spoke. "They don't care about forgeries."

Alessandro pressed the ignition button. "I'm not surprised. No one does."

"They only wanted to know about Paloma's sales roster, names of clients, etc."

"What do you think is going on there?"

"I don't know." Angel looked at his sharp profile as he

eased the car into traffic and wished she wasn't so head over heels for him. "That doesn't help you, though."

"Help with what?"

"Finding the person who forged your grandfather's paintings."

"My brother and Myles both want me to let that go, so maybe I should."

"No," Angel said, a stubborn determination taking hold in her. "I want to help you figure this out."

"No," he said, sounding just as stubborn. "You want to prove something to me. And I don't want you to prove anything."

"Head north on 95," she said, as they approached the junction.

"Why?" he asked. "Don't you want to go home?"

"There's someone we need to speak to first."

His grip on the wheel tightened. "Who?"

"Justine Carr."

Justine lived in a quiet neighborhood in North Miami. Her house was a plain ranch-style home, the kind that cropped up everywhere back in the seventies. At first glance, it did not look like much, a flat roof and a brick facade painted white. When Justine opened for them, holding the door wide, Angel got a view straight through the house to the backyard and noted that it bordered onto a canal complete with dock.

Justine did not look like her clever self, with her corn-yellow hair in a messy bun and her right foot trapped in an orthopedic boot. Her weary blue gaze slid from Angel to Alessandro. Angel felt like the pet cat that had brought a dead rat into the house.

"I don't want to get mixed up in any family drama," she said.

"Well, hello to you, too," Angel replied, wondering what exactly she meant by that.

"Alessandro Cardenas," Justine said, quite obviously sizing him up. "We meet at last."

Alessandro had kept his distance, casting a look around as if he did not trust the neighborhood. Dressed as he was, he looked as if he were playing the role of her bodyguard.

"We spoke on the phone once," he said.

"Simpler times," she said dryly, then stepped aside to let them in. "You're lucky you found me. I just got back from Costco."

She said this as if it were an ordinary day and her list of mundane errands was all that mattered. "That's cool," Angel replied. "I just came back from an FBI interrogation."

Justine rolled her eyes. "Those fools! I told them you had nothing to do with anything."

"They didn't take your word for it," Angel said. "Thanks anyway."

Instead of inviting them into her living room, she led them past her kitchen, a gleaming granite and stainless steel box, straight to the yard where a few rattan chairs were set up around a fire pit. She led them past those, too, and straight to the dock where a cooler and a few throw pillows were stacked. The water that drifted through the canal was a particular shade of blue green. Cobalt green, if sold by the tube at the art supply store.

"What are we drinking?"

It wasn't yet lunchtime. "I…ugh…water?"

That eye roll again. "After the morning you had? They must have gone soft with you. They had me held up for five hours yesterday."

Angel sank down onto the splintered wood dock, allowing her legs to hang over the edge. She grabbed Alessandro by the hem of his T-shirt and drew him down beside her. He draped a protective arm over her shoulders. Angel's mood shifted like sand. As angry and resentful as she was with him, she was still more comfortable with him than any man she'd ever dated. It was as if life was playing a cruel joke.

"Look at you two all cozy," Justine said. "I must have done you a favor of a lifetime when I got hit by that puny car."

She flipped open the cooler and rummaged through the ice for a chilled can of beer from a local brewery. Angel recognized the blue 305 logo. Alessandro raised a hand and she tossed the can to him. He cracked it open.

Everyone was having a swell time.

Angel got back to business. "I need another favor."

"Here!" She tossed Angel a can. "Have a beer instead."

Had Justine always been this wily? Yes, she had.

Using a wood post as support, she slid down next to them and propped her booted foot onto the stack of pillows. Mimicking Alessandro, she cracked open her can.

"Yeah… Paloma screwed us over with those so-called private sales of hers," she said.

Angel set the can down. "What do you know about it?"

"She helped some really sketchy characters to buy and sell art at outrageous prices as a way for money to exchange hands. She got kickbacks for her trouble. Did you see any of that kickback money?"

"No," Angel said. "Did you?"

"No." Justine took a sip of beer. "You know what really bothers me? Those crooks likely tossed those paintings into a ditch when they were done. They didn't care."

A seagull swooped low and flew off. Justine cared about art; Angel knew that much. A graduate of Sotheby's, she was serious about her work and, therefore, excelled.

"Now what am I going to do?" she said. "I was Miss Gallery Six. Everybody knew me from the East Coast to the West as Miss Gallery Six. Now Gallery Six is closed and I'm screwed."

Alessandro had some advice. "Move to a new city. Start over."

Angel disagreed. Moving to LA might have worked out

for him, but her move to Miami was a disaster from start to finish.

"I'm not moving anywhere," Justine said. "This house is home. I've put everything I have into it. I'm going to sit here, drink my beer, feed the alligators and wave to my neighbors as they sail by."

Justine…always so dramatic! "No one ever called the shop asking to speak with Miss Gallery Six. Your clients knew you by name and would only work with you. Reach out and tell them you're flying solo, freelancing. Next thing you'll know, you're back on the scene."

"I guess…" A little smiled teased at the corners of Justine's mouth. "And what about you, little one?"

"Me? I guess I'll move back home."

"Why?"

Justine and Alessandro had shouted the one-word question in unison. They were both glaring at her. All Angel could think to say was "Because!" She might not be Miss Gallery Six, but how could she ever escape it now?

"Don't let your stint at the gallery shape your life. You were nothing but the salesgirl."

"Gee, thanks!" Angel reached for her can of beer and cracked it open. It was lunchtime somewhere.

"I'm serious! When anyone asks you say that you were just the salesgirl, hadn't even worked there a year. You're young and you're pretty and no one will care."

"I'm not that young!" Angel protested.

Justine treated her to yet another epic eye roll. "Just do me a favor," she said. "Do something you really love. You're not really suited at pushing art."

"I'm not really suited at anything!" Angel said, annoyed.

Alessandro was quick to console her. "That's not true!"

"It is true!"

Angel looked up to the sky, at a cluster of clouds in the shape of a continent. She had a lot to figure out, but now wasn't the time. Next to her, Alessandro's body was tight and tense. He must be so confused as to what they were actually doing here, drinking beer on a dock with her former colleague, but he was playing along. She lowered a hand to his thigh and he immediately covered it with one of his own.

They all fell silent for a while, watching the dark blue-green water flow through the canal. It felt good to sit and enjoy the quiet.

Justine stretched her arms over her head. Eyeing them, she said, "I know why you're here and I'm going to help you out."

Angel lit up. "You are?"

"Yup." She took a long sip from her can. "This shitty year is almost over. I should do one kind thing to set things up for next year."

That wasn't how it worked, generally, but Angel was game.

Justine tilted to one side to better catch Alessandro's eyes. "Your niece is selling your granddad's paintings."

If Alessandro hadn't been holding her hand, Angel might have toppled into the canal. His niece, his *beloved* niece, was peddling fake artwork? No, that's not what Justine had said. His beloved niece was selling his grandfather's art. It was possible Justine didn't know that the paintings were fakes. If that were the case, she hoped Alessandro wouldn't say anything to give it away. After all, the less anyone knew, the better.

Alessandro had gone very still. He looked struck, but not surprised. When he slipped off his sunglasses to better meet Justine's gaze, Angel noted that his hand trembled a bit. His voice, though, was even. "Where did she get these paintings from? Do you know?"

"I never asked," Justine replied. "Figured she plucked them off the walls of the family compound. My guess is that she needed the money. Sadly, I see this sort of thing everyday. She dropped your name quite a lot, in case I'd missed the connection."

Angel ran her hand along Alessandro's arm. His jaw was tight and his shoulders bunched up with tension. She felt terrible, understanding for the first time the magnitude of pressure that he'd been under. Alessandro had been working alone to find answers, with no one to rely on but himself. His brother and his best friend had advised him to give up. To discover that his niece, the one person he seemed to cherish, had forged his grandfather's work and used his name to sell it, well…it made her gripes seem like small, shriveled potatoes.

Alessandro's reaction impressed her. He politely thanked Justine for the information and got up on his feet. She blinked up at him towering over her, solid and stable, even after such a brutal blow. She saw him, not through the screen of his fame and fortune, but the rose-tinted lens of any woman in love with any man. He extended a hand and those shifting sands of emotions settled into solid ground. She took his hand and let him lift her up.

Angel helped Justine to her feet and she walked them to her door. "Come back in happier times," she said. "I'll fire up the grill."

Some neighbors had gathered on the sidewalk across the street to check out the gleaming sports car in Justine's driveway. A woman pointed when she recognized Alessandro. They quickly ducked into the car before anyone pulled out a cell phone camera. They drove off in silence. Alessandro kept his eyes on the road, his jaw tight. From time to time, he would run a palm over his rugged cheek. Very soon, a thick, oppressive silence filled the car. It was a relief when, at the press of a button, he lowered the top.

They cruised along Rickenbacker Causeway. He was driving her home, which was what she'd wanted, or so she'd thought. The mystery was solved. The gallery was closed and she had no plans to bail out Paloma from federal custody, if she hadn't made bail already. There wasn't anything for her to do at home except wallow. Yet she'd made such a scene this morning, he was probably reluctant to invite her back. Would he ever invite her back?

They were about to zip past the beach when Alessandro hooked a sharp right, pulling into the public parking lot. He found a spot facing the water, parked and cut off the engine. Angel held her breath, waiting for his next move. He leaned forward and pressed his forehead to the steering wheel and let out a long breath. Her heart ached for him.

"I wanted to tell you, Angel," he said, his voice raw. "I thought I had time. I wanted us to have those days together. Just you and me. Happy. I thought I had time." He paused and exhaled. "I wasn't trying to mislead you. Tell me you won't shut the door on us."

Angel was stunned. After all that he'd just learned, he was *still* focused on her. She released her resentment to the wind. Maybe it was a mistake to trust him again, but it was a mistake she just might have to make.

She snapped off her seatbelt and lunged at him. "Don't worry about any of that."

He cradled her to his chest and, for a while, the rolling sounds of the surf rocked them both.

"You have so much to deal with," she said. "What are you going to do?"

"I'm going to find Sabina and confront her. Let her know that I know what she's up to and that it better stop."

"How will you get your money back?" she asked.

He laughed and it rolled right through her. "Forget the money. She can keep it. Consider it a lifetime of birthday and Christmas gifts wrapped in one."

"Do you want me to go with you when you confront her?"

"No, my angel," he said. "I'm taking you home. I have to do this myself."

"Okay," she said, nestling closer to him. "Take me home, but first give me a minute."

She wanted this time with him.

Twenty-One

On the morning of JD's funeral, Sandro and Eddy had met in their grandfather's art studio, a shed thrown up in the yard of his house without any care for zoning laws or local regulations. The topic of the meeting was money. Funeral expenses had quickly accrued. Even the most modest of services cost money. Previously, they'd decided to split the costs. That morning, Eddy suggested Sandro sell JD's paintings, art supplies and furniture to raise money.

Sandro didn't follow his logic. "Hold a garage sale or something?"

"A garage sale! Bingo!"

"If we sold everything, we probably wouldn't raise more than $500 and that wouldn't put a dent in it."

JD didn't have many prize possessions to offload. The furniture was old and broken and the house in the Little River neighborhood was a rental. He'd lived in it for years and the homeowners, who wanted only a stable renter, had overlooked JD's many breaches to the lease, the least of which was the art studio shed. He owned a truck and a boat that he took out on weekends and holidays. Sandro noticed that Eddy hadn't mentioned selling those big-ticket items.

"I know you want the boat, but if we sold the Ford it would cover everything."

Eddy's face had crumbled. "I have plans for the truck."

"I have plans for the paintings."

"Like what?" Eddy snapped.

"It's personal. I don't expect you to understand."

Sandro would never forget the flash of anger in his brother's eyes and his own gut reaction to it. It didn't help that Eddy had grown into the spitting image of the father they'd both lost, milky white skin, hawk nose and thinning black hair. It was getting tough for Sandro to compartmentalize his feelings for the two men. He was beginning to resent them both.

"I'm opening a business soon. That truck will help."

"The boat is yours," Sandro said. "That's what JD wanted. The truck is for sale. If you want to buy it at a reduced price, we can talk about that."

The discussion had ended there. It was time to head out to the cemetery for the simple graveside ceremony. Afterward, family and friends gathered at the house. The neighbors brought over tons of food. Some of the guys were huddled in the yard, drinking and smoking. Eddy flicked his lit cigarette and fire tore through the shed.

Sandro left Angel with the promise that he'd return later that night. As soon as he pulled out of the gates of the rental community, he got Sabina on the phone.

Her voice spilled out of the car speakers. "Congratulations on the Golden Globe nomination, Tío!"

Christ! That seemed like a decade ago.

"Thanks," he said. "Listen, I need to see you."

"Um... How about a brunch on Sunday?"

"No," he said. *"Ahora mismo."*

"Really?"

"Yes."

"Is it urgent?" she said. "I'm with my boyfriend."

"Ask him to give you ten minutes. It won't take long."

She rattled off a Miami Beach address. Sandro was not interested in creating a stir, pulling up in the flashy sports car. He got Gus on the phone and made arrangements to switch vehicles. A half hour later, he was riding Gus's motorcycle. The helmet worked as the perfect barrier between him and the world.

When he arrived at the given address, Sabina was pacing the sidewalk before a sunny three-story art deco building. She looked lovely, as always, in a cherry-red sundress, glossy chestnut hair straight down her back and eyes hidden behind round sunglasses. She pointed to the motorcycle and smirked. "New toy?"

"A loaner."

"Nice," she said in a breath. "Tío, I'd like to invite you up but…"

Was she kidding? Hot, thirsty and patience running thin, he wasn't up for this. "I don't care where we go, but we can't stay here. We have to speak in private."

Sabina folded her arms across her chest and took a rigid stance. "What's this all about?"

Sandro had no doubt that she knew exactly what this was all about, which explained the stalling tactics. "I'm not getting into it on the sidewalk."

"Hmm…follow me."

She led him up two flights of narrow stairs and down a hall to a black door marked APT A in gold art deco font. Sabina unlocked the door and ushered him inside. The apartment was very much a guy's place. The furniture consisted of glass-top tables and leather seating. "Who's the boyfriend?"

No answer.

"Will I get to meet him?"

"He stepped out."

"So…why couldn't I come up?"

Her cheeks brightened. "He'll be back soon, and you know…"

He didn't know. "Doesn't he know we're related?"

She crossed the room and plopped down on a black leather ottoman. "Just tell me what's so important."

Her harsh tone hurt him. Was he kidding himself for hoping they could resolve this and move on? In reality, his bond with his niece had frayed long ago. Gone were the days when they hung out together, caught a movie and lunch. Even when she stayed on Fisher Island, it was to hang out with the daughter of the trust fund manager who lived in the building.

Sandro dropped his helmet on a bench under a shuttered window. His eye caught a framed painting hanging over a media console with a turntable and a stack of vinyl records. It was a field of sunflowers, faces upturned to the sky, each flower distinct from the other in that distinct JD style.

"You painted that, didn't you?"

"It's a hobby," she said with a slight shrug.

Sandro lowered his head and laughed. "I should have known it was you. The truth was glaring at me the whole time. I was blinded by my love for you, my affection for you..."

Sabina balled her hands into fists. She had ditched her sunglasses when they entered the apartment and she looked young and lost.

"Why?" he asked. "You're so talented. Why use me to sell JD's paintings? You could have had a career of your own."

Sabina shook her head as if she couldn't believe how dense he was. "No one is going to pay top dollar for some Instagrammer's artwork, no matter who they're related to."

"And they'll pay top dollar for the work of a long-dead unknown?"

"Do you want to know why I'm so good at what I do?" His answer would have been no, but she continued. "Social media content is only as good as the story it tells."

Sandro pulled a chair from the dining table and sat facing her. As it so happened, he was in the storytelling business. "If you've got a good story, I'm dying to hear it."

Sabina sat up a little straighter to make up for the inches in height she lacked. It killed him that she saw in him an adversary even though he had come to confront her.

"How does this sound?" she said. "Picture a grandfather, a political exile, who supports his grandchild by peddling paintings of his childhood memories in Cuba. Then lo and behold, that grandchild grows up to be American royalty, a movie star with an Oscar. He lives in Hollywood and his face is on billboards and covers of magazines. It's the god-damn American Dream and people will pay top dollar for it. Do you get it, Tío? It's not the paintings people pay for. It's the mystique."

He had to admit, she told a damn good story. Too bad it was to rip people off. "If you needed money—"

"I don't need money," she said imperiously. "I am doing very well. I did it for Dad."

"What?" Had Eddy put her up to this?

"I don't know if you noticed that last time you rolled through," Sabina said, "but he's not exactly rolling in money up there. He mortgaged his house to finance the shop and he was going to lose both. I came up with the scheme, so don't go blaming him."

Sandro covered his face with a hand, trying to digest it all. The shop had been nearly empty when he'd stopped by, but he'd figured it was a low point in the day. Another thing leaped at him from that day, Eddy's certainty that he would never catch the forger. Had he known that his love for his niece would blind him to the truth?

"Why not come to me? I could've helped out." Just asking him for the money was a far less complicated plan than the one she'd concocted.

"Dad doesn't want your money!"

"Why the hell not?"

"Because you're not the son who should have made it," Sabina said. "I know this sounds terrible, but I might as well tell you the whole truth since you're sitting here. You are the kid that *my* grandfather conceived with some girl he picked up at a bar and here you are today, a movie star! It's eating Dad up inside. It's stupid and it's petty. I don't feel that way. I love you a lot. But he's my father. I had to find a way to help him. Please don't hate me for it."

Sandro hated himself for what he was going to say next. "How much does he need to get out of this?"

Her gaze dropped. "I don't know."

"Give me a number," he growled.

"About eighty grand."

"I'll see what I can do."

She jumped to her feet. "He won't take money from you!"

"But he'll take it from you," Sandro said. "I got a crash lesson on money laundering today and this is what we're going to do. I'll give you the cash, you'll give it to him, and that will be the end of it."

She settled back down. "That might work. I'll tell him I sold more paintings."

"About that," Sandro said. "The paint you've been using wasn't available for commercial use back in the day. At any time any buyer can discover they've been duped. Good thing Gallery Six was raided this morning and the FBI arrested the manager. The blame will likely fall on her. But if any other Valero paintings pop up on the market, I'll know about it. Next time, I won't be this understanding."

Sabina grew pale. "It won't happen again," she said. "I've been sick about it. Why do you think I've been avoiding you?"

Eddy, fucking Eddy... How could he have put his daughter in such a terrible position? After JD's death, Sandro had felt obligated to keep his dwindling family together. He was free of that burden now. Eddy could take the money and go to hell. He hoped it would buy Sabina her freedom. If it didn't, she'd have to fight for it herself. She was, after all, a multitalented young woman. She could handle herself.

Twenty-Two

Angel filled the tub, dropped in a lavender-scented bath bomb, and slipped on a bunny-eared headband. No news from Alessandro. No need to mope around. Initiate full-code #selfcaresunday on a Wednesday! She slathered on a thick coat of green moisturizing mask that promised to tighten and brighten with the use of sea algae. For a split second she wondered whether Chris would approve. And then it hit her.

Oh, God...it's only Wednesday.

Alessandro Cardenas had entered her life exactly one week ago. One week! She had aged during that week. She'd likely sprouted gray hairs; if she searched, she would find some. Angel sank onto the Lucite vanity bench that matched her bathroom's faded 1980s glamour, as did most of the apartment, which kept the rent relatively cheap. One week to turn her life upside down. Now, granted, he wasn't responsible for Paloma's shady shit. It wasn't his fault that she'd stayed on at a job that did not fulfill her, ignoring her own instincts on which path to take. She couldn't blame him that she had failed to define success for herself, letting her mother's voice stoke her fears of failure—as if failing was the worst thing that could happen in the course of a life. But he'd come at a time when the dormant volcano had erupted.

Alessandro's presence had shone a great bright light in the dark corners of her life. Things that she'd wanted to sweep up under the rug—her dependence on Chris, her lack of focus on her future, her irrational fear of failure and her need to feel secure. She had to clean up her act. She could fly without a safety net. She could tell her mother, and her sister, too, for that matter, to back off, and not lose her cool—without losing anything, really. She could do it and move forward. If she failed, she failed. She was still young enough to make mistakes. Life didn't end at thirty. Why could she see a path forward for Justine, but only walled-off corridors for herself?

Angel rested her palms on the cool faux-marble countertop and studied her reflection in the mirror. She looked calm and confident, celery-green face mask and bunny ears and all. *We're going to make some changes around here. Got that?* Then her phone pinged with a message and she tabled the pep talk.

BEST MALE LEAD: I'm here. Just parked.

Angel was in her bra and panties. She grabbed a towel off the rack, wrapped it around her chest and raced out of the apartment. Her heart thundered; she so badly wanted to see him. From the breezeway corridor, she had a view of the parking lot. She searched for the flashy little sports car and, not finding it, noticed the man dismounting a motorcycle. She would have recognized that walk anywhere.

There was her lover...

Angel had her phone with her and she called him. His phone lit up and he raised it to his ear. "Hey!" she said, teasing. "Look at you, easy rider!"

He looked up and spotted her. "No... Look at *you*, little bunny."

She laughed and brought a hand to her bunny ears. "I gave up on you. I was going to take a bath."

His golden voice filled her ears. "That sounds good. May I join you?"

"It's not a big Jacuzzi tub like you're used to."

"You have no idea what I'm used to."

"That's true."

"I stopped by *Diablo* and grabbed your favorites. After a bath we can get dirty and eat with our fingers."

That sounded delicious. "Come on up! The door's unlocked."

Angel rushed back into her bathroom to wash the green paste off her face and gurgle with mouthwash, just in case. She came out to find him in the kitchen, unpacking the bags of takeout and sliding the containers into the refrigerator. He looked at ease in her home and familiar with her kitchen setup. It made her heart smile. How had it been only a week? She had lived in this apartment with Chris for months and it had never felt this good.

Alessandro, though, did not look good. His striking face was marked with fatigue and his bronze complexion had gone ashen. She'd nearly forgotten their day had begun with such fantastic news. They should have gone out to dinner with his friends. They should have celebrated with champagne. Instead, his day had been jam-packed with unpleasant tasks: speeding her back to the mainland, waiting around while she endured an FBI interrogation, learning from Justine that his beloved niece had betrayed him, then having to confront this niece. That was a lot to pack into twenty-four hours.

She went to him and touched his face. "How did it go?"

He took her hand and brought it to his lips. "I don't want to talk about it."

"Understood."

He slid the last container into the refrigerator and swung the door shut with more force than necessary. "No... I want to talk about it."

"Okay." Angel folded her arms across her chest, mainly to hold her towel in place. "I'm listening."

"She did it for the money."

That much Angel had figured out. But as far as get-rich-quick schemes went, this one was pretty elaborate. There had to be easier ways to make fast cash. However, her professional curiosity prevailed. "Who forged your grandfather's work?"

"She did."

His beloved niece was a mastermind forger, too? "Are you sure? That takes skill."

His broad shoulders drooped. "She's a talented artist."

"I don't get it. Why not just sell her own art then?"

"I asked the same question," he replied wearily. "She's not interested in building a career over years and years and years. She wanted fast cash."

Angel winced. That description, minus the criminal element, was how she'd describe herself. She wasn't interested in building a career over years. She'd given up because the struggling artist phase had dragged on for too long and too many people were waiting in the wings for her to fail. Alessandro, who hadn't given up or sought fast cash, who'd worked as a bartender, waiter, janitor and who knows what to bankroll his dreams, was reaping the rewards.

"She's also a talented businesswoman," he said. "Buyers are willing to pay good money for a famous actor's grandfather's secret paintings. She leaked the story and the waitlist got longer."

Angel was overcome with sadness. It was terrible that his niece thought nothing about using him that way.

"The money was for my brother, Eddy. He's in trouble and risks losing his house and his business. The paintings didn't go for much. Fifty grand here. Forty grand there. It was enough to save my brother's house from foreclosure."

"Oh...wow..."

He looked down at his scuffed boots. "Yeah."

Angel waddled over and leaned heavily on him, even though her intention was to lend him support. "What are you going to do?"

"I'm going to give her the money."

"What? No!"

"Yes."

She jerked away "You're rewarding bad behavior! They could have just asked you for a loan, you know. Have you thought about that?"

"You'd think so, but my brother didn't want my dirty money."

Angel was confused. "Repping Rolex watches on the side isn't exactly shameful."

"The money is dirty because I'm dirty. I'm the kid of some woman my dad picked up at a bar during *Calle Ocho Festival*, and I'm not deserving of success."

Angel's skin prickled with revulsion. "She told you this to your face?"

He raised his hands to his head and interlaced his fingers. "I knew they thought that way, but honest to God, Angel…"

"Alessandro…" she whispered. "I'm so sorry. Your family—"

"I don't think I can call them my family, Angel," he said. "They're relatives, not family."

She did not know what to say to that. Rather than offer him empty words of consolation, she let the silence do its work. When the flash of pain had dimmed in his eyes, she took him by the hand. "Come," she said. "Let's get into that bath before it gets cold."

In the bathroom, Angel undressed him and dropped his clothes onto the vanity bench. He stepped into the tub with a splash. She eased in and got settled, her back to his chest. "Hope you like lavender."

"Love it." His hands moved all over her body, roaming everywhere.

Angel twisted around and sought his mouth. She kissed him again and again, deeper and deeper. In need of more, she swiveled onto her knees. Sudsy water splashed onto the pink floral tile. He yanked the headband off her head, tangled his fingers with her hair and pulled her to him. They kissed until it felt as if they were both sinking. Their wet bodies slipped and slid as water swirled around them. All she could hear was her own whimpering, the splash of water against tile, his drowned-out moans. Alessandro gripped her bottom and forced her still. "We have to get out," he said, breathing fast. "I want you now."

Angel kissed him once again before pushing away and rising to her feet. She extended a hand to Alessandro, but his gaze poured over her dripping wet body. When he looked at her like that, she felt beautiful, desirable and bold.

His eyes trailed after her as she stepped out of the tub. The bathmat was soaking wet under her feet. The cold air streaming through the A/C vent hardened her nipples. Angel met his gaze and did not reach for a towel. "When you collect yourself, you'll know where to find me."

Twenty-Three

"Let's eat!" she said.

Angel had set up a buffet on the coffee table. Sandro dropped down on the couch. He'd worked up a healthy appetite, but her greedy grin made him want to propose they do something else entirely. After all, they'd made good use of this couch before. He knew if he tried anything, Angel would stab him with a fork.

She opened a cardboard container and gasped. "The mac and cheese! My favorite!"

Her delight was pure. Grabbing dinner at *Diablo* had been a smart move. It would make what he had to do next so much easier. Maybe.

"Angel, I have to leave in the morning."

"Back to paradise," she teased, and handed him the carton of spicy meatballs.

"Back to work."

His publicist had called again. FastFlix wanted him available for promotional work and Cameron demanded he make up lost ground from the "epic Emmys snub." *We need you out there, reminding the people why they love you.* Any award could potentially be the last. He had to make the most of it. The nomination could raise his profile, his clout, his pay grade and anything else he could possibly raise.

Angel was sitting very still, her fork loaded with mac and cheese suspended halfway between the paper plate on her lap and her lips. She'd piled her wavy hair on the top of her head and held the unruly mass together with a pair of clips. This left her long, slender neck exposed. But if he leaned over to kiss that spot below her ear, she would stab him for real this time.

"I promised you more time..." Angel would not look at him. He pressed on. "The award nomination changes everything. I have to do a lot of press."

"The Golden Globes," she mused. "An amazing opportunity."

Sandro hesitated before taking the plunge. "Would you come with me?"

She set her plate on the coffee table as if the food were poisonous. "Where to?"

He presented his itinerary as if it were the adventure of a lifetime. "Up the coast to New York City, then cross country to LA."

"No."

Her blunt answer wounded him.

"I'm not asking you to move in with me," he said defensively. "Only to hang out a while. We can spend the holidays together."

"My dad is celebrating his sixtieth birthday this Christmas," she said. "Plus I have things to do here."

"What things? The gallery is closed," he reminded her.

"And they can lose my number," she said. "I will never work for them again."

"What then? Orlando?" Did she want to go home? Was that it?

"No," she said. "I'll stay here and sort myself out."

Sandro had lost his appetite. So long, spicy meatballs. "Angel, you don't have to have your life all figured out. Not for my sake, anyway."

"Actually, I do." Her voice was a tortured whisper.

He'd wanted to protest, but the words died in his mouth. Who was he to lecture her? He'd avoided serious relationships all through his twenties for those same reasons. He'd wanted his career on track. It had taken a few hit movies and a variety of awards to get him to slow down enough to allow a woman like Angel into his life.

"This is a good thing," she said. "Do the press, the Globes,

film your movie, all of it. Next time you're in town, we'll
hang out."

She hadn't yet finished her thought and Sandro was shaking his head. "How about you come up with another plan."

She crossed her legs. Her silky robe parted to reveal a
flash of smooth brown thigh. Again he struggled to keep
his hands to himself. As much as he wanted to touch her,
he had to listen. This was important.

"I've been thinking about this. We are no way near what
you're proposing."

Sandro grabbed a napkin to wipe his mouth, but really
just to do something with his hands. She'd been thinking
about them spending time apart? This was news to him.

"Will you fly out for the awards?" he asked. "You're
my date."

"No." She held her ground. "That's something a couple
in a committed relationship would do, don't you think?"

If she needed him to commit, he'd commit, no problem.
"Angel, I—"

She grabbed his arm as if to prevent him from saying
something rash. "None of this was supposed to matter. Remember? You were always meant to leave, and I was always
meant to get on with my life."

Sandro got up to get a beer from the refrigerator. He
needed to cool down. He found the bottle opener in the
utensil draw and snapped off the cap of the *Corona Light*,
the only beer she kept in stock. A strange feeling moved
through him. He felt more at home at her rental apartment
than at Fisher Island or LA. This was a feeling that had
eluded him for years. He hadn't had a home since JD's death.

He abandoned the beer bottle on the countertop and went
to her. Hunching low before her, he anxiously slid his hands
to her waist. He could lose her if he didn't handle this right.
"Querida—"

"NO!" Angel smashed his face between her hands to silence him. "No Spanish! That's not fair!"

He peeled her hands away and kissed them. "Sorry. Didn't know it had that kind of effect on you." He made his feelings known in plain old English. "I don't want to lose you."

Her eyes glazed with tears. "I don't want you to lose me, either. I'm phenomenal."

"Yes, you are."

"And so are you, but I can't dream with you anymore, Alessandro. I've woken up to the truth."

"Angel... I know I hurt you and broke my promise."

We tell each other the things that matter.

He'd had no business making such a promise, unfairly earning her trust, at a time when he was withholding so much from her.

"It doesn't matter any more."

"You're giving up?"

"I told you: we orbit around different suns."

"That doesn't mean anything!"

He could tell by the tilt of her head that there was nothing he could say to reach her.

"Trust me," she said. "It's better this way."

Sandro brushed his lips to hers, wishing to God he could take away the pain he'd caused. When he pulled back, the taste of her tears was on his tongue. He didn't say it, but he committed to her right then and there.

The next morning, they woke up at six, as per her routine. Only this time Sandro didn't protest. It was all arranged. He was flying out to New York City this evening to report at the NBC studios tomorrow at dawn. She agreed that it was better for him to leave before rush hour traffic made moving around the city difficult. He had to return Gus's bike and stop by the restaurant to speak with Myles.

Angel had made coffee and they talked quietly for a while. Then she walked him to the parking lot. The day was fresh. Neighbors on their way to work cast curious glances their way as they drove by, maybe finally recognizing the Hollywood actor that had been coming in and out of their apartment complex. Sandro was oblivious to all that. The breeze played with the palm trees that lined the asphalt lot. Little green lizards darted between the low-cut shrubs. The sprinklers stuttered and sprayed cool water. He hugged Angel tight and breathed in the familiar scent of her skin. He hadn't shaved. She rubbed her cheek against his stubble.

"Can we keep in touch?" he asked sheepishly.

"We can," she said. "Nothing forced though. Whatever feels good."

Sandro groaned. He hated her noncommittal tone.

She tilted her head back and searched his face. "You're going to be on a movie set for months. Have fun!"

"Fun?" he said. "It's work. What do you think I'm going to do? Hook up with extras in my trailer?"

"If you're going to hook up with anybody," she said, "at the very least, make it your costar."

"It's a fantasy thriller. My costars are a robot and a green screen."

"Some of those robots are really sexy!"

"Will they laugh and cry at the same time, though?"

She laughed and brushed back a tear. "Go!" she said. "Go and be amazing."

"What are you going to do?"

"I'm going to be smart for a change."

"Will you remember me, your dumb mistake?"

She gave him a smile as fresh as the day. "Always."

Myles greeted him with a bear hug. "Mr. Golden Globes!"

Sandro had parked in the alley behind the restaurant and found Myles at the back door receiving a delivery of vegetables.

"I'm heading back to LA," Sandro said.

"How long this time?"

"I'll be lucky if I get back before the spring. After the awards, I'm taking off to film in New Zealand."

"Damn." The kitchen smelled like coffee. Myles poured him a cup. "I just got used to you coming around, disrupting my morning routine."

Sandro took his coffee to his usual seat at the prep counter. "I thought you liked peace and quiet."

"Nobody likes that much peace and quiet."

Myles heated up his favorite chocolate pastry and set it before him. "You don't even have to beg this time."

"Thanks, man." Sandro stirred sugar into his coffee and stared blindly into the cup.

"You okay?" Myles asked.

"I'm not okay," Sandro admitted. "Angel is through with me. I've lost her."

Sandro pushed back his coffee cup, breaking into a cold sweat. He'd lost his angel and had no one to blame but himself. He could not have messed up more spectacularly if he'd planned it.

"I don't buy it," Myles said. "Anyway, you two were fast and furious. Maybe it's a good idea to pump the brakes a little, slow it down."

Gigi had said something similar, except she'd used the words *hot and heavy*. She'd managed to spin Angel's refusal to accompany him to the Golden Globes as a positive. "That's a good thing! I'd be far more concerned if she wanted to jump into the limelight with you."

"That means you'll have to jump into the limelight," he said. "I need a date. Please don't make me go with my publicist."

"You can count on me!" Gigi said. "Jumping into the limelight is my favorite sport."

Now Myles was looking at him with a goofy expression. Sandro lost his cool. "She said we orbit around different suns."

"What does that mean?"

"I have no idea!"

"Astrology maybe?"

Sandro glared at Myles.

"Eat your *pain chocolat*," Myles said. "You'll feel better."

Sandro chomped down half of the pastry with one big bite. While he chewed, he observed his childhood friend. He looked okay, but he always looked okay. Something was off. "What's going on with you?"

Myles shrugged. "Same old."

"Don't give me that," Sandro said. "I come here all the time and complain my ass off. The least you can do is give me something. Family, sex life, the restaurant…" Myles shifted slightly, but Sandro caught it. "The restaurant! Bingo!"

Myles circled the empty kitchen. Soon his prep staff would arrive and he would clam up. Sandro cut to the chase. "I risk losing man points by saying this, but here goes. I love you."

"Yo, man points are dead currency," Myles said.

"I'm being sincere," Sandro said. "I want us to grow old together, meet twice a week on a park bench and catch up while our grandkids run around."

Sandro had lost his family on this trip. Maybe his relationship with Sabina could be salvaged. Maybe not. She was not the person he thought she was. They'd have to get reacquainted and start over from zero. He would leave it up to her. His relationships with his friends were a different story. Sandro was prepared to fight to preserve them.

Myles tossed a balled-up dishtowel, aimed at Sandro's head. "What grandkids? I'm not having any kids, let alone grandkids."

"Your granddogs then."

"That's cool."

"What's going on with this place? It's packed every night."

"It's not my place, though, is it?" Myles said. "I put everything I have into it, but it's not mine. I hear the owners are thinking of selling."

Ah... *Diablo* was just one of the many restaurants owned by a faceless conglomerate. Restaurants were risky business. Even rich people weren't rich enough to carry the losses. But Myles had proven that he was bankable.

Sandro had an idea, but first he got Myles up to speed on the Sabina affair. "My niece forged the paintings."

Myles's eyes widened. "No shit?"

"Absolutely none," Sandro said, resigned.

His friend took the wooden stool beside him. "What's the plan?"

"The plan is to shake down my agent and have her line up some endorsement deals. Cars, cologne, Fabergé eggs, I don't care."

"Hey! You have to care!" Myles protested. "You've got a brand to protect."

Sandro waved off his concerns. "Part of that money is going to save my brother's sorry business. And the rest, I could invest in another venture."

Myles face went taut. "I can't take your money."

No one wanted to take his money and frankly he was sick of it. "If you want your own place, you need to raise capital," he said. "Would you rather Sabina whip up a few paintings for you to sell?"

Sandro could hardly finish the sentence, he was laughing so hard. Myles slapped him on the back. "You are one sick dude!"

He had to laugh, even as he pressed the heels of his hands over his eyes to keep from crying. In the past few days, he'd experienced every emotion known to man. It was enough to crack a man in two.

Suddenly, Myles pulled him into a hug that felt like a chokehold. "You're a good friend and a great guy. Something tells me Angeline knows this and you don't have anything to worry about."

Twenty-Four

Alessandro was gone. As Angel watched him speed away on the borrowed bike, panic surged inside her. Unsure that she'd done the right thing, she tried to imagine an alternate ending. None came to mind. She and Alessandro had rushed into something they were not prepared for. Attraction was there, intimacy and friendship, too, but fundamental trust was not.

Back in her apartment, Angel crawled into bed and slept for hours. Her sheets smelled like him and, as the day dragged on, she was reluctant to leave her bed. He'd called on his way to the airport. Although he was up for an acting award, Angel delivered a stellar performance. She chatted happily and sounded upbeat when she wished him a safe trip.

In the evening, she ate their leftovers straight out of the cartons. Call it a miracle, but the creamy, buttery mac and cheese revived her. Bottom line: she would see him again. At some point, he'd return to Miami. When that day came, she did not want to be the woman he'd left behind. She would use this time to change her life.

Angel took a container of roasted brussels sprouts to her computer desk and fired up Google. *Okay! Let's see what's out there for me.*

The first package arrived on Friday. The delivery guy knocked on her door and left the stiff envelope on her doormat. Running late for a job interview, she picked it up and tossed it onto the kitchen table. Later that night, while eating supermarket sushi, she noticed the envelope sitting on top of the stack of mail. She opened it, her fingers sticky with soy sauce. Inside was a single sheet of paper. She slid it out and blinked in disbelief. It was a simple ink sketch of a woman.

Angel grabbed a napkin and wiped her hands. Then with the tip of a finger, she traced the wavy hair, wide-set eyes, long nose, and full lips curled into a faint, enigmatic smile. The drawing was not signed. She checked the envelope again. The sender was "AC Enterprises." After a good laugh, she snapped a photo of the drawing and sent it to Alessandro. He called her right away. On impulse, she answered, forgetting the days of gut-wrenching silence that had followed his departure.

"Hello," she said. "Is this the CEO of AC Enterprises?"

"Speaking."

"You drew this?"

"Sabina didn't get all the talent. I can handle a pen."

"You can handle more than a pen."

"The pen is mightier than whatever you have in mind."

Angel laughed. "I love it so much!"

"I drew it that first morning, after I spotted you running along the dock to catch the ferry. Good times."

"I was so scared that morning," she said in her defense. "The whole experience was too intense."

"Are you still scared?"

"Yes!" she said.

"I've missed you."

There was no way she could express how deeply and desperately she had missed him. She said goodbye and ended the call.

Every Friday after that, an envelope arrived. Each contained a new sketch that pulled her back to the time they had spent together. He drew her laughing, sleeping, reading and sipping a cup of coffee. If she were critiquing this work, she would have noted the obvious pandering to the male gaze. However, in this case, she didn't seem to mind.

She didn't mind when he started calling more regularly,

at the start of his day. While he poured his first cup of coffee, Angel was on her second cup. He'd send her selfies at all hours and gave her virtual tours of the green rooms of every major show he'd booked. When bedtime came around, at least on her coast, they'd text until she fell asleep.

One night, she decided to tease him.

BEST MALE LEAD: So what are you up to?

ANGEL'S PHONE: I'm peeling off my T-shirt because I'm so hot…

Her phone rang immediately. "As much as I love where you're going with this, I want to know what you're up to regarding work."

"Oh." She sat fully dressed on the edge of her bed.

"I haven't pressed you on this because I know you need space," he said.

"Uh-huh." She hadn't brought up work because there was nothing to bring up. She'd gone through a round of interviews and was waiting to hear back.

"Angel, you can talk to me," he said. "I'm not going to judge you. Remember those early years when I was working as a—"

"Bartender/waiter/janitor," she chanted. "Yes, I know."

"Yeah, well," he said. "Going months between acting jobs was tough and humiliating. If I didn't have friends to talk to I would've gone crazy."

Angel knew exactly how he'd felt. She was already dreading the holidays in Orlando.

"I have a few promising leads," she said weakly.

"Let's hear it."

She told him about her interviews for positions at two prominent art museums. These were entry-level positions and would not pay much. But either one would go a long way to erasing the stain of Gallery Six on her résumé.

"Okay." His voice held no trace of enthusiasm.

"One of those museums is the Pérez," she said. "I'd be lucky to get a job there."

"Maybe…" he said. "What would you really want to do, given the chance?" Angel closed her eyes, weary, while he continued. "What about your own art? Why haven't I seen it yet?"

"You've seen my paintings."

"The few on your walls? Weren't you a kid when you painted those?"

"Well…yes."

"Plus they're paintings of a country you've never visited."

"What does it matter? I will someday."

"And I'll visit Cuba someday. Maybe we'll go on a pilgrimage together. My point is: I know what it's like to be haunted by a lost homeland."

More than anything, Angel loved how much they had in common. Their respective family trees had been violently uprooted from the Caribbean and planted on Florida shores without the benefit of a soil study or even fertilizer. As a result, they were hybrid individuals bearing all sorts of odd fruit. But that was where the similarity ended. Alessandro had the freedom to experiment. Angel was trapped in a box. In a desperate attempt to earn her parents' approval, she had limited herself to producing the kind of art they admired and collected. And now she was stuck with the artist's version of writer's block.

"As they say in LA, pretty angel, bloom where you're planted."

She hated to break it to him, but they said that everywhere, though mainly online. "Are you suggesting that I paint Lincoln Road Mall?"

"Or just the view outside your window," he said. "Why not? We're here now. Florida is home."

"Technically, you're in California."

"But where is my heart?"

Angel spilled onto her back and drew her knees to her chest. *Oh, be still, stupid heart!*

Angel knew what Alessandro was doing with his sketches, texts, photos and phone calls and it was working. A few days ago, he'd asked in a soft voice whether she could ever forgive him. She'd said yes. Even so, she wasn't prepared to toss caution in the wind and start up with him again.

"Hey, it's late," he said. "I'll let you get some sleep."

"What if I try again and it doesn't work?" she blurted.

Her question had two layers. The pause before his answer told her that he understood.

"What if it does?"

"Okay, but what if it doesn't?"

"Well then you'd have tried. No regrets."

After they'd said goodnight, Angel tapped on the digital drawing app on her phone and scrolled through her portfolio. She considered sharing her sketches with Alessandro, but compared to her oil paintings, all neatly packed away at her parents' house, these seemed so basic. Would he laugh?

Her gaze drifted to her bedroom walls, which she'd turned into a gallery showcasing the drawings delivered to her door every Friday. Each quick sketch was precious to her. She would never judge them or laugh at his technique. They brought her so much happiness and sparked pinwheels of joy.

Before Angel lost her nerve, she selected a few of her digital sketches and forwarded them along.

Her phone rang immediately.

THE RED CARPET STYLE EVOLUTION OF HOLLYWOOD'S LEADING MAN

Alessandro Cardenas is nominated for acting in a supporting role; nevertheless, he remains our lead-

ing man. The Cuban American actor caused a stir the moment he stepped onto his first red carpet in Armani Privé. He has been turning heads ever since. Here are some of our favorite looks. (Click for slideshow) —@Vanities_Fashion_IG

Twenty-Five

No sketch arrived on the Friday before the Golden Globes. Angel assumed that Alessandro was busy with fittings, press junkets, dinners and after-parties. On Saturday morning, he called to say that he'd be MIA through Sunday. "It's a crazy circus."

"I understand. And I'm rooting for you."

She had rented *Black Market*. His performance as a disillusioned cop had been flawless.

"Thanks, Angel," he said. "Love you."

Her belly tightened. "Love you, too."

Love you was the kind of thing you said to a friend and she refused to read too much into it. Plus, Angel had her own schedule to stick to. She had resumed waking up at six to paint, except this time she left her apartment with only an iPad and a stylus. Her new project was an expansion of her lunch break excursions, only now she ventured past Lincoln Road to Little Haiti, Little Havana, Wynwood and Midtown. She picked a street and drew her surroundings, rendering the buildings and the people as she saw them. The drawings were vivid in a way still life paintings of fruit could never be. In no time, she had developed quite a portfolio. Digital art was a dynamic field. There were no shortage of grants and residencies. Angel applied for a few. She was particularly excited about a residency at a prestigious institute. She could not bring herself to hope and told no one, not even Alessandro, out of fear of jinxing it.

Angel spent Saturday in Coral Gables, sketching a stretch of Ponce de Leon Boulevard. But she could not stop thinking of Alessandro. Did he have a pre-award show ritual? Did it consist of a standard massage, shave and haircut, or was it more elaborate? She imagined him holed up in a Beverly Hills hotel with a team of professionals fussing over him. As his date, would she have received one of those famous goodie bags chock-full of designer items—or was that reserved for the Oscars? Finally, why had she passed on the opportunity to attend an awards show? Likely a once in a lifetime opportunity. By the end of the evening, she could have been hanging out with Tracee Ellis Ross and exchanging contact information with Amal Clooney. *You don't think, Angel. You just feel and react.*

That night, Angel fell asleep with her phone clutched in her hand. At two in the morning, she startled awake and found that she'd missed a text message.

BEST MALE LEAD: You don't know how much I miss you.

On Sunday Angel couldn't hold back. She called him. It was the morning of the Golden Globes and she wanted to hear his voice. She wanted to feel connected with him in some way. And she wanted to wish him luck one last time. She hoped he'd win.

The call went to voice mail.

Angel made breakfast and spent the morning searching the internet for scraps of information. Nothing! Most of the stories focused on what the actors would be wearing to the show, as if anyone cared. Why weren't the tabloids doing their job?

She was drizzling honey in her oatmeal when an email alert popped on her screen. She'd received a message from Art Tech, a resident artists program in Los Angeles. *Oh, God!* She crossed the room and plopped onto her couch. Finally! This was the message that she'd been waiting for, but to receive it on a Sunday... This couldn't be good. Maybe this was the gentle, letting-you-down softly email. The thanks, but no thanks message. There was no way to know until she read it.

Angel reached for a throw pillow and clutched it to her belly for support. What had started as a pipe dream had blossomed into so much more. She wanted this, or something similar. She wanted the opportunity to focus on her art, hone her voice and explore a new medium. If this turned out to be a politely worded rejection, she would howl with disappointment. For a moment, she fought the urge to toss her phone out the window. Angel quickly snapped out of it. She could survive bad news. A little disappointment never killed anyone, but dreading bad news could give her a heart attack.

She held her breath and tapped on the message.

Congratulations! You have been selected for a one-year artist-in-residency program at ART TECH in Los Angeles, California.

Holy shit!
Angel buried her face in the pillow on her lap and screamed. She screamed until her throat ached. At long last, something for her!
I won! I won! I won!

Alessandro won, too. A giddy actress opened a gold envelope and read his name off a card. Angel popped open a bottle of champagne. The overflow spilled onto her pajamas. The camera caught Alessandro's stunned expression. He was seated next to beautiful Gigi Garcia. She drew him into a hug and kissed his cheek. Angel watched as he trotted up the wide steps to the stage. He looked incredibly handsome in a classic black tuxedo. And as happy as she was, as proud as she felt, she couldn't beat away a sour feeling. This had been a big day for both of them and they should have enjoyed it together.

Alessandro could be counted on to put on a show and give the viewers at home what they wanted. He kissed the trophy and held it high, earning more applause. When the cries died down, he spoke into the microphone.

"This award is dedicated to my grandfather, the painter Juan David Valero, who taught me to value my art."

Angel's pajama top was wet with champagne, her face was wet with tears and she was turning into a pile of mush on the floor. But Alessandro wasn't done.

"My angel, I love you and I'm coming home."

The camera panned away. The next thing she knew, Angel was watching a commercial for the new Buick. She raised the champagne bottle to her lips with a shaky hand and gulped down a third.

The 5:00 a.m. knock on her door sent Angel flying out of bed. She'd been in a champagne-induced coma. Was the banging on her door and the buzzing of her phone real or imagined? She tiptoed to her apartment door. Her vision was too blurry for her to see anything through the peephole. Another knock and she jumped back.

"I'll call the police!" she cried, unsure why exactly. For all she knew it could have been her elderly neighbor.

"Oh, Angel, don't do that."

That voice!

Angel fumbled with the lock and swung open the door. There stood her leading man, a little disheveled but still devastatingly handsome in his classic tux. "Sorry," he said, sheepish. "I couldn't stay away a day longer."

She threw herself at him, any trace of shame gone. "I love you! So much!"

"That's a relief!" Laughing, he lifted her off the floor and carried her inside the apartment. He took care to lock the door behind them. "I love you, too. But are you alright?"

She ran a hand through her messy hair. "I had a lot of champagne."

"Told you champagne was overrated. I never touch the stuff."

"Well, I was celebrating!"

"Without me?"

She pouted. "It wasn't the same."

"I bet."

He swooped her up and carried her into the bedroom. They flopped onto her bed, laughing. As he peeled off his jacket, he noticed the framed sketches on the wall. "This is why I love you!" he exclaimed. "Those sketches are not worth the price of IKEA frames."

Angel rested a hand on his cheek. "Those frames are from Michael's. The sketches are priceless to me. I was sad I didn't get one on Friday."

Alessandro rubbed his face into her palm. "Friday was crazy. New Zealand is postponed indefinitely. They've released me from my contract."

She scrambled onto her side. "Are you serious?"

"Yes, and it's fine. I'm glad to be done with it. My grandfather raised me to be an artist, not a hollow movie star. I need to pick my projects more wisely."

Angel was moved beyond words. "He would be so proud of you."

"Thanks." He took her hand and laced their fingers together. "I hope so."

"What are your plans?"

"I've got a meeting with Knight Films—they're local. Maybe I'll move back to Florida full-time. What do you think?"

Angel made a face. He interpreted it the wrong way. "Too fast?"

"No, it's not that. I'm leaving Florida."

"You are?"

"Sorry, yes. I got accepted to a one-year artist residency."

"You have?" Alessandro went ashen gray. "I'm happy for you. Where will you be?"

"Los Angeles."

"Wait." He rolled off the bed and stood before her. "Say that again."

"I'm moving to Los Angeles." She searched his face. A strange mix of emotions was displayed there. "Too fast?"

He held her face between his hands. "Not for us," he said, and kissed her slowly.

Never for us.

Epilogue

LIVESTREAM

"Hey, everyone! Last Sunday at the Globes I forgot to thank a few very important people in my life. Some I've called and thanked privately. But I have to give a big shout out to my agent, Leslie Chapman.

Leslie, you're my rock and I couldn't do any of this without you.

Guys, it's been a crazy few weeks. I'm going to follow my agent's advice and take some time off. Don't come looking! I'm with my Angel in paradise, and we're going dark. I'll check in when we're back in LA. Until then, be good and take care!

@Sandro_Official.

Comments turned off.

* * * * *

CORNER OFFICE SECRETS

SHANNON MCKENNA

One

Vann Acosta stared at the screen, his jaw aching. "Play it again," he said.

Zack Austin, Maddox Hill Architecture's chief security officer, let out a sigh. "We've seen it ten times, Vann. There's not much to unpack in the video itself. Just Sophie Valente, taking pictures of a computer screen. Let's move on to the next step."

"It's not time for that yet," Vann said. "Play it again."

"As many times as you need." Tim Bryce, Maddox Hill's chief technology operator, put his hand on the mouse. "But nothing's going to change. So there's hardly any point."

Vann gave Bryce a cold look. He was not going to let himself be rushed. As chief financial officer of Maddox Hill, he owed it to his employees to get all the facts, and to study them for as long as it took to get clarity.

"I'll make that call," he said.

"Where the hell did you put that camera?" Zack asked. "It looks like it was recorded from directly behind your desk."

"It was." Bryce looked pleased with himself. "The camera is in a picture frame above the desk. I bought it from a spy gadget website. It has photos of my sons in it. Looks perfectly innocent, but it got the job done."

"Don't get ahead of yourself," Vann said. "Sophie Valente's been personally developing our own data loss protection software. She's teaching our IT department to prevent exactly this kind of data leak, right? It's her specialty." He looked at Zack. "Wasn't that the point of hiring her in the first place?"

"Yes, it was," Zack admitted. "And yes, it seems strange."

"Very strange," Vann said. "If she wanted to steal Maddox Hill project specs, she wouldn't fish for them on Tim's desktop computer where she could be seen by anyone. She's smarter than that. It's far more likely she was conducting a random spot test."

Bryce's eyebrows climbed. "On my computer, at twelve thirty on a Friday night? I doubt it. I made a point of talking about the Takata Complex project in front of her last week, and letting her see the documents on my screen. She knew those files weren't watermarked yet. Drew and his team are still fine-tuning them. I just wanted to see if she'd bite, and she did. The files were copies of old, outdated specs, so she got zip. But I nabbed her. Maybe she can wipe herself off our log files, but she can't wipe herself off my video camera."

The smugness in Bryce's voice bothered Vann. This was not a kid's schoolyard game. There were no winners here, only losers. "Play it again," he repeated.

"Be my guest." Bryce set the clip to Play. It was time-and-date-stamped 12:33 a.m. from four days before. For twenty seconds all they saw was a dimly lit office.

Then Sophie Valente, Maddox Hill's new director of information security, appeared in the camera's view frame. The light from the monitor brightened, illuminating her face as she typed into the keyboard. The camera was recording her from behind the screen and slightly to one side. She wore a high-necked white blouse with a row of little buttons on the side of her neck. Vann had memorized every detail of that shirt. The silk fabric was tucked loosely into her dress pants, lapping over the wide leather belt she wore with it. Her hair was wound into its usual thick braid, hanging over her shoulder.

She lifted a cell phone and began taking pictures of the

screen. Her hand moved quickly and smoothly between keyboard and phone as if she'd done it many times before.

But her face looked so focused and serene. That was not the nervous look of a person doing something shady after midnight. She was not shifty-eyed, or looking over her shoulder, or jumping at shadows.

On the contrary. Sophie Valente was in a state of total, blissful concentration.

"Who logged into your computer at that time?" Vann asked.

"Me," Bryce said. "But I wasn't here. I was home watching TV with my wife and son."

Vann stared at the screen. "It doesn't make sense," he said again.

"Facts don't lie." Bryce's voice had a lecturing tone. "I don't say this with a light heart, but Valente is responsible for our data breaches. She knew the documents weren't watermarked. She's avoiding a log trail by taking photos of the screen. What's not to understand? If you're confused, we can go over my data—"

"I understood it the first time around." Vann tried to control his tone, but the look on Maddox Hill's CTO's face set his teeth on edge.

Bryce did not look as sorry as he professed to be. In fact, he looked gleeful.

Still. The man had been at the architecture firm for over twenty years, working his way up the ranks. More than twice as long as Vann had worked there. He'd never been Vann's favorite person, but his opinions had weight.

"What is it that doesn't convince you?" Bryce sounded exasperated.

"Every piece of evidence could be coincidental," Vann said. "We all use multiple computers. She's often here at night. She's responsible for information security. She was thoroughly vetted by the HR department before the hire, and she checked out. We already gave her the keys to the kingdom. Hell, we hired her to code the keys to the kingdom for us. She should be allowed to explain what she was doing before you accuse her."

"Yes, but she—"

"Corporate espionage is a serious charge. We cannot be wrong about this. I won't trash a woman's professional reputation unless we're one hundred percent sure."

"But I am sure!" Bryce insisted. "The data breaches started a month after Valente was hired to head up Information Security. She's fluent in Mandarin. She went to school in Singapore. She has contacts all over Asia, and at least two of the stolen project specs were tracked to an engineering firm in Shenzhen. On top of it all, she's overqualified for her job here. With her credentials, she could make twice as much if she took a job at a multinational bank or a security firm. She had a specific reason to come here, and I think I've figured out what it is. Have you even looked at her file?"

Vann glanced at Sophie Valente's open personnel file, and looked away just as quickly. Yeah, he'd looked at that file. For longer than he'd ever dare to admit.

It was the photo that got to him. It captured her essence as photos rarely did, and it was just an overexposed, throwaway shot, destined for a personnel file or a lanyard.

Sophie Valente's face was striking. High cheekbones, bold dark eyebrows, a straight, narrow nose. Her mouth was somber, unsmiling, but her lips had a uniquely sensual shape that kept drawing his eye back to them. Her thick chestnut hair was twisted into her trademark braid, with shorter locks swaying around the sharp point of her jaw. Large, intense, deep-set topaz-gold eyes with thick, long black lashes gazed straight at the viewer, daring him not to blink.

Or maybe that was just a trick of the light. The effect

of the proud angle of her chin. And the picture didn't even showcase her figure, which was tall, toned. Stacked.

Sophie Valente didn't look like a shifty, dishonest person. On the contrary, she gave the impression of being a disarmingly honest one.

His instincts had never led him astray before. Then again, he'd never gotten a stupid crush on an employee before. Hormone overload could make him blind and thick.

He would not let himself fall into that hole. Oh, hell, no.

"The evidence you've shown me doesn't constitute proof," Vann said. "Not yet."

Zack crossed his arms over his burly chest and gave him a level look. Zack knew him too well. They'd served together in Iraq, and worked together at Maddox Hill for almost a decade. His friend sensed that Vann's interest in Sophie Valente went beyond the strictly professional, and Zack's level gaze made him want to squirm.

"We need more information," Zack said. "I'll talk to the forensic accounting firm I usually use. Meantime, this matter stays strictly between the three of us."

"Of course," Vann said.

"We don't know much about her, beyond the background checks," Zack went on. "Just that she's smart and doesn't miss much, so investigating without her noticing is going to be a challenge. She doesn't fit the profile of a corporate spy. She's not a disgruntled employee with a score to settle, she's not recently divorced, she doesn't have debts, or a drug habit. She doesn't appear to live beyond her means, and she doesn't have a motive to seek revenge. At least, not that we know of."

"How about old-fashioned greed?" Bryce offered. "Those engineering specs are worth millions to outside firms. We should alert Drew and Malcolm and Hendrick. Now."

"I'll handle that when the time is right," Vann said. "When we're sure."

Bryce made an impatient sound. "The time is now, and we *are* sure. I'm not talking about hauling her off in cuffs in front of everyone, Vann. I'm just talking a discreet warning to the bosses. Who will not thank us for keeping them in the dark."

"Malcolm and Hendrick are both in San Francisco for the meeting with the Zhang Wei Group," Vann said. "I'm joining them tomorrow, and Drew's wedding is afterward, at Paradise Point this weekend. Let it wait, Tim. At least until next week, after the wedding. And leave Drew alone. He's busy and distracted right now."

Massive understatement. Drew Maddox was the firm's CEO, but at the moment, he was so wildly in love with Jenna, his bride-to-be, that he was useless for all practical purposes. It was going to be a genuine relief when the guy took off for his honeymoon and got out of everyone's way for a while. At least until he drifted back down to earth.

But Vann couldn't knock his friend. It was great that Drew had found true love. No man alive deserved happiness more. They'd been friends ever since they met in their marine battalion in Fallujah, Iraq, many years before, where Drew, Zack and Vann had shared a platoon. He loved and trusted Drew Maddox.

Still, the upcoming wedding had changed things. Drew had moved into a new phase in his life when he got engaged to Jenna. Vann still belonged to the old phase. It felt lonely and flat back there.

But hey. People grew. People changed. Whining was for losers.

He had nothing to complain about. He liked his job as chief financial officer of an architecture firm that spanned the globe and employed over three thousand people. He hadn't set out to achieve that title. He just did things intensely if he did them at all. An ex-lover once told him he was so laser-focused it bordered on the freakish.

Too freakish for her evidently. That relationship had fizzled fast.

"So how do you intend to investigate her? Is there some way to get her out of the way?" Bryce demanded. "We'll bleed out if we drag our feet on this."

Vann leafed through her file, thinking fast. "You said she speaks Mandarin?"

"Fluently," Bryce said.

"That's perfect," Vann said. "We just found out that they need a last-minute interpreter for tomorrow's meeting in San Francisco with Zhang Wei. Hsu Li just had a family emergency, and Collette is our usual backup, but she's out on maternity leave. If Sophie speaks Mandarin, I could ask her to fill in for Hsu. That way, we get an interpreter, and she'll be out of the investigators' hair. Sophie will be too busy to notice what's going on up here. You know how Malcolm is. He'll keep her running until she drops."

Zack's eyebrow went up. "And have her listen in on all the private details of Malcolm and Hendrick's negotiations with Zhang Wei? You sure that's a good idea?"

"We're not going to negotiate the nuts-and-bolts details of the specs in San Francisco," Vann said. "That's not in the scope of this meeting. It'll be about money and timing, nothing all that useful to an IP thief. It's not ideal, but I think it's worth it, to get her out of the way for your forensic team to do their work. It also gives me a chance to get a sense of who she is."

"Well, they say to keep your friends close and your enemies closer." Bryce chuckled. "Should be no hardship to keep close to that, I'm guessing, eh? Whatever else you could say about the woman, she sure is easy on the eyes."

Vann ground his teeth at the comment. "I'm not yet assuming that she's my enemy," he said. "None of us should be assuming that."

"Uh, no," Bryce amended quickly. "Of course we shouldn't."

Zack nodded. "Okay, then. That's the plan. Keep her busy. Keep your eyes on her."

Like Vann had any choice. Vann glanced back at the computer screen. Sophie Valente's face was frozen in the video clip, her big, clear golden eyes lit by the bluish squares of the reflected computer screen. She seemed to be looking straight at him. It was uncanny.

Bryce got up and marched out of Vann's office, muttering under his breath, but Zack lingered on, frowning as he studied his friend.

"You're tiptoeing around here," he said. "I agree that it's appropriate to be careful. You don't want to ruin her career. Just make sure you're holding back for the right reasons."

"Meaning what exactly?"

"You tell me," Zack said. "Are you involved with her?"

Vann was stung. "No way! I've barely even spoken to the woman!"

"Good," Zack soothed. "Calm down, okay? I had to ask."

"I am calm," he growled.

His friend didn't need to say a word, but after a few moments of Zack's unwavering X-ray stare, Vann had reached his limit. He got to his feet. "I'll go to her now," he said. "I have to tell her we need her for the meeting down in San Francisco."

"You do that," Zack said. "Just watch yourself. Please."

"I always do," Vann snarled as he marched out the door.

Zack was just being thorough. Careful. That was what made him a good chief security officer. But it pissed Vann off to have his professionalism questioned, even by a friend.

Particularly when he was questioning it himself.

He was careful not to catch anyone's eye as he strode

through the halls of Maddox Hill. He needed every neuron buzzing at full capacity to interact with that woman, considering how sweaty and awkward she made him feel.

Sophie Valente stood in her big office near a window that overlooked downtown Seattle. The door was open, and she was talking on the phone. Her voice was low and clear and musical, and she was speaking…what the hell was that? Oh, yeah. Italian.

Vann was competent in Spanish, and Italian was just similar enough to be intensely frustrating to listen to. His father had been second-generation Italian, but food words, body parts and curses were all that he'd picked up from Dad.

Frustrating or not, Italian sounded great coming out of Sophie Valente's mouth.

She sensed his presence and turned, concluding her conversation with a brisk I'll-get-back-to-you-later tone.

She looked hot. Sleek, professional. Her braid was twisted into a thick bun at the nape of her neck today, and slim-cut black pants hugged her long legs and world-class backside. A rust-colored, loosely draped silk shirt was tucked into it. She was already tall, but spike-heeled dress boots made it so that she was just a few inches short of his own six-foot-three frame. Her clothes didn't hide her shape, but they didn't flaunt it, either.

There was no need to flaunt. Her body effortlessly spoke for itself. He had to constantly course-correct the urge to stare.

She laid her phone down. "Mr. Acosta. Can I help you with something?"

"I hope so," he said. "I hear you speak fluent Mandarin. Is that true?"

"Among other things," she said.

"Was that Italian I just heard?"

"Yes. I was talking to the IT department in the Milan office."

Then she just waited. No greasing the conversational wheels with friendly chitchat. That wasn't Sophie Valente's style. She just stood there, calmly waiting for him to cough up whatever the hell he wanted from her.

Most of which was unspeakable. And extremely distracting.

Vann wrenched his mind back to the matter at hand. It took huge effort to keep his gaze from roving down over her body. "I'm going to San Francisco for the negotiations for the Nairobi Towers project," he explained. "Our Mandarin interpreter had a family emergency and we need someone last-minute. I was wondering if you could help us out."

Sophie's straight black brows drew together. "I am fluent in Mandarin, yes. But simultaneous or consecutive interpreting is not my professional specialty. I do know several top-notch specialists in Seattle and the Bay Area, however. It's last-minute, but I could put you in touch. Or call them myself on your behalf."

"I appreciate the offer, but both Malcolm and Hendrick prefer to use in-house interpreters," he told her. "The interpreting doesn't have to be perfect, just serviceable. And it's just Mandarin to English, not English to Mandarin. Zhang Wei will have his own interpreter. His grandson will be with him, too, and the young Zhang Wei speaks fluent English. We'd rather have you do it rather than call someone external."

"If that's their preference, I'm happy to help," she said. "But it will slow down the work we're doing on the watermarking, as well as my plans to implement the new three-step biometric authentication process. I had sessions scheduled all week with the coding team, and the project can't go forward without me. That'll be delayed."

"It's worth it to facilitate Malcolm and Hendrick's meeting with the Zhang Wei Group," Vann told her. "I'll make sure everyone is on board with the new timetable."

She nodded. "Okay. Will we fly down with Malcolm and Hendrick tomorrow?"

"They're already in San Francisco, at Magnolia Plaza," he told her. "Be prepared for an intense couple of days. Hendrick, Malcolm, Drew and I have back-to-back meetings scheduled with Zhang Wei and his people all through Thursday and Friday."

Sophie's mouth curved in a slight smile. "I'm no stranger to hard work or long days."

"Of course not." Vann felt awkward and flustered, his mind wiped blank by that secret smile and what it did to her full lower lip. "My executive assistant, Belinda, has the briefing paper she was going to give to Hsu Li. She'll arrange for a car to pick you up tomorrow morning. Talk to her about the travel details, and I'll see you on the plane."

"Great," she said. "Until tomorrow, then."

He turned and walked away, appalled at himself for feeling so sweaty and rattled. It already felt sleazy to gather information on a colleague without her knowledge.

It would be even worse if he got all hot and bothered while doing it.

But there was no question of getting sexually involved with her. He never got involved with coworkers, much less subordinates. That was begging for disaster.

Vann ran his sex life with the same detachment he used for his professional life. His hookups were organized to never inconvenience him. He never brought his lovers to his own home, and was equally reluctant to go to theirs.

He favored hotels. Neutral ground, where he could make some excuse after he was done and just go, with no drama. And he was careful to sever the connection before his lovers got too attached.

He was a numbers guy. He liked control. He kept his

guard up. That made him a good CFO, and it had made him a good soldier, too. He was chill under fire. He'd learned from the best.

Sex was fun, and giving satisfaction to his lovers was a point of honor, but emotionally, it ended right where it started for him. It never went anywhere.

Which worked for him. He was fine right where he was.

He had no playbook for coping with feelings like this. He didn't even recognize himself. Muddled and speechless. Distracted with sexual fantasies and embarrassing urges.

He had to stay sharp and analytical. Vann didn't buy Tim Bryce's accusation. It just didn't fit with his impression of Sophie Valente.

He needed to find out more about her to defend her innocence effectively, but that was going to be a hell of a challenge, if just listening to that woman speak Italian on the phone reduced him into stammering and staring.

Not a great beginning.

Two

Good thing Sophie's chair was right behind her when Vann Acosta walked out. The adrenaline-fueled starch went right out of Sophie's knees the second he cleared the door and she plopped down onto the seat. Breathless.

Going to San Francisco with Vann Acosta? Hoo boy.

Please. It was ridiculous to get all fluttery. This was a business trip. She was just a resource to be exploited. Besides, she was almost thirty, wise in the ways of the world and thoroughly disillusioned about men. They were more trouble than they were worth, and they always had some fatal flaw or other. In her experience, the more attractive the man, the more fatal the flaw.

If that rule applied to Vann, then his fatal flaw had to be one colossal humdinger.

Still, even if he miraculously had no flaws, he was a C-suite executive at Maddox Hill, which was a flaw itself, for all intents and purposes. She was walking a fine line already, juggling a demanding job with her own secret agenda. The firm's chief financial officer was sexually off-limits. A thousand times over.

But Vann Acosta fascinated her. He was the youngest CFO that Maddox Hill had ever had, and he'd held that title for almost five years now. Company gossip painted him as a numbers god. He could have made far more money than he made at Maddox Hill if he'd gone to work for a hedge fund or opened his own.

If watercooler gossip was to be believed, he stayed out of loyalty to Drew Maddox. They'd been comrades in arms in Iraq, along with Zack Austin, who was in charge of Maddox Hill's security. Both of whom, coincidentally enough, were dreamboat hotties in their own right. The Maddox Hill Heartthrobs, they were called. Every straight woman who worked at Maddox Hill had her favorite of the trio, but from day one, it was Vann Acosta who commanded all of Sophie's attention.

It was late, and she had to scramble to reorganize her week, so she set off, stopping here and there to reschedule meetings and tweak deadlines. In the months that she'd been here, she'd found Maddox Hill a good place to work. She hadn't made close friends yet, since she took her own sweet time with that, but she had lots of pleasant acquaintances.

She leaned into Tim Bryce's office, tapping on the open door. "Hi, Tim."

Surprised, Tim spilled coffee on his hand and cursed, flapping his fingers in the air.

"Oh, no!" she exclaimed. "I'm so sorry. I didn't mean to startle you."

"Not your fault," Tim said tightly. "Just clumsy today."

"I came by to let you know that we have to reschedule the team meetings for tomorrow and Friday," she told him. "I'm going down to San Francisco to fill in for Hsu Li. They need an interpreter for the Zhang Wei negotiations. I'll see you on Monday."

"Tuesday actually. I'll be coming back from the wedding on Monday. I won't be in to work that day." Tim pulled some tissues from a pack on his desk and dabbed at the coffee stain on his sleeve. "I'll have Weston email out a memo and reschedule the team meeting. Tuesday afternoon work for you?"

"Tuesday sounds great. Thanks. Have a great week."

"You, too," he said, rubbing at his sleeve. "We'll miss you. But we all must bow to the will of the masters."

She hesitated. "Tim? Is everything okay? Other than scalding yourself, I mean?"

"Fine," he said emphatically. "Everything's fine."

"I'm glad. Later, then."

Sophie made her way into the open plan area, admiring the walls of glass, the towering ceilings and the lofted walkway that led to the corporate offices above. She liked working in beautiful places. Life was too short to hang out in ugly ones.

Drew Maddox strode by. The Maddox Hill CEO was surrounded by his usual entourage, and all the women in the room tracked his progress hungrily with their eyes. She hardly blamed them. Maddox was gorgeous, as well as rich, famous and talented. He'd designed the building she was standing in, the firm's Seattle headquarters. The striking skyscraper was constructed out of eco-sustainable wood products, and the lattice of red-tinted beams overhead was made of cross-laminated timber, as strong as concrete and steel, but much more beautiful.

Drew Maddox had been the first of the Heartthrob trio to fall, after his highly publicized romance with Jenna Somers. His wedding was this weekend, and scores of female employees were mourning their dashed hopes.

But all was not yet lost. They still had Vann Acosta and Zack Austin to cling to.

Sophie was surprised to be on Acosta's radar at all. She'd been introduced to him, but he'd barely seemed to notice.

Better not to be noticed, she reminded herself. She was keeping a low profile while awaiting her chance to make contact with Malcolm Maddox, the company founder. Malcolm was semiretired, leaving most of the decision-making to his nephew, Drew. He spent most of his time in his luxury home on Vashon Island.

Approaching a reclusive, elderly, world-famous architect who seldom ventured from his island home was easier said than done. And Malcolm Maddox was a grumpy, curmudgeonly old man who, famously, did not suffer fools gladly.

Damn good thing she was nobody's fool.

The assignment this weekend was a perfect opportunity to encounter Malcolm, but it came with a hitch—Vann Acosta looming over her, watching her with his smoldering eyes. Distracting her from her mission while she most needed to keep her wits together.

Laser-sharp focus, please. No forbidden lust allowed.

But damn, it was hard. She was a tall woman, at five-foot-nine, but Vann Acosta made her feel like a little slip of a thing, towering over her at six-foot-three. And those thick shoulders? Mmm. She wanted to sink her fingers into his solid bulk and just squeeze.

She loved his rangy build. All lean, taut muscle and bone, with those huge, big-knuckled hands that looked so capable. Those wide shoulders. Pure, raw physical power vibrated right through his perfectly tailored suit and blazed out of his eyes. It made her nervous, in a restless, ticklish, delicious sort of way. She could get addicted to the feeling.

His face was angular; his nose had a bump on it. He had a strong jaw, and his mouth managed to be both grim and sensual. She loved the dark slashing line of his eyebrows. The glossy texture of his thick dark hair.

She couldn't help but imagine how it would feel to wind her fingers into it…and yank him toward her. *Get over here, you.*

Stop it right now. Not the time or place.

Vann had a huge corner office, and his executive assistant, Belinda Vasquez, guarded it jealously. She was a square-built lady in her late fifties with jet-black hair, and she eyeballed Sophie as she approached, her red mouth puckering in anticipatory disapproval. "Can I help you?"

"I'm Sophie Valente," Sophie said. "I'll be filling in for Hsu Li as translator in San Francisco. Mr. Acosta said to speak to you about the briefing paper and the travel arrangements."

"Ah, yes. He mentioned that. I have that briefing paper for you right here." Belinda reached down into a drawer and pulled out a thick folder with Confidential written across the corner. She pushed it across the desk. "That's for you." She pushed a notepad and pen after it. "And write down your address and cell phone number for me to give to the driver, please. He'll be there to pick you up at 3:45 a.m."

Sophie put the folder under her arm, taken aback. "Wow. That's early."

Belinda smirked. "I know, right? Malcolm and Hendrick like to get an early start. Oh, and clothes. It's regular business wear for the meetings, but there's almost always a reception at the end of the second day, so be sure to bring a nice cocktail dress."

"Will do," Sophie said. "Thanks for the heads-up."

"Ah, there you are!" Belinda's face lit up as she looked at someone over Sophie's shoulder. "I was just squaring away the travel details with Sophie."

"Excellent." Vann's deep, resonant voice sent a ripple of emotion rushing up from someplace deep inside her. She braced herself and turned toward him.

"I was about to tell her to hide some energy bars and Red Bull in her purse," Belinda said. "Collette and Hsu Li tell me horror stories about those interpreting sessions."

Sophie met Vann's eyes with some effort. "Horror stories?"

"Oh, those architects just never stop blabbering." Belinda chuckled, shaking her head. "You'll be at it from morning till night, hon. They'll squeeze you dry like a lemon."

"I can take it," she said. "Let 'em squeeze."

Yikes. That had sounded so terribly suggestive. The nervous silence that followed didn't help. Her face went hot.

Belinda cleared her throat with a prim cough. "Well,

good, then. As long as you're psychologically prepared for a grind. That's all from my end. Your hotel room is all set."

"I'll fill you in on any last-minute details on the plane," Vann said.

"Great," Sophie said, backing away. "I'll go get organized. See you at dawn."

She'd never seen his smile before. It was more devastating than she'd imagined. She set off, trying not to bump into walls and hoping that no one was watching.

But she had to stay focused. Her secret agenda was top priority, and now she was closer than ever to accomplishing her mission: to obtain a specimen of Malcolm Maddox's DNA for the genetics lab. Not that she doubted her mother's word, but Mom was gone now, and couldn't provide the proof Sophie needed. She was all alone with this.

She had proof already, by virtue of the DNA sample she'd gotten from Malcolm's niece, Ava, some weeks before. The lab techs had assured her that the results were conclusive, so getting a sample from Malcolm was overkill at this point.

Still, it was overkill she felt she needed. She wanted a sheaf of hard scientific evidence in her hand before she looked Malcolm Maddox in the eye and told him that she was his biological daughter.

Three

Vann felt his tension rise when the attendant showed Sophie Valente to her seat, across the aisle, in the small private plane. He hadn't slept well. He kept dreaming of Sophie, and waking up agitated and sweaty, heart thudding.

He was accustomed to being in control. He managed his staff smoothly, pulling just the right strings to get what he wanted out of people. And all that hard-won managerial skill went up in smoke whenever this woman walked into a room.

Sophie gave him a cool and distant smile. "Good morning."

A curt answering nod was all he could manage. He tried to focus on the financials on his laptop screen but he couldn't concentrate. His senses were overwhelmed.

Not that she was showing off. If anything, she'd dressed down today. She wore a white silk blouse, a tan pencil skirt and a tailored jacket. Her hair was wound tightly into a sleek updo. Little tasteful swirls of gold rested on her well-shaped earlobes. She wore elegant brown suede pumps on her slender feet.

No stockings. The skin on her calves was bare. Golden, even-toned, fine-grained. It looked like it would be beautifully smooth to the touch.

The ultraprofessional, understated vibe just highlighted her sensual beauty. He could catch an elusive hint of faint, sweet perfume as she took her seat across the aisle. He wanted to lean closer, take a deeper whiff.

He didn't do it. He wasn't a goddamned animal. *Get a grip.*

The plane took off, and when they'd reached cruising

altitude, the attendant came out to offer them coffee and tea. Sophie gazed out the window at the dawn-tinted pink clouds as she sipped her coffee, lost in her own thoughts. Serenely ignoring him.

This would be the perfect time to start a conversation and start learning more about her, but Vann was stuck in a strange paralysis. It felt all too similar to adolescent shyness. Ridiculous, for a grown man. After a long, silent interval, the flight attendant came out to offer them some breakfast, which Sophie declined.

That gave him an opening, which he gratefully seized upon.

"Now would be the time to fuel up," he suggested. "When we touch down, we'll hit the ground running. There won't be any opportunity later."

Her smile was wry. "Thanks, but my stomach isn't awake at this hour," she said. "It wouldn't know what to do with food."

"You changed your hair," he blurted, instantly regretting it. Too personal.

"From the braid, you mean?" She brushed back the loose locks that dangled around her jaw, looking self-conscious. "The braid needs to be periodically refreshed during the course of the day, or it gets frowsy. An updo is lower maintenance. If it holds. Fingers crossed."

"It looks great," he said. "So does the braid, of course."

"It's my go-to," she admitted. "I finish my morning kung fu class before work, and it's the quickest style if I need to hustle to get to the office."

"Kung fu?" he asked. "Every morning?"

"Oh, yes. It's my happy place. A kung fu teacher came to my high school once to give us a self-defense workshop, and I fell in love with it. It keeps me chill."

"Agreed," he said.

"You practice it, too?"

"Not specifically. I studied a very mixed bag of martial arts. I leaned from my dad. He was a marine sergeant, and a combat veteran, and he borrowed from every discipline, from boxing to jujitsu. He even saw American football as a martial arts discipline. Good training in learning to run toward pain and conflict, not away. So I did football, too."

She gave him a quick, assessing glance. "I can see why your high school would have wanted you on their football team."

"I guess," he muttered, wishing he hadn't started a line of conversation that focused on his body. He was far too conscious of both hers and his own right now.

"Lucky you, to learn to fight from your own dad," she said.

He grunted. "*Nice* isn't the word I'd choose. My father was a hard man. I got my ass kicked on a regular basis. But I learned."

The piercing look she gave him felt like she was peering inside his head with a high-powered flashlight. God forbid she thought he was asking her to feel sorry for him.

"How about you?" he asked, just to change the subject. "I bet your father was glad you learned kung fu."

Her eyebrow tilted up. "Why would you think that?"

"The world is full of sleazeball predators and ass-grabbing idiots. If I had a daughter, I'd want her trained to sucker punch and crotch-kick at a moment's notice."

She nodded agreement. "Me, too. But my dad was never in the picture."

He winced inside. *Damn.* "I'm sorry."

"It's okay," she said. "My mother, on the other hand, didn't know what to think of the kung fu. It's not that she disapproved. She just wasn't the warrior type. Her idea of heaven was a hot bath, a silk shirt and a glass of cold Prosecco."

"They don't cancel each other out," he said. "A person can have both."

"Who has the time? My life doesn't allow for hot baths. Lightning-fast showers are the order of the day."

"Me, too," he said. "When I was in the service, we only had a couple of minutes in the water. You learn to make them count."

Damn. From bodies to baths and showers, which was even worse. Time for a radical subject pivot. "Have you met Malcolm and Hendrick yet?"

"I've seen them in passing, but I've never been introduced. What are they like?"

Vann chose his words carefully. "Hendrick will never acknowledge your existence except to lean closer with his good ear to hear you better. But if you're female, he won't look you in the eye."

"Which ear is his good ear?"

"The left one. Hendrick is extremely shy around women. Any woman who isn't his wife, that is. He worships his wife, Bev. So don't take it personally."

She nodded. "Understood. How about Malcolm?"

"Malcolm is tougher. He's moody, and quick to criticize. He thinks that you should just toughen up and learn to take it."

"Take what?"

He shrugged. "Whatever needs to be taken. So don't expect to be pampered. In fact, don't even expect common courtesy. You won't get it."

She nodded thoughtfully. "Understood. I don't need to be pampered."

"Then you'll be fine. With Malcolm, you're guilty until proven innocent. He'll just assume that you're an incompetent idiot who is actively trying to waste his time and money. Until you prove to him that you're not."

"Wow," she said. "That's good to know in advance. Thanks for the heads-up."

"That said, I genuinely do respect the guy. He has incredible talent. Vision, drive, energy. We get along."

"So you passed his test evidently," she said.

He shrugged. "I must have."

She got that flashlight-shining-into-the-dark look in her eyes again. "Of course you did," she said. "You spent your childhood training for exactly that, right? Getting your ass kicked. Learning to run toward pain, instead of away. It doesn't scare you."

He couldn't think of a response to that, but fortunately, just then, the attendant came through for their coffee cups and told them to prepare for landing.

He shut down his laptop, appalled at himself. What a mess he'd made of that conversation. The idea had been to gain her trust, get her to open up. And without ever meaning to, he'd revealed more about himself than he had learned about her.

And now he had those images in his head. Sophie, hot and sweaty from her kung fu class, stripping off her practice gear and stepping into the shower. Steaming water spraying down on her perfect skin. Suds sliding over her strong, sexy curves.

The harder he tried not to see it, the more detailed the image became.

Soon he had to cross his leg and lay his suit coat over his lap.

Four

Sophie sat next to Vann in the limo as it crawled through rush-hour traffic, trying to breathe deeply. Now she was all wound up with anxiety. She had no doubts about her ability to do the job, but damn, she hadn't counted on being hazed by a bad-tempered old tycoon while she was doing it.

And in front of Vann, too. He just stirred her up.

She'd worked hard on her professional demeanor. Steely control and calm competence were the vibe she always went for. And Vann Acosta just decimated it.

She was spellbound by his dark eyes that never flinched away. Her own directness and focus didn't intimidate him at all.

It felt as if they were communicating for real. On a deeper level.

Please. Stop. She had a crush on the man. She was projecting her own feverish fantasies onto him, that was all. Snap out of it already.

She was here to do a spectacular job, earn Malcolm Maddox's good opinion and get a viable DNA sample while she was at it. But the last part might be tough, with Vann Acosta watching her every move. It would be awkward if he saw her slipping Malcolm's salad fork into her purse.

She also had to find the time to monitor the traps she'd set for the IP thief at Maddox Hill. Depending on what kind of intellectual property made the corporate spy rise to the bait, she'd be able to interpolate if it was an inside job, or an outside entity.

She'd discovered the data breach within weeks of starting the job, but she was so new here, with no idea who she could trust. Until she had more definitive data, she'd decided to stay quiet about her investigation. Her best-case scenario was to be able to offer the thief up to Malcolm Maddox on a silver platter, kind of like a hostess gift. To set the tone, before she delivered her bombshell about being his biological daughter.

She wanted to make it crystal clear that she had skills and talents and resources of her own to offer. She was not here to mooch.

Vann was speaking into the phone in a soothing tone. "I know, but the traffic is crazy, and we can't control that. Tell him to calm down... Fine, don't tell him... I know, I know... Yeah, you bet. See you there."

He put his phone in his pocket, looking resigned. "Charles will let us out at the North Tower of Magnolia Plaza and take our bags on to the hotel for us," he said. "We're already late, and Malcolm is having a tantrum."

"Oh, dear," she murmured. "A bad beginning."

"You'll make up for it by being awesome," he told her.

She laughed. "Aw! You sound awfully confident about that."

"I am," he replied.

"How so?" she demanded. "You've never seen me in action."

"I'm a good judge of character," he said. "You're tough and calm, and you don't get rattled. Malcolm likes that. He'll be eating out of your hand by Friday."

"We'll see," she said. "Let's hope."

"This is us," Vann said as the limo pulled up to the curb.

Vann held the car door open for her. He led them through the lobby, and then down a long breezeway across the plaza under an enormous glass dome, all the way to the second tower.

"Is this building one of Maddox Hill's designs?" she asked.

"Yes. It was finished last year. Zhang Wei, the man

we're meeting, is the owner." Vann pushed the door open
and beckoned her inside, waving at a security guard who
waved back with a smile. "They want us to design another
property in Nairobi, similar to the Triple Towers in Can-
berra that we did two years ago. That's what we're nego-
tiating today."

"Yes, all that was in the briefing paper," she said. "I
read it last night."

"Malcolm and Hendrick and Drew are upstairs with
Zhang Wei's team, waiting for us."

"Drew Maddox is here?" She was surprised. "Isn't he
getting married this weekend?"

"Sunday. After this meeting, he heads to Paradise Point,
and the party begins."

"I've heard about Paradise Point," Sophie said. "That's
the new resort on the coast, right? I hope I get a chance to
see it sometime."

"Yes, it's a beautiful property," Vann said. "That's one
of Drew's first lead architect projects. He made a big splash
with it. Got a lot of attention."

The elevator doors hummed open. A woman with curly
gray hair and round gold-rimmed glasses hurried toward
them, her eyebrows in an anxious knot. "Thank God!"

"Sylvia, this is Sophie Valente, our interpreter," Vann
said. "Sophie, this is Sylvia Gregory, Malcolm's executive assistant."

Sylvia shook Sophie's hand and then grabbed it, pulling
Sophie along after her.

"Come on now, both of you!" she said. "He's just beside
himself. Hurry!"

"He'll live, Sylvia," Vann said wryly.

"Easy for you to say," Sylvia fussed. "I wish you two
had gotten here in time to have some coffee or tea or a pastry from the breakfast buffet, but it's too late now. We just

can't keep him waiting any longer. Come on now, pick up the pace, both of you!"

Sophie glanced at her watch. Not even 8:20 yet. The guy was hard-core.

Sylvia pointed at two doors as she hustled them down the corridor. "See those two offices? Take note of the numbers—2406 and 2408. The Zhang Wei Group has made them available to Mr. Maddox and Mr. Hill for the duration. If you're ever called upon to interpret for a private meeting, you'll meet in one of those offices."

Sylvia ushered them into a large conference room with an elegant, minimalist design and a wall of windows. The hum of conversation and clink of china stopped as they entered. On one side of the table was a group of Chinese men. The man seated in the center was very old. Those ranged around him were younger.

There was staff from the Maddox Hill legal department there, as well, but Sophie focused on the three men in the center. She saw Drew Maddox and Hendrick Hill, Malcolm's cofounder. Tall and bald and bony, he gave them a tight-lipped frown.

Then Malcolm Maddox stood up and turned to them.

She'd seen Malcolm in passing, and she'd seen photographs of him online. But this was the first time she'd seen him up close and in the flesh. She finally got why her mother had fallen so hard all those years ago. He was seamed and grizzled now, but still good-looking, with a shock of white hair and deep-set, intense gray eyes. Bold eyebrows, chiseled cheekbones. He would have been tall, if the arthritis hadn't bent him over, and he was trim and wiry for a man with his health problems.

Her mother had fallen for him so hard she'd never recovered. She'd been on a team of interior designers on a project in New York thirty years ago. A luminously pretty, naive twenty-six-year-old with a mane of blond curls and head full of romantic notions.

Malcolm had been over forty. He'd been lead architect on the Phelps Pavilion. Charismatic, seductive, brilliant, charming. Intense.

They'd had a brief, hot affair, and then he'd left, returning to the West Coast.

When Vicky Valente found that she was pregnant, she'd gone to look for him. His wife, Helen, had opened the door when Sophie's mom knocked on it. She'd left without ever making contact with Malcolm. Mortified. Heartbroken.

Malcolm glowered at them, clutching his cane with a hand gnarled from arthritis. "So," he growled. "Finally deigned to make an appearance, eh? Mr. Zhang, I believe you met Vann Acosta at our last meeting, correct?"

"Yes, we did meet," Vann said, nodding in Zhang Wei's direction. "I'm sorry to have kept you waiting, sir."

"You should be," Malcolm barked. "I don't have time to waste. Neither do Mr. Zhang and his team."

Sophie set her purse down and promptly situated her chair behind and between Hendrick's and Malcolm's chairs. "Whenever you're ready, sir." Her voice was calm.

Hendrick's eyes slid over her and skittered away, but Malcolm's eyes bored into her with unfriendly intensity for a moment.

The meeting got under way with some formal speechifying about mutual friendship and regard and Mr. Zhang's best wishes for prosperity for all in their shared undertaking, etc., etc. Sophie interpreted whenever Zhang or one of the others paused for breath, in a clear, carrying voice. After a certain point, Malcolm's patience began to fray. She could tell from how he clicked the top of his ballpoint pen, a rapid tappety-tap-tap.

Funny. She did that herself when she was nervous. In

fact, she'd stopped using ballpoint pens because of that particular nervous habit. She couldn't seem to stop doing it.

Mr. Zhang's speech finally wound up with a flowery expression of best wishes on behalf of the entire Zhang Wei Group for Drew Maddox's upcoming nuptials, and best wishes for the future and wonderful prospects for the happy young couple.

Drew responded with grace, echoing the older man's formal language as he thanked Zhang Wei for his kindness. Finally that part was over, and they got down to business.

It was fortunate that her mind was occupied so completely with translating while she was just inches away from her biological father. Close enough to smell his aftershave, to compare the shape of his ears and his fingernails with her own. His hands were bent by arthritis, so their original shape was impossible to determine, but he had the same broad, square fingernails that she had. The same high cheekbones. Drew had them, too, as well as Malcolm's coloring.

Her intense focus altered her perception of time. She was surprised when they finally broke for lunch. Sylvia approached her as they exited the conference room. "You do know that you'll be interpreting for Mr. Hill and Mr. Maddox during lunch, as well?" she asked, her eyes daring Sophie to say no.

"Of course," Sophie said. "Whenever I'm needed."

"You'll want to arrive before Malcolm and Hendrick get there. I'll show you where to go. Right this way, please."

Sylvia led her onto the elevator and up to the restaurant on the penthouse floor.

When the rest of the party came into the private dining room, Sophie took her place behind Malcolm and Hendrick and interpreted their conversation with Zhang Wei as they ate lunch. She must have done it competently enough, because no one complained, but very little of what they said penetrated her conscious mind. Her stomach had woken up, and the *fettucine ai limone* and stuffed lobster smelled freaking divine.

No pampering. Belinda had warned her to stuff her purse with protein bars. Vann had advised her to grab breakfast. But she'd been all a-flutter to meet Malcolm up close. And in a tizzy from gawking at Vann Acosta's ridiculous hotness. It was her own damn fault.

As if there'd been so much as a single free moment to gnaw a protein bar today, anyhow.

Lunch dragged on. Dessert, then coffee and still more talk. Global international trade, geo-politics, pictures of Zhang Wei's twin great-grandsons, which had to be admired and chatted about. Still more coffee.

On the way back to the conference room, Sophie trailed Malcolm and Zhang Wei and interpreted as they walked. Mr. Zhang waxed eloquent about the poetic significance of empty space in architecture.

All she got was a pit stop in the ladies' room where she splashed her hands and face in the sink before the afternoon session began. It was twice as long as the morning one, and more technical. This involved Zhang Wei and his lawyers facing off with Maddox Hill's legal department. They got deep into the weeds and stayed there for hours.

At some point in the afternoon, her voice got thick and cracked. Malcolm whipped his head around to glare at her as she coughed to clear her throat.

Then a shadow fell over her. She heard a popping sound and turned to find Vann next to her, twisting off the top of a bottle of chilled water. Everyone watched in silence as she took a quick, grateful sip. That was all she dared to take the time for.

The sky was a blaze of pink before they wrapped up the meeting. Dinner plans were announced, this time at the restaurant at the top of the South Tower, on the other end of Magnolia Plaza. Sophie was unsurprised when she walked out to see Sylvia approach her with that now-familiar look on her face.

"Same song and dance for dinner," Sylvia said. "Head over there before Mr. Zhang, Mr. Maddox or Mr. Hill arrive. You don't want them standing around before dinner trying to making small talk with no interpreter to help. Mr. Maddox hates that."

Sophie let out a silent sigh. "Of course."

"Are you familiar with the Magnolia Plaza complex? I'll give you a map if—"

"I know it." It was Vann's deep voice behind her. "I'll make sure she gets there."

Sophie followed Vann into the elevator, too tired to feel self-conscious. Her eyes stung, and her throat was sore. She uncapped the water he'd given her earlier and drank deep. "Wow," she remarked. "Those guys have stamina."

"So do you," Vann said.

Sophie slanted him a wry look as she drained her bottle.

"It's true," he said. "Don't think Malcolm didn't notice."

"Oh, please," she said. "He didn't look at me once the whole day. Except to glare at me for being late this morning. And for coughing. Thanks for the water, by the way."

"That's exactly what I mean," Vann said. "Malcolm doesn't reward perfection. He expects it as his due. He doesn't appear to notice if things go smoothly, but if something doesn't measure up to his high standards, by God you'll hear about it."

"So being ignored by Malcolm Maddox all day is a good sign?"

"Very good," he said. "You're excellent. You never missed a beat. I don't speak Mandarin, so I can't vouch for your language skills, but there was good flow all day long. We got more accomplished than any of us expected. Because of you."

"Hmph." She tucked the bottle back into her purse. "It's kind of you to say so. Is Malcolm always like that?"

"Workaholic, hyperfocused, obsessive? Yes. And he expects the same maniacal focus from everyone who works for him. Which makes for some guaranteed drama."

"I was told he was a hard boss to work for," Sophie said.

"He's infamous," Vann said. "You have to be like him to earn his approval. Drew is, at least before he fell in love. His niece, Ava, is, too, in her own way. So are you."

"Me, like him? An alarming prospect." She said it with a light tone, but Vann's words made her hairs prickle with a shiver of undefinable emotion.

Like him? Maybe they did have some subtle, mysterious genetic similarities. But be that as it may, she couldn't be seduced by the idea of getting to know her birth father. When her mother had learned about her stage IV pancreatic cancer, she'd been so afraid at the thought of Sophie being alone in the world. She'd pressed her daughter very hard for a promise that Sophie would approach Malcolm and his niece and nephew once she was gone.

She'd slipped away so fast. Just a few weeks afterward.

Sophie still remembered Mom's chilly, wasted hand clutching Sophie's fingers. *You have more to give them than you have to gain from them. They'd be lucky to know you. I know I was. My darling girl.*

The memory brought a sharp, tight lump to her throat.

She appreciated Mom's effort. It was a sweet thought. But Malcolm Maddox was famously difficult. Even unlikable, by some accounts. The chance that they would truly connect was small. She couldn't let her own loneliness set her up for almost certain disappointment. She'd just fulfill her promise to Mom, and move on.

Vann was talking again. She forced herself to tune back

in. "…are kind of like him," he was saying. "I've seen the hours you put in at work. You stay late every night."

"That's more a function of not having a social life than being dedicated to my job," she said without thinking. "I stay late because why not, if I'm on a roll. There's no one at home competing for my attention."

"So you're unattached?"

Heat rushed into her face "I'm new in town," she said. "I just got to Seattle a few months ago. I'm still finding my feet."

The elevator door rolled open, a welcome distraction from her embarrassment. They walked in silence on the cool breezeway beneath the great dome between the two towers, which was nearly deserted at this hour.

"I'm sorry you didn't get any lunch," he said.

"I'm fine," she assured him. "No pampering, right?"

He grunted under his breath as the glass elevator in the South Tower arrived and the door opened.

They got in, and the elevator zoomed up the side of the building. The top-floor restaurant had walls of floor-to-ceiling glass. The ambience was hushed and elegant, and the aromas from the kitchen made Sophie's mouth water.

The host led them to a large private dining room bathed in the fading rusty glow of sunset. A long candlelit table was set for sixteen.

But there was no seat for her. She asked the waitstaff for another chair to be brought in, and was positioning it behind two chairs near the head of the table when they heard Malcolm's deep voice outside the door. He was arguing with someone. The door opened, and that someone proved to be Drew Maddox, looking frustrated.

"…don't see why you should be so concerned," Malcolm snapped. "She doesn't strike me as a type who needs coddling. And these young skinny females never eat nowadays, anyway. No fat, no carbs, no this, no that. Ridiculous creatures."

He and Drew caught sight of Sophie at the same moment. Malcolm harrumphed, and made his way to the table with his cane, muttering under his breath. Drew cast her an apologetic look as she took her place behind Malcolm.

The rest of the party lost no time in sitting down to eat. Vann's encouraging compliments had bolstered Sophie quite a bit, but it was harder this time to concentrate on the conversation without gazing with longing at the artichoke tarts, the succulent entrecôte, seared to perfection and cut into juicy pink slices with slivers of Grana Padano, the gemlike cherry tomatoes and scattered arugula leaves, the rosemary-thyme oven-roasted potatoes and the deep red Primitivo wine.

The aromas were dizzying.

Of course, it would be too late for her to order from room service once she got to the room. It would be peanuts from the minibar if she was lucky. Cue the violins. She hoped the clink of cutlery and the hum of conversation would cover the grumbling of her stomach. Suck it up, buttercup.

At long last, the men from the Zhang Wei Group made their farewells and took their leave. Now it was just the executives from Maddox Hill, and Sophie.

Malcolm drained his wine, and turned to give Sophie an assessing look. "Make sure this one is on call for all future meetings that require Mandarin," he said, directing his words to Drew and Vann. "I don't want anyone else from here on out."

"Actually, she's our information security director," Vann informed his boss. "She's just filling in for Hsu Li and Collette. She usually directs the team on cyber—"

"She's a better interpreter than Hsu Li or Collette. Much

better." Malcolm turned his scowl directly on Sophie. "What other languages do you speak?"

"Ah…fluently enough to interpret professionally, only Italian," she told him. "But I'm not actually specialized in—"

"Then it's settled. Whenever we require Italian or Mandarin, you're up."

"Ah…but I—"

"Get some sleep. Tomorrow's another long day. Not as long as I expected, though. We're ahead of schedule." Malcolm frowned, as if fishing in his mind for something to complain about, and then threw up his hands with a grunt of disgust when he couldn't think of anything. "Well, then. Whatever. Good night."

He hobbled out, cane clicking. Drew hurried after to help him to the elevator.

Sophie felt her body sag. She turned to Vann. "How far away is the hotel?"

"Not far," Vann told her. "We're in it already. The first six floors of this building is the Berenson Suites Hotel. Come with me. I'll show you where your room is located."

"Don't we need to go down to the desk? We never checked in."

"Sylvia took care of it. Your bags have been brought up. You're in room 3006, and I've asked for a hotel employee to meet you at your door with a key card."

She gave him a teasing smile as their elevator plunged downward. "What's this I sense? Is this…dare I say it… pampering?"

"It's been a long day," he replied, grinning back at her. "I'd call it survival."

The doors opened onto the third floor and Vann strolled with her down the hall. They turned the corner, and there was room 3006, with a uniformed young man standing by the door, holding an envelope with a key card to her. "Your luggage is inside, miss."

"Thanks so much." She took the envelope and fished out the card.

"And here's your meal," the man said, gesturing at the rolling cart full of silver-topped dishes. "May I take it inside?"

"Meal?" she said blankly. "Ah...no. You must have mixed me up with someone else. I didn't order a meal."

"No, it's not a mistake," Vann said. "I ordered the food."

"You?" Bewildered, she looked at the cart, and then at him.

"From the look on your face in the restaurant, I assumed that tonight's menu would be agreeable," he said. "So I ordered you the same meal. I hope that's okay."

"Oh, dear. Was it so obvious?"

"Only if you were paying attention," he said.

The fraught silence following his reply made her face heat up. She turned away and inserted her key card in the door, opening it and stepping back to let the hotel attendant wheel the cart inside. "I'm ravenous, yes," she admitted. "A hot meal sounds great. But this definitely qualifies as pampering."

"This is just smart management of human capital," he said. "It's stupid to misuse a vital resource just because you always have in the past. Tradition is not a good enough reason to be rude. It's bad business. But Malcolm doesn't listen to me. Not about this, anyway. So this is my imperfect solution."

"Very kind of you," she said. "I like to be considered a vital resource."

"Malcolm certainly thinks that you are."

The hotel employee said good-night and departed, leaving them standing there in awkward silence.

"Well, then," Vann said. "I'll say good-night. Enjoy your meal." He turned to walk away.

"Wait!"

The word flew out of Sophie's mouth against her better judgment.

Too late now. Vann had already turned around, eyebrows up.

"Would you come in and help me eat it?" she asked. "It's a ridiculous amount of food for just one person."

"I had plenty at dinner," he told her. "You've been fasting all day."

"Just have a glass of wine, then," she said. "There's a whole bottle. It's wasted on me alone."

He hesitated, and turned back. "All right. A quick glass of wine."

She had a frantic moment as he followed her in. What had she just implied? Would he misinterpret it? The room was airy and luxurious, with a king-size bed dominating it, but Vann's presence made the place feel breathlessly small.

"Would you excuse me for a moment?" she asked. "I need to pop into the bathroom."

"Of course," he said. "I'll pour the wine in the meantime."

Once she shut the bathroom door behind her, her breath emerged in an explosive rush. She lunged at the mirror over the sink, gasping at the undereye smudges, the worn-off lipstick, the loose wisps around her face and neck. They had gone well beyond the romantically tousled look, and were now officially a straggly mess.

She still had her purse, which was a damn good thing, since it had her makeup wipes and some lip gloss and mascara. But, oh, the hair, the hair. She pulled out all the pins and unwound the coil. The effect, after a day of the tight twist, was wild waves every which way. The quickest solution was a tight over-the-shoulder braid, but she had nothing to fasten the end. The ties were packed in her toiletries case, which was zipped up in the luggage outside. She could put her hair back up, but that would take time. Her hands were cold and shaking. And he was waiting for her out there.

Damn. She'd finger-comb it, shake it out and act like that had been the plan all along.

Sophie fixed her face with the wipes and a little fresh mascara. She put the hotel's courtesy toothpaste and toothbrush to good use and brushed her teeth before putting on a final slick of colorless lip gloss. It was the best she could do under these conditions.

Toothpaste and red wine, yikes. It was an unholy combination, but hey.

A girl had to do what a girl had to do.

Five

Vann poured out two glasses of wine and strolled over to stare out the window at the city lights. No big deal, he kept repeating. Just a quick drink with a colleague to unwind after a high-pressure day, and then he was out of here, leaving her to her well-deserved rest. No weirdness, no agenda, other than learning more about her and keeping her too busy to notice the forensic investigation under way back at headquarters. God knows when it came to that, Malcolm was keeping her busy enough without Vann's help.

Her stamina was incredible. She was classy and tough. Elegant, composed, pulled-together. That voice, wow. It was a problem for him. Constant, relentless sexual stimulation every time she spoke. Like he was being stroked by a seductive invisible hand.

It kept his blood continually racing. He needed to shut. That. Down.

Sophie Valente couldn't be Bryce's IP thief. A woman as accomplished as she was wouldn't waste her time and energy stealing the fruits of other people's labors. She had plenty of fruits to offer herself. She had that rare quality he'd seen in only a few people, his friends Zack and Drew among them. Ava, too, Drew's sister, and Jenna, Drew's soon-to-be wife. They knew who they were and what they were meant to do on this earth, and they just got on with it, no bullshit.

People like that didn't cheat and steal. Entirely aside from their morals and principles, it would just never occur to them to do so. It would bore them.

Insecure, jealous, damaged people cheated and stole. That wasn't Sophie Valente.

The bathroom door opened. The light and fan flicked off. He turned to speak, and forgot whatever he had meant to say.

She hadn't changed. It was the same silky white blouse over the tan pencil skirt. But she'd kicked off her heels and let down her hair. Her bare feet were slender and beautiful. High arches. Nails painted gold. That flirtatious glint on her toenails made the sweat break out on his back.

Her hair was a wild mass of waves swirling down over her shoulders. Her lips gleamed. Her skin looked dewy and soft. Fresh. Kissable.

"Excuse me," she said, her voice uncertain. "Sorry to keep you waiting."

"No, no. Take your time. It's been a hell of a day." He picked up her full wineglass and presented it to her.

She took it and sipped. "Mmm, thank you," she said. "It's very nice."

He gestured toward the table. "Waste no time," he urged her.

"Don't mind if I do," she said, taking her seat.

He sat down across from her as she loaded up her plate and forked up her first bite. "Oh, happy me. Are you sure you don't want some? I'll never manage to eat it all."

"Positive," he assured her. "Am I making you self-conscious?"

"Maybe a bit," she said, popping a cherry tomato into her mouth.

"I could just go," he offered. "And leave you to it."

"Oh, stop." She grabbed a dinner roll and tore a piece off. "This steak is delicious."

"Glad you like it. Drew and I both complained to Malcolm about not giving you a lunch break. But he's got this hazing mentality baked into his system. Everyone has to run the gauntlet and get clobbered to prove their worth. Classic Malcolm for you."

"You shouldn't have said anything. I can take whatever he dishes out."

"Yeah," he said. "We noticed."

Her eyes dropped. "I heard that you met Drew when you two were in the military together. Is that true?"

"Marines," he said. "*Semper Fi.* Two tours in Iraq. Fallujah, the Anbar Province."

She nodded. "And you've been with the firm for how long?"

"I've worked here for over eleven years," he replied. "Since I was twenty-three."

"And you're already the CFO? Of a big global company like Maddox Hill, at age thirty-four? That's really something."

"I started on the bottom," he said. "After I mustered out of the marines, I was at loose ends. So Drew suggested that I take a job at his uncle's architecture firm. He knew I was good with computers. I thought, what the hell? It might keep me out of trouble."

Her eyes smiled over her wineglass. "Did it?"

"More or less," he said. "I started out as an assistant general gofer and computer guy in the accounting department, and they busted my ass down there. Then the finance manager, Chuck Morrissey, took an interest in me. Fast-forward a couple of years, and he arranged for Maddox Hill to pay for me to get a degree in accounting and get myself certified. After that I was off and running. I got an MBA a few years later. Chuck encouraged that, too."

"No college after high school, then?"

He shook his head. "Almost. I was offered a football scholarship my senior year, but then my dad died. My grades tanked and I lost the scholarship. I couldn't afford college without it, and nobody was hiring where I lived. Central Washington is mostly rural. Sagebrush, wheat fields. So I joined the marines."

"A self-made man," she said.

He shrugged. "Not entirely. Chuck mentored me. When he got promoted to CFO, he made me his finance manager. Malcolm and Hendrick took chances on me over and over again. And Drew went to bat for me every single time I was up for a promotion. I wouldn't be where I am now if they hadn't helped."

"Their investment in you paid off a hundredfold. Out of curiosity, why the marines?"

He sipped his wine, considering the question. "It was a way to test myself, I guess," he said finally. "And learn some new skills."

"And did you?"

"Oh, yeah. I even thought about making a career out of it. But Fallujah and the Anbar Province changed my mind. Then Drew got wounded, and they sent him home. After that, it was pretty rough. I lost some good friends there."

Sophie sipped her wine and waited for more, but he couldn't keep up this line of conversation. The more painful details of his time in Iraq were too heavy, and the atmosphere between them was already charged.

"You said that your dad was a marine," she said. "A combat veteran. Did you join up because you wanted to understand his demons better? You followed in his footsteps so you could make some sense out of it all, right?"

He stared into her clear, searching eyes, speechless. Almost hypnotized.

"Did you find out what you needed to know?" she prompted. "Was it worth it?"

The question reverberated inside him. He'd never articulated that wordless impulse she had described, but the insight rang so true.

His eyes dropped. He took another sip of wine, stalling. Unable to speak.

Sophie put down her knife and fork. "I'm sorry," she

said quietly. "That was invasive and presumptuous. Please forget I said it."

"Not at all," he said. "It just took me a while to process it. The answer is yes. That's probably what I was doing, but I didn't know it at the time. And yes, I think it was worth it."

She looked cautiously relieved. "I'll stop making big pronouncements about things that are none of my damn business."

"Don't stop," he urged her. "Make all the pronouncements you want. That way I don't have to rack my brains for small talk. I prefer the crossbow bolts of truth, straight to the chest."

She laughed as she forked up another chunk of her steak. Licked a drop of meat juice off her fingers. As her full, smiling lips closed around it, his whole body tightened and started to thrum. His face felt hot. His back getting damp with sweat.

He had to look away for a second and breathe.

"Your turn," she offered. "You're authorized to ask me any embarrassing question you like. Within the limits of decency, of course."

The limits of decency were feeling about as tight as his pants right now. Vann crossed his leg to protect his male dignity. "Give me a second to think up a good one," he said. "It's a big opportunity. I have to make it count."

She laughed. "Don't think too hard," she said. "It doesn't have to be a zinger."

"Okay, how about this? You talked about being a self-made man. How about you? Are you a self-made woman? How did you come to be so accomplished?"

She nibbled on a roasted potato. "I certainly had financial help," she said. "My mother's parents were well-to-do, and she earned well in her own right, so no expense was spared in my education. But they just assumed I'd do great things as a matter of course. 'From those to whom much is given, much is expected.' That was the general attitude."

"So you're a pathological high achiever," he said.

She snorted into her wine. "I wouldn't go that far. But I ask a lot of myself, I guess. Just like you."

"Do I get a bonus question?" he asked. "Now I'm warmed up. The questions are starting to come thick and fast."

"Go for it," she said. "Ask away."

"Okay. Going back to fathers, what happened to yours? Did he leave?"

Sophie's smile froze and Vann felt a stab of alarm. He'd taken her at her word, and still he'd overstepped. He studied her whiskey-gold eyes, barely breathing.

"He never knew I existed," she said finally. "I can't blame him for being absent."

"His loss."

"I like to think so," she said.

"So it was just you and your mom?"

Sophie's face softened. "Mom was great. I was lucky to have her. She was a brilliant artist. A bright, wonderful person. She was a textile designer, very much in demand. She worked all over the world, but by the time I finished middle school, she'd pretty much settled in Singapore."

"Is she still there?"

Sophie shook her head. "I lost her last year. Pancreatic cancer."

"Oh. I'm so sorry to hear that."

She nodded. "It happened so fast. It took us both by surprise."

"I lost my mom, too," he said. "When I was in Iraq. She had one of those sneaky heart attacks. The kind that seems like an upset stomach. She went to bed to sleep it off and never woke up."

"So you didn't even get to say goodbye," she said. "Oh, Vann. That's awful."

He nodded. "It was hard to find my place again when I came home. Civilian life seemed strange, and I had no one left to care about. So when Drew suggested coming to work here, I thought, what else have I got to do? At least I'd be close to a good friend."

"And the rest is history," she said.

"I guess so. Anyhow, that's my story. What brought you to Maddox Hill?"

Her eyes slid away. "More or less the same thing as you, I guess," she said. "After Mom died, I was out of reference points. I needed new horizons. Fresh things to look at."

"You lived in Singapore before?"

"Mostly. I studied there. Software design. Then a friend of mine who was a biologist had all her research for her doctorate stolen. I was so indignant for her I started learning about computer security and IP theft, and I eventually ended up specializing in it. I learned Mandarin in Singapore."

"How about the Italian?"

"My mom was Italian," she said. "Italian American, rather. Your people must have been Italian, too, with a name like Acosta. I take it Vann is short for Giovanni?"

"You nailed it," he said. "Calabrese. Third generation."

"My grandparents moved from Florence to New York in the seventies, when Mom was in her early teens. She spoke English with no accent, but we spoke Italian at home with my grandparents. I lived with them for half of my childhood. My mom would jet off to do her design jobs, and I'd stay in New York with my *nonno* and *nonna*. My grandfather had a company that shipped marble from Italy. Ital-Marble. A lot of the big buildings on the East Coast are made of the stone he imported."

He was startled. "ItalMarble belonged to your grandfather? Really?"

"You know it?" she asked.

"Of course I know it," he said. "We're up on all the providers of high-end building materials. The company changed hands a few years ago, right?"

"Yes, that was when Nonno retired. He died shortly after that."

"I'm sorry to hear that," he said.

She nodded in acknowledgment. "When I was eleven, I persuaded my mom to rescue me. Take me with her the next time she left."

"Rescue you? From your grandparents? Why? Were they hard on you?"

She twirled some feathery arugula fronds up off the plate with her fork. "The opposite actually. They were very sweet to me. But suffocatingly overprotective."

"Yeah? Were they old-fashioned?"

"Very," she said. "But it was mostly because of my health."

He was taken aback. "Your health? Were you not well?"

"I had a heart condition when I was a toddler," she explained. "I almost died a few times. I had to have open-heart surgery. I spent the better part of two years recuperating. After that my grandparents always treated me like I was fragile, and I couldn't stand it."

Vann gazed at the glowing, vital woman across the table from him, tucking away her roasted potatoes with gusto. He couldn't imagine her having ever been ill.

"You don't seem fragile," he said. "Not with the crack-of-dawn kung fu classes, the high-octane male-dominated career and the killer heels."

"I may have overcompensated a little," she admitted. "I push myself. But I never want to feel weak or helpless ever again."

He lifted his wineglass in a toast. "You've succeeded in your goal."

"Have I?" she said. "A person has to climb that mountain from the bottom every single day, forever. You can't just sit back and rest on your past achievements."

"Wow, what a rigorous mindset," he commented. "Don't you get tired?"

"Sometimes," she admitted. "But you know what? It's a lot easier to have a rigorous mindset when you have a big steak dinner inside of you. It was wonderful. Thanks for thinking of me. I can't believe I ate so much."

"Don't mention it. You up for dessert?"

Her whiskey-colored eyes widened. "Dessert?"

"There was a choice of four different desserts. I went with chocolate cheesecake."

"Ooh. I love cheesecake."

Vann retrieved the plate from the tray and placed it in front of her, removing the cover with a flourish. *"Voilà."*

Sophie admired the generous slab, with multiple gooey layers on a chocolate cookie-crumb crust, swirled with drizzles of raspberry syrup. Fruit was artfully arranged next to it: watermelon, pineapple, kiwi, a cluster of shining red jewellike currants, a succulent strawberry and velvety raspberries.

"You have to help me out," she informed him, popping a raspberry into her mouth. "It's too gorgeous to waste, but if I eat it all, I'll hurt myself."

"Try it," he urged. "You go first."

She scooped up the point of the cheesecake slice and lifted it to her lips.

It was agonizing, watching her pink tongue dart out to catch a buttery chocolate crumb. Seeing the pleasure in her heavy-lidded eyes. He fidgeted on his chair.

"Now you." She fished for another spoon and prepared a generous bite for him.

He leaned forward and opened his mouth. That rush of creamy sweetness nudged him right past all his careful walls and limits and rules. He was so turned on it scared him.

He chewed, swallowed. "Wow," he said hoarsely, trying to recall all the bullet points in his lecture-to-self.

Bryce had accused her of spying. Zack was investigating her. She was an employee. A key employee. He was her superior. He never got involved with coworkers. Especially subordinates. Cardinal rule.

He couldn't remember why that was relevant when he wanted this so badly. He stared hungrily as she took another bite of her dessert.

So. Damn. Beautiful.

"Want another bite?" she was saying.

He dragged his eyes away. "I should go. Tomorrow will be another long day."

Sophie's smile faded. "Thanks again. The meal was lovely."

He was supposed to say something polite, something automatic that he shouldn't even have to think about, but the mechanism wasn't working. In any case, he didn't trust his voice. Or any other part of himself. He had to get the hell out of this room.

Before he said or did something he could never take back.

Six

Sophie preceded him to the door, glad to have her back to him for once. She felt so exposed. All that blushing and giggling and babbling. Things she'd never told anyone. And the inappropriate personal questions she'd asked him? What had come over her?

And was he flirting, or just being gracious? She couldn't work it out.

She usually beat down attempts at flirting with a sledge-hammer. But she couldn't treat Vann Acosta that way. Nor could she quite tell if it was happening or not.

Ordering her a fabulous meal was a seductive move, but he hadn't tried to capitalize on it. She had invited him in and insisted on sharing the wine. He'd made no sexy comments or innuendos; he'd given her no compliments.

At least, other than for her work ethic and professional focus.

But that conversation had gone beyond flirtation. She had such a strange, electric feeling inside. Like they were connecting on a deeper level.

Soul to soul. The intimacy was jarring. And arousing.

It wound her up. Her toes were shaking, clenched in the carpet fibers. Her chest felt tight; she was afraid to breathe. She was acutely aware of him, and of her own body. Her clothes felt heavy on her sensitized skin. Her thighs were clenched. Her heart thudded heavily.

She reached for the door handle—and Vann's hand came to rest on top of hers.

The shock of connection flashed through her. Her heart-beat roared in her ears. It felt like a sultry fog of heat had surrounded her head.

She was drunk with his nearness. Conscious of every delicious detail of him. His scent, his height. The way his clothes fit on his big, muscular body. The ridiculous breadth of his shoulders, blocking the light from the room behind them.

His eyes locked on hers. A muscle pulsed in his jaw.

She had no more doubt. This wasn't a lighthearted *"How 'bout it, babe?"*

This was raw, stark desire.

She glanced down. His desire was visible to the naked eye. He reached up and wound a lock of her hair around his forefinger, tugging it delicately.

She swayed forward, drawn helplessly by his pull. He was so tall. Her neck ached from staring up at him. Then her head fell into the cradle of his warm hand. His heat surrounded her. The scent of his shirt, his cologne, was intoxicating. Just a little closer and their bodies would touch—and she would be lost to all reason.

His hunger called to her own. She craved it. A big, strong, gorgeous guy who was smart and classy and thoughtful and attentive, a man who wasn't afraid to be real with her, a man who rang all her bells like a church on Easter Sunday. Hell, yeah. Give her some of that. Give her a massive double helping, and keep it coming. She wanted to pull him toward her and wrap herself around him like a scarf. The yearning made her ache.

Then she thought of Mom. Her life blighted by one ill-considered affair with her boss. It was swiftly over, and she was quickly forgotten—by him. But Mom hadn't forgotten.

Sophie saw her mother in her mind's eye, sitting on the terrace of the Singapore apartment with a glass of wine and a cigarette. Every evening, quietly watching the sun set on another day, with that remote, dreamy sadness on her face.

Vicky Valente had never recovered from Malcolm. She'd never bonded with any other man. She'd gone on a few dates, had the occasional brief hookup, but the men always drifted away once she started comparing them to Malcolm.

No one else ever measured up, and she could not settle for less.

That affair had marked her forever.

Sophie sensed the same potential for destruction right now. She was so drawn to Vann. More than she'd ever been to anyone. This could leave a scar just like the one Malcolm had left on her mother. A life-altering wound.

She took a step back, bracing herself against the wall. "You're my boss." Her voice was unsteady. "This could blow up in our faces."

Vann let go of her hair, and let his hand drop. He started to speak, stopped himself. "It probably would," he said. "I'm sorry. Good night."

He pulled the door open and left without another word.

Sophie watched as the door swung shut on its own. She felt like yelling in a rebellious rage. Kicking and screaming. What a goddamn waste. Not…freaking…fair.

But the cosmic timing sucked. She was in a state of overload. On the one hand, she was trying to get a DNA sample to verify if Malcolm really was her father. On the other, she was trying to demonstrate to him that she'd be worth having as a daughter.

No one should have to scramble to prove her right to exist. Yet here she was, scrambling for Malcolm's notice and approval and respect. Terrified of not being found worthy. She didn't want to feel that way, but still, she did.

It made her so vulnerable. And that was enough vulnerability for the time being.

She did not need to fish for more.

Seven

Sophie looked as fine today as she had the day before, Vann reflected. She wore closed-toe shoes, but he knew the sexy secret of those gold toenails. She'd left her hair down today, which was a dirty trick. Those heavy locks had slid through his hands like—

Thud. A kick to the side of his foot jolted Vann out of his reverie. He looked around to find Malcolm glaring at him. His boss's gaze flicked to Sophie, who was leaning forward and speaking in a low, clear voice directly into Hendrick's good ear.

Down, boy, Malcolm mouthed.

Nothing slipped past the old man. *Damn.*

Sophie had sensed the interchange, too, and she flashed them a swift, puzzled look while never missing a beat with her interpreting. Thank God they were wrapping it up. They were at the stage of congratulating each other for reaching a mutually satisfactory accord. Zhang Wei had been at it for forty minutes now.

An hour after the meeting concluded they met again for the reception on the observation deck, where the restaurant had laid out a buffet. Sophie was already there when Vann arrived. He stood next to Drew, making conversation with Zhang Wei's grandson while trying not to stare at her. She was dramatically silhouetted against a sky streaked with sunset colors, translating for Hendrick and the elder Zhang Wei. He loved the flounced ivory silk skirt. How it hugged her shape.

Look away from the woman. Damn it.

The atmosphere was finally relaxed. The food and wine were good. After they'd eaten, the younger Zhang Wei was congratulating Drew on his upcoming wedding when Malcolm interrupted, beckoning to both of them imperiously. "Vann! Drew! Come here! I have an idea!"

Vann followed Drew over, careful not to meet Sophie's eyes.

"Mr. Zhang should come to the wedding along with his grandson," Malcolm announced. "They'll both be in the States until the middle of next week, so why not?"

Drew smiled in cheerful resignation. "Great idea, Uncle. The more, the merrier." He gave the elder Mr. Zhang a short bow. "I'd be honored to have you there, sir."

"Damn straight," Malcolm said. "You already have over two hundred and fifty people coming. What are two more? I'll tell Sylvia to arrange a suite. Sophie, too. Mr. Zhang will need to have an interpreter on hand." He turned on Sophie. "You'll make yourself available this weekend? You can go back to the city on Monday."

"Ah…yes, of course," she said after a startled pause. "I'll let them know back at the office."

"Excellent," Malcolm said. "Vann, you didn't have a plus-one for this weekend's extravaganza, right? I remember Ava complaining about it. Now you have one, so it's a win-win for everyone, eh?"

The younger Zhang murmured in his grandfather's ear. "Grandfather is tired," he told them with a smile. "I will escort him to his room." He turned to Drew. "Will you meet me downstairs at the bar later? I must drink to your last days as an unmarried man."

"With pleasure." Drew turned to Vann. "Join us there?"

"Sure," Vann said.

After the Zhangs made their way out, Sophie spoke up. "Since Mr. Zhang no longer needs me, would you gentlemen excuse me?"

"What for?" Malcolm demanded. "Where are you going?"

Sophie's smile was utterly serene. "The call of nature, sir."

Malcolm harrumphed. "Oh, fine. Off you go."

Malcolm, Drew and the others kept talking after Sophie left, but Vann couldn't follow what they said. His entire attention was on Sophie as she retrieved her purse.

She left the room, and after a decent interval, he excused himself and grabbed his jacket from the chair where he'd left it. He slipped out the door just in time to see Sophie at the end of the corridor, turning the corner.

He followed, peering around the corner when he reached it. She'd gone right past the ladies' room and was approaching the office suite that had been assigned to Malcolm.

She started to look back to see if anyone was watching. Instinctively, Vann jerked back behind the corner.

When he peered around it again, Sophie was gone, and the door to Malcolm's office was closing behind her.

Vann's stomach plummeted into a cold, dark place. He strode after her, wondering if Malcolm had left his laptop in there, unprotected. The old man couldn't quite wrap his mind around the realities of modern corporate security.

Various other Maddox Hill project specs were on it, brought along to illustrate possibilities for the Nairobi Towers project for Zhang Wei and his team. That data could be of great value to an IP thief.

He was almost running. Running toward pain, like Dad had coached him to do in his football days. He pushed open the door of the office, looking wildly around.

The room was dark and empty. Malcolm's laptop sat undisturbed.

Water rushed in the sink in the suite's bathroom. Sophie was in there.

Vann let the door fall shut behind him. He felt almost dizzy with relief. Sophie hadn't opened the computer. She couldn't have, in the little time it took him to sprint down the hall. She might have planned to do so after emerging from the bathroom, but a smart spy would take her opportunities fast. She wouldn't dawdle for one…two…three minutes in a bathroom. Almost five minutes now. He waited until the water stopped running.

Light blazed out as the bathroom door opened.

Sophie's fingers shook as she tucked the fork she'd seen Malcolm use to eat fruit trifle that afternoon into the plastic bag and shoved it in her purse. It had been hard to interpret Malcolm's and Zhang's conversation while simultaneously following Malcolm's fork with her eyes, memorizing exactly where it ended up on the tray when he was done using it. Hoping desperately that it would still be there, untouched, when she had a chance to get back in here and swipe it. He'd left it laying crosswise over his dessert plate, while the other forks lay scattered around on the tray.

And they were all still that way, thank God. The cleaning staff hadn't taken anything away yet. A stroke of pure luck.

She tucked the plastic bag down into her purse and headed for the bathroom, setting the water running as soon as she locked the door. No toothbrush or razor in here. She'd only find those items in Malcolm's hotel room, and she couldn't risk trying to get in. She simply didn't have the nerve. But she'd seen him take his blood pressure meds and wash the pills down with a glass that he left in the bathroom. That would work.

Two DNA samples ought to do the job. In truth, it was all unnecessary. She'd already tested Ava's DNA from a champagne glass at the company-wide reception celebrating Drew's engagement. The test had demonstrated an overwhelming probability that they were cousins. The geneticist assured her that the test was conclusive.

But even that wasn't strictly necessary. Her mother had

no reason to lie to her. Not on her deathbed. She'd always refused to talk about Sophie's parentage. It was one of the few things they had argued about.

Mom had never given in. Not until the very end.

But it wasn't about doubting Mom's word. Sophie needed objective proof for the Maddoxes that she wasn't an opportunistic scammer.

Sophie snapped her purse shut, washed her hands and unlocked the door.

"What are you doing in here?" It was Vann's voice.

Sophie shrieked and jerked back, heart pounding. "Oh, my God! You scared me!"

He just stood by the door, his dark eyes gleaming. The only light in the room came from the bathroom, and the city lights outdoors.

"Why are you here?" he asked again.

"I came in to use the bathroom," she said. "Given a choice between a public bathroom and a private one, I'll always choose the private one."

"This is Malcolm's office," he said.

Sophie felt defensive. "I was in and out of here all afternoon, and I watched people from our team come and go the whole time. I was under the impression that the office was available to all of us. But if it makes you uncomfortable, I'll leave. Excuse me."

She strode past him, chin up.

Vann reached out and gripped her wrist. "Sophie."

It was happening again. The slightest touch of his big hand released that feverish swell of heat, the roar in her ears. That clutch in her chest of wild excitement. "What do you want?" She tried to keep her voice from shaking.

"I didn't mean to offend you. I was surprised, that's all."

"Were you following me?"

He just stood there silently, not admitting it, not denying it. She tugged at her wrist, but he wouldn't let go. "Answer me, Vann."

"Yes, I was following you," he admitted.

"What for?" she demanded.

No part of her could resist as his arm slid around her waist. As his hand came to rest at the small of her back. The heat of it burned through the fabric.

"For this," he said as his lips came down on hers.

Eight

Sophie had spent two nights imagining how it would be to kiss that man. Her imagination hadn't come close to reality.

Her body lit up. A blaze of raw power rushed up from her depths, blindingly intense. His lips coaxed her, drawing her deeper into the seductive spell of his kiss. His fingers twisted into her hair. Her arms wound around her neck. Her heart thudded frantically. She came up from the desperate tenderness of that wild, sensual kiss for a quick, whimpering gasp of air, and then she went right back for more.

The world rocked, shifted. She felt a hard surface under her bottom. He'd lifted her up onto the mahogany desk. One of her shoes dangled off her toe. She kicked it off, then the other one, and wrapped her legs around his. He cupped her bottom, pressing her against the stiff bulge of his erection.

She twined around him, bracing her legs around his as their tongues touched. She loved his taste. The hot, sinuous dance of lips and tongue that promised every possible pleasure, multiplied infinitely. She'd never responded to a man this way. She forgot where she was, who she was, what she was doing, what was at stake. All she felt was him.

The door flew open. The light flicked on. Sophie blinked over Vann's shoulder.

Malcolm Maddox stood in the doorway. He looked horrified.

Damn. Vann felt Sophie go rigid and shrink away.

"What in God's name is going on in here?" Malcolm sounded furious. "Vann? What's the meaning of this?"

Vann pulled away from Sophie's warmth, and turned around to face his boss.

Sophie slid off the desk, shaking her skirt down. She knelt to retrieve her shoes, slid her feet back into them and picked up her purse from the floor, shaking her hair defiantly. "Good night, Vann," she said.

She paused near the doorway, waiting for Malcolm to step aside to let her pass.

"My apologies for the spectacle, Mr. Maddox," she said when he didn't move. "We shouldn't have been in here. But I'd like to go now."

"For damn sure you shouldn't have been in here," Malcolm said. "After two days of watching you work, I expected better judgment from you, Ms. Valente."

Her lips tightened. "Agreed," she said. "Excuse me. I'd like to go."

Malcolm stepped aside to let her pass, then closed the door behind her sharply.

Vann braced himself. This was going to hurt.

"And just what the hell do you have to say for yourself?" Malcolm demanded.

"Nothing," Vann said. "I apologize that it happened here. For the record, I initiated what you saw, not her. She never behaved unprofessionally. That's on me."

Malcolm let out a dubious grunt. "Gallant words, but that looked like equal opportunity bad judgment to me. She should have slapped your face and told you to take a cold shower and grow up. You are her superior. This kind of thing is messy and stupid."

"I understand," Vann said stiffly.

"Only when it's convenient for you," Malcolm snapped. "I never expected you to live like a monk, but think long and hard before you indulge with my key employees. Because it will not play out well for you."

"Yes, sir, I understand," he repeated.

"I doubt it," Malcolm said. "You could hurt her, you know. And when it comes to that, she could hurt you, too.

There are very few possible happy endings to a story like this. And all of the unhappy ones reflect badly on my company."

That was true, but Vann didn't want to dwell on it. "I understand," he repeated. "Can I go?"

"That girl," Malcolm said slowly. "She reminds me of someone I knew long ago. Decades ago. Mistakes I made that I still regret."

Vann felt trapped. "Sir, I'm really not sure what that has to do with me."

"I hurt someone back then," Malcolm went on. "I was a selfish dog, thinking of my own enjoyment. I paid the price. I didn't appreciate something special when I found it, and then it was gone. I don't even know why I'm saying this. But I don't want you to make the same...oh, hell. Never mind. Forget I said it."

"If you say so, sir," Vann said.

Malcolm laid his hand on Vann's shoulder. He stared into Vann's eyes with unnerving intensity. "Don't be like me," he said roughly. "Be better than that. You'll thank yourself later."

"Okay," Vann said, bemused. He'd never seen that look in Malcolm's eyes, or ever imagined his boss displaying pain or vulnerability. It was painful to witness. "I will, sir."

Malcolm broke eye contact with a snort. "No, you won't. You'll do as you damn well please. I know it, and you know it."

Vann sidled past him. "Good night, Mr. Maddox."

"Behave yourself," the old man snarled. "Get out of here."

Vann wasted no time in doing so.

Nine

Sophie was surprised at herself. She wasn't in the habit of shedding tears, but getting scolded by Malcolm Maddox when her guard was down—it shook her to her core, and now here she was, blubbering in the shower.

God knows Malcolm was in no position to judge her. But men held women to different standards. Even women they cared about. And she was not in that category.

Nor would she ever be, at this rate. He'd probably written her off already. Decided she was a silly piece of man-crazy fluff who would just wind up embarrassing him.

And that kiss, oh, God. She'd gone molten with desire. She was still dizzy, even after the humiliation of the scene with Malcolm.

What a mess. And she'd thought she was being so slick, whisking away DNA samples. She'd dropped her purse when Vann kissed her. Ker-plop, down it went on the floor with a glass tumbler inside it. Would have served her right if the glass had shattered.

Sophie toweled off, shook her hair down from its damp topknot and wrapped herself in the terry-cloth robe that the hotel had provided. She brushed her hair and teeth, wondering if she should check on the honeypots, traps and snares she had laid out for the corporate spy. She'd been too busy and exhausted yesterday to monitor them. She was too tired tonight, too.

She'd nab that thieving son of a bitch eventually, but it looked like her fond fantasy of impressing Malcolm with her smarts and her skills had just gone up in smoke.

In her own defense, it wasn't a fair fight. Vann Acosta was so gorgeous no one could blame her for getting swept away.

The low knock on the door made excitement flash through her like lightning.

Calm down. Could be housekeeping, bringing fresh washcloths and body soap. For God's sake, breathe.

The knock sounded again.

"Who is it?" she asked.

"It's Vann."

The seconds that followed were charged with uncertainty. Images, sensations and memories swirled through her. She felt Vann's big, hot body pressed against hers. His lips, demanding sensual surrender. That vortex of need pulling her down.

If she gave in, it would pull her in so deep and fast she might never get out.

She opened her mouth to ask what he wanted, and then closed it. There was no point in playing dumb. She either wanted this, with all the risks and potential consequences, or she didn't. She wasn't going to make herself decent. That would be silly.

Vann hadn't come here to see her decent. He came here to get her naked.

She opened the door.

Vann just looked at her. She was acutely conscious of how unprepared she was for this moment. Naked under the robe. Hair damp, flowing loose and wild over the bathrobe. Flushed from the shower. Her face bare of makeup.

No need to state his purpose. She'd stated her own by opening the door. Sophie stepped backward without a word, making room for him to enter.

Vann walked in and turned to face her. "I'm sorry about what happened."

"It wasn't completely your fault," she said. "I didn't exactly shove you away."

"That's why I'm here," he said. "To see if you want this. Because I do. If I read you wrong, or if you've changed your mind, just tell me."

She couldn't speak. Words just wouldn't form in her throat.

"Say something," he insisted. "Please. Tell me where we are with this."

She licked her lips. "It's…a little soon," she said. "Hookups with virtual strangers…it's not my style. I barely know you."

Vann let out a jerky sigh. "I understand." He turned to the door. "I'll go."

"Don't!" she blurted.

He turned back. They gazed at each other in the yawning silence.

There were so many ways to start this. Her breath came quick and shallow, and the air between them felt thick. Time slowed down.

Vann drifted closer. He reached out, touching her lower lip with his forefinger. Stroking it. She vibrated like a plucked string as he slid his hand downward, tugging at the tie of her bathrobe. It came loose and the bathrobe fell open, revealing just a shadowed, vertical stripe of her naked body. Her centerline. Throat, chest, belly, mound.

He had made his move, and now he was waiting for her countermove. Now would be the perfect time for her to say something provocative. To grab his tie, yank him closer. To throw off her robe with a flourish. Ta-da. Take that.

His finger trailed downward. Chin, jaw, throat. He stayed in that strip of space between her robe as he traced the rough, puckered surgical scar on her breastbone, then slid his hand inside her robe to press his palm over her frantically beating heart.

She quivered as his caresses began again. The tender stroke of his fingertips felt so aware, so switched on, so deliberate. Every faint touch felt like a kiss.

Over her belly button. Lower. He brushed the trimmed swatch of dark hair on her mound, then lower, stroking sensitive, hidden folds between. Taking his time. Slow, teasing. He leaned over her shoulder, kissing her throat, his breath warm against her neck. His fingers delved into her secret heat. Petting and probing. Driving her nuts.

She gripped his shoulders to brace herself as she moved against his skillful hand. He coaxed her arousal higher and higher—until the wave crested, and broke.

Pleasure wrenched through her. A torrent of chaotic, beautiful energy. Deep, pulsing throbs, expanding wider and wider, filling her entire consciousness.

Vann's murmur of satisfaction rumbled against her throat.

Sophie felt wide open to the sky. As soft as starlight. She shrugged the robe back and let it fall. No attitude. No bow-down-before-my-celestial-beauty vibe. She just wanted to be seen by him, known by him.

Vann hid his face against her hair. "Sophie," he whispered. "You're perfect."

She leaned against him, shivering with laughter. "Hardly. With my battle scars."

"Your scar is beautiful. It's the reason you're still here. It represents triumph over death. All the effort it took to make yourself whole and strong."

Her throat tightened. "That's a poetic spin on a big old surgical scar. Nicely done."

"I swear, I could not blow smoke at you if I wanted to. You're taking me apart."

"Me? You're the guy with the magic hands." She

looked him over, eyes lingering on the bulge in his pants. "What other secrets have you got hidden away in that bespoke suit of yours? I showed you mine. Now show me yours."

His big grin carved sexy grooves in his lean cheeks as he shrugged out of his suit jacket. He jerked the tie loose, kicked off the shoes, tugged the shirt out of his pants, while Sophie attacked his belt buckle.

He pulled a strip of condoms out of his pocket, and tossed them onto the bed, and then flung his clothing onto the chair. Pants, briefs and socks, whipped off in a few quick gestures.

His naked body exceeded her expectations. She'd seen how tall and broad and solid he was, and she'd felt the intense physical energy he generated. But she hadn't dreamed of the effect his nakedness would have on her. His body was thick-muscled, sinewy and taut and defined. Dark hair arrowed down to his groin. He was beautiful there, too. Stiff, substantial and ready for action. She seized his penis, enjoying the taut firmness, the throbbing pulse, in her palm. The gasp of pleasure he made as she stroked him.

He clamped her hand and held it still. "Stop," he told her, breath hitching. "Let me save it for later. Keep that up and I'll go off like a grenade."

"Sounds exciting," she murmured.

"Oh, it would be, for me. But it's too soon, and I don't want to lead with that."

"No? How do you want to lead?"

His eyes held hers. "Just in case that's a trick question, I don't have to take the lead at all."

"Trick question?" She laughed. "Please. Do I really seem so treacherous?"

"If you'd rather call the shots, just tell me. My master

plan is to make you come until you're too exhausted to roll over. The details don't matter to me. Got me?"

She squeezed his stiff, pulsing hardness once again. "Oh, yes. I've got you," she murmured, delighted at the shudder that racked him. "Right in the palm of my hand. It all sounds great. I don't have any sort of master plan, so I'll just enjoy yours. Carry on."

His grin flashed again, and he turned her to face the mirror, holding her gaze as his hand slid up to cup her breast. Stroking the undercurve. Teasing her nipple.

She sagged back against him with a whimpering gasp. The tip of her breast was a glowing point of concentrated pleasure, and every slow caress racked her with fresh shivers of need. Her thighs clenched as his hand crept lower. His lips were hot against her neck, giving her lazy, seductive kisses that slowed down time. She felt suspended, breathless, as he gripped her hips, caressing her bottom.

She struck a provocative pose, leaning over. "Do you want to do it from behind?"

"Of course," he said. "But not the first time, or maybe even the second time. It's too soon to mess around and be playful. The first time should be…worshipful."

"Oh. So that's what this is? Wow. Being worshipped works for me."

"That's good, because that's what's happening." He pulled the bed covers down and pushed her until she sprawled on her back in the bed. Scooping her hair up, he arrayed it on the pillow, burying his face in it with a wordless groan.

Then he slid down over her body, trailing kisses to the scar on her chest.

She vibrated with emotion as he lingered there, kissing right over her frantically beating heart. Any place he touched began to glow and melt into something shining and liquid. His touch was magic. Transforming her.

After a sweet, languorous eternity of kisses, he trailed them down over her breasts, then her belly. Farther, and then farther down, kissing and licking and nuzzling, until he settled between her thighs and put his mouth to her most sensitive flesh.

And she could do nothing but shiver and gasp.

Ten

Worshipful.

It wasn't a tactic, or a choice. It was a stark truth, a physical necessity, like breathing. His body worshiped hers. Some part inside him bowed before her, dazzled by her beauty. Humbled by the privilege of touching her, pleasing her. Tasting her.

She was so sweet. He'd never imagined anything as exciting as caressing her secret female flesh with his tongue, taking his time. Making it last. Making her wait. The longer he made this last, the bigger the payoff.

Finally, she exploded in another shattering orgasm. He savored it, and kissed his way back up her body, settling himself over her. "You're good?" he asked.

Sophie smiled as her eyes fluttered open. "You couldn't tell?"

"I take nothing for granted with you," he said. "It's too important."

"It's wonderful," she whispered. "It's superdeluxe. Please, proceed with your master plan. As a matter of fact…" She grabbed the pack of condoms that he'd tossed on the bed and opened one. She put the little circle of latex in his hand, and slid her fingers into his chest hair, gripping until he felt the bite of her nails. "Don't make me wait."

Vann was teetering on a tightrope of self-control. He got the condom on with no fumbling. Then she pulled him into her arms, wiggling until she had him right where she wanted him…slowly easing deeper into her tight, clinging heat.

Then the deliberate, rocking surges, jaw clenched, panting for control as he fought the urge to go crazy. Lose control.

No. He was sticking to the plan. Oh-so-slow. Until it was too slow for Sophie, and she was winding her legs around his and insisting with her body. Her nails dug into him. She made those whimpering sounds that made him want to explode…but he hung back. Just a little longer…until her felt her climax start to overtake her.

Then he was lost. The power crashed through him, obliterating thought.

Afterward, he felt her lips against his cheekbone. Her chest jerked and heaved.

Still inside her, he rolled off to let her breathe. He was amazed by her beauty. He could hardly believe she was real. He drew away with extreme reluctance. "I have to get rid of the condom," he said. "Don't go anywhere. Please."

"Don't worry," she murmured. "I can't move."

He slid off the bed and went into the bathroom to take care of it, then slid right back into bed with her, tugging the sheet up over the two of them. Hungry for contact. She was so long and lithe and exquisitely smooth. Her soft curves. Those high, full breasts.

She snuggled up close, and her pink tongue licked his collarbone, making his body instantly stir. "You taste good," she whispered. "So salty."

"You, too," he told her. "You're so sweet. Can't get enough of you."

Her full lips curved in that seductive smile. "Awww." Sophie slid her fingers through his sweat-dampened hair, exploring him. Neck, shoulder. Squeezing and murmuring her approval. "This is going to get us into so much trouble."

"Is it?" he said.

"You saw how Malcolm reacted. He's angry. And disgusted."

"He has the wrong idea about us."

"How so?"

He pulled her closer, wrapping his leg around her body. "He thinks I'm just serving myself. Using you. That's not what's happening here."

She laughed. "If you are using me, then you're doing a damn good job of it."

"All jokes aside, it was never about that," he told her. "This is like nothing I've ever felt before."

"I'm glad. Because honestly? I do not feel used right now."

"What do you feel?" He blurted out the question without considering whether he was ready to hear the answer.

She considered the question for a moment. "Hmm, let me think," she said. "Sexually satisfied. Flattered. Delighted. Infinitely pleasured. And definitely pampered."

"That's a good starting place," he said, relieved.

"Also worried," she added. "About the fallout."

"We'll get through it," he said. "We'll look back on this and laugh."

She gave him a dubious look. "I'm not sure what that means. But it sounds hopeful."

"It is hopeful," he said forcefully. "As a matter of fact, I haven't felt this hopeful in…well, hell. I don't know. Ever, maybe."

Her eyes widened. "Vann. Put the brakes on. We hardly know each other."

"We can fix that," he suggested. "This weekend is the perfect opportunity. We'll accelerate the process. We can work at it every waking moment. I want to learn all your secrets. I want to know everything about you. Hopes, dreams, fears, nightmares."

To his dismay, Sophie pulled away. She sat up, tossing her hair back over her shoulder. "Okay," she said, her voice guarded. "But let's take it easy."

"Easy how?" he demanded. "What does that even mean?"

"I'm not an invited guest, Vann," she reminded him. "I'm hired help, remember? I'm a convenience for Zhang Wei. I'll be at his beck and call, not yours. You won't have a chance to learn my secrets while I'm following Zhang around. And Malcolm will definitely be watching us like a hawk after tonight."

"I don't care." He realized, as the words came out, that they were literally true.

"Well, I still do," she said. "So don't rush me."

Sophie slid off the bed, giving him the opportunity for a long, appreciative look at her backside, that mass of dark hair swinging against her back, the perfect curves of her bottom. The pearl-like luster of her skin. Those long, shapely legs.

She uncorked the wine he'd ordered the night before, and took the paper caps off the two water tumblers that were on the tray, pouring out two glasses. Then she sauntered back, aware of his gaze. Taking her time. Letting him look.

She handed him a glass. "One step at a time," she said. "Let's not get ahead of ourselves."

"Why not?" he demanded, rebellious.

"It's not smart to push our luck."

He shrugged. "I have never felt so lucky in my life."

She sipped her wine as she studied him, gorgeous and enigmatic in the darkness. He suddenly thought of Tim Bryce and his accusations.

They seemed even more ridiculous now. He'd met liars and cheats. Some were attractive, smart, charming, but none of them shone like Sophie. Strength and toughness radiated out of her, impossible to mistake.

Sophie was for real. He'd bet everything he had on that.

"It doesn't scare you?" she asked him. "Feeling so lucky?"

He shrugged. "Sure, it scares me. So what? I'll be brave."

She came closer, placing her glass on the bedside table, and clambered onto the bed, flinging her leg over his thighs. "Okay," she said softly. "Let's be brave. Careful… but brave." She kissed his chest, her gaze flicking up at him with a teasing smile as her kisses trailed lower.

"Whoa," Vann said. "What are you doing?"

"Getting to know you," she said. "Didn't you say you wanted to accelerate the process?"

"Of course. But…ah… I thought you wanted to slow down."

She pressed a kiss to his thigh, her hand caressing his shaft. "But then we decided to be brave, right?"

"Uh…yeah," Vann choked out as she took him in her mouth.

And that was the end of any words.

Sophie floated in bliss. Her body was lapped by it, caressed and cradled and rocked by waves of pleasure as she drifted up, closer to waking consciousness—

Just in time for the explosive burst of release. It welled up from some mysterious source inside her, radiating out into the universe like the sunrise.

Her eyes fluttered open as pleasure echoed through her. She looked down, gasping for breath. Vann lay between her legs, kissing the side of her thigh, petting her tenderly with his fingertips. Smiling at her as he wiped his mouth.

"Couldn't resist," he said. "Thought it might be a good way to start the day."

Wow. She could not voice the word. She just formed it with her lips.

Vann rose up, a condom ready in his hand. "Am I overdoing it?"

She shook her head and held out her arms, and Vann rolled the latex swiftly over his impressive erection. He covered her with his warmth, resting on his elbows. Her body's response was instinctive, immediate. She arched and opened as he pressed slowly inside her.

Their breath was ragged, eyes locked with each slow, surging thrust. Each stroke a caress, a sweet lick of pure delight.

It was harder to look into his eyes in the light of dawn, with the day ahead of them, with all its dangers and uncertainties. The night they'd passed was a wild erotic dream of sensual delights. She'd been so wanton, surrendering to pleasure, over and over again.

He'd awakened a need that got bigger, hotter and wilder every time.

They moved frantically against each other, desperate for release…and came to pieces together.

Vann rolled to the side, breathing raggedly. They lay there, stroking each other's damp skin. Speechless with emotion. He seized her hand, and kissed it.

"You remember that we have a plane to catch this morning, right?" she asked.

He nodded, still kissing her knuckles. "There's still time."

"There's always less than you think," she said. "And remember. Be discreet."

"If you want."

"You don't want? You want to throw caution to the wind? Already?"

He shrugged. "I'm not ashamed," he said.

"Well, I'm not ashamed, either. But for now, I don't want anyone else to know about what's between us. It's new and fresh. Let's protect it from the outside world for a while."

"That's fair."

She laughed at him. "And to that end, you should get back to your room before anybody sees you wandering the halls with bedhead and lipstick stains."

"Do I have lipstick stains?" His eyes widened. "Cool. Where?"

She swung a pillow at him, laughing. "Oh, get out."

"I'm dismissed? Already?" he asked, crestfallen.

"Just for now," she said demurely. "Later, we'll see. Don't you need to pack?"

Vann headed into the bathroom with a long-suffering look. He emerged a few minutes later, hair damp, and pulled on his clothes. "See you downstairs."

"Downstairs," she echoed.

The door shut behind him, and the room felt unbearably empty and quiet.

Sophie rolled over, pressing her face against the pillow to bury a scream of pure emotional overload. Excitement, terror, shock, joy.

And hope. This had been beyond anything she'd ever imagined. She was head over heels in lust. She'd fallen into bed with a guy she hardly knew. She'd given him everything she had to give.

And now all she could do was count the hours until she could do it again.

Eleven

Sophie was good at playing it cool. She greeted Vann at the coffee bar in the hotel restaurant with the same crisp friendliness with which she greeted Drew and the others. No one would have known they had passed a night of searing passion.

Except Drew, who knew him well. As soon as Sophie went to the buffet for some scrambled eggs and fruit, he spoke up.

"Zhang and I missed you last night at the bar," he said. "I thought you said you'd meet us. We waited for you for quite some time."

"Oh. Ah, yeah." Vann had completely forgotten. "Sorry. I ended up getting involved in some work stuff in my room."

"Yeah? I texted you. Several times." Drew's voice was carefully nonchalant.

"Sorry I missed it."

"Came by your room, too, on my way to bed. Knocked on your door. Pretty loudly. Guess you must have crashed hard. Long day yesterday, hmm?"

"I was wearing headphones," Vann said through his teeth. "I blast heavy metal when I'm looking at numbers. It keeps me focused."

"Oh. I see." Drew's eyes flicked over to Sophie, and then back to Vann. "Well, good luck with those numbers. I hope they all add up for you."

Vann's phone chimed. When he got it out he saw the four messages from Drew from the night before. And one from Bryce that had just arrived.

Learn anything about SV?

Tension gripped him. It offended him that Bryce was so convinced that Sophie was the spy. As if Bryce had accused Vann himself.

Nothing, he texted back. Not her. One hundred percent sure of that.

He could feel Bryce's irritation in the quickness of the man's response.

Didn't try too hard, did you?

Vann texted back rapidly. Malcolm invited her to the wedding to interpret for the Zhangs. Suspend everything. You're barking up the wrong tree. Look elsewhere.

Wrong tree, my ass, Bryce texted back. SV at P Point this weekend is perfect. We'll settle this. I'll call a meeting with Malcolm, Hendrick, Drew and SV when you get to P Point. Do not tip her off.

Don't do this, Vann texted. Not at the wedding. Not the place or time.

Bryce did not respond. *Shit.*

"Vann?"

He looked up at the sound of Sophie's voice, and thumbed the app closed. "Yes?"

"The others are waiting in the car," she said. "Time to go."

"On my way." He slid his phone into his pocket and followed her.

Sylvia was in the lobby, looking harassed as always. "There you are! I had them go ahead and load your luggage. Malcolm is getting agitated!"

Vann suppressed a rude suggestion about what Malcolm could do with his agitation. "Thanks, Sylvia," he said. "I appreciate your help."

"Thank God someone does," Sylvia snapped.

The one free spot in the limo was right next to Sophie.

Her sweet scent was dangerously overstimulating. Drew sat in the front, while Hendrick, the Zhangs and Malcolm were in the other car.

"They don't need me to interpret over there?" Sophie asked.

"Zhang's grandson can manage," Drew said. "At the wedding he'll probably do most of the interpreting for his grandfather, anyway. You won't have to work like you did these last couple days. You'll be able to relax and enjoy yourself."

Sophie looked doubtful. "Ah. Well, in that case, should I even go at all?"

"Yes, by all means," Drew urged. "For backup. Just in case. At this point, my uncle would pitch a fit if you pulled out. You can be Vann's plus-one. He's always throwing off the seating arrangements by refusing to bring a date."

Sophie gave Vann a quick, teasing glance and patted his knee. That tiny brush of contact made his heart race and his face flush.

Bryce could not be allowed to mess with her. He'd never met anyone so clear and honest and real, and he was going to make damn sure all the people who counted knew it.

But it made his guts chill to think how Sophie would feel if she knew that doubts had been cast on her character. She'd feel mortified and betrayed.

If he could shield her from that, he would. If he was careful, she might never even know.

They were picked up at the Sea-Tac Airport by another pair of limos, and they set off straight to Paradise Point. As they drove, Sophie pondered the relative merits of the two cocktail dresses she'd brought, longing for fresh wardrobe options. Neither dress was perfect for the occasion, but that was just too damn bad. She'd probably go with the dusty-pink one with the chiffon wrap.

Her phone beeped, and she checked it. It was a message from Tim Bryce.

Heard you were going to be at Paradise Point. Calling a quick emergency meeting this morning before the rehearsal dinner. See you there. Tim.

She looked at Vann. "No rest for the wicked, I'm afraid. Tim called a meeting. Five o'clock. What could possibly be so urgent, I wonder."

"Count me out," Drew said. "I've been waiting to see Jenna for days. The minute I get to Paradise Point, I'm officially unavailable until after the honeymoon."

"Right," Vann said. "The rest of us grunts can pick up the slack."

"Don't even try to guilt me." Drew grinned widely over his shoulder. "Wasted effort. I'm too buzzed to notice or care."

The car had turned onto a long driveway through a blaze of spectacular spring wildflowers. Evening sunshine slanted through them, lighting up the blossoms like stained glass, glinting around the edges of the clouds over the ocean.

The entrance to the Paradise Point Resort was a glassed-in reception hall with a wooden roof made of big interlocking geometric triangles. A wall of glass at the end of the building looked out on a terrace, the grounds and the ocean cliffs.

Malcolm turned to them. "I've been told that Tim Bryce just called a meeting, God knows why. The resort has kindly made the southwest conference room available to us. The rehearsal dinner begins in less than two hours, so let's get this dealt with."

Tim Bryce was waiting in the conference room. He jumped up as they came in.

"Congratulations, sir," he said to Malcolm. "I heard the negotiations went well."

"They were fine," Malcolm snapped. "So what in God's name is so important that it can't wait until next week?"

"Ah, well, sir, when I learned that Mr. Zhang was here, it occurred to me that now was the best opportunity to show him the latest eco-engineering that Drew's team developed for the Johannesburg project," Tim said. "There's a lot of overlap. We've been keeping them in the vault until the new security technology is in place, but being able to show them to Mr. Zhang was worth the risk." He indicated the laptop on the table. "So here they are."

"And this couldn't have waited until after the rehearsal dinner?"

"I thought it was better to know right away, so that you could schedule—"

"Thanks, Tim." Malcolm snatched up the laptop. "I'll take this for safekeeping." He looked at Sophie. "Our interpreter will make herself available to discuss these plans with Mr. Zhang whenever we can carve out a free hour."

"Of course, sir," she assured him.

"Excellent. Sylvia has your number. She'll let you know when we need you." He clapped his hands. "So! We're done, correct? Or is there more?"

"That was the main issue, but I also—"

"Good. Then let's get ready for this rehearsal dinner." Malcolm squinted at Sophie. "You come, too. You're Vann's plus-one."

"Me?" she said, alarmed. "Why? Do I need to interpret? Will Mr. Zhang be there?"

"No, he'll be resting," Malcolm said. "Come to the dinner, anyway."

"But I barely know the groom, and I've never even met the bride!"

"You're Vann's plus-one, and I want you there," Malcolm said testily. "Don't be late." He stomped out, the laptop clutched under his arm.

Sophie turned to Vann. "This is awkward. A rehearsal dinner is an intimate gathering. It's already strange that I'm at this wedding at all."

"Don't bother arguing," Vann advised. "You'll only hurt yourself. And don't worry about the crowd. They're all nice people, and they understand how Malcolm is. You'll like them."

"I'd better go make myself decent," Sophie said.

"I'll be waiting for you in the front hall at eight thirty," he told her.

She gave him a grateful smile and set off, consulting the map of the grounds the reception staff had given her. She was in number 82, the Fireweed Cabin. Wooden walkways led out from the main reception hall like the branches of a tree out from the trunk, each winding branch leading to a cluster of individualized cabins.

It was a beautiful walk. The wooden pathway led around jagged rock formations, ferns sprouting below the walkway, vines and flowers sprawling over the wooden boards. Flowers were everywhere. Much of the walkway was shaded with huge, fragrant pines and firs, and stunted, wind-twisted madrone trees. The sinking sun outlined the clouds with shining gold, and the sea's constant roar in the distance filled her ear.

She found the Fireweed Cabin, unlocked the door—and jerked back with a gasp.

Someone was already inside.

The woman shrieked, dropping something on the floor. "Oh, God! You scared me half to death!"

Sophie looked at the number written on her card. "Excuse me, but my card envelope says 82. Am I in the wrong room? This is 82, right? Fireweed Cabin?"

"Yes, it is, and no, you are not in the wrong room." The

woman was young and rosy-cheeked with a high, bouncing blond ponytail. "I'm resort staff."

Sophie registered the maroon jacket and black pants, as well as the name tag on the woman's ample chest. "Oh. I see. I'm sorry I startled you."

"Not at all," the woman said. "I gave you a scare, too, I imagine. I was just bringing your bags to your room from the reception hall."

Sophie realized belatedly that the stuff spread over the bed were her own clothes. "Why are my things out on the bed?"

"Oh, I'm so sorry about that." The woman gave her an anxious smile. "Your garment bag slid off the luggage cart and fell into one of the swampy bits. It rained last night, see, and there's some bits that don't drain very well. Your bag got mud on it, so I was just getting your things out and making sure they were okay before water seeped through and stained them. I know it's kind of strange, but I figured, if it was me, I'd prefer having my stuff rescued than finding a wardrobe crisis on my hands."

"I see." The woman's name tag read "Julie," she saw as she came inside. She leaned to touch the garment bag, unzipped on the floor. It was sodden, as Julie had said.

"I took a washrag and sponged off the mud," Julie explained. "I'm so sorry this happened. I hope you don't mind me taking the liberty of trying to save your clothes."

"No, I guess I appreciate the effort," she said. "Did anything get ruined?"

"No, thank God." Julie's toothy smile blazed at full wattage. "Everything seems just fine! Shall I hang your clothes up for you?"

"No, thanks," Sophie said. "I'll take it from here. Have a nice evening."

"You, too!" Julie crouched down and grabbed a smartphone up off the floor, slipping it into her pants pocket. "Sorry. I was so startled I dropped it when you came in."

Sophie watched the woman leave with mixed feelings. She didn't care for having her private things handled by a stranger, but in Julie's position, she might have made the same call, even if it was an invasion of privacy.

Sophie draped the sodden garment bag over the luggage rack to dry and hung her clothes up. She'd thought she was overdoing it when she packed three days ago. Now she wished she'd brought a much wider selection.

She took a quick shower, then let her hair down and shook it loose. The tight twist gave it enough curl and movement so that it looked quasi-styled. She put on the bronze knit top and white flounced silk skirt that she'd worn yesterday. Drew, Malcolm and Vann had already seen it, but if she wanted a fresh dress for the wedding, she had to recycle this one tonight.

After freshening up her makeup, dabbing on perfume and sliding on her heels, she was ready. Malcolm had insisted, so there was no help for it.

Time to crash her long-lost cousin's wedding.

Twelve

Vann lingered by the entrance to the dining room, keeping his eyes trained on the walkway outside. Sophie was already at a disadvantage tonight. He wasn't letting her walk into a room full of strangers all alone.

Tim Bryce strolled in, caught sight of Vann and started toward him.

Hmm. This might get interesting.

The other man stopped at a safe distance. "You're not doing yourself any favors, you know."

"What the hell is that supposed to mean?" Vann asked.

Bryce smiled thinly. "You know exactly what I'm talking about."

Vann's hands had balled into fists. He forced them to relax. "What you're doing is a pointless waste of time and resources. I've already told you it's not her. This is supposed to be a celebration. Do not mess it up."

"I won't ruin Drew's precious wedding," Bryce said. "I'll be discreet. The fallout can wait." He gave Vann a meaningful look. "Unless you tip her off, that is."

Rage made the hair prickle on his neck. "What are you implying?"

Bryce shrugged. "It just seems strange. You've been her biggest champion, from the very start. You really, really don't want it to be her. And anyone with half a brain could figure out why. That makes your judgment suspect."

"She doesn't need a champion," Vann said through his teeth.

"Well, be that as it may. You'd better not say anything to her. Because she's the one, Vann. There's no doubt in my mind. The truth will come out, and when it does, you'll be implicated. And it will not go well for you."

Vann's jaw ached. "Whatever you're plotting, she won't take the bait."

"Shhh." Bryce's gaze fixed over Vann's shoulder, at someone behind him.

"Good evening, gentlemen." It was Sophie's voice, coming up behind him.

Vann turned around. The sight of her was like a punch to the chest. Her gold-kissed skin, her luxurious hair swirling loose, those let-me-fall-into-your-infinitely-deep eyes. She wore the same outfit as yesterday, and he liked it even better tonight. Her smiling lips shone with a shimmery, gold-toned lipstick. She looked like a goddess.

He caught the expression on Bryce's face as the man looked away. That knowing smirk, like Bryce had something over him. *Bastard.*

"Hey, Tim," Sophie said. "Are you coming to the rehearsal dinner, too?"

"No, not me," Bryce replied. "I'm just out here waiting for my son Richard. He drove up from LA, and should be arriving soon. He and I are having dinner later on."

"Oh. So your son knows Drew?" she asked.

"They went to high school together," Bryce told her. "Now Richard works on CGI for a movie studio down in Hollywood."

"That's wonderful," Sophie said. "I look forward to meeting him tomorrow."

Bryce turned a meaningful gaze on Vann. "Have a good time at the rehearsal dinner. Remember what I said. Not one word." He nodded at Sophie, and walked away.

Sophie gazed after him, puzzled. "What was that about?"

Vann shook his head. "Nothing," he muttered. "Just some accounting stuff. Shall we go on in?" He offered her his arm.

She took it, smiling. "Thanks for waiting for me."

Vann introduced her to people as they circled the table. Bev, Hendrick's wife. Jenna, the bride. Then Ava, Drew's sister, and Cherise, one of Jenna's bridesmaids.

Sophie was seated between Vann and Cherise. Today Cherise was sporting a bright purple and crimson forelock that dangled playfully between her eyes. She had a mechanical arm decorated with flashing accent lights, and it seemed to do anything she wanted it to do. Cherise had gotten her bionic arm from Jenna's foundation, Arm's Reach. She'd since become one of Jenna's closest friends. Several other people Vann had met from Jenna's foundation were also at the table.

"Nice work, Vann," Cherise said, eyeing Sophie with approval. "She's a hottie. Let me load you guys up with some of this fabulous bubbly." She poured everyone champagne, demonstrating total mastery of her state-of-the-art prosthetic. Sophie couldn't help but be in awe.

His friends toasted Cherise's progress while giving him and Sophie that considering look. Drew must have said something to Jenna about them and God only knew what Jenna had said, and to whom.

Fortunately, Cherise kept Sophie too busy to notice the speculative glances.

By the end of the meal, after numerous touching speeches, toasts and roasts, everyone in the room was buzzed on excellent food and fine wine, and Sophie was talking and laughing with his friends as if she'd known them for years. He'd never seen her this way before. He'd only ever seen her in work mode, cool and focused, or else alone with him.

He could just stare for hours, but people would notice. Hell, they already had.

Sophie looked as if she belonged in the wedding party.

He wished he could enjoy himself as much as she seemed to, but Bryce's scheming made him tense.

He felt cheated. He was in a beautiful place, surrounded by the people he loved most in the world, in the company of the most sexy, fascinating woman he'd ever encountered.

It would have been perfect, if someone hadn't been trying to prove that his new lover was a liar, a thief and a spy. And warning her about it would only make it worse.

No matter how he sliced it, it felt like betrayal.

Sophie was surprised at how much fun she was having. This was her first real opportunity to observe Ava and Drew Maddox at close range, and she liked them. Ava and Jenna made a big effort to draw her out, and she let them do it.

Everyone was so warm and welcoming. They really seemed to care about each other. And she had more in common with her cousins than she'd thought. They were all orphans, since Drew and Ava had lost their parents in a plane crash when they were in their teens. But Malcolm had looked after them, in his gruff, clumsy way, and they had turned out fine. It seemed like a wonderful family to belong to.

She wondered if that would change if she came forward with her claim. If they would close ranks against her. It was a painful thought and hard to imagine now, with everyone so relaxed and happy because of the wedding.

Except for Vann, for some reason. Vann was unusually quiet, and his expression was grim. As the dinner began to wind down, and people started pushing their chairs back to leave, Drew stood up.

"Public service announcement, everyone," he said. "Jenna and I arranged for perfect weather for you all. The moon's almost full, there's no rain and not much wind. Perfect night for a walk on the beach. That's where we'll be. You're welcome."

Jenna stood, and the two of them came together in a swift, intense kiss. Then they waved at the crowd and strolled together, arms around each other's waists, out the dining room exit onto the terrace outside.

Sophie caught that tormented look on Vann's face again. "Everything okay?"

"Sure," he replied. "Why wouldn't it be?"

"You tell me," she said. "You seem off tonight. Too quiet. And tense."

Vann drained his wineglass. "It's been a long day," he said tersely.

"Understood," Sophie said, standing up. "Go rest, then. See you in the morning."

He caught her wrist as she started to leave the table. "Wait. Where are you going?"

"To the beach. I've never walked on a beach on this side of the Pacific before."

"Not alone," he said.

"Oh, please," she said. "I bet almost everyone at this table apart from Malcolm will end up out there on the beach. It's perfectly safe. Go to bed. Don't trouble yourself."

"Hell, no," he said. "I'm going with you."

She rolled her eyes. "Fine, then. Suit yourself."

The terrace outside segued into a walkway leading to an observation deck that overlooked the sea cliffs. A staircase to the beach below was bolted to the cliff face. The gleaming expanse of wet sand was lapped by the wide, foamy waves, and broken at intervals by jagged humps and spires of black volcanic rock. There was a bright, eerie glow on the water as the almost full moon lit up the night.

Vann led her to the head of the stairway. "There's a wooden shelf here where you can leave your shoes," he said.

Sweet relief, to slip off her heels. Vann took off his own shoes, and they made their way down the sandy staircase, zigging and zagging until they reached the bottom.

Their feet sank into the cool, dry sand as they slowly worked their way over to the water. The foam was icy cold when it first rushed over Sophie's feet, and she gasped and laughed. Vann stopped to roll up the legs of his pants.

At some point, she stumbled on a rock that poked up out of the sand. Vann caught her arm to steady her, and his hand slipped down to clasp her fingers, squeezing them as the cold water had numbed away the pain of her stubbed toes.

The contact made the memories of their passionate night flare through her body, making her weak with fresh yearning. She tugged her hand free. "We can't."

"Why not?"

"Don't you dare play dumb," she said. "We've been through this. Your best friend is getting married. His uncle is your boss. Let's nix any potential drama and concentrate on what's important here, which is Drew's wedding."

"There's nothing shocking or dramatic about holding hands on a moonlit beach."

Sophie took a step away from him. "Depends on the context. And the audience."

They looked around. As Sophie had predicted, several people had taken Drew and Jenna's suggestion. The happy couple were a tiny bit farther up on the beach. They were madly kissing each other, not caring who saw.

Lucky them.

"What would it take to get us to the point where we could hold hands on a beach?" Vann demanded. He sounded almost angry.

Sophie's chin went up. "We'd have to do the work," she said. "It's not instant. It's not automatic. You know, the way sex can be sometimes. Maybe that was a mistake."

"No," he said. "That was the farthest thing from a mistake I ever felt."

"Nice to hear, but even so," Sophie said. "We'd need transformation before hand-holding on a beach could happen. We'd have to make some big choices. Come to some conclusions about things. Otherwise, nothing. So stop it. You're bugging me tonight."

"I didn't mean to piss you off," Vann said.

"It's fine." She turned her back on him and walked away.

Vann trailed along behind her for a while before catching up and walking next to her again. The silence was starting to weigh on her, so she threw out a conversation opener as a peace offering.

"Your friends seem wonderful," she commented. "What a fun group of people."

"Yes, they are. I'm lucky. Drew and Zack are like brothers to me. Not that I had brothers as a kid, but I like to imagine it would be like my relationship with them."

"I have good friends like that, but they're scattered all over the world," she said. "One's still in Singapore, one is in Hong Kong, one got married to a guy from Sydney. A couple of them are in Europe. I never see them all together. And I hardly ever see any of them face-to-face. Just phone calls, or Skype."

"That's tough," he said. "It must be lonely."

Sophie didn't reply. For a moment, she couldn't trust her own voice. Her throat felt hot and soft. Admitting to loneliness was taking this instant intimacy a little too far. She didn't want him to feel sorry for her.

She turned away from him, staring out at the streak of moonlight on the sea and the surges of surf. They'd almost reached the end of this expanse of beach, and were coming to a more jagged, rocky place full of tide pools. Without a word, they turned and started back the way they came. They were quiet this time, but she was intensely aware of Vann's tall, brooding presence. The water boiled and frothed around her toes and ankles. The salty breeze whipped her skirt and lifted her hair like a banner.

His spell was working on her again. Being out in the infinite hugeness of this beautiful place…it fed that part of her that yearned for freedom, wildness. The same part of her that hungered for Vann. His power, his energy. His sexual generosity.

Sophie climbed back up the many long flights of steps that hugged the cliff side. Her shoes had gone clammy and sticky in the humid sea air, so she didn't bother putting them back on her sandy feet, but just walked down the wooden walkway barefoot.

Vann walked her to the door of her cabin. "Wait," he said as she reached for her key card.

"What?"

"Look at this. For sandy feet." Vann stepped on a small wooden pallet placed near the stepstone, and grabbed a small, retractable spray hose coiled up there.

He rinsed the sand off his own feet, and then gestured for her to step on the pallet.

Once she did so, Vann aimed the stream of cool water over her feet.

It was yet another one of his seductive tricks. The rush of cool water was soothing. He brushed the sticky sand off, caressing her feet with his hands.

The contact made her speechless and flustered. She fumbled for her key card. Fumbled again as she tried to find the switch that turned on the lights. Vann waited silently outside the door.

She turned around and beckoned impatiently for him to enter. "Oh, just get in here before someone sees you lurking."

He came inside and shut the door, but didn't walk into the room. "You're still mad at me," he said.

"Yes," she said. "Because you're still sulking. And you won't tell me why."

"Do you want me to leave?" he asked.

"No," she said. "I want to know what the hell your problem is. So I can understand if it's fixable or not."

"I'm not sure what you mean." His voice was guarded.

She flapped her hand at him angrily. "You're different tonight. All wound up. Negative. You weren't like that last night, so what's changed?"

He shook his head. "I don't know. I'm sorry if I'm pissing you off."

She waited for more, then shook her head in frustration. "You can't say what's wrong?"

"No," he said. "Sorry. I don't know what else to say."

She tried to read his face, but it was an impenetrable mask. "Did I say or do something that bothered you?"

"Not at all," he said. "You're perfect."

She snorted. "Hardly that. Then what is it?"

He turned toward the door. "I think I'd better go."

"Stop it," she snapped. "I already told you to come in. I want you here, but not the whole night. I don't want people seeing you leave in the morning, and have to deal with the snickering and the side-eye. I'm at a disadvantage here as it is. Understand?"

He set his shoes down. "As you command."

She gave him a narrow look. "Are you making fun of me?"

"Hell, no," he said. "I wouldn't dare."

Sophie put her hands on her hips. "Before anything else happens," she said. "Let's discuss a couple logistical details. We got carried away last night, and we never talked about safe sex. I trust you have more condoms with you?"

"Only one. I didn't have a chance to buy more. But I'll make that one count."

"You'd better," she said. "But while we're talking about this, I'll take this opportunity to tell you that I haven't been with anyone for a long time, and I've had bloodwork done since then. I'm disease free. Just so you know."

"Thanks for bringing it up, and so am I," he told her. "I always use condoms. I get tested regularly, and I've been tested since the last time I was involved with someone."

Sophie bit her lip thoughtfully as she weighed the risks and temptations. He did not strike her as dishonest. By no means. Moody, yes. Mysterious, yes. But not a liar.

"In that case, shall we dispense with the latex?" she said, her voice tentative. "I have a contraceptive implant, and it's good for another year or so."

Vann's throat worked. "Whoa," he muttered. "That would be…incredible. I would love it. I'm honored that you trust me that much."

"I haven't done that with anyone, ever," she told him. "I never wanted to risk it before. But tonight, for some reason, I do."

"Thank you," he said.

They gazed at each other in a moment of confused shyness.

Sophie shook it off with some difficulty. "So, Vann," she said. "Since yesterday's adventure started with me naked and you fully clothed, let's switch it up. Your turn, buddy. Strip. Let's see your stuff."

Vann's lips twitched, but he undressed quickly. Shirt, belt, pants. In moments, he stood there, stark naked, and ready to play from the looks of his stiff erection.

He reached out, sliding the silk jacket off her shoulders. "Your turn," he said.

He took his time with peeling off the close-fitting knit top. He explored the contours of the balcony-lace demi bra that propped up her bosom, his thumb sliding across her nipple, taut and dark against the lace. He slid his hands to her waist and sank down to his knees, pressing his face against her belly. The warmth of his breath heated the chiffon fabric of her skirt. He stroked his big, hot hands slowly up her legs beneath her skirt. Hooking her panties, he eased them down.

She stepped out of them, gasping as he pushed the front of her skirt up and pressed his face against her. Kissing, caressing, opening her with lips and tongue.

She watched the shockingly intimate scene in the mirror. Her in just her skirt and bra, him naked on his knees, her skirt bunched up at her belly as he pleasured her. The back view of him would have taken her breath away if she had any breath to take.

She clutched his shoulders, swaying on her feet, panting with shocked delight at the tender swirl and flick of his tongue against her most sensitive flesh. She wound her fingers into his warm hair as the wild sensations lifted her—and then sent her flying.

Vann was on his feet, holding her steady. She barely noticed as he peeled the rest of her clothes off. She just felt gravity shifting and was aware of being lifted. Then cool sheets pressed against her back, and his scorching heat came down next to her.

"Wait," she said.

He went still, eyes narrowed. "Yeah? What for?"

"You lie down on your back," she said. "I want to look at you."

He rolled over, head propped on the pillow. She feasted her eyes on that gorgeously strong male body, draped lazily across the bed. He held his stiff erection in his hand. He stroked it slowly as he smiled, his dark, sultry bedroom eyes saying, *Come and get it. If you dare.*

His self-assurance aroused her. Without ever seeming

arrogant, he had complete confidence that he could please her. He instinctively knew how.

It switched her on like nothing ever had.

Sophie clambered over him, swinging her leg over his until she had him right where she needed him. She slowly took him inside…undulating, rising and falling, until the pleasure surged up, hot and sweet and wrenching.

When she came back up for air, Vann had rolled her over onto her back, folding her legs high. He propped himself up on his elbows as he once again pushed inside her clinging warmth and began to move. Surging, rocking. She was so primed, after what had come before. Slick and soft and sensitized. Every slow, gliding thrust made her whimper with delight.

The bed shook as their rhythm quickened. Sophie writhed, digging her nails into him, goading him on. That hugeness was opening up in her mind again, the endless space and power that she'd felt on the beach with the stars and the sky and the sea. Wild magic, wild mystery. Pleasure exploding, flinging them into that enormous nowhere together.

Sophie floated in the glow of residual pleasure. When she opened her eyes, she turned to look at Vann with a lazy, satiated smile.

He didn't smile back.

He almost looked like he was bracing himself.

A chill settled into her, someplace very deep.

She tried to breathe down the hurt, but she had no barriers right now. Her walls were down, but he'd kept his own walls as high as ever. That hurt.

Be a grown-up, she lectured herself. He'd made no promises to her. This was just a fun, hot thing for him. Women must throw themselves at him all the time.

She was the one making it stupid by getting all emotional. Like a shivering virgin falling like a ton of bricks for the first guy who ever touched her.

She was careful to keep her tone light. "There you go again. All down in the mouth. What is it with you tonight, Vann?"

Vann shook his head, but he didn't deny it. "I can't seem to shake it."

Sophie rolled onto her back and stared at the ceiling. "If what just happened can't make you feel better, nothing will," she said. "If you're so miserable, why are you here?"

"Because I'm starving for more," he said. "Because I never want it to stop."

She was taken aback by his stark intensity. And confused. "You just got more," she said slowly. "A lot more. And you've still got that sad look on your face."

Vann clapped his hand over his eyes. "I'm sorry," he ground out. "There's nothing I can do about it. I can't control the way I feel. It just happens."

"I understand." Sophie slid off the bed. "That settles it. Go sulk in your own room. That was hot and fabulous, but we're done, Vann. Like always, it's been real."

"Sophie—"

"I'm getting into the shower. When I'm out, I want the room to myself."

"I didn't mean to make you angry."

"You say you can't control the way you feel. Well, neither can I. Good night."

She made it into the bathroom just in time and set the shower running, hand pressed to her quivering lips. She welcomed the hot spray coming down on her face.

She wished she could wash away those inconvenient feelings. Be empty and free of them. Then the shower door creaked. A rush of cool air kissed her skin.

Vann stepped inside with her. His big body took up all the space, making the huge shower stall suddenly feel cramped. She dashed water from her face, and opened her mouth to tell him to back the hell off—and then she saw his eyes. Pain he couldn't express.

She recognized that nameless pain. She'd felt it herself. "Vann—"

He cut her off with a kiss. It was too sweet and too hot to resist.

Vann hit the faucet to switch the shower off. In the steamy, dripping quiet she could hear her own heart thudding in her ears, her own breathless, helpless whimpering gasps. The sounds of absolute sensual surrender.

He spun her around, placing her hands flat against the wall, and then pulled her hips back and nudged her feet apart. She opened to him, arching her back as he reached around with his hand to expertly caress her as he sank his thick shaft slowly inside her.

She rocked back, trying to take him deeper, but he kept his surging rhythm slow and relentless. The heavy, gliding thrusts were delicious, each one stoking her excitement until she wanted to claw and scream at him.

He finally gave in to her demands and moved faster, harder, rising to meet the power building up inside her.

She cried out as the intense sensations raging through her body wiped her out.

Vann stayed inside her afterward, his face pressed to her neck. He bit her shoulder gently, then tenderly licked the spot. "I know I was supposed to go," he said. "I just can't seem to pry myself away."

"You are the master of mixed signals, you know that?"

"I know," he said. "I'm sorry."

"I'm sick of your apologizing," she said. "Go back to your room now."

"Do I have to?"

"Yes," she said. "There are some definitions to get straight. There's scenario A, a secret workplace affair.

That's a specific set of rules and expectations. Then there's scenario B, a boyfriend. Totally different rules and expectations. You're mixing them up. You're not my boyfriend. Don't act like you are. That's a whole other level of intimacy."

"This feels pretty intimate to me," he said.

She squirmed out of his grip, and turned the water back on, soaping herself up without looking at him. "My job is important to me," she said. "Don't threaten it."

"I never meant to," he said.

She met his eyes. "You're pushing too hard. I need a break. I'll see you at breakfast. Good night, Vann. Off you go."

Vann didn't look at her as he toweled off and left the bathroom. Something inside her snapped when she heard the cabin door close a couple of minutes later. Alone at last, just like she'd insisted.

She promptly fell to pieces.

Thirteen

Vann had to stop himself from jumping up to get Sophie's attention at breakfast. He had to abide by the rules. But the rules felt like a jacket that was two sizes too small.

"Sophie! There you are!" Jenna called out. "I was wondering where you were."

Sophie gave Jenna a smile as she approached the table where Vann sat with Ava, Drew, Zack and the bride-to-be. She looked amazing, in a stretchy sunshine-yellow top that wrapped smoothly over her breasts and showed off her narrow waist, and wide-legged white linen pants. Her hair was still down. He could smell her fresh scent from across the table.

A stern glance from Sophie told him he was staring. He looked away.

"Good morning," Sophie said, smiling at Drew and Jenna. "I see the weather is holding for you. My phone told me it's going to be sunny and warm this afternoon."

"I know, right? And the beach last night was wonderful," Ava said. Her curious gaze flicked from Sophie to Vann, but thankfully, Sophie didn't seem to notice as she sat down. "Did you sleep in?"

"No, I've just been running around, getting organized," Sophie said. "I went to see when Mr. Zhang might need me. His grandson tells me that Malcolm and Hendrick have the conference room scheduled for eleven. That gives me plenty of time for breakfast."

"Good," Ava said. "Relax and enjoy. I hear Uncle Malcolm was doing his best Dickensian supervillain routine down in San Francisco. He's so annoying when he does that."

She shrugged. "It wasn't that bad. I lived."

"We're glad you did," Jenna told her. "Fuel up. We've got a long day of celebrating ahead of us."

"Hey, Richard," said Ava with a bright smile. "How nice to see you again!"

Vann glanced up and saw Richard Bryce standing there. He'd met Tim's son a couple of other times over the years. Richard was a tall, good-looking man with a buzz cut and a neatly trimmed beard. From the way Richard looked at Sophie, Vann suspected that Bryce had already shared his suspicions about her with his son.

Then again, any guy could be excused for staring at Sophie.

But then Richard slid into the seat opposite Sophie and proceeded to talk her ear off as she ate her breakfast, trying to impress her with his clout as a budding Hollywood mogul. As the minutes passed, all desire to be charitable and understanding with Richard Bryce swirled down the drain.

"Yeah, it's intense," Rich was saying to Ava. "There are always at least a hundred people ready to stab me in the back so they can take my job. I have to stay on my toes."

"Hmm," Sophie murmured. "Sounds stressful. Do you like the work at least?"

"God, yes," Rich said. "It's what I was born for." As Rich spoke, his eyes drifted down to Sophie's chest. "I've won six awards in the last two years. I get offers from headhunters every day. People try to poach me all the time."

"That's great, Rich," Ava said. "I'm so glad it's working out for you."

Rich turned his attention to Sophie. "Everyone in this crowd is in the wedding party except for you and me," he said. "Let's leave them to it and go down to the beach until it's time for the ceremony. There are some amazing tide pools I'd love to show you."

"She's working," Vann said. "Interpreting for Malcolm and Hendrick."

Rich blinked at him, as if startled to realize that Vann existed. His smile widened. "Ah! Dude, I get it. My apologies. I didn't mean to move in on your territory."

"Not at all," Sophie said. "No territory here. And I can speak for myself." She gave Vann a sharp look. "But it's true," she said to Rich. "I'm busy this morning."

"Well, all right. Looks like you all have lots to do, so I'll just get out of your hair." Rich got up. "See you at the ceremony."

After Rich was halfway across the room, Ava smacked her forehead with the heel of her hand and glared at Drew. "Remind me why you invited him?"

Drew shrugged. "Uncle Malcolm insisted. To make Tim Bryce happy, I guess? Tim is convinced that Rich and I were the best of friends all through our tender boyhood. You know. Childhood memories, summers on the lake and all that?"

Ava snorted. "Yeah, him constantly trying to undo the strings of my bikini top," she said. "He was a bra-snapping dweeb back then, and surprise, surprise, he still is."

"Ignore him," Drew said. "We've all got better things to think about."

"We certainly do." Ava turned a misty look on Jenna. "I still can't believe it. My two favorite people in the world, coming together. It's a dream come true."

Ava and Jenna dissolved into tears and wrapped each other in a big, sniffling hug. Sophie caught Vann's eye. "I should go get ready for Malcolm and Mr. Zhang," she said.

"I'll walk you to the conference room," Vann said.

"You're drawing attention to us," Sophie said as they walked through the dining room.

"I'm just walking beside you," he said under his breath.

"I'm not touching you. Surely that's not suspicious. We're colleagues, right?"

"And fending off that guy at the breakfast table? What was that all about?"

He shrugged defensively. "He pissed me off. Tide pools, my ass."

"I don't need protection," Sophie told him. "I'm capable of decimating any man who gives me unwanted attention with no help from you. You're acting like a jealous boyfriend, and it's visible from miles away. Please, stop it."

Vann stopped in the corridor. "I can't get anything right with you."

"Not if you draw attention to us in public like that," she said crisply. "I know the way to the conference room. I'll take it from here. Later, Vann."

As Sophie walked away, he stood there, stung.

Banished to the doghouse.

Malcolm, Hendrick and Zhang discussed the Nairobi Towers project for well over two hours before a knock finally sounded on the door.

Ava poked her head in, giving the men a brilliant smile. "I hate to interrupt you gentlemen, but just a heads-up. The ceremony is in two hours, and Bev sent me to nudge you." She winked at Hendrick. "So blame her and not me. She wants everything to run on time."

"Bev is, as always, the ultimate authority," Malcolm said, his voice surprisingly jovial as he snapped the laptop shut. "We can continue tomorrow, I suppose. Don't keep your wife waiting, Hendrick."

After the men left the conference room, Sophie hurried back to her room to look through her much depleted wardrobe. The choice was clear. The last dress standing.

She slipped on the dusty-rose dress. It was bias-cut silk chiffon with a long, filmy wrap. The underdress faded from dark on the clinging bodice to light at the skirt, and the wrap was a couple of shades lighter, with a loose, floppy chiffon rose at the hooked closure. She put on her spike-heeled strappy sandals made of black velvet, and freshened her makeup. Then she transferred phone, tissues and room card to her beaded evening bag with a chiffon rose that matched the wrap.

And that was it. She'd done all she could.

At least the bride and groom in question were incredibly sweet about her crashing their wedding. She hoped that someday she'd be able to claim those people as friends. Maybe even family. A girl could hope, but hope was a risky enterprise. The chance of this going sour was very high.

With Vann. With the Maddoxes. She had to stay chill, or she could hurt herself.

She'd tried to tame her hair with the blow dryer and the curling iron, but the minute she stepped outside, the wind whipped it around madly. The wedding was to be held out on a relatively sheltered swath of lawn in the lee of a big rocky outcropping near the reception hall of the resort. Beyond the lawn, the turf segued into waist-deep fields of wildflowers that covered the rest of the countryside.

Once she got there, the worst of the wind would be blocked, but her hair was already a casualty.

The day was warm for spring on the coast. She was fine in the clingy sleeveless dress and the filmy chiffon wrap. As she drew near to the main building, a woman came out, dressed in the tailored maroon jacket and black trousers of the resort staff.

It was Julie, she realized. The woman spotted her and hurried in her direction, her ponytail bobbing wildly.

"Ms. Valente! I'm so glad I caught you!" she called out. "I called your room, but you must have just left!"

"You're looking for me?" Sophie asked. "Why?"

"Mr. Maddox needs you urgently, for a quick interpretation job," Julie said. "You're supposed to go to his room immediately."

"Now?" Sophie glanced at her watch. "But…the wedding's about to begin."

"I know! Which is why you have to hurry! The room number is 156, the Madrone Suite." Julie held out a brochure with a map. She'd scribbled with a ballpoint pen to mark the way, and circled cabin 156. "See? It's this big one, at the end of the main walkway."

Sophie took the brochure, still perplexed. "Are you sure—"

"Absolutely! You'd better hurry. You don't want to hold them up."

"Okay. Thanks for telling me."

Sophie was tempted to take off her shoes to run back to Malcolm's cabin. She'd certainly make better time. But she didn't want to spend the day with sand between her toes.

The walkways were deserted. The timing was strange but Malcolm Maddox was the boss. Maybe he was so eccentric and egoistic he figured everyone and everything could wait upon his pleasure. Including his nephew's wedding.

Still, what on earth could be urgent enough for such a delay?

Whatever. It was not her call, nor was it her problem. She was just a lackey, so she'd do her job and shut up about it. But damn, the wind was tossing her hair around. She was going to look like she'd been flying through a storm on a broomstick by the time she got back to the ceremony. She spotted the cabin up ahead, peeked at her watch and half ran on the balls of her feet to the door. She knocked.

She waited for a moment for a response, then knocked again. "Mr. Maddox?" she called. "Are you in there?"

No response. The seconds ticked by. She tried again, knocking for the third time, loudly enough so that it might seem rude to anyone inside. He was an old man, but she hadn't gotten the impression that he was hard of hearing. "Mr. Maddox?" she yelled. "Are you in there?"

Could he be in the bathroom? Or, God forbid, having some kind of health emergency? But she had no way to go inside and check on him.

The best thing would be to run like hell back to the main hall and let someone else know that Malcolm was in his room, but not responding. So he could get help.

She checked her watch again, shoving her hair back impatiently, and trotted back the way she came as quickly as she could. Hoping that everything was okay with Malcolm.

When she got to the main building, she was in a cold sweat, scared for him.

She could see the crush of the wedding party through the picture window at the end of the building, the tents and streamers.

Then she saw Malcolm there, clutching his cane. Jenna was on his arm. He was starting up the grassy aisle with slow, halting steps. Giving away the bride.

He'd never been in his room at all. What the *hell*? So this Julie character had sent her on a fool's errand. The directions were too specific to be a mistake. Was it some sort of lame prank?

She turned around, fuming, and went to the front desk. "Excuse me," she said to the woman behind the desk. "Could you put me in touch with your colleague Julie?"

The woman gave her a blank look. "Um, who?"

Sophie's patience was at the breaking point. Her voice got louder. "Julie? Short, blond ponytail? She just sent me off to my boss's room and told me he was waiting for me there. But he wasn't, because he's outside right now, giving away the bride. I really need to talk to her and find out what the hell just happened."

The woman, whose name tag read "Debra," looked

frightened. "Ah, ma'am... I'm supersorry, but I don't know what you mean. We don't have a Julie on our staff."

Sophie stared at her, mouth open. "Excuse me?"

"We have a Gina and a Jennifer," Debra said. "And a Julian, on the maintenance staff, but he's a man in his sixties."

"But I saw...but she had a name tag like yours," Sophie said blankly. "She wore the uniform. She knew my name, and that I worked for Mr. Maddox. How is that possible?"

"I have no idea, ma'am. I promise you, I have absolutely no idea," Debra said. "I've never met a Julie since I've been here, and this is my third year. Do you want me to call the general manager? Maybe she can tell you something more."

Sophie was opening her mouth to say yes, by all means, do call the general manager, when a voice from behind made her jump.

"Sophie! What are you doing here? The ceremony's already begun!" It was Rich Bryce, poking his head inside the door. "Aren't you coming out?"

"Ah...sure. I'm just confused. Someone told me to meet Mr. Maddox in his room just now. But when I got there—"

"Meet Malcolm? Any fool knew that he'd be here, giving away the bride."

"I know," Sophie said through her teeth. "But—"

"It must have been some kind of mix-up. Come on, or we'll miss the whole thing."

Sophie glanced back at the wide-eyed Debra. "After the wedding, I would like to speak to your general manager. Would you let her know I want a meeting?"

"Of course! I'll let her know right away," Debra assured her. "I'm so sorry!"

Rich took her by the arm, pulling her so abruptly she tottered on her heels. Sophie jerked her arm back. "I'll walk at my own pace, thanks," she said frostily.

Rich lifted his hands with an apologetic grin. "Sorry. It's just that you're late."

"Don't concern yourself," she said. "It's my problem, not yours."

But Rich wasn't easy to shake. He followed on her heels as she made her way across the wide swath of green lawn to the crowd.

Rich took her arm as she stepped onto the grass. She snatched it away again. She was forced to pull so hard the gesture was evident to everyone around them.

Sophie joined the edge of the big crowd and Rich took up a position uncomfortably close to her, the front of his body touching the back of hers, forcing her to inch forward again and again. Their position suggested that they were together.

As-freaking-if. She edged away. He oozed after her. This was all her reputation needed, now that people had noticed the energy between her and Vann. Showing up late for the wedding trailing yet another man in her wake? Just call her the Harlot of Maddox Hill.

And, of course, Vann's gaze locked on to her the second she was in his line of vision. He had a perfect view up there on the raised dais, flanking Drew along with Zack, and looking absolutely smashing in his tux. Malcolm had brought Jenna up the aisle, and had gone back to the front row to sit down next to Bev and Hendrick.

Jenna and her bridesmaids took their places. The bride looked stunning in her white lace and long train, holding a bouquet of wildflowers, her hair a curly strawberry blond cloud crowned with yet more flowers. She was followed by Ava and Cherise, both looking great in clinging midnight-blue wrap dresses. Cherise's bionic arm was decorated with blinking lights of every shade of blue. The ring bearer, a preteen Arm's Reach client Sophie had met at the dinner last night, was holding a pillow with two rings pinned to it, a big smile on his face.

Sophie slid between two of the other guests to put

space between herself and Rich, but it didn't work. Rich just shamelessly elbowed them out of the way to reclaim his place beside her, to the accompaniment of hissing and muttered complaints.

The only way to get away from him was to be harsh, bitchy and loud. To make a big, unattractive spectacle of herself and risk marring the wedding.

What a way to endear herself to her new cousins.

Fourteen

Zack nudged Vann's arm. He'd zoned out during his best friend's wedding, first wondering where the hell Sophie was, then wondering why in holy hell she'd ended up coming out so late, and in the company of that asshat Rich Bryce.

He dragged his attention back to the celebrant, who was saying something sentimental about mutual trust. Jenna and Drew had that drunk-on-happiness look that used to make him nervous and uncomfortable, and now just made him envious.

Nervous and uncomfortable had been preferable.

He was going to schedule a meeting with Hendrick and Malcolm as soon as possible when they were back in Seattle on Tuesday. Lay it all out for them. He wanted to take this relationship with Sophie to the next level.

And he wasn't going to let Bryce's bullshit hold him back.

The crowd erupted in cheers and applause. Drew and Jenna were kissing passionately. When they came up for air, they beamed at each other.

Zack nudged him again. Time to process out after the new bride and groom. They'd practiced the choreography after breakfast, but it was all gone from his head.

Zack and Ava went first, and then Cherise took the lead, grabbing his arm and towing him along after them.

Sophie looked at him intently as he passed, as if she were trying to tell him something with her eyes, but he couldn't grasp what it was, not with Rich Bryce hanging over her with that self-satisfied look on his face, like he'd gotten away with something.

Postwedding chaos followed. Tears, showers of flower petals and eco-friendly bird feed over the bride. A crush of wedding guests descended on the receiving line.

He couldn't find Sophie in all the hubbub afterward, but he kept looking.

He finally found her on one of the cliff overlooks. She'd gotten a glass of champagne, and was gazing out on the surf as she sipped it.

Vann grabbed a glass from a passing waiter's tray and joined her. "There you are."

She gave him a guarded smile and lifted her glass. "Well, they did it. Beautiful ceremony."

"It was," he said, clinking it with his own. "To Jenna and Drew."

They drank, and leaned their elbows on the railing, gazing out at the sea together.

"Where were you when the ceremony started?" he asked.

Sophie shook her head. "It was the strangest thing," she said. "I was on my way there, but right when I got to the door of the reception hall, this woman dressed like hotel staff told me that Malcolm urgently needed me in his hotel room."

"What?"

"I know, right? She said he needed me to interpret. The timing seemed bizarre, but she was very insistent, so I just hightailed it up there and knocked on his door. But he wasn't there. Of course, because he was here all along. Obviously. The wedding was about to start. Which means that someone was jerking me around. So I hurried back, and asked at the desk to speak to the person who's sent me on this fool's errand—Julie's her name. And the woman tells me there is no Julie on the resort staff. Never has been in the three years she's worked here."

"That is bizarre," Vann said.

"I know," Sophie agreed fervently. "And it's not the first

time I saw her. She was in my room last night when we got here. She'd delivered my bags while we were in that meeting with Tim. She said she dropped my garment bag and got it wet, so she was laying my clothes out on the bed. Now they tell me this person I've interacted with twice never worked here? It gives me the shivers."

Vann shook his head. "I don't like the sound of it."

"Me, neither. I'm hesitant to talk to the general manager about it now. Out of embarrassment. It sounds…weird. Like I'm delusional. Or seeing ghosts."

"You're as solid as a rock," he assured her. "Trust yourself. I certainly do."

She gave him a grateful smile. "Thanks. I appreciate your faith in my sanity."

"So, ah…" he said after a moment's silence. "How is it that you ended up arriving at the ceremony with Rich Bryce?"

Vann had kept his voice neutral, but Sophie still gave him a withering look. "For real, you are asking me that?"

"Just wondering," he said innocently.

"I ran across him in the resort lobby when I was asking about this mysterious Julie, if you must know," she said. "He attached himself to me like a leech. I literally had to pry him loose a couple times. So don't waste my time being jealous about that guy. I have far more urgent problems. He does not even make the cut. Clear?"

Vann felt his chest relax. "Crystal clear. Shall I kick his ass?"

"Not funny," she said. "I want no more drama. Spectral hotel staff are more than enough stress for me to deal with."

"Oh, so that's where you two are hiding!" Ava broke in after bursting out the door of the reception hall. Her blond hair was tousled around her flushed, beautiful face. "Come back in! Bev and Malcolm are about to start speechifying. You guys can whisper and canoodle later."

Busted. He shot Sophie a guilty glance, but she ignored him as she followed Ava inside, her skirt fluttering in the breeze.

It was strange. In spite of all her issues, plus the mysterious, disappearing Julie, Sophie was actually having a good time. The happiness around her was infectious. Drew and Jenna were ecstatic to be married to each other, and everyone else basked in the reflected glory.

The party had a natural momentum. Everything was beautiful. The surroundings were gorgeous, the food was fabulous and abundant, the wine was excellent and the music was amazing. The band played three long and very danceable sets, and the music was a perfect blend of high-energy pieces to get everyone dancing and heart-melting romantic ballads.

Sophie didn't usually dance, but she couldn't say no when Ava dragged her out onto the floor to be part of a chorus line. It left her breathless and damp and pink, and intensely aware of Vann watching from the table where he sat with Zack.

"Single ladies, single ladies! All the single ladies gather around!"

Oh, no, no, no. Bev Hill was on the warpath. Hendrick's wife was the honorary benevolent matriarch of this event, since both Drew's and Jenna's mothers were gone. She was hustling around, rousting out the unmarried women and herding them into the center of the room. No way was Sophie getting roped into the bouquet toss.

Sophie tried to melt out of sight, but Bev swung around and pointed an accusing finger at her. "And just where do you think you're going, young lady?"

"Oh, no. Not me," Sophie protested. "I'm only here in a

professional capacity. I wasn't even invited to this wedding. So I certainly shouldn't participate in the—"

"Nonsense. You just get your patootie right out here with the other girls," Bev directed. "This only counts if everybody plays along. Come on, now!"

So it was that Sophie found herself in the midst of twenty sweaty, giggling young woman, all high on dancing and champagne. They were herded into a tight formation, she and Ava shooting each other commiserating glances as Bev jockeyed Jenna into position.

The rest of the crowd ringed the group, laughing and cheering them on as Jenna positioned herself, turned around…and flung her bouquet high into the air.

It arced, turning and spinning…right toward Sophie's head.

She put up her hand to shield her face. It bounced off her fingers like a volleyball, and then thudded down onto her chest, where she caught it instinctively. Oh, God. No.

The room erupted in riotous cheers.

"Woo-hoo! You're next," Ava shouted over the din. "Good luck with that!"

Sophie couldn't reply, being thronged with hugs and squeals and teasing best wishes.

Vann kept his distance during the ordeal, thank God, but he'd watched the whole thing. She was too self-conscious to go near where he was sitting, so she let Bev lead her over to a table where Ava and Jenna were resting their feet.

She sat down gratefully. There was a steep price to be paid for dancing in high-heeled sandals. She needed a break from the implacable force of gravity right about now.

Bev pulled a bottle of champagne out of the ice bucket and poured them all fresh chilled glasses. "Drink up, hon! Fate has chosen you to be next."

Sophie couldn't hold back the snort. "Fate may have a rude surprise in store," she said. "I'm a tough nut to crack."

"Nonsense." Bev patted her hand. "A gorgeous young thing like you must have the suitors lined up out the door."

"It's never easy, Bev," Jenna reminded her.

"I suppose you're right," Bev admitted. "My romance with Hendrick was rather rocky at first. He was quite the bad boy, back in the day."

"Hendrick?" Sophie repeated, disbelieving. "A bad boy?"

Bev, Ava and Jenna burst out laughing at the tone of her voice.

"Yes!" Bev said. "Believe it or not, Hendrick was quite the player. I had to treat him very, very badly for a while. But I got him in line. Elaine helped me with that. Drew and Ava's mother. She was the one who got us together, forty-six years ago. She's been gone for over eighteen years now, and I still miss her so much."

Sophie looked from the rounded little lady with her white pixie cut, eyes dreamy behind her rimless glasses, over to the bald, tight-lipped Hendrick, sitting at a table with Malcolm, the elder Mr. Zhang and his grandson. Hendrick was leaning his good ear to hear young Zhang's interpretation, scowling in concentration. It was hard to imagine him as a focus of romance, but Bev's eyes were misty with sentimental memories.

"Congratulations," Sophie said. "On forty-six years of happiness." She looked over at Jenna, and lifted her glass. "May you be just as lucky."

They drank, and Bev pulled out a tissue and dabbed at the tears leaking from below her glasses. She grabbed Jenna's hand. "This was Elaine's engagement ring," she told Sophie, lifting Jenna's hand. "Doesn't it just look perfect on her?"

Sophie admired the night-blue sapphire, nested in a cluster of small diamonds, that adorned Jenna's slender hand. "It is lovely."

"I can just feel Elaine's presence here tonight." Bev's voice was tear-choked. "She would have been so happy to see Drew with you. She was so proud of her children."

Ava dug into her purse for a tissue and mopped up her own eyes. "I should have worn waterproof mascara. What was I thinking?"

"Oh, honey, I didn't mean to make you cry."

"It's okay, Bev," Ava said. "It's just that I actually felt her, you know? Just a flash of her. It's been such a long time. I was afraid that I'd forgotten the way she made me feel forever. But I haven't. And you helped me remember."

Bev scooted closer and grabbed Ava in a tight hug.

Then they all broke down in tears. Sophie's eyes stung, and her throat was so tight it ached.

She missed Mom so badly. Mom would have known just what to say to transform all the tears into cathartic laughter, but Sophie hadn't inherited that gift.

"Was Malcolm ever married?" Sophie asked after Bev had wiped her eyes and blown her nose.

"Briefly," Ava said. "To Aunt Helen. It only lasted a few years. She got bored easily, if you know what I mean. Though Uncle Malcolm is anything but boring."

"No one really liked her." Bev's voice hardened. "We all knew it was a mistake. Sure enough, she ended up running off." She turned to Ava. "That was before you were born. Drew was just a toddler."

"And he never married again?" Sophie asked.

"He never wanted to risk it," Bev said sadly. "In spite of all the choices he had. And he could have had his pick. Oh, he had his adventures. Nothing serious, though. He left a trail of broken hearts in his wake. But all that's long past now."

Sophie looked over at Malcolm. She thought about Bev, and her forty-six-year marriage with Hendrick. Of her own mother, staring at the sunset on the terrace with her glass of wine, and her regrets.

Vicky Valente had been a one-man woman, just like Bev. She should have had what Bev had. Weddings and births and graduations and funerals and all the messy, complicated business in between. But fate had not been kind.

Sophie pushed her chair back and got up, babbling something incoherent to Ava, Jenna and Bev. They looked up, blinking back tears, calling after her as she left.

She didn't register what they said. They were probably asking if she was okay, or if there was anything they could do. But she wasn't okay. And there was nothing anyone could do.

She just had to get someplace private, before she disgraced herself.

Fifteen

Where the hell had Sophie run off to?

Vann excused himself and headed toward the door he'd seen her leave through. Once outside on the walkways, he caught a flutter of her dark pink skirt before the path turned and the foliage hid her from view.

People on the walkway stared as he ran by. A big guy in a tux sprinting down the wooden walkway at top speed must look strange.

He hit the branch in the path. One way led to Malcolm's room, and Bryce's baited trap, whatever it might be. The other way led to Sophie's cabin. He turned in that direction, only slowing down when he got there. He tried to get his breathing calmed down before he knocked.

"No housekeeping, please," Sophie called from inside.

Vann was so relieved he practically floated off the ground. "Sophie? It's Vann."

There was a long pause. "It's not a great time."

"Are you okay?"

"I'm fine. I just need to be alone. I'll catch up with you later."

"Please," he insisted. "Let me talk to you. Just for a minute."

The silence was endless. Finally, to his huge relief, the door opened a crack.

He pushed it open and went inside. Sophie was in there, standing with her back to him. "What's so important that it can't wait a few hours?" she asked.

He shut the door. "What's wrong?"

"Oh. That's why you're invading my privacy? Because you're curious?"

"Just concerned," he said.

She blew her nose loudly. "I didn't ask for your concern."

"Too bad," Vann said. "You're getting it, anyway. Please tell me what's wrong."

She turned to face him. Her wet topaz eyes blazed. "Fine," she said. "Here it is, Vann. The shocking truth. I miss my mom."

He had no idea how to respond to that. "Ah…"

"Yes, I know," she said. "And that's the sum total of what's going on in here. Happy now?"

"I wouldn't say happy," he said carefully. "What brought that on?"

Sophie fished another tissue out of the pack. "It was a sneak attack," she said, blowing her nose. "Bev was going on about how sad it was that Drew's mom couldn't be here for the wedding. Ava started to cry, then Jenna piled on, then Bev, too, and the whole thing just got out of hand. But I'm not part of their club, and I didn't feel comfortable indulging in a cry with them. So I bailed. My clever plan was to have my sobfest in the privacy of my own room, where nobody could see me or judge me or, God forbid, feel sorry for me. But no, it was not to be. I have to do it in front of you."

"Not part of the club?" he asked. "What club?"

"Oh, you know," she said impatiently. "The inner sanctum. The family circle. I'm just hired help. It didn't seem appropriate. But I just miss her so much…" Sophie pressed her hand to her mouth.

"I'm so sorry you can't have what you want," he said. "I wish I could change that."

"Me, too," she whispered. "Thanks for wanting to."

He had hesitated to touch her—she seemed so raw and charged with electricity—but the impulse was too strong now. He pulled her into his arms, and waited until the tension vibrating through her relaxed, and her soft weight settled against his chest.

After a few moments, she rubbed her eyes. "I'll ruin your shirt."

"I don't care," he said.

"Wow," she whispered. "That just blindsided me. It was so hard last year, losing her. It happened so fast. I thought I was handling it, and suddenly, kaboom. I fall to pieces."

"I think it's normal," he said. "Family gatherings, holidays, weddings. They can really slip past your guard."

"Exactly," Sophie said. "My guard is usually miles high. It's the organizing principle of my professional life, you know? That's what I do. I help people keep up their guard. But the last few days, my guard has been like Swiss cheese. And my mom is the biggest hole of all. She's the reason I'm here."

Vann waited for more, but Sophie stopped speaking.

She pulled away with an incoherent apology, and went into the bathroom and bent over the sink, splashing her face.

He followed her and slid his arms around her waist from behind as she straightened up, dabbing at her face with the towel.

"What does that mean? That your mom is the reason you're here?" he asked.

She wouldn't meet his eyes. "I told you, remember? That's why I moved to Seattle. I needed a fresh start after she was gone."

Vann waited for more. Sophie finally met his eyes in the mirror.

"What?" she demanded, almost angrily.

"You're always straight with me, so I have a good baseline reading on you for honesty," he said. "And this doesn't ring true. What is it about your mom?"

She made a frustrated sound. "You are all up in my face tonight, Vann."

"Yes," he said. "And I'm not backing down."

Sophie let out a sharp sigh. Her eyes looked almost defiant. "All right," she said. "Here goes nothing. If I tell you a secret, will you promise not to tell a soul?"

Vann felt himself go ice cold inside. He couldn't think of what to say. "Ah…"

Sophie laughed out loud. "Oh, my God, your face," she said. "Relax, Vann. I'm not confessing to murder or anything shocking."

"Even so, I can't make that promise blind," he said carefully. "How do I know what you'll say?"

Sophie sighed. "How about if I promise in advance that my secret will not compromise you morally? It will not sully your honor to keep my promise. It's just private, that's all."

He nodded. "I see."

"So? Do you promise?"

Vann let out a slow breath, and braced himself. "I promise."

Sophie spun inside the circle of his arms, and placed both her hands on his chest. She looked like she was working up her courage.

"Is this about your mother?" he prompted.

Sophie nodded. "She was the one who wanted me to go to Seattle," she said. "It was her dying wish for me to come here."

Vann waited for the rest, unable to breathe. "And why is that?"

Sophie raised her eyes to his. "Because Malcolm Maddox is my father."

Vann looked blank. Stunned. But not dismayed, which was heartening.

"Whoa," he whispered at last. "No way. For real?"

"Absolutely for real," she said. "I didn't even know myself until right before Mom died. She always put me off when I asked about my father. It was the one thing we ever fought about. But when she got her terminal diagnosis, she changed her mind."

"So, it's a sure thing? You know this for a fact?"

Sophie nodded. "Mom had an affair with Malcolm thirty years ago, in New York. It happened while he was working on the Phelps Pavilion. My mother was on the team working on the interiors. They had a wild affair, for just a couple of weeks. She fell madly in love with him."

"And she never told him about you?"

"She tried," Sophie said. "She went to his house in Seattle. His wife, Helen, met her at the door. She was mortified. She left, and she never came back."

Vann stared at her, fascinated. "Yeah. I can see the family resemblance, now that I'm looking for it. To Ava, to Drew, to Malcolm. It's in the shape of the eyes, the eyebrows. It's so obvious. I can't believe I didn't notice it before."

"So you believe me? You don't think I'm some grifter trying to con them?"

He looked shocked. "Hell, no. Why would you lie about a thing like this?"

She laughed at him. "Oh, come on, Vann. Malcolm is rich and famous in his field, and he was known to get around in his wild youth. He probably has paternity suit insurance, for God's sake. Not that it's in any way relevant. I'm not after his money, or any sort of notoriety. On the contrary."

"It would never occur to me that you were after Malcolm's money," Vann said. "If you wanted money, you'd go make it yourself. You have the skills."

"Well, thank you," Sophie said. "That's a lovely compliment. To tell you another secret, I actually inherited quite a considerable sum of money from my grandparents. Ital-

Marble made my grandfather a very rich man. So I would never need to bother Malcolm at all if money was all that I cared about."

"What do you care about?"

"It's hard to put my finger on," she said. "It was important to Mom. Fulfilling my promise made me feel closer to her. My grandparents died several years ago, and my mother was an only child, like me. And there's no one else in my family. So she was worried. Poor little Sophie, all alone in the world. She thought maybe Malcolm could at least offer me fellowship and family."

"So you're sure that it's him? There's no doubt in your mind?"

"I don't think Mom would have led me astray about something like that on her deathbed," Sophie said. "But I still tested Ava's DNA. I swiped a champagne glass at the reception announcing their engagement. She's definitely my cousin. This trip to San Francisco was my first chance to get close enough to Malcolm to get a sample from him."

"And did you?"

She gave him a sheepish smile. "I did, actually. The other night, when you found me in his office? I was in the bathroom, stealing his water glass. I'd already swiped his dessert fork. They're wrapped up in bubble wrap, packed in my suitcase. So if it looked like I was sneaking around in there, I guess I was. Stealing flatware and glassware."

"Wow," he murmured.

"I needed hard objective proof," she explained. "I didn't want to have to defend my mom's truthfulness, of my own. So I'm covering all my bases. But truthfully? I don't know if I can stand to wait any longer. It took almost four weeks to get results that last time, for Ava's DNA."

"No, don't wait any longer," Vann said. "Just do it."

"I've been taking my time, just watching them," Sophie

said. "Some families are poisonous. But from the looks of this wedding, the Maddoxes aren't."

"No, they are not," Vann said. "They're solid. Not perfect, but solid."

Sophie crossed her arms over her chest. She felt vulnerable...but hopeful. "You know these people well. So you don't think they'd ride me out of town on a rail if I come forward with this?"

"By no means," he said. "I think you'd be a great addition to their family. You'd fit right in. You're smart, tough, talented, accomplished, gorgeous. You'd just be another jewel in their crown."

"Oh, please," she scoffed.

"It's the objective truth," Vann said. "As far as looks are concerned, they've got great genes going for them, and you are no exception to that rule."

Sophie walked out of the bathroom, sat down on the bed and unbuckled the ankle strap on her sandal. "I know that Malcolm raised Ava and Drew after their parents were killed," she said. "I was afraid that if I came out of nowhere and claimed to be Malcolm's daughter, they might get jealous and possessive. Protective, even. He's like their dad, in every way that counts. I'd understand if they did."

Vann shrugged. "Who can say how they'll feel? People are complicated. But they'll get over it because they're not stupid or spiteful. And they'll do the right thing because that's who they are. In the end, they'll be glad they did."

Sophie was so relieved at Vann's reaction her eyes were fogging again. She wiped away the tears, laughing. "Wow. That's an extremely positive spin on this whole situation."

"That's how I see it," he said. "Drew's my best friend. I trust him. I respect Malcolm. I don't know Ava as well, but I like her, and Drew worships his baby sister. I know

SHANNON McKENNA 129

you. You're amazing. What's not to be positive about? It's a win/win for everyone."

"That's sweet, Vann, but it would be silly to think there's no downside."

"I don't see it," he said. "Having you in their lives is like finding buried treasure."

"Aww! Don't go overboard," she warned him. "I'm already overwhelmed from the party. Thinking about how it might have been if Mom had been a part of the Maddox family. And me, for that matter. I could have been one of them. It just got to me somehow. All the lost chances. Brothers or sisters I might have had. It's silly, I know."

"It's not silly at all." Vann sat down on the bed and clasped her hand.

"I know that the past is gone," she said. "The mistakes are over and done with. There's no point in thinking about them."

"Except to learn from them," he said. "To not repeat them."

She gave him a wry look. "I'm not having an affair with a married man, Vann. Nor will I find myself with a surprise pregnancy."

"Actually, I was thinking about my own father," he said. "He never let down his guard. Not with my mom and not with me. It was probably his PTSD, but it marked him forever. Maybe it was that way for your mom, too. And Malcolm."

Sophie nodded. "Mom never let down her guard, either," she said quietly. "She had the occasional date now and again, but she couldn't let herself care that much about anyone again. Except for me."

"That won't be us." Vann pressed his lips to her hand.

Sophie let out a shaky laugh. "It's so strange," she said. "But I just can't keep up my guard with you. No matter how I try."

Vann shook his head, gazing into her eyes. "So don't try."

The moment was so fragile. Delicate. A rainbow-tinted bubble, made of longing and possibility. With feelings so powerful she could barely stand their charge.

They made her shake with fear. And hope.

She stroked Vann's face, memorizing every tiny detail. He moved her, excited her. So beautiful, with those serious dark eyes.

He reached out slowly to unfasten her dress, working loose the hook she'd sewn under the fabric rose. He opened it and pushed the light, sheer wrap off.

Sophie tossed her hair back, but couldn't help a self-conscious glance down at the frilly neckline of the under-dress, dipping low to show the entire length of the scar on her chest. Her hand drifted up to cover it.

Vann's hand covered it first. Her heart felt like it was thudding against her ribs.

"Beautiful," he whispered.

"What?" she asked.

"Your heart," he said. "It's been through so much, but it's so strong."

She smiled at him. "It's galloping like a racehorse." She tugged the soft fabric of her bodice, peeling it down over her breasts, freeing her arms.

"Mine, too," he said hoarsely. He slid his hands down from her shoulders to cup her breasts.

Her hunger was too urgent to put up with teasing games. She reached back and unhooked the bra, tossing it aside.

He got up and stripped off his tux, tossing item after item in the general direction of the chair. Some hit, some missed. He didn't seem to care. Sophie pushed the covers down and then took off her dress and panties. Soon he was pressing her into the sheets.

Oh, *yes*. The heat of his big body was a shock to her

system. He tasted so good. Like whiskey and coffee. Hot and wet. She gasped with pleasure as he situated himself over her. The length of his hot, stiff shaft rested against her most sensitive folds without entering her. Just slowly caressing her. Sliding and teasing. Driving her mad as he ravaged her mouth with those frantic kisses.

Sophie moved against him, sensually at first, but it soon turned to moaning desperation, fighting to get him where she needed him—deep inside her.

"Take it easy," he murmured. "The longer you wait, the better it will be."

She laughed with what breath she could. "Please don't tease."

"Not tonight." Vann shifted his weight, nudging himself inside her.

They sighed in agonized delight as he slowly pushed inside. Every moment of it was an exquisite, shuddering bliss. Every part of her so sensitive, alive to sensation. As if she were being painted with light, and every stroke made her glow brighter.

Every deep, surging stroke made her crazy for the next one. A frenzy of need. An explosion of bliss. She lost herself in it.

As she came back to earth, she was afraid to open her eyes. That it would be like the night before. She'd be floating on air, and he would have those grim shadows in his eyes.

But he didn't. He was smiling.

"Hey," he said. "There you are at last. I was about to send out a search party."

She felt almost weak with relief. "I was destroyed. Beautifully destroyed."

"Same." He stroked his hand slowly over her hip. "Incredible."

"So, ah…what's different tonight?"

His hands stopped. "Meaning?"

"For you," she specified. "Yesterday the sex was amazing, but you weren't happy. What changed for you?"

His grin dug gorgeous, sexy grooves into his cheeks. "Maybe I'm letting my guard down, too."

"You seem relieved," she said.

A puzzled line formed between his brows. "In what way?"

"I think I scared you, asking you to keep my deep dark secret," she said. "What on earth where you afraid I was going to say?"

"In my experience, long-kept secrets usually aren't happy things," Vann said. "Otherwise, why would they be secret?"

"Like our hot affair?" She batted her eyes at him teasingly.

"I can't keep that a secret anymore," he said. "I'm sorry, but I just can't."

She gave him a stern look. "You will not add to my burden right now."

"But I want to stay here all night," he said. "I want to walk out with you in the morning and go to breakfast. Brazenly. Holding hands."

"In your tux?" she teased. "You naughty boy."

He laughed. "Fine, so I'll get a change of clothes. But that's not the point. I want to sit with you at the breakfast table. Pour your champagne. Peel your grapes."

She laughed at him. "Whoa! Serious stuff!"

"Remember what you said on the beach? When I asked what it would take to be able to hold your hand?"

"I remember," she said.

"I'm ready," he said. "I want to do the work. Whatever needs to be done so I have the right to hold your hand on the beach, or hover over you at the breakfast buffet, or be stuck to you, any damn place we want."

"Slow down," she said gently.

"Why?" he demanded. "Why waste time? I want to show you off. You're a prize. I want to flaunt you to the world. I can't play it cool. I want to court you."

"I like being courted," she said, her hand trailing down over his belly until it reached his erection. "I suggest that you start by demonstrating exactly what I stand to gain from your offer."

"You got it," he said as he covered her mouth with his.

Sixteen

"Noon would be fine," Vann told the employee at the car rental employee. He finished his business, closed the call and pushed the bathroom door open.

Sophie was awake and smiling at him. Morning sunlight spilled through the lofted skylight. The light showed the deep red highlights in her glossy brown hair. She stretched luxuriously, and the movement made the sheet twist and tighten around her gorgeous body. "Who are you talking to?" she asked.

"Sorry I woke you," he said.

She saw the clock and jerked up with a gasp. "Oh, God. The limo! We're so late!"

"No, we're not," Vann said.

"It's supposed to leave in fifteen minutes, and I'm not even packed!"

"You don't have to take the limo," he told her. "I just rented a car. A convertible. I got online this morning, while you were still asleep. They're driving it over for me. I figured, no one expects us at work today, and the weather's holding, so maybe we could spend the day exploring the coast together. We can make our way back to Seattle this evening." He paused, and added delicately, "Or not. If you're in a hurry to get back."

A belated smile broke out all over her face. "That sounds like a blast."

"Great," he said. "They're dropping it off at noon. That gives us time for breakfast."

"Time for the walk of shame, eh?" she teased. "Back to change the tux?"

"I'll live," he said, but flushed as memories of last night's erotic play flashed through his mind.

"Well, then." She stretched, letting the sheet drop to her waist. "Why don't you go get dressed and get your suitcase ready, and I'll do the same. Then come on back, and we'll go in to breakfast together."

He grinned as he buttoned his shirt. "Do I get to hold your hand as we go in?"

She tilted her head to the side, considering her answer carefully. "If you like," she conceded. "But you're not peeling my grapes. A girl's got to draw the line somewhere."

"No grapes," he agreed swiftly.

She got up, sauntered over to him naked and kissed him.

"You're making it hard for me to leave," he murmured, his voice thick.

"Your problem," she whispered. "Not mine."

He seized her. "Aw, hell. The walk of shame can wait."

The breakfast crowd had thinned out by the time they finally got to the dining room. Many of the wedding guests had left already but there were more than enough people still there to notice the grand entrance. Holding hands, at Vann's insistence. It made her face hot, but it was a symbolic thing. A milestone.

Drew and Jenna noticed immediately. Drew grinned, Jenna looked delighted and Ava fluttered her fingers and winked. Even Bev, sitting with Hendrick in the corner, blew Sophie a benevolent kiss.

Tim Bryce was there, with Rich. Both men gave her a cold stare. She wasn't too surprised. She'd been curt with Rich the day before. She didn't regret it.

"It looks like Malcolm's gone back," she said. "He must have caught the limo. I was going to ask if I could schedule a meeting for tomorrow. I'm going to take your advice, and meet with him now. The testing can wait. If he needs proof."

"There's Sylvia, having breakfast," Vann said. "Have her set up a meeting. He would have told you to talk to her, anyway. Let's ask her right now."

Wow, this was all getting very real, very fast. She felt rushed, but there was no reason she could think of to put it off, so they walked over to Sylvia's table.

Sylvia's eyes had a speculative twinkle over the rim of her coffee cup as they approached.

"Good morning, Vann," she said. "Looks like you've been busy."

"Always am, Syl. Sophie needs to schedule a meeting with Malcolm as soon as possible," Vann said. "Will he be in the office tomorrow?"

Sylvia pulled a tablet out of her bag, opened a scheduling app and flicked through it. "You're in luck," she said. "Usually he doesn't come in on Tuesdays, but he's playing catch-up after the wedding and San Francisco. I could put you in for ten thirty."

"That's great," Sophie said faintly.

"Done." Sylvia tapped the keypad with a stylus. "See you tomorrow."

They seated themselves near the window. Vann studied Sophie's face as they waited for the waiter to bring coffee. "You look nervous," he observed. "Don't be."

"It just hit me," she said. "I wasn't expecting things to move this fast. The documentation phase was easier. Guess I'm more chicken than I knew. I almost regret not waiting for another test."

"Do you want me to be there tomorrow?" he offered.

Sophie smiled at him. "Thanks, but this should be just between me and him."

"In any case, let's meet for lunch after," Vann said. "That way you can debrief me."

Sophie gladly agreed to that. Their eggs Benedict arrived, and they took their time with their breakfast before getting on their way.

The day that followed was perfect in every way. Not just because of the sexy little car, the beautiful weather, the stunning scenery.

It was the way she felt. The melting warmth all through her body. The company of this man made her tingle and glow and laugh constantly. They had long, winding conversations about everything that popped into their minds. There were no awkward pauses. Even the pauses seemed right and natural, full of their own proper significance.

The sky was cloudy, but there was no rain, just stunning moments when sun burst through the clouds, illuminating the sea. They stopped at every scenic vantage point, strolled barefoot on every beach. When they got hungry, they picked up some fish and chips and cold beers at a boardwalk restaurant and ate on the sand on a beach blanket that Vann had bought at the first tourist shop they came across.

That was followed by double-decker ice-cream cones, and a lively difference of opinion about the relative merits of milk chocolate versus dark chocolate. The dispute was never resolved, but the argument required multiple taste tests, which soon turned into chilled, chocolatey kisses. After a few minutes of that, someone drove past them and yelled, "Get a room!"

Vann pulled away with some difficulty. "We could," he murmured.

"Get a room, you mean?"

"In a heartbeat," he said.

"I'd love it," she said. "But tomorrow is a big day for me, and I don't want to get back to the city late."

"I guess we should hit the road, then. As it is, we'll reach Seattle after dark."

"I hate to go," she said. "Hey, watch out. Ice cream is dripping on your shoes."

They set out again. With the top down, it was too noisy for conversation, but Vann held her hand whenever he didn't need it on the gearshift or the wheel. The feeling that hummed between them transcended words.

The occasional glance or smile was enough. No barriers.

Vann turned to her when they got close to the city. "I'll take you home if you want," he said. "But my house is close. On Lake Washington."

She hesitated, thinking about tomorrow's meeting. But being with Vann made her feel brave and fearless, and naturally lovable. She could use every last drop of that feeling. It would give her courage. "I have one last outfit in my bag that would be acceptable in a work setting," she said.

"Do you need to get any lab documentation from home?" he asked. "Like the test on Ava's DNA?"

"I have the documents on my computer at home, but I also have them on my tablet, right here in my bag," she told him. "I'm all set for this meeting."

"So you'll stay with me? Can I take you home?"

After a single suspended breath, she smiled at him.

"Yes," she said softly. "Take me home."

Seventeen

Vann's house didn't seem big from the road that circled the lake, but on the other side, it opened up and revealed itself to be larger than it seemed, with a terrace looking out over the water. The entrance led to the upper floor, and corridors led to bedrooms on either side. Then a wide, shallow staircase in the foyer under a big skylight led down to a huge central space that opened off into a dining room, living room and kitchen, all with spectacular walls of glass to showcase the view.

"What a beautiful place," Sophie murmured.

"I can't take credit for it," he said. "Drew designed it. I told him in broad strokes what I wanted, and he made it happen. Better than my wildest dreams. One of the perks of having a best buddy who's a world-class architect."

He hung up her coat and turned the lights on in the kitchen. "I'm too distracted to cook," he said. "But I've got some take-out favorites I can recommend. A Thai place, a Japanese place, a Middle Eastern restaurant, Indian. And some really excellent Italian."

"I'm fussy about Italian, since it's my heritage," she teased. "Excellent?"

"You won't know until you try," he said.

"Then I opt for the Italian," she said.

Vann picked out a menu from the bundle in his drawer. "Want to take a look?"

"You know their dishes," she said. "You pick this time."

He grabbed his smartphone and dialed as he uncorked a bottle of red wine. "Hello?… Yes, this is Vann Acosta. I'd like an order delivered to the usual address. Let's start with the smoked salmon. Fresh artichoke salad, stuffed mushroom, batter-fried spring vegetables, the half-moon smoked cheese ravioli with butter and sage. Fresh greens with orange and fennel. Grilled cacciatore sausage. Panna cotta with blackberry topping for dessert. All of this is for two... Excellent... Yes. Put it on the usual card."

Sophie gave him a shocked look. "That's a lot of food. Overdoing it much?"

He poured the wine. His hungry, lingering glance made her nipples tighten. "I'm burning off the calories just looking at you." He held out the glass. "Come on back to the lake."

She followed him out into the water-scented air on the terrace, listening in the stillness for the hollow sound of water slapping the pebbles on the beach. City lights gleamed on the dark ripples. Wind ruffled the water's surface like a stroking hand.

"It's beautiful," she murmured. "So peaceful."

"I was actually the first one to buy waterfront property here," he said. "Then Drew decided he liked the lake, too, and he found another piece of land. So he's my neighbor, just mile or so up that way." He pointed.

"How wonderful, to have a friend nearby. Do you guys hang out on weekends?"

He snorted. "What weekends? We see each other mostly at work. At least until he met Jenna, at which point I basically stopped seeing him at all. Not that I begrudge him his happiness." Vann smiled at her. "Now less than ever."

Sophie raised her glass. "To Drew and Jenna. May their love endure forever."

"To Drew and Jenna," Vann echoed.

They clinked glasses, and drank. He reached out to stroke the side of her cheek with his knuckle. "So soft," he said. "It's amazing how soft your skin is."

"Usually I feel as hard as glass," she said. "You make me feel soft."

He reached down to grab her hand. "We have to stay close enough to the house to hear the doorbell," he told her. "They usually don't make me wait very long for the food."

They'd only just finished their first glass of wine when the delivery arrived. Vann brought in the food and set the table, dragging out some candles and candleholders.

They spread the containers out, and feasted by candlelight.

At a certain point, the conversation wound down into long, speaking silences. They gazed at each other, feeling the sweet, delicious anticipation build.

This looked and felt so…well…real. This fantasy of happiness, pleasure and love. It felt like a future. A family. Something she'd never quite been able to envision for herself.

Against all odds, this actually seemed to be real.

Vann stood up and held out his hand. "Are you ready to go upstairs?"

She got up and took his hand. "Lead the way," she said.

The night was a feverish erotic fantasy. After the first few wild, frenzied times they made love, they slowed down, dozing from time to time, tightly twined together.

Vann was too happy to sleep. He just stroked Sophie's hair, his throat too tight to speak, his chest bursting with emotion. He craved more of her. Now and forever.

Dawn was lightening the sky outside. Tendrils of mist rose off the lake, creating an ethereal, otherworldly realm where nothing could intrude on their love. They gazed at each other until gazing wasn't enough, and it turned to kissing, tasting, stroking. She caressed him boldly, guiding him into her tight, slick warmth. They rocked together in a surging dance of pleasure that crested into yet another explosion of delight.

They lay together afterward, lost in each other's eyes.

Sophie's hands moving over his chest, fingertips sliding through the hair that arrowed down from his chest to his belly.

"It's such a strange feeling," she said.

"Which one?" he asked. "I'm fielding a lot of them."

"Being so open," she admitted. "I let my guard down so far, I don't even know where I left it."

"Me, too," he admitted.

"Does it feel good?" she asked hesitantly.

"Great," he assured her. "Let's never put our guard back up. Not with each other."

Sophie put her hand to her lips, kissing his knuckles. "It's a deal," she whispered.

He felt like his heart was too big for his chest as the meaning of her whispered words sank in. They were taking a step into something so rare and pure and precious. He was humbled, dazzled to realize it. She trusted him. It was such a gift.

He wanted to be a better man. To fully deserve that trust.

"What time is it?" she asked.

"Really early," he said. "But I'm too jacked up to sleep any longer. It's a big day. I'll make you a good breakfast."

He bounded out of bed, threw on a pair of sweatpants and went down to get to work.

The dining room was a mess from last night's feast, but the breakfast nook was still pristine, so he set up there. By the time Sophie came down, swathed in his blue terry-cloth bathrobe, her hair a mass of damp waves, he had breakfast sausages, English muffins, OJ and coffee on the table, and was tipping a panful of eggs, two for her, four for him, onto the plates. He hadn't felt this hungry since he was a teenager.

"Wow," she said, impressed. "Look at you, pampering me. Don't tell anyone."

He poured her coffee. "I don't care who sees me," he said. "I'll do it out in front of God and everyone."

"Whew." She sank into her chair and sipped her coffee, smiling. "Scandal."

"Bring it on," he said. "I'm so wound up. I'll try to chill."

"No, don't. I like you like this. It excites me."

Their eyes locked. The air ignited.

Sophie looked away first, laughing. "Not now, for God's sake! There's no time!"

"Soon," he promised. "I'll pamper you again. Until you can't even see straight."

"Mmm, something to look forward to."

He realized, over halfway through the meal, that having breakfast with a lover was a first for him. He never stayed with anyone all through the night. Never wanted to.

But everything about Sophie was different. New.

After breakfast they got dressed. Sophie was as stunning as ever when she was all put together, in a silver-gray linen tunic over matching wide-legged trousers and gray suede pumps. Her hair was loose, styled in long waves and curls. Her lips were a glossy red, and her whiskey-colored eyes were full of mystery as she looked him over. "Nice suit," she said. "I think we're both presentable."

"Should we take the convertible to go to work?"

"I wish." She shook her head with a regretful smile. "I'd ruin my hair. Not today."

"No problem," he assured her. "We can take my Jag."

Morning traffic was what it always was in Seattle, but he was too euphoric to be frustrated today. It meant more time with Sophie. And as early as they'd risen, they got there with time to spare.

"Can you let me out at the front entrance?" Sophie asked as they got closer to the downtown office. "I need to take care of some things before the rest of the staff gets in."

He pulled over in front of the building. "I'll be at your office at 12:15."

She had a shadow of lingering doubt on her face. "Shouldn't we just meet at the restaurant? For now, anyway?"

He shook his head, resolute. "We're through with that now. Onward."

She gave him a smile that made his body tingle. "You are just on fire today, Vann."

"You lit the flame," he said.

Her laughter sounded happy. "Okay, fine. My office, then. Later."

"Good luck with the meeting," he called. "I know it'll be fine. He's a lucky man."

Her smile left him just staring helplessly after her until the cars started beeping impatiently behind him.

Vann floated through the morning in a haze. Then Zack leaned inside his office.

"Hey," he said. "Do you have a quick debrief for me before I go to Malcolm's office?"

Vann looked at him blankly. "Debrief about what?"

Zack frowned. "Your info-gathering project? Sophie Valente? The IP theft?"

"Oh, that. I'll give you the short version. Not her. Look elsewhere."

Zack's face froze. Then he stepped inside and closed the door behind him. "You're sure of this?" he said. "You have proof?"

"You need to prove guilt, not innocence," Vann said. "I know her now."

"What, in the biblical sense?"

Vann stood up. "What the hell is that supposed to mean?"

"Sorry," Zack said. "I guess that wasn't appropriate."

"No, it wasn't," Vann said through his teeth. "What I

meant was, I know exactly what Sophie Valente is after here at Maddox Hill. And it's not money."

"So what is it?"

Vann hesitated. "I'll leave that for her to reveal. It's not my place to tell."

"She'd better hurry up about it," Zack said. "And she better be prepared to defend herself. From what I heard Bryce say, he's got her in the bag."

A chill seized him. "Bryce is full of shit."

"I won't say you're wrong, but if he has the ironclad proof he says he has, Sophie's in trouble."

"Bryce can't have proof," Vann said. "He's going down a dead end."

"Be that as it may, he's meeting with Malcolm now," Zack told him. "Explaining his discoveries."

"But Sophie was supposed to meet with him. In just a few minutes, in fact. We were supposed to talk with Malcolm and Bryce about all this tomorrow."

"Malcolm got in early," Zack said. "I heard him complaining about Sylvia scheduling back-to-back meetings this morning. Evidently Bryce couldn't wait until tomorrow. He looked buzzed. I was just going there, but I wanted to check in with you first."

"He can't be showing Malcolm what he discovered," Vann repeated. "There's nothing to discover! I'll go and tell Malcolm myself."

"Steady, now," Zack cautioned. "You're not currently in the best position to come to Sophie Valente's defense. Keep that in mind."

"Because I'm in love with her, you mean?" Vann said. "I'm not ashamed of it."

Zack winced. "This is worse than I thought."

Vann was already out the door. Zack caught up and kept pace with him as he made his way to Malcolm's office. Sylvia gave him a disapproving look as he approached.

"I'm going in to see Malcolm," he said.

"And a pleasant good morning to you, too, Vann. I'm sorry, but you can't quite go in yet! Tim Bryce is in there with him. Vann…hey! Vann, he's in a meeting!"

Malcolm's office door flew open. Malcolm poked his head out. "Sylvia!" he bawled. "Get Zack and Vann in here right—oh, there you are. Get your butts in here this instant."

Vann and Zack filed past Sylvia. She leaned in the door. "Do you gentlemen need coffee or—"

"They can drink coffee on their own damn time," Malcolm snarled. "Leave us."

Sylvia quickly closed the door. Malcolm's face was splotchy with anger as he rounded on them. "You two have been keeping secrets from me, eh?"

"No, we haven't," Zack said evenly. "We've been taking care of business, just like we always do."

Malcolm gestured at Vann. "I've seen some of his business lately. I'm not impressed."

"You've got it wrong, Malcolm," Vann said.

"No, he doesn't," Bryce said. "On the contrary, I think he's nailed it. Quite literally." Bryce chortled at his own joke, but the snickering died out as Vann fixed his icy gaze on him. "It's her," he said, his voice triumphant. "What I just showed Malcolm is airtight."

Vann breathed down the urge to punch that smug, self-satisfied look right off Bryce's smirking face. "What do you think you've got on her?"

"I don't think it, I know it. Look for yourself. I have a video of Sophie Valente stealing documents out of Malcolm's laptop."

"That's impossible," Vann said.

"It's a fact," Malcolm said heavily. "I saw it. The video is time-stamped. She's in the dress she wore at the wedding. I recognize my hotel room. There's no mistaking her. To think I invited a lying thief to my own nephew's wedding and let her mix with all the people I care most about. And the sensitive information she heard in the Zhang Wei meetings, God help us."

"I thought Vann's plan was to get more information before we went any further with our investigation." Bryce's voice was oily with insinuation. "Looks like he took the job more literally than we ever dreamed."

Zack blew out a sharp breath. "I want to see that video, right now."

They circled the desk and gathered around the monitor. Bryce edged closer but kept the length of the desk between himself and Vann. "I rigged cameras on the walkway leading to your room at Paradise Point," Bryce began.

"I doubt that's legal," Zack said. "Privacy laws—"

"Shut up and watch," Malcolm said. "Show them the clip from the walkway."

Bryce tapped the mouse and set the video clip to play. The camera was trained on one of the wooden walkways at Paradise Point, the rhododendron branches swaying gently and casting shadows on the weathered planks.

Sophie appeared, walking briskly and purposefully. She paused, frowning, and lifted her arm to check the time on her glittering gold wristwatch. She moved swiftly out of the camera's frame.

"You will all agree that's Sophie Valente. Correct?" Bryce said.

Vann ignored the question. "What time was it?"

"The video clock shows that it was 3:51," Bryce replied. "The ceremony began less than ten minutes later. She picked her time carefully. Everyone was already assembled on the lawn for the wedding. Now look at this." He fast-forwarded until there was another flash of pink, then ran the video back and set it to Play.

It was Sophie again, coming back the other way. Still

frowning. The wind tossed her hair over her face. This time, she was almost running.

"Four minutes and twenty-five seconds," Bryce said. "Just a couple of minutes after that, Rich saw her in the entrance hall and told her she was late for the ceremony. The two of them came in together, as I'm sure you noticed."

Vann looked into Bryce's face, his gaze unwavering. "Sophie told me that a woman who claimed to be on the resort staff told her to go to Malcolm's suite right before the wedding was scheduled to begin."

Malcolm made a derisive sound. "My suite? Right before the ceremony? What for? That's absurd!"

"She thought so, too," Vann said. "This mystery person told her that you were there and that you needed her to interpret something. Obviously, she found no one in the room. She said she knocked, waited for a couple of minutes—"

"Four minutes and twenty-five seconds, to be exact," Bryce said. "That's how long she was inside his suite."

"She never went inside," Vann said. "She and I discussed it. And they told her at the front desk that the woman who sent her to Malcolm's room had never worked there."

"Well now," Malcolm said. "Isn't that convenient."

"Are you interested in seeing what happened in Malcolm's room during that interval, or not?" Bryce asked.

"For God's sake, Tim, just play the damn thing," Malcolm growled. "Gloating is in poor taste, and I'm not in the mood."

Bryce tapped on the keyboard for a moment. "I'm emailing a courtesy copy of these clips to both of you," he said. "Review them at your leisure." He shot a sly glance at Vann. "Something to remember her by?"

"Tim!" Malcolm barked. "What did I just say?"

"Sorry." Bryce hit Play and stepped back. "Enjoy."

The video was shot from the wall behind the desk. The

room was dimly lit. At 4:34, they saw a dark silhouette position herself on the desk chair in front of the open laptop.

The figure reached out to hit the mouse, and the computer came to life, flooding the figure in the chair with cool blue light.

It was Sophie, in that same silk chiffon thing she'd worn at the wedding. She stared into the screen, seeming serene and absorbed, typed rapidly for a moment and then lifted her phone, as she'd done in the video Bryce had shown them the previous week, before the San Francisco trip. She was taking pictures of the screen.

"I loaded the laptop with dummy files," Bryce said. "Just for her. They look very convincing, but all the details and calculations have been scrambled. Her buyer is going to be very angry. I'm afraid our bad little girl is in for quite a spanking."

"Don't talk about her that way," Vann growled.

"Not another word out of you," Malcolm said. "You're in no position to criticize."

The video continued. Just Sophie looking calmly into the screen. She would lift the phone, focus, snap the picture. Lift, focus, snap. Her long hair hung over her shoulders, the waves and curls smoothly arranged.

At a certain point, she dropped her phone into her beaded bag and put the computer to sleep. A blurry shifting of shadows in the dark, a brightening as she opened the door to leave—and it was over.

Vann felt rooted to the ground. His brain seemed frozen. It wouldn't process this information. The woman he knew, the woman he was in love with—she could not have done this. It just…wasn't…possible.

"Well?" Bryce said. "Does that satisfy you?"

"*Satisfy* is not the word I'd use," Malcolm said slowly. "But it's certainly damning evidence. I don't think I need anything more to be convinced of her guilt. Not much more to say about it, eh, Vann?"

"You have to let her defend herself," Vann said. "She may have an explanation. Something we don't know about. Something we've overlooked."

"What explanation can she have for being inside my private room?" Malcolm demanded. "Now that I think about it, she turned up in my guest office in the San Francisco meeting, too. Remember? That's where I found the two of you, as I recall. Did she go in before you went in, Vann?"

Vann had to force himself to speak. "Yes. A couple of minutes before me. I saw her heading in there, and chased after her to see if she was up to anything. She wasn't."

"So she hadn't told you to meet her there," Malcolm persisted.

"No," Vann admitted reluctantly. "I surprised her."

"And she distracted you by coming on to you," Bryce said, smirking. "Well, that's a classic move. Nothing like sex to distract a man. I hardly blame you. Except that I do."

"Shut up, Tim," Malcolm said. "There is nothing amusing about this situation. So she might have been snooping around on my computer in there, too."

"No," Vann said. "She didn't go near your computer. She was in the bathroom."

"Really?" Malcolm grunted. "Public ladies' room not good enough for her, then?"

Vann didn't answer. His face felt numb.

"Well, Vann?" Malcolm said. "You've got your work cut out for you."

Vann looked at him, baffled. "Come again? What work?"

"You're the one who has to do it," Malcolm went on. "You know her best."

"Do what?"

Malcolm made an impatient sound. "Stop playing dumb.

Get her to come clean about everything she's done up to now. Every detail, every dollar. Do it, if you care about her at all. Persuade her to cooperate. I'll be as lenient as I possibly can if she does."

His mouth was bone-dry. He forced out a rasping croak. "I can't."

"It has to be you," Malcolm said. "Would you rather she spend the best years of her life in jail? Don't make me be the bad guy here, Vann. Help me out. Help her out."

The intercom buzzed. "Mr. Maddox?" Sylvia said. "Ms. Valente is here for your ten-thirty meeting. Shall I have her wait until you gentlemen have finished, or shall I reschedule her for later on?"

"No, Sylvia, send her on in," Malcolm said.

"Are you sure?" Sylvia sounded baffled. "With everyone still there?"

"Exactly." Malcolm glared around at each of them. "Why drag this out?"

The worst-case scenario was unfolding before Vann's eyes with terrifying speed. His belly clenched with dread. Then the door opened and Sophie walked in.

Suddenly, all at once, Vann remembered the powerful rationale he'd always instinctively understood for keeping up one's guard. Love had made him forget that basic, elemental rule of nature.

You kept up your guard to not get annihilated.

Eighteen

Sophie stopped the minute she entered Malcolm's office, startled to see so many people there. Including Vann.

He didn't smile. In fact, his face was a blank, tight mask. It reminded her of something sad, something painful. It came to her after a split second.

Mom's face, that last, terrible week before she died. It was the bloodless tension in a person's expression when they were trying not to show intense pain. She almost asked Vann if he was okay, but then Malcolm spoke.

"Good morning, Ms. Valente."

She turned back to Malcolm, who was behind his desk with Zack Austin and Tim Bryce, of all people. "Sorry to interrupt," she said. "I can find a better time if—"

"Not at all," Malcolm said. "Go on. Say whatever you need to say."

Sophie was taken aback. Something was off, and she was smack-dab in the middle of it, with no clue. "Are you sure—"

"I am. Please, just say it, whatever it is. Out with it."

Oh-kayyyy…fine. She took a careful, calming breath. "Actually, what I wanted to discuss with you is of a private nature. I'd prefer to speak with you alone."

Malcolm studied her from under heavy, furrowed eyebrows. "I think not," he said. "Anything you have to say can certainly be said in front of these people."

This was all wrong, and it gave her chills. But it wasn't like she could retreat in confusion. That would look mealymouthed and cowardly and just…well, weird. As if she were somehow in the wrong. Trying to hide something, trying to pull something.

What the hell. She'd do this for Mom. If this bombed, she'd just leave this place forever and start fresh elsewhere. She gave Vann another swift glance, hoping for a smile, a signal. Any sign of solidarity.

He wasn't even looking at her. It was starting to scare her.

"I came in to see you because I have something important and very personal to tell you," she said. "It involves us both."

"Tell it," Malcolm said. But he did not beckon for her to move closer to his desk, nor did he offer her a chair.

Tim grabbed a chair and sat down, looking at her like she was the main attraction. What on earth?

"Bryce," Zack said under his breath. "Do not start."

"I didn't say a word," Tim said. "Don't mind me. I'm just watching the show."

That pissed her off too much to keep silent. "I didn't come in here to put on a show for you, Tim."

"I guess that remains to be seen, hmm?"

Sophie turned her attention from him and approached Malcolm's desk despite his marked lack of an invitation. She'd be damned if she was going to cower by the door, ready to bolt like a scared little bunny.

She squared her shoulders. "I asked for this meeting because I have decided to tell you that I am your biological daughter," she announced.

Malcolm's face was absolutely blank as seconds of painful silence ticked by.

She wanted to break the silence, but it was his place to make the next move. Tim's mouth hung open. Zack looked startled. The only one who didn't look shocked was Vann—but he still looked like he was hiding mortal agony behind a mask.

She looked back at Malcolm. His eyes were downcast now.

"I see. So… Vicky," he said hoarsely. He coughed to

clear his throat. "You're Vicky Valente's daughter, correct? You look like her. I noticed your surname when you were introduced. It's not an uncommon name, so I never dreamed you might be related to her."

And to you. "So you remember her?"

He put his hand up to his eyes. "Of course I remember Vicky. How is she?"

"She died, not long ago," Sophie said. "April of last year. Pancreatic cancer."

Malcolm covered his eyes again. Almost a minute went by before he cleared his throat with a sharp cough. "I'm very sorry to hear that," he said. "You have my sincere condolences."

"Thank you," Sophie said, bemused. And then she just stood there, in the awkward silence. Waiting.

This was so weird. The hard part was done. He hadn't thrown her out, or yelled at her, or laughed in her face, or called her a liar. He hadn't denied ever knowing her mother. Those were the outcomes she had feared, and none of them had come to pass.

So why did the air still feel so thick in here? And why did Vann and Zack look like they were being forced to witness an execution?

Tim, on the other hand, looked like he should be munching buttered popcorn.

"So you believe my claim?" she asked. "I was born in New York City, nine months after you and she worked together on the Phelps Pavilion."

"I do not disbelieve it." Malcolm's voice was expressionless.

Sophie pulled her tablet out of her bag, opening the files. "This is my birth certificate. I got a sample of Ava's DNA several weeks ago. I had it analyzed by a local genetics lab, and these are the results. As you can see, there's an overwhelming probability that she's my close relative. At least a cousin."

"I see." Malcolm didn't even lean forward to look at the birth certificate or the genetics lab test results. Which was not promising.

"I also took the opportunity to get a sample of your DNA when we were in San Francisco," she said. "Not because of any doubts I had, since I believe what Mom told me, but just because I wanted objective proof, for your sake. I took a fork and a water glass from your office in San Francisco. But then I decided I couldn't wait to have the results analyzed to speak to you. The stress of keeping this secret was getting to me."

"This explains a lot," Tim said.

"Your contribution was not requested, Tim," Malcolm said.

Tim made a lip-zipping gesture. Sophie looked around at all the men present in the room and threw up her hands. "This explains what?" she demanded.

But no one answered. "Come on, people!" she said. "What the hell is going on in here? What aren't you telling me?"

"One thing at a time," Malcolm said. "Why didn't you tell me immediately? You've been working here for months. Why not come to me before?"

"I wanted to line up objective, scientific proof," Sophie said. "Plus, I had to work up the nerve. I couldn't just pop out of nowhere with an announcement like that."

"I see," he said. "And what exactly did you hope to gain from this revelation?"

Sophie flinched inwardly. It wasn't a surprise, of course, but it still hurt, that he would automatically assume that her motives were just money-grubbing avarice.

"Nothing financial, if that's what you're wondering," she said. "I have many hard-won and highly marketable professional skills. I could make an excellent living any-where in the world that I chose to go. I also have inherited a considerable amount of money and property from my mother's side of the family. I own homes in Singapore, New York City, the Catskills, Florence and Positano. I don't need one penny from you. I wouldn't even need to work, strictly speaking, but I wasn't cut out to be a bored social-ite. I need challenge in my life."

Malcolm cleared his throat. "It's a lot to take in all at once. So if you are independently wealthy as you say, then what do want from me, Ms. Valente?"

Damn. It was a bad sign if he had to ask.

"Please, call me Sophie," she said stiffly. "My mother asked me to come to you. It was a deathbed request. She wanted us to know each other. She was worried about the fact that I have no living family left. It's mostly for her sake that I'm here. I promised her I'd come and tell you about myself."

She and Malcolm stared at each other. Her heart sank. Malcolm didn't look angry, or defensive, or even suspi-cious. Just sad.

"I would be satisfied just to be known to you," she said hesitantly. "And acknowledged by you. I would be open to us getting to know each other as people, if that interests you. I've enjoyed my time working here, and I've done my best for the company. I'd also like to get acquainted with my cousins. Ava and Drew seem well worth knowing."

"That they are," he said.

Sophie tapped on the tablet, opening the file of pho-tographs. "I have pictures of my mother and me over the years, if you'd care to take a look."

For this, Malcolm did lean forward. He swiped through more than fifty pictures, studying each one for many long moments. Finally, he closed the file, pushing the tablet sharply away. "You can take that back."

She slid the device back into her bag, chilled. "So where do we go from here?"

Malcolm wrapped his arms over his chest. "That depends entirely upon you."

"Me?" She shook her head, confused. "Not at all, Mr. Maddox. I've made my move. It's your turn, to either respond to it or not. As you prefer."

Once again, that cool stare, like he was waiting for something more from her.

Something that he thought he was owed.

Which seemed backward. She'd given him everything she had to offer. She'd displayed her most intimate memories, for God's sake. Showing him that file was like pulling a piece of her heart out of her chest and handing it over to a stranger. Not knowing if it would be flung back into her face or not.

Malcolm made an impatient huffing sound. "Come on now, Ms. Valente. Is there anything else important that you need to tell us today?"

She was confused. "Excuse me? Does this issue not seem important enough to warrant a private meeting with you?"

"Skip the snark, please. Do you have anything else to say, beyond your genetic revelation?"

Sophie studied each of the people in the room in turn. She had the uncomfortable feeling that some inexplicable trap was about to spring shut on her.

She shook her head. "Nothing," she said. "This was the sum total of my agenda for today."

"Oh, enough of your bullshit." Malcolm slapped his hand down on the desk, making everything on it rattle.

Sophie jerked back, startled. "What on earth? What bullshit?"

"Come on, girl! For your mother's sake, and for everything that I should have done for you while you were growing up, I'll give you a pass. But you've got to come clean!"

"Come clean about what? A pass on what? Explain yourself, for God's sake!"

Malcolm shook his head. "Don't play dumb with me. I'll go easy on you, on the condition that you cooperate completely with our internal investigative team, and then swear never to contact me or my family ever again. But for that, you have to confess."

"But...what are you suggesting that I—"

"God knows, I'd want to get back at me, too, if I were you," he said.

"Get back at you? Hold on." Sophie sucked in a shocked breath. "Oh, my God. You think I'm the one who's been selling Maddox Hill proprietary IP to China?"

"Oh, so you know about that!" Malcolm's voice rang out in challenge.

"Of course I know! I found out right after I got here. But I didn't know who I could trust here, so my plan was to unearth the thief myself and serve you his head on a plate before I even told you we were related. But it turned out to be a slower business than I anticipated."

Tim shook his head in disbelief. "Can you believe this?" he said. "She's still playing the innocent. She waltzes in here, gets a job on false pretenses—"

"I never misrepresented myself!" she said sharply. "I gave one hundred percent to my work here!"

Tim snorted. "A little more than a hundred percent, from what I can tell."

"Shut up, Bryce," Vann said. "You don't know what you're talking about."

Malcolm turned his fulminating glare on Vann. "You shut up. You've mishandled this from the start. You took advantage of not just my trust but also hers, which was truly despicable, whether she deserved it or not. It was very badly done, and I'm disgusted. Clear out your desk. Right now. I don't want to see your face around here any longer."

With those words, the bottom fell out of Sophie's whole world.

She turned to stare at Vann, horrified.

"You knew," she said, her voice hollow. "Even before San Francisco. You knew they thought I was the thief. You were setting a trap the whole time."

"No!" he said swiftly. "I was defending you! I never for one second believed that you could—"

"Do not hammer away at this false narrative, either one of you," Malcolm said. "We're not stupid, Ms. Valente. We have you red-handed. Video footage of you sneaking into my room at Paradise Point, taking photos of documents from my laptop."

"I was never in your room!" Sophie said curtly. "I was sent to your suite by a woman who claimed to be on the hotel staff. I was standing outside that door, knocking and yelling for you like an idiot, but I never went inside. Why would I?"

"Please." Malcolm put his hand to his head as if it hurt him. "Please, Sophie. We saw you on the video. Inside my room. Sitting at my computer. Please, just stop this."

"You may have seen something, Mr. Maddox, but you did not see me, because I was never…freaking…*there*!" Her voice rose in pitch and volume no matter how hard she tried to control it. "As if I would need to break into your hotel room to steal from you. Hah! I could reach into your system and pull out all your deepest, darkest secrets in no time, from anywhere in the world, without leaving a trail. But I didn't, because I'm not a thief, or a spy! I have no reason to be one!" She rounded on Malcolm. "You really think this is about money?"

"In my experience, it usually is," Malcolm said. "And it looks like you got your pound of flesh, so keep it. Just take it, with my apologies. My blessing, even. Consider it your inheritance, your back child support, your payoff, however you want to label it, as long as you never show your face around here again. Do not come anywhere near me and my family. If you do, I will come after you with the full force of the law."

Sophie had to take a moment to control her expression. Tears welled up in her eyes. Anger, hurt, confusion rampaged through her. There were too many things that were breaking her heart and outraging her pride right now. She was overloaded.

She slung her purse over her shoulder and straightened up. "I'm not your thief," she said. "But I doubt anyone here has the brains to figure that out. I hope that bastard bleeds you dry. It's what you deserve."

"Goodbye, Ms. Valente," Malcolm said. "We're done here."

She turned, tear-blinded, and marched in the general direction of the door. Zack opened it for her. She was grateful not to be forced to fumble and grope for the handle. Once outside, she dug in her purse for tissues.

Sylvia called after her. "Ms. Valente? Are you all right?"

She waved her hand, shaking her head as she hurried away. No point in saying anything to the other woman. Sylvia would know soon enough. Everyone would know.

Her reputation would be trashed in this firm in a matter of minutes. And the news would spread like wildfire. She would never work in her chosen field again.

But that was something to mourn at another moment. One damn thing at a time.

"Sophie." It was Vann's voice behind her. He put his hand on her shoulder.

She didn't think or reason, just spun around and slapped him in the face with all the force in her arm.

He didn't block her, or even flinch. "Sophie, please listen—"

"You lying scumbag!" she hissed.

He reached out to her. "I swear to God, I never—"

"Do not touch me! You *bastard*!"

Their audience was growing by the second. All chatter subsided. Heads popped up to peep over cubicles.

"I never believed it was you," Vann insisted. "Never for a second, and I still don't. From the very start."

"You set me up! Deliberately! What kind of monster would do that to somebody? Why, Vann? What have I ever done to you?"

"Sophie, I didn't do that! I never—"

"You maneuvered me into a firing squad! Knowing that they'd pinned the IP theft on me. You never warned me. Oh, yes, go tell Malcolm, you said. He'll welcome you with open arms. It'll be all flowers and rainbows. You set me up to get emotionally destroyed. Deliberately. That's a special kind of evil."

"I swear, I never—"

"You thought I was a liar and a thief, but you seduced me, anyway, because you could. So why not just squeeze the situation for everything you could get out of it, right?"

"No! I never thought you were a—"

"If you'd trusted me, you would have warned me!" she yelled.

"I didn't know Tim had that video, or that he was going to show it to Malcolm before he saw you. We were supposed to meet about that tomorrow, and I was going to explain that you couldn't possibly be—"

"Stop!" She backed away from him. "Just stop. I don't want to hear it. If your master plan was to inflict maximum pain and humiliation on me, then congratulations, it was executed perfectly. Quickly, too. What did that take, ten minutes? You couldn't have done any more concentrated personal harm unless you'd hired a hit man and had me shot. Next time, maybe. Practice makes perfect, right?"

"Sophie, please," he begged. "You have to listen to me."

"No, Vann." She backed away. "I don't have to do a damn thing for you."

"Please," he said roughly. "I believe in you. I'll do anything on earth to help untangle this for you. If you would just tell me what in God's name you were doing in Malcolm's hotel room at Paradise Point. I'm not saying you're a thief. I just need to understand why you were there, so I can organize your defense. I'm on your side, I swear. Just please. Make me understand. Spell it out for me. Why were you in there?"

Sophie backed away, wiping her stinging eyes. "I wasn't," she whispered. "I was never there."

His face contracted. "Oh, God. Sophie. Please. Help me out here."

She shook her head. "Burn in hell," she whispered as she turned and fled.

Nineteen

Vann stared after Sophie. Her gleaming hair swung as she walked. The no-nonsense click of her heels faded away as she turned the corner and was lost to his sight.

People began to murmur and stir as they realized the show was over. Those nearest him, who had been frozen in fear, began sidling discreetly away.

He had to get to his office. Tell his personal staff. Make them understand what had happened. Not that he understood it himself.

He couldn't seem to move. It was as if moving would propel him into this new, awful future where Sophie had lied, cheated, stolen. Connived to cheat his employer. Used him to cover her misdeeds. A future where Sophie had been banished and disgraced, and he'd been part of it. Participating in it.

Moving, taking any kind of step…it would make this awful future real somehow.

So would standing still. Time ground forward with or without his participation.

It wasn't true. His gut, his instincts, his heart, they all refused this new data utterly.

Vann lurched forward. Left foot, right foot. The truth didn't care if he accepted it or not. He moved down the corridor toward his office. Belinda was already on her phone, eyes wide and horrified. She'd heard.

She laid her phone down. "Oh, Vann." Her voice was thin. "I'm so sorry."

"Me, too," he said dully.

"This is just…it's insane."

"I'll tell Zack and Drew to look out for your job," he said. "They'd be stupid to lose you."

Belinda sank down into her chair and burst into tears. "I don't understand it! How can he fire you? You're the best thing that ever happened to this place. Just because some thieving little slut decided to use you for her—"

"She's not a thief, or a slut," he said sharply. "She's innocent."

Belinda clapped a tissue to her reddened nose and gave him a look that was hard to misunderstand, even with her eyes overflowing with tears. It was pity.

He turned away without a word and went into his office.

He took in the floor-to-ceiling window, the deluxe furniture, the fancy decorating. This office signaled that he'd moved up the ladder in life. That he'd achieved something.

It was all gone now. The office, the job, his whole life. Up in flames, along with his love for Sophie. Everything was burning in hell, just like she'd invited him to do.

The dissonance paralyzed him, the gap between the Sophie he knew and the conniving creature that Tim had painted her to be. And Tim had somehow painted Vann to be just as bad. A lying user, out for what he could get. Capable of getting a woman's trust, using her sexually and then stabbing her through the heart.

The videos literally hurt his head, as if someone had wrung out his brain like a wet towel. What was up with that? How could it be?

The thought of watching them again made his stomach heave, but he turned grimly to his computer. Following his dad's stern training. Run straight toward pain. Like he had at high school football practice. Like when he'd been out on patrol in Fallujah.

Same thing now. He had to run straight toward the pain and the fear. Not away.

He opened his email program. The last highlighted, unopened email in his list, the one from Bryce, had two video attachments. His jaw ached from being clenched so hard.

He played the first one.

It was Sophie on the walkway outside Malcolm's room, her luxuriant hair tossed back by the wind. He fast-forwarded all the way through the hotly disputed four minute and twenty-five second window when she was in the room, and then watched Sophie come back the other way. Her hair was now tossed forward over her face by the wind. She brushed it back and took off, moving as fast as heels like hers would permit. Definitely Sophie.

Then Vann set the other clip to Play. He watched the dark, shadowy figure come into the room, sit down and wake the computer up.

In this video, she seemed different. It was Sophie's face, yes, but her expression was out of sync with the video he'd seen of her outside. Outside, she had looked worried, agitated, angry. In this video, she looked calm and unhurried. It was the look of a person in the blissful zone of pure concentration. Not looking at her watch, no shifty eyes or nervous gestures, no lip-biting or shoving her hair from her forehead. No hint of urgency or stress. Or guilt.

Of course she wouldn't be looking at her watch. There was a clock on the computer screen. But her hair? It didn't look wind-tousled at all. It was smoothed over her shoulders in perfect, freshly styled ringlets arranged decorously over her shoulders. He'd just seen her finger-comb them back off her face moments before.

This was all wrong. The look on her face. The calmness, the unhurried air. Her hair, unruffled by wind or fingers, curling over her chest.

Which was on full display. Luscious cleavage popped up over the neckline of the crinkly edge of the chiffon bodice. The fabric encased her breasts like flower petals.

He didn't remember admiring Sophie's cleavage during

the party. It was the type of sexy detail that would burn itself permanently into the long-term memory of any straight man with a pulse. But it hadn't registered on his.

His hand shook as he guided the mouse to click back on the previous video of Sophie outside the room.

No cleavage here. Because the floppy pink chiffon rosette was positioned right at the level of her breasts. Not below.

He observed the indoor clip again. In this image, the rosette was much lower. Hooked loosely closed at waist level, leaving her chest uncovered.

It wasn't adding up.

But something told him that drawing Malcolm's attention to Sophie's luscious cleavage was not going to earn him any points. He'd just look like the balls-for-brains idiot that he was, wildly in love with the woman that he'd just stabbed through the heart. That wasn't going help her cause, if he—

Wait.

Stabbed. Through the heart.

Oh, God. Sophie's *heart*.

His own heart started thudding so loudly he had to bend over for a moment. The searing flash of emotion almost wiped him out for a second. Then he was out the door. Belinda leaped to her feet as he raced past.

"Vann!" she called. "What is it? Did anything happen? Can I help?"

He turned, still moving. "Yes! Tell them all that it's not Sophie. Tell everyone. It's not her, and I know it for a goddamn fact. I have hard proof!"

"Um… Vann, slow down! I'm not sure it's a good idea to rush back into—"

"I have proof," he repeated. "The video they're using was a fake. And I know who did it, too. He framed her, and he defamed her. And now he is going down."

Belinda hurried after him, panting. "But...but where are you going?"

"To beat that lying bastard to a pulp," Vann said.

Rage bore him along like jet fuel, all the way back to Malcolm's office. He heard Sylvia's squeak of protest behind him as he burst through the door.

Malcolm's face darkened. "What are you doing back here? I already dismissed you! Get gone!"

"Not until I'm done," Vann said. "I have something to say to all of you."

Zack stepped in front of Malcolm. "Calm down, Vann," he said.

"Sophie is not your thief," Vann announced.

Malcolm grunted. "For God's sake, stop letting your little head do your thinking for you. She's been exposed. Lying won't help her now. Don't embarrass yourself."

"I don't have to lie," Vann said. "I'm in love with her, yes. I'm crazy about her, and I'm not embarrassed to admit it. But it's not necessary to lie for her. The woman in the video taken inside your hotel room is not Sophie. The outdoor images are genuine, and they dovetail with Sophie's account of what happened on the day of the wedding. She was set up. This whole operation was carefully planned. But the woman at the computer? Not Sophie."

"Vann." Malcolm's voice was pained. "Don't insult my intelligence. I saw her with my own eyes. It's very clearly Sophie Valente."

"You saw a doctored video," Vann said.

"Vann, please," Bryce scoffed. "Don't do this. You saw her come to the ceremony twelve minutes after it started. You saw the videos. She has no alibi, because we were all at the wedding. It's a slam dunk. I'm sad, too, but it's time to accept it and move on."

Vann lunged before Bryce had finished talking.

Crack. His fist connected with Bryce's jaw. The other

man careened backward, arms flailing as he hit Malcolm's antique Persian rug with a heavy thud.

Malcolm stared in shock. "Vann!" he barked. "How dare you?"

Zack grabbed him from behind before he could do any more damage. "Easy now," his friend muttered into his ear. "Stop it right now. Not the place or time."

Vann went still, breathing hard. He jerked his chin in Bryce's direction. "It was him, Malcolm," Vann said. "Bryce doctored the video. It's a deepfake."

"That's a lie!" Bryce blustered, dabbing at the blood from his split lip. He cowered back as Vann jerked toward him, but Vann was still restrained by Zack's hard grip.

"Keep that thug away from me!" Bryce said, his voice high and shaky. "He's gone nuts!"

"It's not a lie," Vann said. "The woman in that video was dressed like Sophie, and she'd styled her hair like Sophie's, but she is not Sophie."

"Don't try to confuse me, boy," Malcolm said. "What the hell are you saying?"

"It's a video of another woman, with old footage of Sophie's face incorporated into it," Vann said. "It's called deepfake technology. It's done with artificial intelligence. It's hard to spot. But that's what happened here."

"You're grasping at straws, Vann," Malcolm told him. "Why should you conclude that the woman in the video is not Sophie? She's in the same clothes."

"The woman in the video has no scar," Vann said.

Malcolm's eyes narrowed. "Excuse me?"

"Sophie had open-heart surgery when she was a toddler," Vann said. "She has an eight-inch surgical star over her sternum. That's why you've never seen her wear anything low-cut. If you look at the outdoor video, you can see that the fabric rose is holding the wrap closed right at the level of her chest. But whoever played Sophie's body double in the video had her wrap closed at the waist. And there's no scar to be seen. It's not Sophie. It's not even necessary to investigate the video itself, but if you did slow it down, you'd find the splices. It's a fake." He glared at Bryce. "His son, the one who was looking for Sophie before the wedding. Isn't he a CGI expert? He doctored that video. Bryce is your thief, Malcolm. Not Sophie."

Malcolm leaned heavily on his cane, looking appalled. "My God," he said, his voice hollow. "Tim. Is this true?"

Tim's face tightened, and it took him a long time to answer. "I... I'm sorry."

Malcolm shoulders slumped. He sank down into the chair. "Oh, Tim. What in God's name have you done?"

"I'm sorry," Tim repeated brokenly. "I had no choice. It was Richie. He got into drugs down there in LA. He got into trouble with his dealers. He owed them money. Mobster types. A whole lot of money. They were going to hurt him."

"And instead of coming to me and asking for my help, after twenty-five years of working together, you decide to steal from me," Malcolm said. "And to set up an innocent woman to take the fall. For the love of God, Tim. How could you do that to her?"

"You sleazebag liar," Vann said. "Sophie could have gone to prison for years."

"I had to keep them from going after Richie." Bryce pushed himself up onto his elbow. "Try to understand, Malcolm. Those men who were after him—"

"Get back down on the floor," Vann snarled. "If you get up, I'll hit you again."

Bryce looked up at Zack, who deliberately lifted his arms, freeing Vann. "I won't stop him," Zack said coldly. "You're on your own, Bryce."

Bryce's face crumpled, and he collapsed back onto the carpet. "I was afraid they would kill Richie," he said thickly. "I knew it was wrong, and of course I was sorry to do that to her, but imagine yourself in my place. Would you rather see some random woman spending a few years in a medium-security prison for a white-collar crime, or see your son tortured or murdered?"

Vann's fists shook. He looked over at Zack. "Please, get this piece of garbage out of my sight. For his own safety."

Zack nodded. "On your feet, Tim," he said. "Let's go get this thing started."

Tim struggled upright, swaying on his feet. Vann and Malcolm watched Zack lead the shambling, slump-shoul-dered man out of Malcolm's office.

The door fell shut behind him. The two men gazed at each other.

"So, then," Vann said flatly. "That's settled. I'll be on my way."

"I take it you're going to follow her?" Malcolm asked.

"Of course I am," Vann said. "Not that it's your busi-ness. She's already told me to burn in hell. She thinks I set her up for this horror show. I have you to thank for that."

"Me? Hah!" Malcolm snorted. "I didn't do a damn thing! You were the one who misbehaved and got caught with your hand in the cookie jar, so watch your mouth!"

"I don't see why I should," Vann replied. "You fired my ass, Malcolm. There's no reason for me to watch my mouth with you any longer."

"Don't be such a drama queen," Malcolm scoffed. "I was overwrought. Things are not what they seemed a short while ago. You may now consider yourself officially un-fired. For now at least. If you behave."

Vann shook his head. "I'm not in the mood to behave, or to be unfired. I have more important things to do right now than work for you, and I don't know how long they're going to take. Go ahead and hire someone to replace me. Screw this job."

"Don't be a fool, Vann," Malcolm blustered.

"I love that woman, you know that?" Vann said forcefully. "I want her to be my wife. The mother of my children. Till death do us part. You and Bryce killed that."

"Well, guess what, boy? You're not the only one who lost something today," Malcolm said. "Sophie came to me in good faith, and I attacked her, brutally. I destroyed my chance to makes things right with her. Vicky's girl. My own flesh and blood."

"I sure do hope that you're not asking me to feel sorry for you," Vann said. "Because you caught me on a bad day for that."

"Oh, shut up," Malcolm snapped. "Take your smart ass and your superior attitude and get out of my face. Go get her. And good luck with it."

Vann headed for the door.

"Vann!" Malcolm called as he pulled it open. "When you find her, please tell her that I hope she'll give me another chance."

Vann turned to look at the older man. "Hunt her down and tell her yourself if you give a damn," he said. "It'll mean more to her if you do. I'm not your errand boy."

"Out!" Malcolm roared. "I've had enough of your lip! Get gone!"

Vann did exactly that, his pace quickening with every step he took. By the time he reached the parking lot, he was running as if his life depended on it.

Twenty

Sophie jerked out of the nightmare, a scream caught in her throat.

God. Every time she drifted off, she had the same ugly dream. She was naked in a cage and people filed by, peering through the bars like she was an animal on display. She huddled, hiding her nakedness under her tangled, matted hair.

Then she saw Vann, standing beyond the crowd. Their eyes met. He shook his head slowly, then turned his back and walked away.

Every time, she leaped up and rattled the bars, screaming his name. But Vann never turned around. He didn't seem to hear her.

Her own scream woke her every time, and she was freshly furious at herself for being so vulnerable, even in a dream. He wasn't worth her tears, damn it.

She swung her legs over the lounge chair and sat up. She'd fallen asleep reading an article on becoming a security consultant while lying under a canopy of drooping wisteria blossoms, and the afternoon light sifted through them, bathing her in a luminous lavender-tinted glow. Every puff of the scented breeze showered her with flower petals. A fountain gurgled in the courtyard.

She got up, stretched and climbed up to the terrace that overlooked the sea. The breeze blew her hair back and fluttered her crumpled linen dress. The ancient villa was built right on the edge of a sea cliff that overlooked the colorful, gorgeous scenic town of Positano, which clung to the side of the stunning Amalfi Coast. The sea was an endless, aching blue. Puffy clouds floated in the afternoon sky. Behind her, the courtyard was a mass of lemon and orange trees, their tender, pale new leaves fluttering in the breeze.

It should be easier to breathe here. Her happiest memories were in this place. But she'd had fantasies of showing this place to Vann. A lovers' paradise.

That was uniquely depressing right now.

To think that she'd come to Positano to cheer herself up. The Palazzo Valente in Florence was magnificent and beautiful, but too grand in scale for a single woman to rattle around in. It was made for a dynasty. She should probably sell it to some big sprawling family. Being alone in it felt like a personal failure.

But one thing at a time. There was so much to stress about. Her broken heart, her hurt pride, her damaged dignity, her trashed career, her crushed hopes. Whether anyone on earth would ever want to hire her again. She could take her pick of disasters.

But right now, her main challenge was just remembering how to breathe.

She hadn't known how attached to the family fantasy she'd actually become. Initially she'd done it for Mom, of course. Asking Sophie to approach Malcolm had been Mom's final attempt to heal that ancient wound. Sophie respected that, and had wanted to honor it.

But it had backfired in such a spectacular way. She'd been publicly rejected, in every way. By her father, her lover, even her workplace. Humiliated, disgraced, banished.

It had been too much to hope for. The family she'd hoped to join. The man she'd hoped to marry. She'd fallen like overripe fruit for the happy daydream of Sophie and Vann, blissful together. Sprinkle on some more fantasy ingredients: Malcolm welcoming her, wanting to know her. Cousins Drew and Ava drawing her into their inner circle. The noise and laughter of a big extended family. Love and sex and babies. Life's adventures and milestones, all faced together with a partner. Growing old together, hand in hand.

Right. She'd abandoned Rule Number One. She'd known it back in her smarter days, but love had made her willfully forget it. The more attractive the man, the more fatal the flaw. And setting her up to get destroyed by Malcolm— hell, damn.

A flaw just couldn't get more fatal than that.

She'd blocked all her Maddox Hill contacts on social media, and changed her phone number. This increased her isolation, but seeing online gossip about her professional reputation was more than she could bear right now.

Staring at the beautiful sunsets over the sea just reminded her of Mom, on the terrace every evening, pining for Malcolm. Letting all of her other chances at love and marriage pass her by, one after the other.

And here she was, Vicky Valente's luckless daughter, staring dolefully at the sunset all alone. History was repeating itself.

But no. Screw those bastards. She wouldn't give into it. They could sit on it and spin. The whole stupid pack of them. Fate, destiny and all the rest.

She was changing this story, and she'd start by taking better care of herself. Buying some decent food, cooking it with care. Treating herself more tenderly. She'd give a damn about Sophie Valente, even if no one else did.

She collected her canvas shopping bags, slipped on her sneakers and headed out to pick up some basic ingredients for quick, tasty, extremely easy meals. Three stops would do the job—the fruit and veggie place, the deli for cheese, cured meats and a bottle of wine, and the butcher's shop. Operation Self Care had begun.

Usually when she was in Italy, she loved the intimacy of shopping in places where she was recognized by all the shopkeepers. Today, it was salt in the wound. Three different worried old ladies fussed over her and tried to tempt her with samples of this or that. Signora Ippolita, the butcher's wife, even insisted on wrapping up a thick Florentine steak for her, despite her protests that it was too much for a single person to eat.

She stopped for a moment outside, to rearrange the contents of her bags. When she looked up, she saw Vann across the road.

She dropped the bags. The wine bottle clanked on the cobblestones, and began rolling noisily downhill. Vann was still there. He was not a dream, or an apparition.

Vann intercepted the wine bottle before it could roll any farther. He picked it up and brushed it off as he walked toward her. "Sophie," he said quietly.

"What are you doing here?" she demanded. "How did you find me?"

"I had to see you," he said. "I've been looking for you for weeks."

"*Ehi! Onofrio!*" Ippolita poked her head out the door and bawled for her husband. "Get out here! There's a man bothering Signorina Sofia!"

"*Che cosa?*" Onofrio, a tall, burly guy with a blood-smeared apron stretched over his large belly, stepped out onto the street, holding a huge meat cleaver in his hand. "Signorina Sofia, *va tutto bene*? Is this idiot bothering you?"

Sophie gave the older couple a reassuring smile. "Don't worry," she soothed. "He isn't a problem for me."

"I could chase him away," Onofrio offered. "Put the fear of God into him."

"Or chop a few parts off," Ippolita offered. "If he's the one who made you look so sad."

"I'm fine," she assured. "It won't be necessary to chop anything off." She held out her hand for the wine bottle. "I'll take that back now."

Vann gave it to her. She tucked it into a shopping bag and picked them up.

"Can I carry those for you?" he asked.

"No, thank you." She turned back to wave at the butcher and his wife.

"Everything's fine," she reassured them with another smile. "Really. *Buona sera.*"

He fell into step beside her as she walked up into the big wooden door that opened into the villa. She glanced back, and noticed that Onofrio and Ippolita were still standing on the street outside their shop, watching her anxiously. Three or four other people in the square had also taken notice.

She cursed under her breath, held out the bags. "Hold these while I get my keys."

He silently did so. When the door swung open, she gestured impatiently for him to enter.

She pulled the door shut behind them.

"Thanks for letting me come in," Vann said. "I think the butcher wanted to hack me into stewing chunks."

"You're only in here because I don't want an audience," Sophie said. "It's not for your sake, that's for sure."

She led the way through the shadowy stone arch and out into the center courtyard. Vann followed, and set the grocery bags down on the pavement next to the burbling fountain.

It was unfair, how good Vann looked in those slouchy tan cargo pants and a crumpled white linen shirt that set off his tan. His dark eyes were full of emotion that bewildered and infuriated her. After what he had done, he had no right to look at her that way.

"You're not welcome here," she told him.

"I know," he said. "Please hear me out. That's all I ask."

"I don't remember ever telling you about this place. Or giving anyone the address."

Vann's big shoulders lifted. "You told us that last day,

in Malcolm's office. That you had property in Singapore, New York City, the Catskills, Florence and Positano. That, and the name Valente, was all I needed."

"And you figured I'd come here? Good guess."

"I've been to all of your houses," he said. "Staking them out. Watching for you."

That startled her. "All? You mean, you've been flying all over the world? What about your job?"

He shook his head. "That's over," he said. "I'm between jobs right now."

"So he really did fire you," she said. "Seems like your time would be better served job hunting than chasing around after me. I'm sure you wouldn't want my criminal taint to wear off onto you. Hardened felon that I am."

"No," he said. "Malcolm knows it wasn't you."

She froze in place. Any news that good had to be a trap. Some fresh new cruelty.

"How on earth could that be?" she asked. "They were so sure."

"Your name has been cleared. I wanted you to hear it from me. I also thought you should know that Malcolm feels guilty as hell about what he said to you."

She crossed her arms over her chest. "So he should. How did all this come about?" She kept her voice cool and remote.

"It was the videos," he explained. "That girl who sent you to Malcolm's room? She was on their team. The thieves' team, I mean. Tim and Rich Bryce hired her. Bryce was selling the IP, and setting you up to take the fall. The girl you saw had to get you into position outside Malcolm's room at that exact time. Inside the room was another woman, already dressed up like you. They deep-faked your face onto that woman's image. Rich is a special-effects guy. But I don't think it's that hard to do anymore, even for laymen."

"Ah," she said slowly. "So when I found Julie in my room that first night, she was checking out my wardrobe. I remember that she dropped her phone when I came in. She must have been taking pictures of all my stuff."

"Yes," Vann said. "After you left, I studied the videos until I finally saw it. The body double's boobs were spilling out of her dress. Her wrap closed at her waist."

"I see," Sophie said slowly, putting her hand over her heart. "So. Saved by the scar. Again."

"Yes," he said. "Malcolm was mortified."

"Good," she said crisply. "Rightly so."

In the silence, the birds twittered madly in the lemon and orange trees. Swallows swooped and darted. She had a hot lump in her throat. She coughed to clear it.

"So, Vann," she said in a formal tone. "I'm glad to know that my reputation is intact, and that I don't need to change careers. I appreciate you telling me. But it would have been cheaper and simpler for you to send a letter to my lawyer."

"I needed to see you," he said.

She shrugged. "The feeling is not mutual." She couldn't bear to look into his eyes.

"We have something between us," he persisted.

"We did have something," she corrected. "Then you ran over it with a truck."

"Please, let me finish," he said. "I never thought you were the thief. The more time I spent with you, the more convinced I was. You would never take a sleazy shortcut. You don't have weak spots and fault lines and holes inside you. You're complete. Sure of your own inner power. You know who you are and what you can do. People like that don't lie, cheat and steal. They can't be bothered."

She let out a bark of bitter laughter. "I hate to disappoint you, but I'm not exactly a poster child for inner power and self-confidence right now."

"I told Bryce that I knew it wasn't you when we got to

Paradise Point," Vann went on. "But I never imagined he was framing you for theft. I just thought, if it's not you, then you're safe. I figured, let Bryce bait all the traps he wants. You'd never take the bait. So when I told you to go to Malcolm and tell him you were his daughter, I swear, I had no idea you were in danger. By the time I knew what was going on, Malcolm had already called you into his office."

She let out a shaky breath. "Did you ever believe it was me?" she asked. "When you saw that doctored video, I mean?"

He shook his head. "Never," he said. "I was confused, but I never thought you were the thief. But I hate that I didn't come to your defense fast enough. If I'd been smarter and quicker, if I'd caught the detail of the scar in time, I could have spared you all that pain. I'm so sorry, Sophie. Please forgive me."

Oh, no. Not again. The slightest little thing and down came the tears.

"Damn it, Vann," she snapped. "This isn't fair."

"No, it wasn't. None of it. You were treated so badly. And it just kills me."

"Well." She sniffed back her tears with a sharp laugh. "Please, don't die. God only knows what they'd accuse me of then."

A smile flashed across his face, but he just stood there with that look on his face. Like she was supposed to pass judgment, make some sort of declaration to him.

"I don't know what you want me to say," she said. "I accept your apology. Satisfied?"

He was silent for a long moment. "No," he said.

Tension buzzed between them. He was doing it again. Playing her, with his seductive energy. After everything, he still had the nerve. It made her furious.

"I hope that doesn't mean you're hoping to get your

sexual privileges reinstated," she said. "Because you'll be very disappointed."

"I want more than that," he said.

She stared at him, her heart racing. "Um…"

"What would it take to make you trust me again?" he asked.

Sophie pressed her hand to her shaking mouth. "I have no idea. I've never been hurt this badly. It's uncharted ground."

"Then let's start the journey of exploration." He sank down onto one knee. "Sophie Valente, I love you. I want to be your man. I want to marry you, have children with you, explore the world with you, grow old with you. You're the most beautiful, fascinating, desirable woman I have ever known. You excite me on every level of my being. Please be my bride, and I promise, I will try to be worthy of your trust until the day I die."

Her mouth was a helpless O of shock.

"Wait," he said, digging into his pocket. "Damn. Important detail." He pulled out a small, flat box covered with gray silk and tied with a gray silk bow. He pulled the bow loose, and opened it. "Here."

It was a stunning square-cut emerald ring, in a classic, gorgeous design, flanked by pearls and tiny diamonds, fit for a duchess or a queen.

"Oh, God, Vann," she whispered.

"I remember you saying something on the beach, about making choices, coming to conclusions," he said. "I've made my choice. I'm sure. I want you."

"But I…" Her voice trailed off. She pressed her hand over her shaking mouth.

"After I finished in New York and Singapore, I headed to Florence and staked out the Palazzo Valente for about a week," he said. "So I was walking over the Ponte Vecchio with all its jewelry shops twice a day, going to and from my *pensione*. All those jewelers on the bridge knew me by first name by the end of that week. I know it's risky, buying something so personal without getting your input, but I felt like I couldn't come here without a ring in my hand. I had to demonstrate commitment on every level. We could always get you something else if you prefer a different style or stone."

"It's…it's incredibly beautiful," she whispered. "But… I just can't…"

"Can't what? Can't trust me?" He grabbed her hand and kissed it. "Then I'll be patient. And persistent. I'll just hang around until you can. Years, if that's what it takes."

Her face crumpled.

Vann placed a tissue in her hand, but he stayed on his knees, patiently waiting. This was embarrassing. She needed so badly to be tough, and here she was, melting down.

"I'm a mass of bruises inside," she said. "I just…don't know if I can."

"I'll wait as long as it takes," he said. "My mind's made up. You're the only one for me. You're everything I could ever need or want. I'm a goner."

She laughed through her tears and tugged on his hand. "Get up, you. It makes me nervous, having you down there."

Vann rose to his feet, and without thinking, she was suddenly touching him. His arms wrapped around her, and, oh, God, it felt wonderful. A flash flood of feelings, tearing through her. It was so intense it hurt. In a good way.

After a while, she leaned against his chest, which by now was rather soggy. She felt emptied out, but not embarrassed anymore. If Vann was going to make all those fancy promises about forever, he could start proving himself by seeing her when she ugly-cried.

When the tears eased off, she felt so soft inside. Buoyant. Like she could waft up into the sky like one of those floating lanterns. Lit up, lighter than air.

She wiped her eyes again. "Got another tissue?"

Vann whipped out the pack. "As many as you need."

"Big talk, mister," she said, mopping up the mess. "I hate crying in front of people. Now you've seen me lose it, what, three times now? A record only my mom could beat."

"It's a privilege," he said solemnly. "An honor. I'll try to be worthy."

Her face crumpled again, and she covered it with the tissue. "Oh, damn."

"What? What is it?" he asked.

"Mentioning my mom," she said. "It set me off. I've been thinking so much about how she must have felt after Malcolm left her. But she had to raise a kid alone on top of it, while feeling all of that. It must have been so hard. She had to be so strong for me."

"I'm so sorry, baby." He kissed her hand again.

She blew her nose. "That day in Malcolm's office, I thought it was like a curse, and I got caught in it somehow."

"Malcolm did, too," he said. "So did I. But we broke the spell. I've been thinking about my father these last weeks. He was so defensive he alienated his wife and kid. He died like that. Cold, hard and alone. I want better than that for myself. I'll do whatever it takes. I'll learn, I'll grow. Whatever I need to do."

"Hmph." She mopped away her tears, and looked up. "Well. That's lovely to hear. I'm glad for you. I want to grow, too. But I'm not sure I'm ready to forgive Malcolm yet."

"Never mind Malcolm," Vann said. "How about me?"

She straightened up, gazing straight into his eyes. "Swear to me," she said. "Never, ever leave me in the dark about something important. Ever again. Not to protect my feelings, or to spare me hurt, or pain, or embarrassment, or fear. Not to avoid a fight. Not for any reason. You have to promise to be brave. Swear to me. On your honor."

His eyes burned with intensity. "I swear it," he said. "I'll be brave for you. But you have to swear the same thing right back to me. We'll learn to be brave for each other."

She nodded. "I swear."

Vann pulled the ring out of the box. "So you'll wear my ring? You'll marry me?"

She tried to speak, but her voice broke. She just nodded.

He slid the ring onto her finger. It fit perfectly. He kissed her hand, his lips lingering, reverent. "My love," he whispered. "My bride. Damn, Sophie. I'm so happy right now I'm scared. I mean, out of my mind scared. Like this can't possibly be true, and I'm going to wake up."

She laughed through her tears. "Aw. Do you want me to pinch you?"

The wind gusted, and wisteria blossoms swirled around them in a pale purple cloud, fluttering gently down to kiss the pavement stones around them.

"Oh, please," Vann said. "Just stop it. A shower of flower petals? That's total overkill, and it's not helping me believe that this is not a dream."

She laughed. "You have no idea what you're in for, Vann. Wait until I get you up to the bedroom with the Juliet balconies overlooking the sea and the vaulted ceilings frescoed with naked pink cherubs and chubby shepherdesses. I will show you overkill like you never imagined. Get ready, big guy."

His grin was radiant. "Cherubs, shepherdesses, angels, rainbows, unicorns, I don't care. Bring 'em on. Have at it."

"Ah…you mean now?"

He shrugged. "Anytime, anywhere. I'm all yours. Lead the way."

"Well. In that case…" She took his hand and tugged

him toward the wide marble staircase that led to the upper floors. "Follow me."

"To the ends of the earth," he told her.

"How about just my bed for now? The ends of the earth can wait."

Their time in the bedroom left them exhausted and famished, which turned Sophie's thoughts to the goodies she'd procured on her shopping trip.

Delicious tender mozzarella knots. A wedge of aged pecorino cheese. Salt-cured smoked ham. Spicy olives. Delicious crusty bread. Ripe plum tomatoes still on the vine. Freshly grilled artichokes drenched in lemon and olive oil. Cherries, those fat shiny deep red ones. A bottle of good red wine. And Signora Ippolita's thick Florentine beef steak.

By the time the wine was poured and the table laden with the rest of their meal, Vann had finished grilling the steak. It was resting on a platter, seared to perfection. Vann served them each a big, juicy pink-tinged chunk of it, and they fell to. Food had never tasted so wonderful.

They were just starting to slow down when she heard a rhythmic buzzing sound. A text message notification. Not her phone. It came from under the table.

Vann fished his phone out from the pocket of his cargo pants. "Sorry, I'll turn it off. Just let me see if—whoa, wait. It's Malcolm."

Sophie was startled. "But didn't he fire you? Why is he texting you?"

"He did fire me, but he…wait. Hold on." He read the text. "Oh, God, he's here."

"Here meaning…where?"

"In Italy," Vann said glumly. "On his way down from Rome to Positano right now. To see you."

"Me?" Her voice broke off into a squeak.

"Yes. Evidently Drew and Zack have been passing along

my progress reports. I can hardly blame the old man for wanting to see you, but his timing sucks. I wanted you all to myself for a while."

Sophie wiped her mouth, her heart thudding. "What does he say?"

"Oh, he's just busting my balls." He held his phone out. "Here, read it. Be entertained."

Sophie scrolled through the long message.

Vann. Twelve hours of silence means one of two things. A) You found Sophie, she spit in your eye and you have thrown yourself off the sea cliff in despair, or B) You found Sophie, she fell prey to your slick line and you are taking advantage of the situation like the dirty dog that you are. Ava and I will soon arrive in Positano. In the case of option A, we will make arrangements for your broken body to be sent home for burial. Otherwise, you and Sophie will join us for dinner tomorrow at eight, at Buca di Bacco.

I await confirmation.

Sophie blew out a sharp breath. "Oh, my God."

"And so it begins," Vann grumbled. "Ball-breaking of monumental proportions. My own fault for losing my temper. He asked me to tell you that he hoped you'd give him a second chance, but I was so pissed I told him I wasn't his errand boy and he could tell you himself. So that's exactly what he did. Now here he is."

She couldn't help laughing at the chagrin on Vann's face. "Well, wow," she murmured. "I'm touched that he cared enough to come all this way."

"Oh, yes," Vann said. "He cares. But he used me first. Shamelessly. He bided his time and monitored my progress while I hauled ass all over the globe, the sneaky old bastard. You wanted family? You've got it now, by the truckload. You will now have the unique pleasure of Malcolm's advice, opinions and judgment about every single aspect of your life going forward. Lucky, lucky you." Then his eyes widened.

"What?" she demanded. "What's that face all about? Is something wrong?"

"It just hit me," he said, his voice hollow. "Malcolm Maddox is going to be my father-in-law. God give me strength."

"Oh, you poor thing. How will you manage, I wonder." She set down her wineglass and selected a plump, gleaming cherry. He watched, fascinated, as she slowly ate it.

"Sophie Valente, you are a dangerous woman," he said, his voice a sensual rasp.

"Probably," she said. "But if you're afraid…if you just can't face it…it's not too late to reconsider."

He shook his head. "You're wrong," he said. "It was too late from the first moment I saw you. My fate was sealed in a heartbeat."

The energy between them made her face heat up.

Vann reached for the phone without breaking eye contact. "Let's wrap this up so I can turn this thing off. So? Do you forgive Malcolm? Your call. No judgment either way from me."

Sophie pondered the question. "Tonight, I think I could forgive just about anything of just about anybody."

"Lucky Malcolm," he said. "So. I'm confirming the dinner reservation?"

"Yes."

Vann tapped the screen. Okay. Option B, duly confirmed, he typed. He thumbed the phone off, and placed it facedown on the table. "And now, I've got you all to myself until eight o'clock tomorrow evening. Malcolm can't bother us until then."

Sophie pushed her chair back, and rose to her feet, licking the cherry juice off her fingers, then slowly running her hand down the front of her dressing gown until the pressure loosened the knot of the silken tie. She spread it open, displaying herself to him.

"We should use the time well," she said. "So? Take advantage of the situation. Make me fall prey to your slick line. Lay it on me, you bad, seductive bastard."

"Oh, man," he said hoarsely, staring at her naked body. "You're so gorgeous. I still can't believe this is real."

She held out her arms. "Then get over here right now, and let me prove it to you."

* * * * *

COMING SOON!

We really hope you enjoyed reading this book.
If you're looking for more romance, be sure to
head to the shops when new books are
available on

Thursday 10th June

To see which titles are coming soon, please visit

millsandboon.co.uk/nextmonth

LET'S TALK
Romance

For exclusive extracts, competitions
and special offers, find us online:

- facebook.com/millsandboon
- @MillsandBoon
- @MillsandBoonUK

Get in touch on 01413 063232

MILLS & BOON

THE HEART OF ROMANCE

A ROMANCE FOR EVERY READER

MODERN

Prepare to be swept off your feet by sophisticated, sexy and seductive heroes, in some of the world's most glamourous and romantic locations, where power and passion collide.

HISTORICAL

Escape with historical heroes from time gone by. Whether your passion is for wicked Regency Rakes, muscled Vikings or rugged Highlanders, awaken the romance of the past.

MEDICAL

Set your pulse racing with dedicated, delectable doctors in the high-pressure world of medicine, where emotions run high and passion, comfort and love are the best medicine.

True Love

Celebrate true love with tender stories of heartfelt romance, from the rush of falling in love to the joy a new baby can bring, and a focus on the emotional heart of a relationship.

Desire

Indulge in secrets and scandal, intense drama and plenty of sizzling hot action with powerful and passionate heroes who have it all: wealth, status, good looks…everything but the right woman.

HEROES

Experience all the excitement of a gripping thriller, with an intense romance at its heart. Resourceful, true-to-life women and strong, fearless men face danger and desire - a killer combination!

To see which titles are coming soon, please visit

millsandboon.co.uk/nextmonth